D1439640

TEXAS BORN

BY
DIANA PALMER

MILLS & BOON

Published in Great Britain 2014
by Mills & Boon, an imprint of Harlequin (UK) Limited,
Eton House, 18-24 Paradise Road, Richmond, Surrey, TW9 1SR

© 2014 Diana Palmer

ISBN: 978-0-263-91322-4

23-1014

Harlequin (UK) Limited's policy is to use papers that are natural, renewable and recyclable products and made from wood grown in sustainable forests. The logging and manufacturing processes conform to the legal environmental regulations of the country of origin.

Printed and bound in Spain
by Blackprint CPI, Barcelona

For our friends Cynthia Burton and Terry Sosebee

Chapter One

Michelle Godfrey felt the dust of the unpaved road all over her jeans. She couldn't really see her pants. Her eyes were full of hot tears. It was just one more argument, one more heartache.

Her stepmother, Roberta, was determined to sell off everything her father had owned. He'd only been dead for three weeks. Roberta had wanted to bury him in a plain pine box with no flowers, not even a church service. Michelle had dared her stepmother's hot temper and appealed to the funeral director.

The kindly man, a friend of her father's, had pointed out to Roberta that Comanche Wells, Texas, was a very small community. It would not sit well with the locals if Roberta, whom most considered an outsider, was disrespectful of the late Alan Godfrey's wishes that he be buried in the Methodist church cemetery beside his first wife. The funeral director was soft-spoken but eloquent.

He also pointed out that the money Roberta would save with her so-called economy plans, would be a very small amount compared to the outrage she would provoke. If she planned to continue living in Jacobs County, many doors would close to her.

Roberta was irritated at the comment, but she had a shrewd mind. It wouldn't do to make people mad when she had many things to dispose of on the local market, including some cattle that had belonged to her late husband.

She gave in, with ill grace, and left the arrangements to Michelle. But she got even. After the funeral, she gathered up Alan's personal items while Michelle was at school and sent them all to the landfill, including his clothes and any jewelry that wasn't marketable.

Michelle had collapsed in tears. That is, until she saw her stepmother's wicked smile. At that point, she dried her eyes. It was too late to do anything. But one day, she promised herself, when she was grown and no longer under the woman's guardianship, there would be a reckoning.

Two weeks after the funeral, Roberta came under fire from Michelle's soft-spoken minister. He drove up in front of the house in a flashy red older convertible, an odd choice of car for a man of the cloth, Michelle thought. But then, Reverend Blair was a different sort of preacher.

She'd let him in, offered him coffee, which he refused politely. Roberta, curious because they never had visitors, came out of her room and stopped short when she saw Jake Blair.

He greeted her. He even smiled. They'd missed Michelle at services for the past two weeks. He just wanted to make sure everything was all right. Michelle didn't reply. Roberta looked guilty. There was this strange rumor he'd heard, he continued, that Roberta was preventing her stepdaughter from attending church services. He smiled when he said it, but there was something about him that was strangely chilling for a religious man. His eyes, ice-blue, had a look that Roberta recognized from her own youth, spent following her father around the casinos in Las Vegas, where he made his living. Some of the patrons had that same penetrating gaze. It was dangerous.

"But of course, we didn't think the rumor was true," Jake Blair continued with that smile that accompanied the unblinking blue stare. "It isn't, is it?"

Roberta forced a smile. "Um, of course not." She faltered, with a nervous little laugh. "She can go whenever she likes."

"You might consider coming with her," Jake commented. "We welcome new members in our congregation."

"Me, in a church?" She burst out laughing, until she saw the two bland faces watching her. She sounded defensive when she added, "I don't go to church. I don't believe in all that stuff."

Jake raised an eyebrow. He smiled to himself, as if at some private joke. "At some point in your life, I assure you, your beliefs may change."

"Unlikely," she said stiffly.

He sighed. "As you wish. Then you won't mind if my daughter, Carlie, comes by to pick Michelle up for services on Sunday, I take it?"

Roberta ground her teeth together. Obviously the minister knew that since Michelle couldn't drive, Roberta had been refusing to get up and drive her to church. She almost refused. Then she realized that it would mean she could have Bert over without having to watch for her stepdaughter every second. She pursed her lips. "Of course not," she assured him. "I don't mind at all."

"Wonderful. I'll have Carlie fetch you in time for Sunday school each week and bring you home after church, Michelle. Will that work for you?"

Michelle's sad face lit up. Her gray eyes were large and beautiful. She had pale blond hair and a flawless, lovely complexion. She was as fair as Roberta was dark. Jake got to his feet. He smiled down at Michelle.

"Thanks, Reverend Blair," she said in her soft, husky voice, and smiled at him with genuine affection.

"You're quite welcome."

She walked him out. Roberta didn't offer.

He turned at the steps and lowered his voice. "If you ever need help, you know where we are," he said, and he wasn't smiling.

She sighed. "It's just until graduation. Only a few more months," she said quietly. "I'll work hard to get a scholarship so I can go to college. I have one picked out in San Antonio."

He cocked his head. "What do you want to do?"

Her face brightened. "I want to write. I want to be a reporter."

He laughed. "Not much money in that, you know. Of course, you could go and talk to Minette Carson. She runs the local newspaper."

She flushed. "Yes, sir," she said politely, "I already did. She was the one who recommended that I go to college and major in journalism. She said working for a magazine, even a digital one, was the way to go. She's very kind."

"She is. And so is her husband," he added, referring to Jacobs County sheriff Hayes Carson.

"I don't really know him. Except he brought his iguana to school a few years ago. That was really fascinating." She laughed.

Jake just nodded. "Well, I'll get back. Let me know if you need anything."

"I will. Thank you."

"Your father was a good man," he added. "It hurt all of us to lose him. He was one of the best emergency-room doctors we ever had in Jacobs County, even though he was only able to work for a few months before his illness forced him to quit."

She smiled sadly. "It was a hard way to go, for a doctor," she replied. "He knew all about his prognosis and he explained to me how things would be. He said if he hadn't been so stubborn, if he'd had the tests sooner, they might have caught the cancer in time."

"Young lady," Jake said softly, "things happen the way they're meant to. There's a plan to everything that happens in life, even if we don't see it."

"That's what I think, too. Thank you for talking to her," she added hesitantly. "She wouldn't let me learn how to drive, and Dad was too sick to teach me. I don't really think she'd let me borrow the car, even if I could drive. She wouldn't get up early for anything, especially on a Sunday. So I had no way to get to church. I've missed it."

"I wish you'd talked to me sooner," he said, and smiled. "Never mind. Things happen in their own time."

She looked up into his blue eyes. "Does it…get better? Life, I mean?" she asked with the misery of someone who'd landed in a hard place and saw no way out.

He drew in a long breath. "You'll soon have more control over the things that happen to you," he replied. "Life is a test, Michelle. We walk through fire. But there are rewards. Every pain brings a pleasure."

"Thanks."

He chuckled. "Don't let her get you down."

"I'm trying."

"And if you need help, don't hold back." His eyes narrowed and there was something a little chilling in them. "I have yet to meet a person who frightens me."

She burst out laughing. "I noticed. She's a horror, but she was really nice to you!"

"Sensible people are." He smiled like an angel. "See you."

He went down the steps two at a time. He was a tall man, very fit, and he walked with a very odd gait, light and almost soundless, as he went to his car. The vehicle wasn't new, but it had some kind of big engine in it. He started it and wheeled out into the road with a skill and smoothness that she envied. She wondered if she'd ever learn to drive.

She went back into the house, resigned to several minutes of absolute misery.

"You set that man on me!" Roberta raged. "You went over my head when I told you I didn't want you to bother with that stupid church stuff!"

"I like going to church. Why should you mind? It isn't hurting you...."

"Dinner was always late when you went, when your father was alive," the brunette said angrily. "I had to take care of him. So messy." She made a face. In fact, Roberta had never done a thing for her husband. She left it all to Michelle. "And I had to try to cook. I hate cooking. I'm not doing it. That's your job. So you'll make dinner before you go to church and you can eat when you get home, but I'm not waiting an extra hour to sit down to a meal!"

"I'll do it," Michelle said, averting her eyes.

"See that you do! And the house had better be spotless, or I won't let you go!"

She was bluffing. Michelle knew it. She was unsettled by the Reverend Blair. That amused Michelle, but she didn't dare let it show.

"Can I go to my room now?" she asked quietly.

Roberta made a face. "Do what you please." She primped at the hall mirror. "I'm going out. Bert's taking me to dinner up in San Antonio. I'll be very late," she added. She gave Michelle a worldly, patronizing laugh. "You wouldn't know what to do with a man, you little prude."

Michelle stiffened. It was the same old song and dance. Roberta thought Michelle was backward and stupid.

"Oh, go on to your room," she muttered. That wide-eyed, resigned look was irritating.

Michelle went without another word.

She sat up late, studying. She had to make the best grades she could, so that she could get a scholarship. Her father had left her a little money, but her stepmother had control of it until she was of legal age. Probably by then there wouldn't be a penny left.

Her father had been lucid at the end because of the massive doses of painkillers he had to take for his condition. Roberta had influenced the way he set up his will, and it had been her own personal attorney who'd drawn it up for her father's signature. Michelle was certain that he hadn't meant to leave her so little. But she couldn't contest it. She wasn't even out of high school.

It was hard, she thought, to be under someone's thumb and unable to do anything you wanted to do. Roberta was always after her about something. She made fun of her, ridiculed her conservative clothes, made her life a daily misery. But the reverend was right. One day, she'd be out of this. She'd have her own place, and she wouldn't have to ask Roberta even for lunch money, which was demeaning enough.

She heard a truck go along the road, and glanced out to see a big black pickup truck pass by. So he was back. Their closest neighbor was Gabriel Brandon. Michelle knew who he was.

She'd seen him for the first time two years ago, the last summer she'd spent with her grandfather and grandmother before their deaths. They'd lived in this very house, the one her father had inherited. She'd gone to town with her grandfather to get medicine for a sick calf. The owner of the store had been talking to a man, a very handsome man who'd just moved down the road from them.

He was very tall, muscular, without it being obvious, and he had the most beautiful liquid black eyes she'd ever seen. He was built like a rodeo cowboy. He had thick, jet-black hair and a face off of a movie poster. He was the most gorgeous man she'd ever seen in her life.

He'd caught her staring at him and he'd laughed. She'd never forgotten how that transformed his hard face. It had melted her. She'd flushed and averted her eyes and almost run out of the store afterward. She'd embarrassed herself by staring. But he was very good-looking, after all—he must be used to women staring at him.

She'd asked her grandfather about him. He hadn't said much, only that the man was working for Eb Scott, who owned a ranch near Jacobsville. Brandon was rather mysterious, too, her grandfather had mused, and people were curious about him. He wasn't married. He had a sister who visited him from time to time.

Michelle's grandfather had chided her for her interest. At fifteen, he'd reminded her, she was much too young to be interested in men. She'd agreed out loud. But privately she thought that that Mr. Brandon was absolutely gorgeous, and most girls would have stared at him.

By comparison, Roberta's friend, Bert, always looked greasy, as if he never washed his hair. Michelle couldn't stand him. He looked at her in a way that made her skin crawl and he was always trying to touch her. She'd jerked away from him once, when he'd tried to ruffle her hair, and he made a big joke of it. But his eyes weren't laughing.

He made her uncomfortable, and she tried to stay out of his way. It would have been all right if he and Roberta didn't flaunt their affair. Michelle came home from school one Monday to find them on the sofa together, half-dressed and sweaty. Roberta had almost doubled up with laughter at the look she got from her stepdaughter as she lay half across Bert, wearing nothing but a lacy black slip.

"And what are you staring at, you little prude?" Roberta had demanded. "Did you think I'd put on black clothes and abandon men for life because your father died?"

"He's only been dead two weeks," Michelle had pointed out with choking pride.

"So what? He wasn't even that good in bed before he got sick," she scoffed. "We lived in San Antonio and he had a wonderful practice, he was making loads of money as a cardiologist. Then he gets diagnosed with terminal cancer and decides overnight to pull up stakes and move to this flea-bitten wreck of a town where he sets up a free clinic on weekends and lives on his pension and his investments! Which evaporated in less than a year, thanks to his medical bills," she added haughtily. "I thought he was rich…!"

"Yes, that's why you married him," Michelle said under her breath.

"That's the only reason I did marry him," she muttered, sitting up to light a cigarette and blow smoke in Michelle's direction.

She coughed. "Daddy wouldn't let you smoke in the house," she said accusingly.

"Well, Daddy's dead, isn't he?" Roberta said pointedly, and she smiled.

"We could make it a threesome, if you like," Bert offered, sitting up with his shirt half-off.

Michelle's expression was eloquent. "If I speak to my minister…"

"Shut up, Bert!" Roberta said shortly, and her eyes dared him to say another word. She looked back at Michelle with cold eyes and got to her feet. "Come on, Bert, let's go to your place." She grabbed him by the hand and had led him to the bedroom. Apparently their clothes were in there.

Disgusted beyond measure, Michelle went into her room and locked the door.

She could hear them arguing. A few minutes later they came back out.

"I won't be here for dinner," Roberta said.

Michelle didn't reply.

"Little torment," Roberta grumbled. "She's always watching, always so pure and unblemished," she added harshly.

"I could take care of that," Bert said.

"Shut up!" Roberta said again. "Come on, Bert!"

Michelle could feel herself flushing with anger as she heard them go out the door. Roberta slammed it behind her.

Michelle had peeked out the curtains and watched them climb into Bert's low-slung car. He pulled out into the road.

She closed the curtains with a sigh of pure relief. Nobody knew what a hell those two made of her life. She had no peace. Apparently Roberta had been seeing Bert for some time, because they were obviously obsessed with each other. But it had come as a shock to walk in the door and find them kissing the day after Michelle's father was buried, to say nothing of what she'd just seen.

The days since then had been tense and uncomfortable. The two of them made fun of Michelle, ridiculed the way she dressed, the way she thought. And Roberta was full of petty comments about Michelle's father and the illness that had killed him. Roberta had never even gone to the hospital. It had been Michelle who'd sat with him until he slipped away, peacefully, in his sleep.

She lay on her back and looked at the cieling. It was only a few months until graduation. She made very good grades. She hoped Marist College in San Antonio would take her. She'd already applied. She was sweating out the admissions, because she'd have to have a scholarship or she couldn't afford to go. Not only that, she'd have to have a job.

She'd worked part-time at a mechanic's shop while her father was alive. He'd drop her off after school and pick her up when she finished work. But his illness had come on quickly and she'd lost the job. Roberta wasn't about to provide transportation.

She rolled over restlessly. Maybe there would be something she could get in San Antonio, perhaps in a convenience store if all else failed. She didn't mind hard work. She was used to it. Since her father had married Roberta, Michelle had done all the cooking and cleaning and laundry. She even mowed the lawn.

Her father had seemed to realize his mistake toward the end. He'd apologized for bringing Roberta into their lives. He'd been lonely since her mother died, and Roberta had flattered him and made him feel good. She'd been fun to be around during the courtship—even Michelle had thought so. Roberta went shopping with the girl, praised her cooking, acted like a really nice person. It wasn't until after the wedding that she'd shown her true colors.

Michelle had always thought it was the alcohol that had made her change so suddenly for the worse. It wasn't discussed in front of her, but Michelle knew that Roberta had been missing for a few weeks, just before her father was diagnosed with cancer. And there was gossip that the doctor had sent his young wife off to a rehabilitation center because of a drinking problem. Afterward, Roberta hadn't been quite so hard to live with. Until they'd moved to Comanche Wells, at least.

Dr. Godfrey had patted Michelle on the shoulder only days before the cancer had taken a sudden turn for the worse and he was bedridden. He'd smiled ruefully.

"I'm very sorry, sweetheart," he'd told her. "If I could go back and change things…"

"I know, Daddy. It's all right."

He'd pulled her close and kissed her forehead. "You're like your mother. She took things to heart, too. You have to learn how to deal with unpleasant people. You have to learn not to take life so seriously…."

"Alan, are you ever coming inside?" Roberta had interrupted petulantly. She hated seeing her husband and her stepdaughter together. She made every effort to keep them apart. "What are you doing, anyway, looking at those stupid smelly cattle?"

"I'll be there in a moment, Roberta," he called back.

"The dishes haven't been washed," she told Michelle with a cold smile. "Your job, not mine."

She'd gone back inside and slammed the screen.

Michelle winced.

So did her father. He drew in a deep breath. "Well, we'll get through this," he said absently. He'd winced again, holding his stomach.

"You should see Dr. Coltrain," she remarked. Dr. Copper Coltrain was one of their local physicians. "You keep putting it off. It's worse, isn't it?"

He sighed. "I guess it is. Okay. I'll see him tomorrow, worrywart."

She grinned. "Okay."

Tomorrow had ended with a battery of tests and a sad prognosis. They'd sent him back home with more medicine and no hope. He'd lasted a few weeks past the diagnosis.

Michelle's eyes filled with tears. The loss was still new, raw. She missed her father. She hated being at the mercy of her stepmother, who wanted nothing more than to sell the house and land right out from under Michelle. In fact, she'd already said that as soon as the will went through probate, she was going to do exactly that.

Michelle had protested. She had several months of school to go. Where would she live?

That, Roberta had said icily, was no concern of hers. She didn't care what happened to her stepdaughter. Roberta was young and had a life of her own, and she wasn't going to spend it smelling cattle and manure. She was going to move in with Bert. He was in between jobs, but the sale of the house and land would keep them for a while. Then they'd go to Las Vegas where she knew people and could make their fortune in the casino.

Michelle had cocked her head and just stared at her

stepmother with a patronizing smile. "Nobody beats the house in Las Vegas," she said in a soft voice.

"I'll beat it," Roberta snapped. "You don't know anything about gambling."

"I know that sane people avoid it," she returned.

Roberta shrugged.

There was only one real-estate agent in Comanche Wells. Michelle called her, nervous and obviously upset.

"Roberta says she's selling the house," she began.

"Relax." Betty Mathers laughed. "She has to get the will through probate, and then she has to list the property. The housing market is in the basement right now, sweetie. She'd have to give it away to sell it."

"Thanks," Michelle said huskily. "You don't know how worried I was…." Her voice broke, and she stopped.

"There's no reason to worry," Betty assured her. "Even if she does leave, you have friends here. Somebody will take the property and make sure you have a place to stay. I'll do it myself if I have to."

Michelle was really crying now. "That's so kind…!"

"Michelle, you've been a fixture around Jacobs County since you were old enough to walk. You spent summers with your grandparents here and you were always doing things to help them, and other people. You spent the night in the hospital with the Harrises' little boy when he had to have that emergency appendectomy and wouldn't let them give you a dime. You baked cakes for the sale that helped Rob Meiner when his house burned. You're always doing for other people. Don't think it doesn't get noticed." Her voice hardened. "And don't think we aren't aware of what your stepmother is up to. She has no friends here, I promise you."

Michelle drew in a breath and wiped her eyes. "She thought Daddy was rich."

"I see," came the reply.

"She hated moving down here. I was never so happy," she added. "I love Comanche Wells."

Betty laughed. "So do I. I moved here from New York City. I like hearing crickets instead of sirens at night."

"Me, too."

"You stop worrying, okay?" she added. "Everything's going to be all right."

"I will. And thanks."

"No thanks necessary."

Michelle was to remember that conversation the very next day. She got home from school that afternoon and her father's prized stamp collection was sitting on the coffee table. A tall, distinguished man was handing Roberta a check.

"It's a marvelous collection," the man said.

"What are you doing?" Michelle exclaimed, dropping her books onto the sofa, as she stared at the man with horror. "You can't sell Daddy's stamps! You can't! It's the only thing of his I have left that we both shared! I helped him put in those stamps, from the time I was in grammar school!"

Roberta looked embarrassed. "Now, Michelle, we've already discussed this...."

"We haven't discussed anything!" she raged, red-faced and weeping. "My father has only been dead three weeks and you've already thrown away every single thing he had, even his clothes! You've talked about selling the house... I'm still in school—I won't even have a place to live. And now this! You...you...mercenary gold digger!"

Roberta tried to smile at the shocked man. "I do apologize for my daughter…."

"I'm not her daughter! She married my father two years ago. She's got a boyfriend. She was with him while my father was dying in the hospital!"

The man stared at Michelle for a long moment, turned to Roberta, snapped the check out of her hands and tore it into shreds.

"But…we had a deal," Roberta stammered.

The man gave her a look that made her move back a step. "Madam, if you were kin to me, I would disown you," he said harshly. "I have no wish to purchase a collection stolen from a child."

"I'll sue you!" Roberta raged.

"By all means. Attempt it."

He turned to Michelle. "I am very sorry," he said gently. "For your loss and for the situation in which you find yourself." He turned to Roberta. "Good day."

He walked out.

Roberta gave him just enough time to get to his car. Then she turned to Michelle and slapped her so hard that her teeth felt as if they'd come loose on that side of her face.

"You little brat!" she yelled. "He was going to give me five thousand dollars for that stamp collection! It took me weeks to find a buyer!"

Michelle just stared at her, cold pride crackling around her. She lifted her chin. "Go ahead. Hit me again. And see what happens."

Roberta drew back her hand. She meant to do it. The child was a horror. She hated her! But she kept remembering the look that minister had given her. She put her hand down and grabbed her purse.

"I'm going to see Bert," she said icily. "And you'll get

no lunch money from me from now on. You can mop floors for your food, for all I care!"

She stormed out the door, got into her car and roared away.

Michelle picked up the precious stamp collection and took it into her room. She had a hiding place that, hopefully, Roberta wouldn't be able to find. There was a loose baseboard in her closet. She pulled it out, slid the stamp book inside and pushed it back into the wall.

She went to the mirror. Her face looked almost blistered where Roberta had hit her. She didn't care. She had the stamp collection. It was a memento of happy times when she'd sat on her father's lap and carefully tucked stamps into place while he taught her about them. If Roberta killed her, she wasn't giving the stamps up.

But she was in a hard place, with no real way out. The months until graduation seemed like years. Roberta would make her life a living hell from now on because she'd opposed her. She was so tired of it. Tired of Roberta. Tired of Bert and his innuendoes. Tired of having to be a slave to her stepmother. It seemed so hopeless.

She thought of her father and started bawling. He was gone. He'd never come back. Roberta would torment her to death. There was nothing left.

She walked out the front door like a sleepwalker, out to the dirt road that lead past the house. And she sat down in the middle of it.

Chapter Two

Michelle felt the vibration of the vehicle before she smelled the dust that came up around it. Her back was to the direction it was coming from. Desperation had blinded her to the hope of better days. She was sick of life. Sick of everything.

She put her hands on her knees, brought her elbows in, closed her eyes, and waited for the collision. It would probably hurt. Hopefully, it would be quick....

There was a squealing of tires and a metallic jerk. She didn't feel the impact. Was she dead?

Long, muscular legs in faded blue denim came into view above big black hand-tooled leather boots.

"Would you care to explain what the hell you're doing sitting in the middle of a road?" a deep, angry voice demanded.

She looked up into chilling liquid black eyes and grimaced. "Trying to get hit by a car?"

"I drive a truck," he pointed out.

"Trying to get hit by a truck," she amended in a matter-of-fact tone.

"Care to elaborate?"

She shrugged. "My stepmother will probably beat me when she gets back home because I ruined her sale."

He frowned. "What sale?"

"My father died three weeks ago," she said heavily. She figured he didn't know, because she hadn't seen any signs of life at the house down the road until she'd watched his truck go by just recently. "She had all his things taken to the landfill because I insisted on a real funeral, not a cremation, and now she's trying to sell his stamp collection. It's all I have left of him. I ruined the sale. The man left. She hit me...."

He turned his head. It was the first time he'd noticed the side of her face that looked almost blistered. His eyes narrowed. "Get in the truck."

She stared at him. "I'm all dusty."

"It's a dusty truck. It won't matter."

She got to her feet. "Are you abducting me?"

"Yes."

She sighed. "Okay." She glanced at him ruefully. "If you don't mind, I'd really like to go to Mars. Since I'm being abducted, I mean."

He managed a rough laugh.

She went around to the passenger side. He opened the door for her.

"You're Mr. Brandon," she said when he climbed into the driver's seat and slammed the door.

"Yes."

She drew in a breath. "I'm Michelle."

"Michelle." He chuckled. "There was a song with that

name. My father loved it. One of the lines was 'Michelle, *ma belle.*'" He glanced at her. "Do you speak French?"

"A little," she said. "I have it second period. It means something like 'my beauty.'" She laughed. "And that has nothing to do with me, I'm afraid. I'm just plain."

He glanced at her with raised eyebrows. Was she serious? She was gorgeous. Young, and untried, but her creamy complexion was without a blemish. She was nicely shaped and her hair was a pale blond. Those soft gray eyes reminded him of a fog in August...

He directed his eyes to the road. She was just a child, what was he thinking? "Beauty, as they say, is in the eye of the beholder."

"Do you speak French?" she asked, curious.

He nodded. "French, Spanish, Portuguese, Afrikaans, Norwegian, Russian, German and a handful of Middle Eastern dialects."

"Really?" She was fascinated. "Did you work as a translator or something?"

He pursed his lips. "From time to time," he said, and then laughed to himself.

"Cool."

He started the truck and drove down the road to the house he owned. It wasn't far, just about a half mile. It was a ranch house, set back off the road. There were oceans of flowers blooming around it in the summer, planted by the previous owner, Mrs. Eller, who had died. Of course, it was still just February, and very cold. There were no flowers here now.

"Mrs. Eller loved flowers."

"Excuse me?"

"She lived here all her life," she told him, smiling as they drove up to the front porch. "Her husband worked as a deputy sheriff. They had a son in the military, but he was killed overseas. Her husband died soon afterward. She planted so many flowers that you could never even see the house. I used to come over and visit her when I was little, with my grandfather."

"Your people are from here?"

"Oh, yes. For three generations. Daddy went to medical school in Georgia and then he set up a practice in cardiology in San Antonio. We lived there. But I spent every summer here with my grandparents while they were alive. Daddy kept the place up, after, and it was like a vacation home while Mama was alive." She swallowed. That loss had been harsh. "We still had everything, even the furniture, when Daddy decided to move us down here and take early retirement. She hated it from the first time she saw it." Her face hardened. "She's selling it. My stepmother, I mean. She's already talked about it."

He drew in a breath. He knew he was going to regret this. He got out, opened the passenger door and waited for her to get out. He led the way into the house, seated her in the kitchen and pulled out a pitcher of iced tea. When he had it in glasses, he sat down at the table with her.

"Go ahead," he invited. "Get it off your chest."

"It's not your problem…"

"You involved me in an attempted suicide," he said with a droll look. "That makes it my problem."

She grimaced. "I'm really sorry, Mr. Brandon…."

"Gabriel."

She hesitated.

He raised an eyebrow. "I'm not that old," he pointed out.

She managed a shy smile. "Okay."

He cocked his head. "Say it," he said, and his liquid black eyes stared unblinking into hers.

She felt her heart drop into her shoes. She swallowed

down a hot wave of delight and hoped it didn't show. "Ga…Gabriel," she obliged.

His face seemed to soften. Just a little. He smiled, showing beautiful white teeth. "That's better."

She flushed. "I'm not…comfortable with men," she blurted out.

His eyes narrowed on her face, her averted eyes. "Does your stepmother have a boyfriend?"

She swallowed, hard. The glass in her hand trembled.

He took the glass from her and put it on the table. "Tell me."

It all poured out. Finding Roberta in Bert's arms just after the funeral, finding them on the couch together that day, the way Bert looked and her and tried to touch her, the visit from her minister…

"And I thought my life was complicated," he said heavily. He shook his head. "I'd forgotten what it was like to be young and at the mercy of older people."

She studied him quietly. The expression on his face was…odd.

"You know," she said softly. "You understand."

"I had a stepfather," he said through his teeth. "He was always after my sister. She was very pretty, almost fourteen. I was a few years older, and I was bigger than he was. Our mother loved him, God knew why. We'd moved back to Texas because the international company he worked for promoted him and he had to go to Dallas for the job. One day I heard my sister scream. I went into her room, and there he was. He'd tried to…" He stopped. His face was like stone. "My mother had to get a neighbor to pull me off him. After that, after she knew what had been going on, she still defended him. I was arrested, but the public defender got an earful. He spoke to my sister. My stepfather was arrested, charged, tried. My mother stood by him, the whole time. My sister was victimized by the defense attorney, after what she'd already suffered at our stepfather's hands. She was so traumatized by the experience that she doesn't even date."

She winced. One small hand went shyly to cover his clenched fist on the table. "I'm so sorry."

He seemed to mentally shake himself, as if he'd been locked into the past. He met her soft, concerned gaze. His big hand turned, curled around hers. "I've never spoken of it, until now."

"Maybe sometimes it's good to share problems. Dark memories aren't so bad when you force them into the light."

"Seventeen going on thirty?" he mused, smiling at her. It didn't occur to her to wonder how he knew her age.

She smiled. "There are always people who are in worse shape than you are. My friend Billy has an alcoholic father who beats him and his mother. The police are over there all the time, but his mother will never press charges. Sheriff Carson says the next time, he's going to jail, even if he has to press charges himself."

"Good for the sheriff."

"What happened, after the trial?" she prodded gently.

He curled his fingers around Michelle's, as if he enjoyed their soft comfort. She might have been fascinated to know that he'd never shared these memories with any other woman, and that, as a rule, he hated having people touch him.

"He went to jail for child abuse," he said. "My mother was there every visiting day."

"No, what happened to you and your sister?"

"My mother refused to have us in the house with her. We were going to be placed in foster homes. The public defender had a maiden aunt, childless, who was suicidal. Her problems weren't so terrible, but she tended to depression and she let them take her almost over the edge. So he thought we might be able to help each other. We went to live with Aunt Maude." He chuckled. "She was not what you think of as anybody's maiden aunt. She drove a Jaguar, smoked like a furnace, could drink any grown man under the table, loved bingo parties and cooked like a gourmet. Oh, and she spoke about twenty languages. In her youth, she was in the army and mustered out as a sergeant."

"Wow," she exclaimed. "She must have been fascinating to live with."

"She was. And she was rich. She spoiled us rotten. She got my sister into therapy, for a while at least, and me into the army right after I graduated." He smiled. "She was nuts about Christmas. We had trees that bent at the ceiling, and the limbs groaned under all the decorations. She'd go out and invite every street person she could find over to eat with us." His face sobered. "She said she'd seen foreign countries where the poor were treated better than they were here. Ironically, it was one of the same people she invited to Christmas dinner who stabbed her to death."

She winced. "I'm so sorry!"

"Me, too. By that time, though, Sara and I were grown. I was in the...military," he said, hoping she didn't notice the involuntary pause, "and Sara had her own apartment. Maude left everything she had to the two of us and her nephew. We tried to give our share back to him, as her only blood heir, but he just laughed and said he got to keep his aunt for years longer because of us. He went into private practice and made a fortune defending drug lords, so he didn't really need it, he told us."

"Defending drug lords." She shook her head.

"We all do what we do," he pointed out. "Besides, I've known at least one so-called drug lord who was better than some upright people."

She just laughed.

He studied her small hand. "If things get too rough for you over there, let me know. I'll manage something."

"It's only until graduation this spring," she pointed out.

"In some situations, a few months can be a lifetime," he said quietly.

She nodded.

"Friends help each other."

She studied his face. "Are we? Friends, I mean?"

"We must be. I haven't told anyone else about my stepfather."

"You didn't tell me the rest of it."

His eyes went back to her hand resting in his. "He got out on good behavior six months after his conviction and decided to make my sister pay for testifying against him. She called 911. The police shot him."

"Oh, my gosh."

"My mother blamed both of us for it. She moved back to Canada, to Alberta, where we grew up."

"Are you Canadian?" she asked curiously.

He smiled. "I'm actually Texas born. We moved to Canada to stay with my mother's people when my father was in the military and stationed overseas. Sara was born in Calgary. We lived there until just after my mother married my stepfather."

"Did you see your mother again, after that?" she asked gently.

He shook his head. "Our mother never spoke to us again. She died a few years back. Her attorney tracked me down and said she left her estate, what there was of it, to the cousins in Alberta."

"I'm so sorry."

"Life is what it is. I had hoped she might one day realize what she'd done to my sister. She never did."

"We can't help who we love, or what it does to mess us up."

He frowned. "You really are seventeen going on thirty."

She laughed softly. "Maybe I'm an old soul."

"Ah. Been reading philosophy, have we?"

"Yes." She paused. "You haven't mentioned your father."

He smiled sadly. "He was in a paramilitary group overseas. He stepped on an antipersonnel mine."

She didn't know what a paramilitary group was, so she just nodded.

"He was from Dallas," he continued. "He had a small ranch in Texas that he inherited from his grandfather. He and my mother met at the Calgary Stampede. He trained horses and he'd sold several to be used at the stampede. She had an uncle who owned a ranch in Alberta and also supplied livestock to the stampede." He stared at her small hand in his. "Her people were French-Canadian. One of my grandmothers was a member of the Blackfoot Nation."

"Wow!"

He smiled.

"Then, you're an American citizen," she said.

"Our parents did the whole citizenship process. In short, I now have both Canadian and American citizenship."

"My dad loved this Canadian television show, *Due*

South. He had the whole DVD collection. I liked the Mountie's dog. He was a wolf."

He laughed. "I've got the DVDs, too. I loved the show. It was hilarious."

She glanced at the clock on the wall. "I have to go. If you aren't going to run over me, I'll have to fix supper in case she comes home to eat. It's going to be gruesome. She'll still be furious about the stamp collection." Her face grew hard. "She won't find it. I've got a hiding place she doesn't know about."

He smiled. "Devious."

"Not normally. But she's not selling Daddy's stamps."

He let go of her hand and got up from his chair. "If she hits you again, call 911."

"She'd kill me for that."

"Not likely."

She sighed. "I guess I could, if I had to."

"You mentioned your minister. Who is he?"

"Jake Blair. Why?"

His expression was deliberately blank.

"Do you know him? He's a wonderful minister. Odd thing, my stepmother was intimidated by him."

He hesitated, and seemed to be trying not to laugh. "Yes. I've heard of him."

"He told her that his daughter was going to pick me up and bring me home from church every week. His daughter works for the Jacobsville police chief."

"Cash Grier."

She nodded. "He's very nice."

"Cash Grier?" he exclaimed. "Nice?"

"Oh, I know people talk about him, but he came to speak to my civics class once. He's intelligent."

"Very."

He helped her back into the truck and drove her to her front door.

She hesitated before she got out, turning to him. "Thank you. I don't think I've ever been so depressed. I've never actually tried to kill myself before."

His liquid black eyes searched hers. "We all have days when we're ridden by the 'black dog.'"

She blinked. "Excuse me?"

He chuckled. "Winston Churchill had periods of severe depression. He called it that."

She frowned. "Winston Churchill…"

"There was this really big world war," he said facetiously, with over-the-top enthusiasm, "and this country called England, and it had a leader during—"

"Oh, give me a break!" She burst out laughing.

He grinned at her. "Just checking."

She shook her head. "I know who he was. I just had to put it into context is all. Thanks again."

"Anytime."

She got out and closed the door, noting with relief that Roberta hadn't come home yet. She smiled and waved. He waved back. When he drove off, she noticed that he didn't look back. Not at all.

She had supper ready when Roberta walked in the door. Her stepmother was still fuming.

"I'm not eating beef," she said haughtily. "You know I hate it. And are those mashed potatoes? I'll bet you crammed them with butter!"

"Yes, I did," Michelle replied quietly, "because you always said you liked them that way."

Roberta's cheeks flushed. She shifted, as if the words, in that quiet voice, made her feel guilty.

In fact, they did. She was remembering her behavior

with something close to shame. Her husband had only been dead three weeks. She'd tossed his belongings, refused to go to the funeral, made fun of her stepdaughter at every turn, even slapped her for messing up the sale of stamps which Alan had left to Michelle. And after all that, the child made her favorite food. Her behavior should be raising red flags, but her stepdaughter was, thankfully, too naive to notice it. Bert's doing, she thought bitterly. All his fault.

"You don't have to eat it," Michelle said, turning away.

Roberta made a rough sound in her throat. "It's all right," she managed tautly. She sat down at the table. She glanced at Michelle, who was dipping a tea bag in a cup of steaming water. "Aren't you eating?"

"I had soup."

Roberta made inroads into the meat loaf and mashed potatoes. The girl had even made creamed peas, her favorite.

She started to put her fork down and noticed her hand trembling. She jerked it down onto the wood and pulled her hand back.

It was getting worse. She needed more and more. Bert was complaining about the expense. They'd had a fight. She'd gone storming up to his apartment in San Antonio to cry on his shoulder about her idiot stepdaughter and he'd started complaining when she dipped into his stash. But after all, he was the one who'd gotten her hooked in the first place.

It had taken more money than she'd realized to keep up, and Alan had finally figured out what she was doing. They'd argued. He'd asked her for a divorce, but she'd pleaded with him. She had no place to go. She knew Bert wouldn't hear of her moving in with him. Her whole family was dead.

Alan had agreed, but the price of his agreement was that she had to move down to his hometown with him after he sold his very lucrative practice in San Antonio.

She'd thought he meant the move to be a temporary one. He was tired of the rat race. He wanted something quieter. But they'd only been in his old family homestead for a few days when he confessed that he'd been diagnosed with an inoperable cancer. He wanted to spend some time with his daughter before the end. He wanted to run a free clinic, to help people who had no money for doctors. He wanted his life to end on a positive note, in the place where he was born.

So here was Roberta, stuck after his death with a habit she could no longer afford and no way to break it. Stuck with Cinderella here, who knew about as much about life as she knew about men.

She glared at the girl. She'd really needed the money from those stamps. There was nothing left that she could liquidate for cash. She hadn't taken all of Alan's things to the landfill. She'd told Michelle that so she wouldn't look for them. She'd gone to a consignment shop in San Antonio and sold the works, even his watch. It brought in a few hundred dollars. But she was going through money like water.

"What did you do with the stamps?" Roberta asked suddenly.

Michelle schooled her features to give away nothing, and she turned. "I hitched a ride into town and asked Cash Grier to keep them for me."

Roberta sucked in her breath. Fear radiated from her. "Cash Grier?"

Michelle nodded. "I figured it was the safest place. I told him I was worried about someone stealing them while I was at school."

Which meant she hadn't told the man that Roberta had slapped her. Thank God. All she needed now was an assault charge. She had to be more careful. The girl was too stupid to recognize her symptoms. The police chief wouldn't be. She didn't want anyone from law enforcement on the place. But she didn't even have the grace to blush when Michelle made the comment about someone possibly "stealing" her stamp collection.

She got up from the table. She was thirsty, but she knew it would be disastrous to pick up her cup of coffee. Not until she'd taken what she needed to steady her hands.

She paused on her way to the bathroom, with her back to Michelle. "I'm… I shouldn't have slapped you," she bit off.

She didn't wait for a reply. She was furious with herself for that apology. Why should the kid's feelings matter to her, anyway? She pushed away memories of how welcoming Michelle had been when she first started dating Alan. Michelle had wanted to impress her father's new friend.

Well, that was ancient history now. She was broke and Alan had died, leaving her next to nothing. She picked up her purse from the side table and went into the bathroom with it.

Michelle cleaned off the table and put the dishes into the dishwasher. Roberta hadn't come out of the bathroom even after she'd done all that, so she went to her room.

Michelle had been surprised by the almost-apology. But once she thought about it, she realized that Roberta might think she was going to press charges. She was afraid of her stepmother. She had violent mood swings and she'd threatened to hit Michelle several times.

It was odd, because when she'd first married Dr. Alan Godfrey, Michelle had liked her. She'd been fun to be around. But she had a roving eye. She liked men. If they went to a restaurant, someone always struck up a conversation with Roberta, who was exquisitely groomed and dressed and had excellent manners. Roberta enjoyed masculine attention, without being either coarse or forward.

Then, several months ago, everything had changed. Roberta had started going out at night alone. She told her husband that she'd joined an exercise club at a friend's house, a private one. They did aerobics and Pilates and things like that. Just women.

But soon afterward, Roberta became more careless about her appearance. Her manners slipped, badly. She complained about everything. Alan wasn't giving her enough spending money. The house needed cleaning, why wasn't Michelle doing more when she wasn't in school? She wasn't doing any more cooking, she didn't like it, Michelle would have to take over for her. And on it went. Alan had been devastated by the change. So had Michelle, who had to bear the brunt of most of Roberta's fury.

"Some women have mood swings as they get older," Alan had confided to his daughter, but there was something odd in his tone of voice. "But you mustn't say anything about it to her. She doesn't like thinking she's getting on in years. All right?"

"All right, Daddy," she'd agreed, with a big smile.

He'd hugged her close. "That's my girl."

Roberta had gone away for a few weeks after that. Then, not too long after her return, they'd moved to Comanche Wells, into the house where Michelle had spent so many happy weeks with her grandparents every summer.

The elderly couple had died in a wreck only a few years after Michelle's mother had died of a stroke. It had been a blow. Her father had gone through terrible grief. But then, so had Michelle.

Despite the double tragedy, Comanche Wells and this house seemed far more like home than San Antonio ever had, because it was so small that Michelle knew almost every family who lived in it. She knew people in Jacobsville, too, of course, but it was much larger. Comanche Wells was tiny by comparison.

Michelle loved the farm animals that her grandparents had kept. They always had dogs and cats and chickens for her to play with. But by the time Alan moved his family down here, there was only the small herd of beef cattle. Now the herd had been sold and was going to a local rancher who was going to truck the steers over to his own ranch.

Her door opened suddenly. Roberta looked wild-eyed. "I'm going back up to San Antonio for the night. I have to see Bert."

"All…" She had started to say "all right," but the door slammed. Roberta went straight out to her car, revved it up and scattered gravel on the way to the road.

It was odd behavior, even for her.

Michelle felt a little better than she had. At least she and Roberta might be able to manage each other's company until May, when graduation rolled around.

But Gabriel had helped her cope with what she thought was unbearable. She smiled, remembering his kindness, remembering the strong, warm clasp of his fingers. Her heart sailed at the memory. She'd almost never held hands with a boy. Once, when she was twelve, at a school dance. But the boy had moved away, and she was far too shy and old-fashioned to appeal to most of the boys in her high school classes. There had been another boy, at high school, but that date had ended in near disaster.

Gabriel was no boy. He had to be at least in his mid-twenties. He would think of her as a child. She grimaced. Well, she was growing up. One day…who knew what might happen?

She opened her English textbook and got busy with her homework. Then she remembered with a start what she'd told Roberta, that lie about having Cash Grier keep the stamp book. What if Roberta asked him?

Her face flamed. It would be a disaster. She'd lied, and Roberta would know it. She'd tear the house apart looking for that collection…

Then Michelle calmed down. Roberta seemed afraid of Cash Grier. Most people were. She doubted very seriously that her stepmother would approach him. But just to cover her bases, she was going to stop by his office after school. She could do it by pretending to ask Carlie what time she would pick her up for church services. Then maybe she could work up the nerve to tell him what she'd done. She would go without lunch. That would give her just enough money to pay for a cab home from Jacobsville, which was only a few miles away. Good thing she already had her lunch money for the week, because Roberta had told her there wouldn't be any more. She was going to have to do without lunch from now on, apparently. Or get a job. And good luck to that, without a car or a driver's license.

She sighed. Her life was more complicated than it had ever been. But things might get better. Someday.

Chapter Three

Michelle got off the school bus in downtown Jacobsville on Friday afternoon. She had to stop by the newspaper office to ask Minette Carson if she'd give her a reference for the scholarship she was applying for. The office was very close to police chief Grier's office, whom she also needed to see. And she had just enough money to get the local cab company to take her home.

Minette was sitting out front at her desk when Michelle walked in. She grinned and got up to greet her.

"How's school?" she asked.

"Going very well," Michelle said. "I wanted to ask if I could put you down as a reference. I'm applying for that journalism scholarship we spoke about last month, at Marist College in San Antonio."

"Of course you can."

"Thanks. I'm hoping I can keep my grades up so I'll have a shot at it."

"You'll do fine, Michelle. You have a way with words." She held up a hand when Michelle looked as if she might protest. "I never lie about writing. I'm brutally honest. If I thought you didn't have the skill, I'd keep my mouth shut."

Michelle laughed. "Okay. Thanks, then."

Minette perched on the edge of her desk. "I was wondering if you might like to work part-time for me. After school and Saturday morning."

Michelle's jaw dropped. "You mean, work here?" she exclaimed. "Oh, my gosh, I'd love to!" Then the joy drained out of her face. "I can't," she groaned. "I don't drive, and I don't have cab fare home. I mean, I do today, but I went without lunch…." Her face flamed.

"Carlie lives just past you," she said gently. "She works until five. So do we. I know she'd let you ride with her. She works Saturday mornings, too."

The joy came back into her features. "I'll ask her!"

Minette chuckled. "Do that. And let me know."

"I will, I promise."

"You can start Monday, if you like. Do you have a cell phone?" Minette asked.

Michelle hesitated and shook her head with lowered eyes.

"Don't worry about it. We'll get you one."

"Oh, but…."

"I'll have you phoning around town for news. Junior reporter stuff," she added with a grin. "A cell's an absolute necessity."

"In that case, okay, but I'll pay you back."

"That's a deal."

"I'll go over and talk to Carlie."

"Stop back by and let me know, okay?"

"Okay!"

She didn't normally rush, but she was so excited that her feet carried her across the street like wings.

She walked into the police station. Cash Grier was perched on Carlie's desk, dictating from a paper he held in his hand. He stopped when he saw Michelle.

"Sorry," Michelle said, coloring. She clutched her textbooks to her chest almost as a shield. "I just needed to ask Carlie something. I can come back later...."

"Nonsense," Cash said, and grinned.

She managed a shy smile. "Thanks." She hesitated. "I told a lie to my stepmother," she blurted out. "I think you should know, because it involved you."

His dark eyebrows arched. "Really? Did you volunteer me for the lead in a motion picture or something? Because I have to tell you, my asking price is extremely high...."

She laughed with pure delight. "No. I told her I gave you my father's stamp collection for safekeeping." She flushed again. "She was going to sell it. She'd already thrown away all his stuff. He and I worked on the stamp collection together as long as I can remember. It's all I have left of him." She swallowed. Hard.

Cash got up. He towered over her. He wasn't laughing. "You bring it in here and I'll put it in the safe," he said gently. "Nobody will touch it."

"Thanks." She was trying not to cry. "That's so kind..."

"Now, don't cry or you'll have me in tears. What would people think? I mean, I'm a big, tough cop. I can't be seen standing around sobbing all over the place. Crime would flourish!"

That amused her. She stopped biting her lip and actually grinned.

"That's better." His black eyes narrowed quizzically.

"Your stepmother seems to have some issues. I got an earful from your minister this morning."

She nodded sadly. "She was so different when we lived in San Antonio. I mean, we went shopping together, we took turns cooking. Then we moved down here and she got mixed up with that Bert person." She shivered. "He gives me cold chills, but she's crazy about him."

"Bert Sims?" Cash asked in a deceptively soft tone.

"That's him."

Cash didn't say anything else. "If things get rough over there, call me, will you? I know you're outside the city limits, but I can get to Hayes Carson pretty quick if I have to, and he has jurisdiction."

"Oh, it's nothing like that...."

"Isn't it?" Cash asked.

She felt chilled. It was as if he was able to see Roberta through her eyes, and he saw everything.

"She did apologize. Sort of. For hitting me, I mean."

"Hitting you?" Cash stood straighter. "When?"

"I messed up the sale of Daddy's stamps. She was wild-eyed and screaming. She just slapped me, is all. She's been excitable since before Daddy died, but now she's just...just...nuts. She talks about money all the time, like she's dying to get her hands on some. But she doesn't buy clothes or cosmetics, she doesn't even dress well anymore."

"Do you know why?"

She shook her head. She drew in a breath. "She doesn't drink," she said. "I know that's what you're thinking. She and Daddy used to have drinks every night, and she had a problem for a little while, but she got over it."

Cash just nodded. "You let me know if things get worse. Okay?"

"Okay, Chief. Thanks," she added.

The phone rang. Carlie answered it. "It's your wife," she said with a big grin.

Cash's face lit up. "Really? Wow. A big-time movie star calling me up on the phone. I'm just awed, I am." He grinned. Everybody knew his wife, Tippy, had been known as the Georgia Firefly when she'd been a supermodel and, later, an actress. "I'll take it in my office. With the door closed." He made a mock scowl. "And no eavesdropping."

Carlie put her hand over her heart. "I swear."

"Not in my office, you don't," he informed her. "Swearing is a misdemeanor."

She stuck out her tongue at his departing back.

"I saw that," he said without looking behind him. He went into his office and closed the door on two giggling women.

"He's a trip to work for," Carlie enthused, her green eyes sparkling in a face framed by short, dark, wavy hair. "I was scared to death of him when I interviewed for the job. At least, until he accused me of hiding his bullets and telling his men that he read fashion magazines in the bathroom."

Michelle laughed.

"He's really funny. He says he keeps files on aliens in the filing cabinet and locks it so I won't peek." The smile moderated. "But if there's an emergency, he's the toughest guy I've ever known. I would never cross him, if I was a criminal."

"They say he chased a speeder all the way to San Antonio once."

She laughed. "That wasn't the chief. That was Kilraven, who worked here undercover." She leaned forward. "He really belongs to a federal agency. We're not supposed to mention it."

"I won't tell," Michelle promised.

"However, the chief—" she nodded toward his closed door "—got on a plane to an unnamed foreign country, tossed a runaway criminal into a bag and boated him to Miami. The criminal was part of a drug cartel. He killed a small-town deputy because he thought the man was a spy. He wasn't, but he was just as dead. Then the feds got involved and the little weasel escaped into a country that didn't have an extradition treaty with us. However, once he was on American soil, he was immediately arrested by Dade County deputies." She grinned. "The chief denied ever having seen the man, and nobody could prove that it was him on the beach. And," she added darkly, "you never heard that from me. Right?"

"Right!"

Carlie laughed. "So what can I do for you?"

"I need a ride home from work."

"I've got another hour to go, but…"

"Not today," Michelle said. "Starting Monday. Minette Carson just offered me a part-time job, but I don't have a way to get home. And she said I could work part-time Saturday, but I can't drive and I don't have a car."

"You can ride with me, and I'd welcome the company," Carlie said easily.

"I'll chip in for the gas."

"That would really help! Have you seen what I drive?" She groaned. "My dad has this thing about cars. He thinks you need an old truck to keep you from speeding, so he bought me a twelve-year-old tank. At least, it looks like a tank." She frowned. "Maybe it was a tank and he had it remodeled. Anyway, it barely gets twelve miles to a gallon and it won't go over fifty." She shook her head. "He drives a vintage Ford Cobra," she added with a scowl. "One of the neatest rides on the planet and I'm not allowed to touch it, can you believe that?"

Michelle just grinned. She didn't know anything about cars. She did recall the way the minister had peeled out of the driveway, scattering gravel. That car he drove had one big engine.

"Your dad scared my stepmother." Michelle laughed. "She wasn't letting me go to church. Your dad said I could ride with you." She stopped and flushed. "I really feel like I'm imposing. I wish I could drive. I wish I had a car…."

"It's really not imposing," Carlie said softly, smiling. "As I said, I'd like the company. I go down lots of back roads getting here from Comanche Wells. I'm not spooky or anything, but this guy did try to kill my Dad with a knife." She lowered her eyes. "I got in the way."

Michelle felt guilty that she hadn't remembered. "I'll learn karate," she promised. "We can go to a class together or something, and if anybody attacks us we can fight back!"

"Bad idea," Cash said, rejoining them. "A few weeks of martial arts won't make you an expert. Even an expert," he added solemnly, "knows better than to fight if he can get away from an armed man."

"That isn't what the ads say," Carlie mused, grinning.

"Yes, I know," Cash replied. "Take it from me, disarming someone with a gun is difficult even for a black belt." He leaned forward. "Which I am."

Carlie stood up, bowed deeply from the waist, and said, "Sensei!" Cash lost it. He roared with laughter.

"You could teach us," Michelle suggested. "Couldn't you?"

Cash just smiled. "I suppose it wouldn't hurt. Just a few basics for an emergency. But if you have an armed opponent, you run," he said firmly. "Or if you're cornered, scream, make a fuss. Never," he emphasized, "get into a car with anyone who threatens to kill you if you don't. Once he's got you in a car, away from help, you're dead, anyway."

Michelle felt chills run down her spine. "Okay."

Carlie looked uncomfortable. She knew firsthand about an armed attacker. Unconsciously, she rubbed the shoulder where the knife had gone in. She'd tried to protect her father. Her assailant had been arrested, but had died soon afterward. She never knew why her father had been the target of an attack by a madman.

"Deep thoughts?" Michelle asked her.

She snapped back. "Sorry. I was remembering the guy who attacked my father." She frowned. "What sort of person attacks a minister, for goodness' sake!"

"Come on down to federal lockup with me, and I'll show you a baker's dozen who have," Cash told her. "Religious arguments quite often lead to murder, even in families. That's why," he added, "we don't discuss politics or religion in the office." He frowned. "Well, if someone died in here, we'd probably say a prayer. And if the president came to see me, and why wouldn't he, we'd probably discuss his foreign policy."

"Why would the president come to see you?" Michelle asked innocently.

Cash pursed his lips. "For advice, of course. I have some great ideas about foreign policy."

"For instance?" Carlie mused.

"I think we should declare war on Tahiti."

They both stared at him.

"Well, if we do, we can send troops, right?" he continued. "And what soldier in his right mind wouldn't want to go and fight in Tahiti? Lush tropical flowers, firedancing, beautiful women, the ocean…"

"Tahiti doesn't have a standing army, I don't think," Michelle ventured.

"All the better. We can just occupy it for like three weeks, let them surrender, and then give them foreign aid." He glowered. "Now you've done it. You'll repeat that everywhere and the president will hear about it and he'll never have to come and hear me explain it. You've blown my chances for an invitation to the White House," he groaned. "And I did so want to spend a night in the Lincoln bedroom!"

"Listen, break out those files on aliens that you keep in your filing cabinet and tell the president you've got them!" Carlie suggested, while Michelle giggled. "He'll come right down here to have a look at them!"

"They won't let him," Cash sighed. "His security clearance isn't high enough."

"What?" Carlie exclaimed.

"Well, he's only in the office for four years, eight tops. So the guys in charge of the letter agencies—the really secretive ones—allegedly keep some secrets to themselves. Particularly those dealing with aliens." He chuckled.

The girls, who didn't know whether to believe him or not, just laughed along with him.

Michelle stopped back by Minette's office to tell her the good news, and to thank her again for the job.

"You know," she said, "Chief Grier is really nice."

"Nice when he likes you," Minette said drily. "There are a few criminals in maximum-security prisons who might disagree."

"No doubt there."

"So, will Monday suit you, to start to work?" Minette asked.

"I'd really love to start yesterday." Michelle laughed. "I'm so excited!"

Minette grinned. "Monday will come soon enough. We'll see you then."

"Can you write me a note? Just in case I need one?" She was thinking of how to break it to Roberta. That was going to be tricky.

"No problem." Minette went to her desk, typed out an explanation of Michelle's new position, and signed it. She handed it to the younger woman. "There you go."

"Dress code?" Michelle asked, glancing around the big open room where several people were sitting at desks, to a glass-walled room beyond which big sheets of paper rested on a long section like a chalkboard.

"Just be neat," Minette said easily. "I mostly kick around in jeans and T-shirts, although I dress when I go to political meetings or to interviews with state or federal politicians. You'll need to learn how to use a camera, as well. We have digital ones. They're very user-friendly."

"This is very exciting," Michelle said, her gray eyes glimmering with delight.

Minette laughed. "It is to me, too, and I've done this since I was younger than you are. I grew up running around this office." She looked around with pure love in her eyes. "It's home."

"I'm really looking forward to it. Will I just be reporting news?"

"No. Well, not immediately, at least. You'll learn every aspect of the business, from selling ads to typing copy to composition. Even subscriptions." She leaned forward. "You'll learn that some subscribers probably used to be doctors, because the handwriting looks more like Sanskrit than English."

Michelle chuckled. "I'll cope. My dad had the worst handwriting in the world."

"And he was a doctor," Minette agreed, smiling.

The smile faded. "He was a very good doctor," she said, trying not to choke up. "Sorry," she said, wiping away a tear. "It's still hard."

"It takes time," Minette said with genuine sympathy. "I lost my mother, my stepfather, my stepmother—I loved them all. You'll adjust, but you have to get through the grief process first. Tears are healing."

"Thanks."

"If you need to talk, I'm here. Anytime. Night or day."

Michelle wiped away more tears. "That's really nice of you."

"I know how it feels."

The phone rang and one of the employees called out. "For you, boss. The mayor returning your call."

Minette grimaced. "I have to take it. I'm working on a story about the new water system. It's going to be super."

"I'll see you after school Monday, then. And thanks again."

"My pleasure."

Michelle went home with dreams of journalism dancing in her head. She'd never been so happy. Things were really looking up.

She noted that Roberta's car was in the driveway and she mentally braced herself for a fight. It was suppertime and she hadn't been there to cook. She was going to be in big trouble.

Sure enough, the minute she walked in the door, Roberta threw her hands up and glared at her. "I'm not cooking," she said furiously. "That's your job. Where the hell have you been?"

Michelle swallowed. "I was in…in town."

"Doing what?" came the tart query.

She shifted. "Getting a job."

"A job?" She frowned, and her eyes didn't seem to quite focus. "Well, I'm not driving you to work, even if somebody was crazy enough to hire you!"

"I have a ride," she replied.

"A job," she scoffed. "As if you're ever around to do chores as it is. You're going to get a job? Who's going to do the laundry and the housecleaning and the cooking?"

Michelle bit her tongue, trying not to say what she was thinking. "I have to have money for lunch," she said, thinking fast.

Roberta blinked, then she remembered that she'd said Michelle wasn't getting any more lunch money. She averted her eyes.

"Besides, I have to save for college. I'll start in the fall semester."

"Jobs. College." Roberta looked absolutely furious. "And you think I'm going to stay down here in this hick town while you sashay off to college in some big city, do you?"

"I graduate in just over three months…"

"I'm putting the house on the market," Roberta shot back. She held up a hand. "Don't even bother arguing. I'm listing the house with a San Antonio broker, not one from here." She gave Michelle a dirty look. "They're all on your side, trying to keep the property off the market. It won't work. I need money!"

For just one instant, Michelle thought about letting her have the stamps. Then she decided it was useless to do that. Roberta would spend the money and still try to sell the house. She comforted herself with what the local Realtor had told her—that it would take time for the will to get through probate. If there was a guardian angel, perhaps hers would drag out the time required for all that. And even then, there was a chance the house wouldn't sell.

"I don't imagine a lot of people want to move to a town this small," Michelle said out loud.

"Somebody local might buy it. One of those ranchers." She made it sound like a dirty word.

That made Michelle feel better. If someone from here bought the house, they might consider renting it to her. Since she had a job, thanks to Minette, she could probably afford reasonable rent.

Roberta wiped her face. She was sweating.

Michelle frowned. "Are you all right?"

"Of course I'm all right, I'm just hungry!"

"I'll make supper." She went to her room to put her books away and stopped short. The place was in shambles. Drawers had been emptied, the clothes from the shelves in the closet were tossed haphazardly all over the floor. Michelle's heart jumped, but she no*f*ticed without looking too hard that the baseboards in the closet were still where they should be. She looked around but not too closely. After all, she'd told Roberta that Chief Grier had her father's stamp collection. It hadn't stopped Roberta from searching the room. But it was obvious that she hadn't found anything.

She went back out into the hall, where her stepmother was standing with folded arms, a disappointed look on her face. She'd expected that the girl would go immediately to where she'd hidden the stamps. The fact that she didn't even search meant they weren't here. Damn the luck, she really had taken them to the police chief. And even Roberta wasn't brash enough to walk up to Cash Grier and demand the stamp collection back, although she was probably within her legal rights to do so.

"Don't tell me," Michelle said, staring at her. "Squirrels?"

Roberta was disconcerted. Without meaning to, she burst out laughing at the girl's audacity. She turned away, shaking her head. "All right, I just wanted to make sure the stamp collection wasn't still here. I guess you were telling the truth all along."

"Roberta, if you need money so much, why don't you get a job?"

"I had a job, if you recall," she replied. "I worked in retail."

That was true. Roberta had worked at the cosmetics counter in one of San Antonio's most prestigious department stores.

"But I'm not going back to that," Roberta scoffed. "Once I sell this dump of a house, I'll be able to go to New York or Los Angeles and find a man who really is rich, instead of one who's just pretending to be," she added sarcastically.

"Gosh. Poor Bert," Michelle said. "Does he know?"

Roberta's eyes flashed angrily. "If you say a word to him…!"

Michelle held up both hands. "Not my business."

"Exactly!" Roberta snapped. "Now, how about fixing supper?"

"Sure," Michelle agreed. "As soon as I clean up my room," she added in a bland tone.

Her stepmother actually flushed. She took a quick breath. She was shivering. "I need…more…" she mumbled to herself. She went back into her own room and slammed the door.

They ate together, but Michelle didn't taste much of her supper. Roberta read a fashion magazine while she spooned food into her mouth.

"Where are you getting a job? Who's going to even hire a kid like you?" she asked suddenly.

"Minette Carson."

The magazine stilled in her hands. "You're going to work for a newspaper?"

"Of course. I want to study journalism in college."

Roberta looked threatened. "Well, I don't want you working for newspapers. Find something else."

"I won't," Michelle said firmly. "This is what I want to do for a living. I have to start somewhere. And I have to save for college. Unless you'd like to volunteer to pay my tuition...."

"Ha! Fat chance!" Roberta scoffed.

"That's what I thought. I'm going to a public college, but I still have to pay for books and tuition."

"Newspapers. Filthy rags." Her voice sounded slurred. She was picking at her food. Her fork was moving in slow motion. And she was still sweating.

"They do a great deal of good," Michelle argued. "They're the eyes and ears of the public."

"Nosy people sticking their heads into things that don't concern them!"

Michelle looked down at her plate. She didn't mention that people without things to hide shouldn't have a problem with that.

Roberta took her paper towel and mopped her sweaty face. She seemed disoriented and she was flushed, as well.

"You should see a doctor," Michelle said quietly. "There's that flu still going around."

"I'm not sick," the older woman said sharply. "And my health is none of your business!"

Michelle grimaced. She sipped milk instead of answering.

"It's too hot in here. You don't have to keep the thermostat so high!"

"It's seventy degrees," Michelle said, surprised. "I can't keep it higher or we couldn't afford the gas bill." She paid the bills with money that was grudgingly supplied by Roberta from the joint bank account she'd had with Michelle's father. Roberta hadn't lifted a finger to pay a bill since Alan had died.

"Well, it's still hot!" came the agitated reply. She got up from the table. "I'm going outside. I can't breathe in here."

Michelle watched her go with open curiosity. Odd. Roberta seemed out of breath and flushed more and more lately. She had episodes of shaking that seemed very unusual. She acted drunk sometimes, but Michelle knew she wasn't drinking. There was no liquor in the house. It probably was the flu. She couldn't understand why a person who was obviously sick wouldn't just go to the doctor in the first—

There was a loud thud from the general direction of the front porch.

Chapter Four

Michelle got up from her chair and went out onto the porch. It sounded as if Roberta had flung a chair against the wall, maybe in another outburst of temper.

She opened the door and stopped. Roberta was lying there, on her back on the porch, gasping for breath, her eyes wide, her face horrified.

"It's all right, I'll call 911!" She ran for the phone and took it outside with her while she pushed in the emergency services number.

Roberta was grimacing. "The pain!" she groaned. "Hurts…so…bad! Michelle…!"

Roberta held out her hand. Michelle took it, held it, squeezed it comfortingly.

"Jacobs County 911 Center," came a gentle voice on the line. "Is this an emergency?"

"Yes. This is Michelle Godfrey. My stepmother is

complaining of chest pain. She's short of breath and barely conscious."

"We'll get someone right out there. Stay on the line."

"Yes, of course."

"Help me," Roberta sobbed.

Michelle's hand closed tighter around her stepmother's. "The EMTs are on the way," she said gently. "It will be all right."

"Bert," Roberta choked. "Damn Bert! It's…his…fault!"

"Please don't try to get up," Michelle said, holding the older woman down. "Lie still."

"I'll…kill him," Roberta choked. "I'll kill him…!"

"Roberta, lie still," Michelle said firmly.

"Oh, God, it hurts!" Roberta sobbed. "My chest…. my chest…!"

Sirens were becoming noticeable in the distance.

"They're almost there, dear," the operator said gently. "Just a few more minutes."

"Yes, I hear them," Michelle said. "She says her chest hurts."

There was muffled conversation in the background, on the phone.

Around the curve, the ambulance shot toward her leaving a wash of dust behind it. Roberta's grip on Michelle's hand was painful.

The older woman was white as a sheet. The hand Michelle was holding was cold and clammy. "I'm…sorry," Roberta bit off. Tears welled in her eyes. "He said it wasn't…pure! He swore…! It was too…much…" She gasped for breath. "Don't let Bert…get away…with it…" Her eyes closed. She shivered. The hand holding Michelle's went slack.

The ambulance was in the driveway now, and a man and a woman jumped out of it and ran toward the porch.

"She said her chest hurt." Michelle faltered as she got out of the way. "And she couldn't breathe." Tears were salty in her eyes.

Roberta had never been really kind to her, except at the beginning of her relationship with Michelle's father. But the woman was in such pain. It hurt her to see anyone like that, even a mean person.

"Is she going to be all right?" Michelle asked.

They ignored her. They were doing CPR. She recognized it, because one of the Red Cross people had come to her school and demonstrated it. In between compressions one EMT ran to the truck and came back with paddles. They set the machine up and tried to restart Roberta's heart. Once. Twice. Three times. In between there were compressions of the chest and hurried communications between the EMTs and a doctor at the hospital.

After a few minutes, one EMT looked at the other and shook his head. They stood up. The man turned to Michelle. "I'm very sorry."

"Sorry. Sorry?" She looked down at the pale, motionless woman on the dusty front porch with a blank expression. "You mean, she's…?"

They nodded. "We'll call the coroner and have him come out, and we'll notify the sheriff's department, since you're outside the city limits. We can't move her until he's finished. Do you want to call the funeral home and make arrangements?"

"Yes, uh, yes." She pushed her hair back. She couldn't believe this. Roberta was dead? How could she be dead? She just stood there, numb, while the EMTs loaded up their equipment and went back out to the truck.

"Is there someone who can stay with you until the

coroner gets here?" the female EMT asked softly, staring worriedly at Michelle.

She stared back at the woman, devoid of thought. Roberta was dead. She'd watched her die. She was in shock.

Just as the reality of the situation really started to hit her, a pickup truck pulled up into the driveway, past the EMT vehicle, and stopped. A tall, good-looking man got out of it, paused to speak to the male EMT and then came right up to the porch.

Without a word, he pulled Michelle into his arms and held her, rocked her. She burst into tears.

"I'll take care of her," he told the female EMT with a smile.

"Thanks," she said. "She'll need to make arrangements…."

"I'll handle it."

"We've notified the authorities," the EMT added. "The sheriff's department and the coroner should arrive shortly." The EMTs left, the ambulance silent and grim now, instead of alive with light and sound, as when it had arrived.

Michelle drank in the scent that clung to Gabriel, the smells of soap and spicy cologne, the leather smell of his jacket. Beneath that, the masculine odor of his skin. She pressed close into his arms and let the tears fall.

Zack Tallman arrived just behind the coroner. Michelle noted the activity on the front porch, but she didn't want to see Roberta's body again. She didn't go outside.

She heard Gabriel and the lawman and the coroner discussing things, and there was the whirring sound a camera made. She imagined that they were photographing Roberta. She shivered. It was so sudden. They'd just had supper and Roberta went outside because she was hot. And then Roberta was dead. It didn't seem real, somehow.

A few minutes later, she heard the coroner's van drive away. Gabriel and Zack Tallman came in together. Zack was handsome, tall, lean and good-looking. His eyes were almost as dark as Gabriel's, but he looked older than Gabriel did.

"The coroner thinks it was a heart attack," Zack was saying. "They'll have to do an autopsy, however. It's required in cases of sudden death."

"Hayes told me that Yancy Dean went back to Florida," Gabriel said. "He was the only investigator you had, wasn't he?"

"He was," Zack said, "so when he resigned, I begged Hayes on my knees for the investigator's position. It's a peach of a job."

"Pays about the same as a senior deputy," Gabriel mused, tongue in cheek.

"Yes, but I get to go to seminars and talk to forensic anthropologists and entomologists and do hard-core investigative work," he added. He chuckled. "I've been after Yancy's job forever. Not that he was bad at it—he was great. But his parents needed him in Florida and he was offered his old job back with Dade County SO," he added, referring to the sheriff's office.

"Well, it worked out for both of you, then," Gabriel said.

"Yes." He sobered as Michelle came into the living room from the kitchen. "Michelle, I'm sorry about your stepmother. I know it must be hard, coming so close on the heels of your father passing."

"Thanks, Mr. Tallman," she replied gently. "Yes, it

is." She shook her head. "I still have to talk to the funeral director."

"I'll take care of that for you," Gabriel told her.

"Thanks," she added.

"Michelle, can you tell me how it happened?" Zack asked her.

"Of course." She went through the afternoon, ending with Roberta feeling too hot and going out on the porch to cool off.

He stopped her when she mentioned what Roberta had said about Bert and had her repeat Roberta's last words. He frowned. "I'd like to see her room."

Michelle led the way. The room was a mess. Roberta never picked anything up, and Michelle hadn't had time to do any cleaning. She was embarrassed at the way it looked. But Zack wasn't interested in the clutter. He started going through drawers until he opened the one in the bedside table.

He pulled out his digital camera and shot several photos of the drawer and its contents before he put on a pair of gloves, reached into it and pulled out an oblong case. He dusted the case for fingerprints before he opened it on the table and photographed that, too, along with a small vial of white powder. He turned to Gabriel who exchanged a long look with him.

"That explains a lot," Zack said. "I'll take this up to the crime lab in San Antonio and have them run it for us, but I'm pretty sure what it is and where she got it."

"What is it?" Michelle asked, curious.

"Something evil," Zack said.

Michelle wasn't dense. "Drugs," she said icily. "It's drugs, isn't it?"

"Hard narcotics," Zack agreed.

"That's why she was so crazy all the time," Michelle

said heavily. "She drank to excess when we lived in San Antonio. Dad got her into treatment and made her quit. I was sure she was okay, because we didn't have any liquor here. But she had these awful mood swings, and sometimes she hit me..." She bit her lip.

"Well, people under the influence aren't easy to live with," Zack replied heavily. "Not at all."

Zack sat down with Michelle and Gabriel at the kitchen table and questioned Michelle further about Roberta's recent routine, including trips to see Bert Sims in San Antonio. Roberta's last words were telling. He wrote it all down and gave Michelle a form to fill out with all the pertinent information about the past few hours. When she finished, he took it with him.

There was no real crime scene, since Roberta died of what was basically a heart attack brought on by a drug overdose. The coroner's assistant took photos on the front porch, adding to Zack's, so there was a record of where Roberta died. But the house wasn't searched, beyond Zack's thorough documentation of Roberta's room.

"Bert Sims may try to come around to see if Roberta had anything left, to remove evidence," Zack said solemnly to Michelle. "It isn't safe for you to be here alone."

"I've got that covered," Gabriel said with a smile. "Nobody's going to touch her."

Zack smiled. "I already had that figured out," he mused, and Gabriel cleared his throat.

"I have a chaperone in mind," Gabriel replied. "Just so you know."

Zack patted him on the back. "I figured that out already, too." He nodded toward Michelle. "Sorry again."

"Me, too," Michelle said sadly.

* * *

Michelle made coffee while Gabriel spoke to his sister, Sara, on the phone. She couldn't understand what he was saying. He was speaking French. She recognized it, but it was a lot more complicated than, "My brother has a brown suit," which was about her level of skill in the language.

His voice was low, and urgent. He spoke again, listened, and then spoke once more. *"C'est bien,"* he concluded, and hung up.

"That was French," Michelle said.

"Yes." He sat down at the table and toyed with the thick white mug she'd put in front of him. There was good china, too—Roberta had insisted on it when she and Alan first married. But the mug seemed much more Gabriel's style than fancy china. She'd put a mug at her place, as well. She had to have coffee in the morning or she couldn't even get to school.

"This morning everything seemed much less complicated," she said after she'd poured coffee. He refused cream and sugar, and she smiled. She didn't take them, either.

"You think you're going in a straight line, and life puts a curve in the way," he agreed with a faint smile. "I know you didn't get along with her. But she was part of your family. It must sting a bit."

"It does," she agreed, surprised at his perception. "She was nice to me when she and Daddy were dating," she added. "Taught me how to cook new things, went shopping with me, taught me about makeup and stuff." She grimaced. "Not that I ever wear it. I hate the way powder feels on my face, and I don't like gunking up my eyes and mouth with pasty cosmetics." She looked at him and saw an odd expression on his face. "That must sound strange…."

He laughed and sipped coffee before he spoke. "Actually, I was thinking how sane it sounded." He quietly studied her for a couple of moments. "You don't need makeup. You're quite pretty enough without it."

She gaped at him.

"Michelle, *ma belle,*" he said in an odd, soft, deep tone, and he smiled.

She went scarlet. She knew her heart was shaking her to death, that he could see it, and she didn't care. He was simply the most gorgeous man she'd ever seen, and he thought she was pretty. A stupid smile turned her lips up, elongating the perfect bow shape they made.

"Sorry," he said gently. "I was thinking out loud, not hitting on you. This is hardly the time."

"Would you like to schedule a time?" she asked with wide, curious eyes. "Because my education in that department is really sad. This one boy tried to kiss me and missed and almost broke my nose. After that, I didn't get another date until the junior prom." She leaned forward. "He was gay and so sweet and shy about it…well, he asked me and told me the reason very honestly. And I said I'd go with him to the prom because of the way my other date had ended. I mean, he wasn't likely to try to kiss me and break my nose and all… Why are you laughing?"

"Marshmallow," he accused, and his smile was full of affectionate amusement.

"Well, yes, I guess I am. But he's such a nice boy. Several of us know about him, but there are these two guys on the football squad that he's afraid of. They're always making nasty remarks to him. He thought if he went with a girl to a dance, they might back off."

"Did they?" he asked, curious.

"Yes, but not because he went with me," she said. She glowered at the memory. "One of them made a nasty remark to him when we were dancing, next to the refreshment table, and I filled a big glass with punch and threw it in his face." She grinned. "I got in big trouble until the gym coach was told why I did it. His brother's gay." The grin got bigger. "He said next time I should use the whole pitcher."

He burst out laughing. "Well, your attitude toward modern issues is…unique. This is a very small town," he explained when her eyebrows went up.

"Oh, I see. You think we treat anybody different like a fungus." She nodded.

"Not exactly. But we hear things about small towns," he began.

"No bigots here. Well, except for Chief Grier."

He blinked. "Your police chief is a bigot?"

She nodded. "He is severely prejudiced against people from other planets. You should just hear him talk about how aliens are going to invade us one day to get their hands on our cows. He thinks they have a milk addiction, and that's why you hear about cattle mutilations… You're laughing again."

He wiped his eyes. She couldn't know that he rarely laughed. His life had been a series of tragedies. Humor had never been part of it. She made him feel light inside, almost happy.

"I can see the chief's point," he managed.

"Cow bigot," she accused, and he almost fell on the floor.

She wrapped her cold hands around her mug. "I guess I shouldn't be cracking jokes, with Roberta dead…" Her eyes burned with tears. "I still can't believe it. Roberta's gone. She's gone." She drew in a breath and sipped coffee. "We've done nothing but argue since Daddy died. But she wanted me to hold her hand and she was scared. She said she was sorry." She looked at him. "She said it was Bert's fault. Do you think she was delirious?"

"Not really," he replied quietly.

"Why?"

"That can wait a bit." He grew somber. "You don't have any other family?"

She shook her head. She looked around. "But surely I can stay here by myself? I mean, I'm eighteen now…"

He frowned. "I thought you were seventeen."

She hesitated. Her eyes went to the calendar and she grimaced. "I just turned eighteen. Today is my birthday," she said. She hadn't even realized it, she'd been so busy. Tears ran down her cheeks. "What an awful one this is."

He caught her hand in his and held it tight. "No cousins?"

She shook her head. "I have nobody."

"Not quite true. You have me," he said firmly. "And Sara's on her way down here."

"Sara. Your sister?"

He nodded.

"She'll stay with me?" she asked.

He smiled. "Not exactly. "You'll stay with us, in my house. I won't risk your reputation by having you move in with just me."

"But…we're strangers," she pointed out.

"No, we're not," he said, and he smiled. "I told you about my stepfather. That's a memory I've never shared with anyone. And you won't mention it to Sara, right?"

"Of course not." She searched his black eyes. "Why would you do this for me?"

"Who else is there?" he asked.

She searched her mind for a logical answer and

couldn't find one. She had nobody. Her best friend, Amy, had moved to New York City with her parents during the summer. They corresponded, and they were still friends, but Michelle didn't want to live in New York, even if Amy's parents, with their five children, were to offer her a home.

"If you're thinking of the local orphanage," he said, tongue in cheek, "they draw the line at cow partisans."

She managed a laugh. "Oh. Okay."

"You can stay with us until you graduate and start college."

"I can't get in until fall semester, even if they accept me," she began.

"Where do you want to go?"

"Marist College in San Antonio. There's an excellent journalism program."

He pulled out his cell phone, punched a few buttons and made a phone call. Michelle listened with stark shock. He was nodding, laughing, talking. Then he thanked the man and hung up.

"You called the governor," she said, dumbfounded.

"Yes. We were in the same fraternity in college. He's on the board of trustees at Marist. You're officially accepted. They'll send a letter soon."

"But they don't have my grades…!"

"They will have, by the time you go. What's on the agenda for summer?" he continued.

"I… Well, I have a job. Minette Carson hired me for the rest of the school year, after school and on Saturdays. And I'm sure she'll let me work this summer, so I can save for college."

"You won't need to do that."

"What?"

He shrugged. "I drive a truck here because it helps

me fit in. But I have an apartment in San Antonio with a garage. In the garage, there's a brand-new Jaguar XKE." He raised an eyebrow. "Does that give you a hint about my finances?"

She had no idea what an XKE was, but she knew what a Jaguar was. She'd priced them once, just for fun. If it was new…gosh, people could buy houses around here for less, she thought, but she didn't say it.

"But, I'm a stranger," she persisted.

"Not for long. I'm going to petition the court to become your temporary legal guardian. Sara will go with us to court. You can wear a dress and look helpless and tragic and in desperate need of assistance." He pursed his lips. "I know, it will be a stretch, but you can manage it."

She laughed helplessly.

"Then we'll get you through school."

"I'll find a way to pay you back," she promised.

He smiled. "No need for that. Just don't ever write about me," he added. It sounded facetious, but he didn't smile when he said it.

"I'd have to make up something in order to do that." She laughed.

She didn't know, and he didn't tell her, that there was more to his life than she'd seen, or would ever see. Sara knew, but he kept his private life exactly that—private.

Just for an instant, he worried about putting her in the line of fire. He had enemies. Dangerous enemies, who wouldn't hesitate to threaten anyone close to him. Of course, there was Sara, but she'd lived in Wyoming for the past few years, away from him, on a ranch they co-owned. Now he was putting her in jeopardy along with Michelle.

But what could he do? The child had nobody. Now that her idiot stepmother was dead, she was truly on her own. It was dangerous for a young woman to live alone, even in a small community. And there was Roberta's boyfriend, Bert.

Gabriel knew things about the man that he wasn't eager to share with Michelle. The man was part of a criminal organization, and he knew Michelle's habits. He also had a yen for her, if what Michelle had blurted out to him once was true—and he had no indication that she would lie about it. He might decide to come and try his luck with her now that her stepmother was out of the picture. That couldn't be allowed.

He was surprised by his own affection for Michelle. It wasn't paternal. She was, of course, far too young for anything heavy, being eighteen to his twenty-four. She was a beauty, kind and generous and sweet. She was the sort of woman he usually ran from. No, strike that, she was no woman. She was still unfledged, a dove without flight feathers. He had to keep his interest hidden. At least, until she was grown up enough that it wouldn't hurt his conscience to pursue her. Afterward…well, who knew the future?

At the moment, however, his primary concern was to make sure she had whatever she needed to get through high school and, then, through college. Whatever it took.

Sara called him back. She wouldn't be able to get a flight to Texas for two days, which meant that Michelle would be on her own at night. Gabriel wasn't about to leave her, not with Bert Sims still out there. But he couldn't risk her reputation by having her stay alone with him.

"You don't want to be alone with me," Michelle guessed when he mentioned Sara's dilemma and frowned.

"It wouldn't look right," he said. "You have a spotless reputation here. I'm not going to be the first to put a blemish on it."

She smiled gently. "You're a very nice man."

He shrugged. "Character is important, regardless of the mess some people make of theirs in public and brag about it."

"My dad used to say that civilization rested on the bedrock of morality, and that when morality went, destruction followed," she recalled.

"A student of history," he said approvingly.

"Yes. He told me that first go the arts, then goes religion, then goes morality. After that, you count down the days until the society fails. Ancient Egypt. Rome. A hundred other governments, some more recently than others," she said.

"Who's right? I don't know. I like the middle of the road, myself. We should live the way that suits us and leave others to do the same."

She grinned. "I knew I liked you."

He chuckled. He finished his coffee. "We should stop discussing history and decide what to do with you tonight."

She stared at her own cooling coffee in the thick mug. "I could stay here by myself."

"Never," he said shortly. "Bert Sims might show up, looking for Roberta's leftovers, like Zack said."

She managed a smile. "Thanks. You could sleep in Roberta's room," she offered.

"Only if there's someone else in the house, too." He pursed his lips. "I have an idea." He pulled out his cell phone.

Carlie Blair walked in the door with her overnight bag and hugged Michelle close. "I'm so sorry," she said. "I know you and your stepmother didn't get along, but it's got to be a shock, to have it happen like that."

"It was." Michelle dashed away tears. "She apologized when she was dying. She said one other thing," she added, frowning, as she turned to Gabriel. "She said don't let Bert get away with it. You never told me what you thought that meant."

Gabriel's liquid black eyes narrowed. "Did she say anything else?"

She nodded slowly, recalling the odd statement. "She said he told her it wasn't pure and he lied. What in the world did that mean?"

Gabriel was solemn. "That white powder in the vial was cocaine," he explained. "Dealers usually cut it with something else, dilute it. But if it's pure and a user doesn't know, it can be lethal if they don't adjust the dose." He searched Michelle's eyes. "I'm betting that Bert gave her pure cocaine and she didn't know."

Carlie was surprised. "Your stepmother was using drugs?" she asked her friend.

"That's what they think," Michelle replied. She turned back to Gabriel. "Did he know it was pure? Was he trying to kill her?"

"That's something Zack will have to find out."

"I thought he cared about her. In his way," she faltered.

"He might have, even if it was only because she was a customer."

Michelle bit her lower lip. "That would explain why she was so desperate for money. I did wonder, you know, because she didn't buy new clothes or expensive cosmetics or things like she used to when Daddy was alive." She frowned. "She never bought anything, but she never had any money and she was always desperate for more. Like when she tried to sell my father's stamp collection."

"It's a very expensive habit," Gabriel said quietly.

"But…Bert might have meant to kill her…?"

"It's possible. Maybe she made threats, maybe she tried to quit or argued over the price. But, whether he meant to kill her or not, he's going to find himself in a lot of hot water pretty soon."

"Why?" Michelle asked curiously

He grimaced. "I'm sorry. That's all I can say. This is more complicated than it seems."

She sighed. "Okay. I won't pry. Keep your secrets." She managed a smile. "But don't you forget that I'm a reporter in training," she added. "One day, I'll have learned how to find out anything I want to know." She grinned.

"Now you're scaring me," he teased.

"Good."

He just shook his head. "I have to go back to my place and get a razor. I'll be right back. Lock the door," he told Michelle, "and don't open it for anybody. If Bert Sims shows up, you call me at once. Got that?"

"Got it," she said.

"Okay."

He left. Carlie got up from the sofa, where she'd been perched on the arm, and hugged Michelle. "I know this is hard for you. I'm so sorry."

"Me, too." Michelle gave way to tears. "Thanks for coming over. I hope I'm not putting you in any danger."

"Not me," Carlie said. "And neither of us is going to be in danger with that tall, dark, handsome man around. He is so good-looking, isn't he?" she added with a theatrical sigh.

Michelle dried her tears. "He really is. My guardian angel."

"Some angel."

She tried to think of something that might restore a little normalcy into her routine. Roberta was lying heavily on her mind. "I have to do dishes. Want to dry?"

"You bet!"

Chapter Five

Carlie and Michelle shared the double bed in Michelle's room, while Gabriel slept in Roberta's room. Michelle had insisted on changing the bed linen first. She put Roberta's clothes in the washing machine, the ones that had been scattered all over the room. When she'd washed them, she planned to donate them to charity. Michelle couldn't have worn them even if she'd liked Roberta's flamboyant style, which she didn't.

The next morning, Gabriel went to the local funeral home and made the arrangements for Roberta. She had an older sister in Virginia. The funeral home contacted her, but the woman wanted nothing to do with any arrangements. She and Roberta had never gotten along, and she couldn't care less, she said, whether they cremated her or buried her or what. Gabriel arranged for her to be cremated, and Reverend Blair offered a plot in the cemetery of his church for her to be interred. There would be no funeral service, just a graveside one. Michelle thought they owed her that much, at least.

Reverend Blair had invited Michelle to come and stay at his house with Carlie, but Michelle wanted familiar things around her. She also wanted Gabriel, on whom she had come to rely heavily. But she couldn't stay with Gabriel alone. It would not look right in the tiny community of Comanche Wells, where time hadn't moved into the twenty-first century yet.

"Sara will be here tomorrow," Gabriel told the girls as they sat down to supper, which Michelle and Carlie had prepared together. He smiled as he savored hash browns with onions, perfectly cooked, alongside a tender cut of beef and a salad. "You two can cook," he said with admiration. "Hash browns are hard to cook properly. These are wonderful."

"Thanks," they said in unison, and laughed.

"She did the hash browns," Carlie remarked, grinning at Michelle. "I never could get the hang of them. Mine just fall apart and get soggy."

"My mother used to make them," Michelle said with a sad smile. "She was a wonderful cook. I do my best, but I'm not in her league."

"Where do your parents live, Gabriel?" Carlie asked innocently.

Gabriel's expression went hard.

"I made a cherry pie for dessert," Michelle said, quickly and neatly deflecting Carlie's question. "And we have vanilla ice cream to go on it."

Carlie flushed, realizing belatedly that she'd made a slight faux pas with her query. "Michelle makes the best cherry pie around," she said with enthusiasm.

Gabriel took a breath. "Don't look so guilty," he told

Carlie, and smiled at her. "I'm touchy about my past, that's all. It was a perfectly normal question."

"I'm sorry, just the same," Carlie told him. "I get nervous around people and I babble." She flushed again. "I don't…mix well."

Gabriel laughed softly. "Neither do I," he confessed.

Michelle raised her hand. "That makes three of us," she remarked.

"I feel better," Carlie said. "Thanks," she added, intent on her food. "I have a knack for putting my foot into my mouth."

"Who doesn't?" Gabriel mused.

"I myself never put my foot into my mouth," Michelle said, affecting a haughty air. "I have never made a single statement that offended, irritated, shocked or bothered a single person."

The other two occupants of the table looked at her with pursed lips.

"Being perfect," she added with a twinkle in her eyes, "I am unable to understand how anyone could make such a mistake."

Carlie picked up her glass of milk. "One more word…" she threatened.

Michelle grinned at her. "Okay. Just so you remember that I don't make mistakes."

Carlie rolled her eyes.

It was chilly outside. Michelle sat on the porch steps, looking up at the stars. They were so bright, so perfectly clear in cold weather. She knew it had something to do with the atmosphere, but it was rather magical. There was a dim comet barely visible in the sky. Michelle had looked at it through a pair of binoculars her father had given her. It had been winter, and most hadn't been visible to the naked eye.

The door opened and closed behind her. "School is going to be difficult on Monday," she said. "I dread it. Everyone will know…you sure you don't mind giving me rides home after work?" she added.

"That depends on where you want to go," came a deep, amused masculine voice from behind her.

She turned quickly, shocked. "Sorry," she stammered. "I thought you were Carlie."

"She found a game show she can't live without. She's sorry." He chuckled.

"Do you like game shows?" she wondered.

He shrugged. He came and sat down beside her on the step. He was wearing a thick black leather jacket with exquisite beadwork. She'd been fascinated with it when he retrieved it from his truck earlier.

"That's so beautiful," she remarked, lightly touching the colorful trim above the long fringes with her fingertips. "I've never seen anything like it."

"Souvenir from Canada," he said. "I've had it for a long time."

"The beadwork is gorgeous."

"A Blackfoot woman made it for me," he said.

"Oh." She didn't want to pursue that. The woman he mentioned might have been a lover. She didn't want to think of Gabriel with a woman. It was intensely disturbing.

"My cousin," he said, without looking down at her. "She's sixty."

"Oh." She sounded embarrassed now.

He glanced at her with hidden amusement. She was so young. He could almost see the thoughts in her mind.

"You need somebody young to cut your teeth on, kid. They'd break on my thick hide."

She flushed and started to jump up, but he caught her hand in his big, warm one, and pulled her gently back down.

"Don't run," he said softly. "No problem was ever solved by retreat. I'm just telling you how it is. I'm not involved with anyone. I haven't been for years. You're a bud, just opening on a rosebush, testing the air and the sunlight. I like my roses in full bloom."

"Oh."

He sighed. His fingers locked into hers. "These one syllable answers are disturbing," he mused.

She swallowed. The touch of his big, warm hand was causing some odd sensations in her young body. "I see."

"Two syllables. Better." He drew in a long breath. "Until you graduate, we're going to be living in close proximity, even with Sara in the house. I'll be away some of the time. My job takes me all over the world. But there are going to have to be some strict ground rules when I'm home."

"Okay," she faltered. "What?"

"No pajamas or nightgowns when you walk around the house. You put them on when you go to bed, in your room. No staying up late alone. Stuff like that."

She blinked. "I feel like Mata Hari."

"You feel like a spy? An old one, at that." He chuckled.

"A femme fatale, then," she amended. "Gosh, I don't even own pajamas or a gown…"

"You don't wear clothes in bed?" He sounded shocked.

"Oh, get real," she muttered, glad he couldn't see her face. "I wear sweats."

"To bed?" he exclaimed.

"They're comfortable," she said. "Nobody who wanted

a good night's sleep ever wore a long gown, they just twist you up and constrict you. And pajamas usually have lace or thick embroidery. It's irritating to my skin."

"Sweats." Of all the things he'd pictured his young companion in at night, that was the last thing.

She looked down at his big hand in the light from the living room. It burned out onto the porch like yellow sun in the darkness, making shadows of the chairs behind them on the dusty boards of the porch. He had good hands, big and strong-looking, with square nails that were immaculate. "I guess the women you know like frilly stuff."

They did, but he wasn't walking into that land mine. He turned her hand in his. "Do you date?"

Her heart jumped. "Not since the almost-broken-nose thing."

He laughed softly. "Sorry. I forgot about that."

"There aren't a lot of eligible boys in my school who live in the dark ages like I do," she explained. "At least two of the ones who go to my church are wild as bucks and go to strip parties with drugs." She grimaced. "I don't fit in. Anywhere. My parents raised me with certain expectations of what life was all about." She turned to look at him. "Is it wrong, to have a belief system? Is it wrong to think morality is worth something?"

"Those are questions you should be asking Carlie's dad," he pointed out.

"Do you believe in…in a higher power?"

His fingers contracted around hers. "I used to."

"But not anymore?"

His drawn breath was audible. "I don't know what I believe anymore, *ma belle*," he said softly. "I live in a world you wouldn't understand, I go to places where you couldn't survive."

"What kind of work do you do?" she asked.

He laughed without humor. "That's a discussion we may have in a few years."

"Oh, I see." She nodded. "You're a cannibal."

He stilled. "I'm…a what?"

"Your work embarrasses you," she continued, unabashed, "which means you don't work in a bank or drive trucks. If I had a job that embarrassed me, it would be involved with cannibalism."

He burst out laughing. "Pest," he muttered.

She grinned.

His big thumb rubbed her soft fingers. "I haven't laughed so much in years, as I do with you."

She chuckled. "I might go on the stage. If I can make a hardcase like you laugh, I should be able to do it for a living."

"And here I thought you wanted to be a reporter."

"I do," she said. She smiled. "More than anything. I can't believe I'm actually going to work for a newspaper starting Monday," she said. "Minette is getting me my own cell phone and she's going to teach me to use a camera…it's like a dream come true. I only asked her for a reference for college. And she offered me a job." She shook her head. "It's like a dream."

"I gather you'll be riding with Carlie."

"Yes. I'm going to help with gas."

He was silent for a minute. "You keep your eyes open on the road, when you're coming home from work."

"I always do. But why?"

"I don't trust Roberta's boyfriend. He's dangerous. Even Carlie is in jeopardy because of what happened to her father, so you both have to be careful."

"I don't understand why someone would want to harm

a minister," she said, shaking her head. "It makes no sense."

He turned his head toward her. "Michelle, most ministers started out as something else."

"Something else?"

"Yes. In other words, Reverend Blair wasn't always a reverend."

She hesitated, listening to make sure Carlie wasn't at the door. "What did he do before?" she asked.

"Sorry. That's a confidence. I never share them."

She curled her hand around his. "That's reassuring. If I ever tell you something dreadful in secret, you won't go blabbing it to everyone you know."

He laughed. "That's a given." His hand contracted. "The reverse is also applicable," he added quietly. "If you overhear anything while you're under my roof, it's privileged information. Not that you'll hear much that you can understand."

"You mean, like when you were talking to Sara in French," she began.

"Something like that." His eyes narrowed. "Did you understand what I said?"

"I can say, where's the library and my brother has a brown suit," she mused. "Actually, I don't have a brother, but that was in the first-year French book. And it's about the scope of my understanding. I love languages, but I have to study very hard to learn anything."

He relaxed a little. He'd said some things about Michelle's recent problems to Sara that he didn't want her to know. Not yet, anyway. It would sound as if he were gossiping about her to his sister.

"The graveside service is tomorrow," she said. "Will Sara be here in time, do you think?"

"She might. I'm having a car pick her up at the airport and drive her down here."

"A car?"

"A limo."

Her lips parted. "A limousine? Like those long, black cars you see politicians riding around in on television? I've only seen one maybe once or twice, on the highway when I was on the bus!"

He laughed softly at her excitement. "They also have sedans that you can hire to transport people," he told her. "I use them a lot when I travel."

He was talking about another world. In Michelle's world, most cars were old and had plenty of mechanical problems. She'd never even looked inside a limousine. She'd seen them on the highway in San Antonio. Her father told her that important businessmen and politicians and rich people and movie stars rode around in them. Not ordinary people. Of course, Gabriel wasn't ordinary. He'd said he owned a new Jaguar. Certainly he could afford to ride in a limousine.

"Do you think they'd let me look inside, when it brings her here?" she asked.

Gabriel was amused at her innocence. She knew nothing of the world at large. He couldn't remember being that young, or that naive about life. He hoped she wouldn't grow up too quickly. She made him feel more masculine, more capable, more intriguing than he really was. He liked her influence. She made him laugh. She made him want to be all the things she thought he was.

"Yes," he said after a minute. "Certainly you can look inside."

"Something to put in my diary," she mused.

"You keep a diary?" he asked, with some amusement.

"Oh, yes," she said. "I note all the cows I've seen ab-

ducted, and the strange little men who come out of the
pasture at night…"

"Oh, cool it." He chuckled.

"Actually, it's things like how I did on tests, and memories I have of my father and mother," she confessed.
"And how I feel about things. There's a lot about Roberta and Bert in there, and how disgusting I thought
they were," she added.

"Well, Roberta's where she can't hurt you. And Bert
is probably trying to find a way out of the country, if
he's smart."

"What do you mean?" she asked.

He stood up and pulled her up beside him. "That's
a conversation for another time. Let's go see if Carlie's
game show is off."

"Don't you like game shows?" she wondered aloud.

"I like the History Channel, the Nature Channel, the
Military Channel, and the Science Channel."

"No TV shows?"

"They're not TV shows. They're experiments in how
to create attention deficit disorders in the entire population with endless commercials and ads that pop up right
in the middle of programs. I only watch motion pictures
or DVDs, unless I find something interesting enough to
suffer through. I like programs on World War II history
and science."

She pondered that. "I guess there's five minutes of
program to fifteen minutes of commercials," she agreed.

"As long as people put up with it, that will continue,
too." He chuckled. "I refuse to be part of the process."

"I like history, too," she began.

"There was this big war…" he began with an exaggerated expression.

She punched his arm affectionately. "No cherry pie and ice cream for you."

"I take it back."

She grinned up at him. "Okay. You can have pie and ice cream."

He smiled and opened the door for her.

She hesitated in the opening, just staring up at him, drinking in a face that was as handsome as any movie star's, at the physique that could have graced an athlete.

"Stop ogling me, if you please," he said with exaggerated patience. "You have to transfer that interest to someone less broken."

She made a face at him. "You're not broken," she pointed out. "Besides, there's nobody anywhere who could compare with you." She flushed at her own boldness. "Anyway, you're safe to cut my teeth on, and you know it." She grinned. "I'm off-limits, I am."

He laughed. "Off-limits, indeed, and don't you forget it."

"Spoilsport."

She went inside ahead of him. He felt as if he could fly. Dangerous, that. More dangerous, his reaction to her. She was years too young for anything more than banter. But, he reminded himself, the years would pass. If he lived long enough, after she graduated from college, who knew what might happen?

There was a grim memorial service at the Comanche Wells Cemetery. It was part of the land owned by the Methodist church where Reverend Blair was the minister. He stood over the small open grave, with an open Bible in his hands, reading the service for the dead. The urn containing Roberta's ashes was in the open grave, waiting for the funeral home's maintenance man, standing nearby, to close after the ceremony.

Gabriel stood beside Michelle, close, but not touching. He was wearing a suit, some expensive thing that fit him with delicious perfection. The navy darkness of the suit against the spotless white shirt and blue patterned tie only emphasized his good looks. His wavy black hair was unruly in the stiff breeze. Michelle's own hair was tormented into a bun because of the wind. But it blew tendrils down into her eyes and mouth while she tried to listen to the service, while she tried even harder to feel something for the late Roberta.

It was sad that the woman's own sister didn't care enough to even send a flower. Total strangers from Jacobs County had sent sprays and wreathes and potted plants to the funeral home that had arranged for the cremation. The flowers were spread all around the grave. Some of them would go to the local hospital and nursing home in Jacobsville, others for the evening church service here. A few of the potted plants would go home with Michelle.

She remembered her father, and how much he'd been in love with Roberta at first. She remembered Roberta in the days before Bert. More recently, she remembered horrible arguments and being slapped and having Roberta try to sell the very house under her feet. There had been more bad times than good.

But now that part of her life was over. She had a future that contained Gabriel, and the beginning of a career as a journalist. It was something to look forward to, something to balance her life against the recent death of her father and Roberta's unexpected passing.

Sara's plane had been held up due to an electrical fault. She'd phoned Gabriel just before he and Michelle went to the funeral with Carlie, to apologize and give an updated arrival time. Michelle looked forward to meeting her. From what Gabriel had said about his sister, she sounded like a very sweet and comfortable person.

Reverend Blair read the final verses, closed the Bible, bowed his head for prayer. A few minutes later, he paused to speak to Michelle, where she stood with Gabriel and Carlie, thanking the few local citizens who'd taken time to attend. There hadn't been time for the newspaper to print the obituary, so services had been announced on the local radio station. Everybody listened to it, for the obituaries and the country-western music. They also listened for the school closings when snow came. That didn't happen often, but Michelle loved the rare times when it did.

"I'm sorry for your loss," Reverend Blair said, holding Carlie's hand and smiling gently. "No matter how contrary some people are, we get used to having them in our lives."

"That's true," Michelle said gently. "And my father loved her," she added. "For a time, she made him happy." She grimaced. "I just don't understand how she changed so much, so quickly. Even when she drank too much…" she hesitated, looking around to make sure she wasn't overheard before she continued, "she was never really mean."

Gabriel and the minister exchanged enigmatic glances.

Michelle didn't notice. Her eyes were on the grave. "And she said not to let Bert get away with it," she added slowly.

"There are some things going on that you're better off not knowing about," Reverend Blair said softly. "You can safely assume that Bert will pay a price for what he did. If not in this life, then in the next."

"But what did he do?" Michelle persisted.

"Bad things." Reverend Blair smiled.

"My sister will be here in an hour," Gabriel said, reading the screen of his cell phone, with some difficulty because of the sun's glare. He grinned at the reverend. "You can have your daughter back tonight."

Reverend Blair grinned. "I must say, I miss the little touches. Like clean dishes and laundry getting done." He made a face. "She's made me lazy." He smiled with pure affection at his daughter, who grinned.

"I'll make you fresh rolls for supper," Carlie promised him.

"Oh, my, and I didn't get you anything," he quipped.

She hugged him. "You're just the best dad in the whole world."

"Pumpkin, I'm glad you think so." He let her go. "If you need anything, you let us know, all right?" he asked Michelle. "But you're in good hands." He smiled at Gabriel.

"She'll be safe, at least." Gabriel gave Reverend Blair a complicated look. "Make sure about those new locks, will you? I've gotten used to having you around."

The other man made a face. "Locks and bolts won't keep out the determined," he reminded him. "I put my trust in a higher power."

"So do I," Gabriel replied. "But I keep a Glock by the bed."

"Trust in Allah, but tie up your camel."

Everybody looked at Michelle, who blushed.

"Sorry," she said. "I was remembering something I read in a nonfiction book about the Middle East. It was written by a former member of the French Foreign Legion."

Now the stares were more complicated, from the two males at least.

"Well, they fascinate me," she confessed, flushing a

little. "I read true crime books and biographies of military men and anything I can find about the Special Air Services of Great Britain and the French Foreign Legion."

"My, my," Gabriel said. He chuckled with pure glee, a reaction that was lost on Michelle.

"I lead a sheltered life." Michelle glanced at the grave. The maintenance man, a little impatient, had started to fill the grave. "We should go."

"Yes, we should." Reverend Blair smiled. "Take care."

"Thanks. The service was very nice," Michelle said.

"I'm glad you thought so."

Gabriel took her arm and led her back to the car. He drove her home first, so that she could change back into more casual clothes and get her overnight bag. Then he drove her to his own house, where Sara was due to arrive any minute.

Michelle had this picture of Sara. That she'd be dark-haired and dark-eyed, with a big smile and a very tender nature. Remembering what Gabriel had told her in confidence, about the perils Sara had survived when they were in school, she imagined the other woman would be a little shy and withdrawn.

So it came as something of a shock when a tall, beautiful woman with long black hair and flashing black eyes stepped out of the back of the limousine and told the driver where he could go and how fast.

Chapter Six

"I am very sorry, lady," the driver, a tall lanky man, apologized. "I truly didn't see the truck coming…"

"You didn't look!" she flashed at him in a terse but sultry tone. "How dare you text on your cell phone while driving a customer!"

He was very flushed by now. "I won't do it again, I swear."

"You won't do it with me in the car, and I am reporting you to the company you work for," she concluded.

Gabriel stepped forward as the driver opened the trunk. He picked up the single suitcase that Sara had brought with her. Something in the way Gabriel looked at the man had him backing away.

"Very sorry, again," he said, flustered. "If you'd just sign the ticket, ma'am…"

He fetched a clipboard and handed it to her, eyeing Gabriel as if he expected him to leap on him any second.

Sara signed it. The man obviously knew better than to look for a tip. He nodded, turned, jumped into the car and left a trail of dust as he sped away.

"That could have gone better," Sara said with a grim smile. She hugged Gabriel. "So good to see you again."

"You, too," he replied. His face changed as he looked at the younger woman. He touched her hair. "You only grow more beautiful with age."

"You only think so because you're my brother." She laughed musically. She looked past him at Michelle, who stood silent and wary.

"And you must be Michelle." Sara went to her, smiled and hugged her warmly. "I have a nasty temper. The silly man almost killed us both, texting some woman."

"I'm so glad he didn't," Michelle said, hugging her back. "It's very kind of both of you to do this for me," she added. "I…really don't have anyplace to go. I mean, the Reverend Blair said I could stay with him and Carlie, but…"

"You certainly do have someplace to go," Gabriel said with a grin. "Sara needed the change of scenery. She was vegetating up in Wyoming."

Sara sighed. "In a sense, I suppose so, although I like it better there than in British Columbia. I left our foreman in charge at the ranch in Catelow. That's in Wyoming," Sara told Michelle with a smile. "Anything that needs doing for the sale, I can do online." Her black eyes, so like Gabriel's, had a sad cast. "The change of scenery will do me good. I love to ride. Do you?" she asked the younger woman.

"I haven't been on a horse in years," Michelle confessed. "Mostly, horses try to scrape me off or dislodge me. I'm sort of afraid of them."

"My horses are very tame," Gabriel told her. "They'll love you."

"I hope you have coffee made," Sara sighed as they made their way into the sprawling house. "I'm so tired! Flying is not my favorite mode of travel."

"I've never even been on a plane," Michelle confessed.

Sara stopped and stared at her. "Never?"

"Never."

"She wanted to look inside the limo." Gabriel chuckled. "She's never seen one of those, either."

"I'm so sorry!" Sara exclaimed. "I made a fuss…"

"You should have made a fuss," Michelle replied. "There will be other times."

"I'll make sure of that." Sara smiled, and it was like the sun coming out.

School had been rough in the days after Roberta's death. People were kind, but there were so many questions about how she died. Gossip ran rampant. One of the girls she sat near in history class told her that Roberta's boyfriend was a notorious drug dealer. At least two boys in their school got their fixes from him.

Now the things Roberta had said started to make sense. And Michelle was learning even more about the networks and how they operated from Minette since she'd started working for the Jacobsville newspaper.

"It's a vile thing, drug dealing," Minette said harshly. "Kids overdose and die. The men supplying the drugs don't even care. They only care about the profit." She hesitated. "Well, maybe some of them have good intentions…"

"A drug dealer with good intentions?" Michelle laughed. "You have got to be kidding."

"Actually, I'm not. You've heard of the man they call El Jefe?"

"Who hasn't?" Michelle replied. "We heard that he helped save you and Sheriff Carson," she added.

"He's my father."

Michelle gaped at her. "He's...?"

"My father," Minette repeated. "I didn't know who my real father was until very recently. My life was in danger, even more than Hayes's was when he was shot, because my father was in a turf war with a rival who was the most evil man I ever knew."

"Your life is like a soap opera," Michelle ventured.

Minette laughed. "Well, yes, it is."

"I wish mine was more exciting. In a good way," she clarified. She drew in a long breath. "Okay, what about this camera?" she asked. It had more dials and settings than a spaceship.

"I know, it's a little intimidating. Let me show you how it works."

She did. It took a little time, and when they finished, a phone call was waiting for Minette. She motioned to Michelle. "I have a new reporter. I'm going to let her take this down, if you don't mind. Her name is Michelle.... That's right. It's a deal. Thanks!" She put her hand over the receiver so that the caller wouldn't hear. "This is Ben Simpson. He's our Jacobs County representative in District 3 for the Texas Soil and Water Conservation Board. He wants us to do a story on a local rancher who won Rancher of the Year for the Jacobs County Soil and Water Conservation District for his implementation of natural grasses and ponds. The award was made just before Christmas, but the rancher has been out of the country until now. I'm going to let you take down the details, and then I'll send you out to his ranch to take a photo of him with the natural grasses in the background. Are you up to it?" she teased.

Michelle was almost shaking, but she bit her lip and nodded. "Yes, ma'am," she said.

Minette grinned. "Go for it!"

Michelle was used to taking copious notes in school. She did well in her schoolwork because she was thorough. She took down the story, pausing to clarify the spelling of names, and when she was through she had two sheets of notes and she'd arranged a day and time to go out to photograph the rancher.

She hung up. Minette was still in the doorway. "Did I do that okay?" she asked worriedly.

"You did fine. I was listening on the other phone. I took notes, too, just in case. You write the story and we'll compare your notes to mine."

"Thanks!" Michelle said fervently. "I was nervous."

"No need to be. You'll do fine." She indicated the computer at the desk. "Get busy." She smiled. "I like the way you are with people, even on the phone. You have an engaging voice. It will serve you well in this business."

"That's nice of you to say," Michelle said.

"Write the story. Remember, short, concise sentences, nothing flowery or overblown. I'll be out front if you need me."

She started to thank Minette again, but it was going to get tedious if she kept it up, so she just nodded and smiled.

When she turned in the story, she stood gritting her teeth while Minette read it and compared it with her own notes.

"You really are a natural," she told the younger woman. "I couldn't have done better myself. Nice work."

"Thank you!"

"Now go home," she said. "It's five, and Carlie will be peeling rubber any minute to get home."

Michelle laughed. "I think she may. I'll see you tomorrow, then. Do I go out to photograph the man tomorrow, too?"

"Yes."

Michelle bit her lip. "But I don't have a license or own a car...there's only Roberta's and she didn't leave it to me. I don't think she even had a will...and I can't ask Carlie to take off from work...." The protests came in small bursts.

"I'll drive you out there," Minette said softly. "We might drop by some of the state and federal offices and I'll introduce you to my sources."

"That sounds very exciting! Thanks!" She sounded relieved, and she was.

"One more thing," Minette said.

"Yes?"

"I'm printing the conservation story under your own byline."

Michelle caught her breath. "My first one. That's so kind of you."

"You'll have others. This is just the first." She grinned. "Have a good night."

"I will. Sara's making homemade lasagna. It's my favorite."

"Sara?"

"Gabriel's sister. She's so beautiful." Michelle shook her head. "The two of them have been lifesavers for me. I didn't want to have to pick up and move somewhere else. I couldn't have stayed here to finish school without them."

"Not quite true," Minette replied. "You could have

come to us. Even Cash Grier mentioned that they could make room for you, if you needed a place to stay."

"So many," Michelle said, shaking her head. "They hardly know me."

"They know you better than you think," was the reply. "In small communities like ours, there are no secrets. Your good deeds are noted by many."

"I guess I lived in the city for too long. Daddy had patients but no real friends, especially after Roberta came into our lives. It was just the three of us." She smiled. "I love living here."

"So do I, and I've been here all my life." She cocked her head. "Gabriel seems an odd choice to be your guardian. He isn't what you think of as a family man."

"He's not what he seems," Michelle replied. "He was kind to me when I needed it most." She made a face. "I was sitting in the middle of the road hoping to get hit by a car. It was the worst day of my life. He took me home with him and talked to me. He made everything better. When Roberta…died…he was there to comfort me. I owe him a lot. He even got Sara down here to live with him so that he could be my legal guardian with no raised eyebrows around us."

Minette simply said, "I see." What she did see, she wasn't going to share. Apparently Gabriel had a little more than normal interest in this young woman, but he wasn't going to risk her reputation. It was going to be all by the book. Minette wondered what he had in mind for Michelle when she was a few years older. And she also wondered if Michelle had any idea who Gabriel really was, and how he earned his living. That was a secret she wasn't going to share, either. Not now.

"Well, I'll see you tomorrow, then," Michelle added.

"Tomorrow."

* * *

Carlie was waiting for her at the front door the next morning, which was Friday. She looked out of breath.

"Is something wrong?" Michelle asked.

"No. Of course not. Let's go."

Carlie checked all around the truck and even looked under it before she got behind the wheel and started it.

"Okay, now, what's going on?" Michelle asked.

"Daddy got a phone call earlier," Carlie said, looking both ways before she pulled carefully out of the driveway.

"What sort of call?"

"From some man who said Daddy might think he was out of the woods, but somebody else was coming to pay him a visit, and he'll never see it coming." She swallowed. "Daddy told me to check my truck out before I drove it. I forgot, so I looked underneath just in case." She shook her head. "It's like a nightmare," she groaned. "I have no idea in this world why anyone would want to harm a minister."

"It's like our police chief said," Michelle replied quietly. "There are madmen in the world. I guess you can't ever understand what motivates them to do the things they do."

"I wish things were normal again," Carlie said in a sad tone. "I hate having to look over my shoulder when I drive and look for bombs under my car." She glanced at Michelle. "I swear, I feel like I'm living in a combat zone."

"I know the feeling, although I've never been in any real danger. Not like you." She smiled. "Don't you worry. I'll help you keep a lookout."

"Thanks." She smiled. "It's nice, having someone to ride with me. These back roads get very lonely."

"They do, indeed." Michelle sighed as she looked out

over the barren flat landscape toward the horizon as the car sped along. "I just wrote my first story for the newspaper," she said with a smile. "And Minette is taking me out to introduce me to people who work for the state and federal government. It's the most exciting thing that's ever happened to me," she added, her eyes starry with pleasure. "I get my own byline." She shook her head. "It really is true…"

"What's true?" Carlie asked.

"My dad said that after every bad experience, something wonderful happens to you. It's like you pay a price for great happiness."

"I see what you mean." She paused. "I really do."

Minette drove Michelle out to the Patterson ranch, to take photographs for her story and to see the rancher's award for conservation management. She also wanted a look at his prize Santa Gertrudis bull. The bull had been featured in a cattle magazine because he was considered one of the finest of his breed, a stud bull whose origins, like all Santa Gertrudis, was the famous King Ranch in Texas. It was a breed native to Texas that had resulted from breeding Shorthorn and Hereford cattle with Brahman cattle. The resulting breed was named for the Spanish land grant where Richard King founded the cattle empire in the nineteenth century: Santa Gertrudis.

Wofford Patterson was tall, intimidating. He had jet-black hair, thick and straight, and an olive complexion. His eyes, surprisingly, were such a pale blue that they seemed to glitter like Arctic ice. He had big hands and big feet and his face looked as if it had been carved from solid stone. It was angular. Handsome, in its way, but not conventionally handsome.

There were scars on his hands. Michelle stared at them

as she shook his hand, and flushed when she saw his keen, intelligent eyes noting the scrutiny.

"Sorry," she said, although she hadn't voiced her curiosity.

"I did a stint with the FBI's Hostage Rescue Team," he explained, showing her the palms of both big hands. "Souvenirs from many rappels down a long rope from a hovering chopper," he added with a faint smile. "Even gloves don't always work."

Her lips fell open. This was not what she'd expected when Minette said they'd take pictures of a rancher. This man wasn't what he appeared to be.

"No need to look threatened," he told her, and his pale eyes twinkled as he shoved his hands into the pockets of his jeans. "I don't have arrest powers anymore." He scowled. "Have you done something illegal? Is that why you look intimidated?"

"Oh, no, sir," she said quickly. "It's just that I was listening for the sound of helicopters." She smiled vacantly.

He burst out laughing. He glanced at Minette. "I believe you said she was a junior reporter? You didn't mention that she was nuts, did you?"

"I am not nuts, I have read of people who witnessed actual alien abductions of innocent cows," she told him solemnly. But her eyes were twinkling, like his.

"I haven't witnessed any," he replied, "but if I ever do, I'll phone you to come out and take pictures."

"Would you? How kind!" She glanced at Minette, who was grinning from ear to ear. "Now about that conservation award, Mr. Patterson..."

"Mr. Patterson was my father," he corrected. "And he was Mister Patterson, with a capital letter. He's gone now, God rest his soul. He was the only person alive I was really afraid of." He chuckled. "You can call me Wolf."

"Wolf?"

"Wofford...Wolf," he said. "They hung that nickname on me while I worked for the Bureau. I have something of a reputation for tracking."

"And a bit more," Minette interrupted, tongue in cheek.

"Yes, well, but we mustn't put her off, right?" he asked in return, and he grinned.

"Right."

"Come on and I'll show you Patterson's Lone Pine Red Diamond. He won a 'bull of the year' award for conformation, and I'm rolling in the green from stud fees. He has nicely marbled fat and large—" he cleared his throat "—assets."

Minette glanced at Michelle and shook her head when Wolf wasn't looking. Michelle interpreted that as an "I'll tell you later" look.

The bull had his own stall in the nicest barn Michelle had ever seen. "Wow," she commented as they walked down the bricked walkway between the neat wooden stalls. There was plenty of ventilation, but it was comfortably warm in here. A tack room in back provided any equipment or medicines that might be needed by the visiting veterinarian for the livestock in the barn.

There were two cows, hugely pregnant, in two of the stalls and a big rottweiler, black as coal, lying just in front of the tack room door. The animal raised his head at their approach.

"Down, Hellscream," he instructed. The dog lay back down, wagging its tail.

"Hellscream?" Michelle asked.

He grinned. "I don't have a social life. Too busy with the bloodstock here. So in my spare time, I play World of Warcraft. The leader of the Horde—the faction that fights the Alliance—is Garrosh Hellscream. I really don't like him much, so my character joined the rebellion to throw him out. Nevertheless, he is a fierce fighter. So is my girl, there," he indicated the rottweiler. "Hence, the name."

"Winnie Kilraven's husband is a gaming fanatic," Minette mused.

"Kilraven plays Alliance," Wolf said in a contemptuous tone. "A Paladin, no less." He pursed his lips. "I killed him in a battleground, doing player versus player. It was very satisfying." He grinned.

"I'd love to play, but my husband is addicted to the Western Channel on TV when he's not in his office being the sheriff," Minette sighed. "He and the kids watch cartoon movies together, too. I don't really mind. But gaming sounds like a lot of fun."

"Trust me, it is." Wolf stopped in front of a huge, sleek red-coated bull. "Isn't he a beaut?" he asked the women, and actually sighed. "I'd let him live in the house, but I fear the carpets would never recover."

The women looked at each other. Then he laughed at their expressions, and they relaxed.

"I read about a woman who kept a chicken inside once," Michelle said with a bland expression. "I think they had to replace all the carpets, even though she had a chicken diaper."

"I'd like to see a cow diaper that worked." Wolf chuckled.

"That's a product nobody is likely to make," Michelle said.

"Can we photograph you with the bull?" Michelle asked.

"Why not?"

He went into the stall with the bull and laid his long arm around his neck. "Smile, Red, you're going to be even more famous," he told the big animal, and smoothed his fur.

He and the bull turned toward the camera. Michelle took several shots, showing them to Minette as they went along.

"Nice," Minette said. She took the digital camera, pulled up the shots, and showed them to Wolf.

"They'll do fine," Wolf replied. "You might want to mention that the barn is as secure as the White House, and anyone who comes here with evil intent will end up in the backseat of a patrol car, handcuffed." He pursed his lips. "I still have my handcuffs, just in case."

"We'll mention that security is tight." Minette laughed.

"He really is a neat bull," Michelle added. "Thanks for letting us come out and letting us take pictures."

He shrugged broad shoulders. "No problem. I'm pretty much available until next week."

"What happens next week?" Michelle asked.

"A World Event on World of Warcraft," he mused. "The 'Love Is in the Air' celebration. It's a hoot."

"A world event?" Michelle asked, curious.

"We have them for every holiday. It's a chance for people to observe them in-game. This is the equivalent of Valentine's Day." He laughed. "There's this other player I pal around with. I'm pretty sure she's a girl. We do battlegrounds together. She gets hung on trees, gets lost, gets killed a lot. I enjoy playing with her."

"Why did you say that you think she's a girl?" Michelle asked.

"People aren't what they seem in video games," he replied. "A lot of the women are actually men. They think of it as playing with a doll, dressing her up and stuff."

"What about women, do they play men?" she persisted.

He laughed. "Probably. I've come across a few whose manners were a dead giveaway. Women are mostly nicer than some of the guys."

"What class is your Horde character?" Minette broke in.

"Oh, you know about classes, huh?"

"Just what I overheard when Kilraven was raving about them to my husband," she replied, chuckling.

"I play a Blood Elf death knight," he said. "Two-handed sword, bad attitude, practically invincible."

"What does the woman play?" Michelle asked, curious.

"A Blood Elf warlock. Warlocks cast spells. Deadliest class there is, besides mages," he replied. "She's really good. I've often wondered where she lives. Somewhere in Europe, I think, because she's on late at night, when most people in the States are asleep."

"Why are you on so late yourself?" Michelle asked.

He shrugged. "I have sleep issues." And for an instant, something in his expression made her think of wounded things looking for shelter. He searched her eyes. "You're staying with the Brandons, aren't you?"

"Well, yes," she said hesitantly.

He nodded. "Gabriel's a good fellow." His face tautened. "His sister, however, could drop houses on people."

She stared at him. "Excuse me?"

"I was backing out of a parking space at the county courthouse and she came flying around the corner and hit the back end of my truck." He was almost snarling. "Then she gets out, cussing a blue streak, and says it's my fault! She was the one speeding!"

Michelle almost bit her tongue off trying not to say what she was thinking.

"So your husband—" he nodded to Minette "—comes

down the courthouse steps and she's just charming to him, almost in tears over her poor car, that I hit!" He made a face. "I get hit with a citation for some goldarned thing, and my insurance company has to fix her car and my rates go up."

"Was that before or after you called her a broom-riding witch and indicated that she didn't come from Wyoming at all, but by way of Kansas...?"

"Sure, her and the flying monkeys," he muttered.

Michelle couldn't keep from laughing. "I'm sorry," she defended herself. "It was the flying monkey bit..." She burst out laughing again.

"Anyway, I politely asked her which way she was going and if she was coming back to town, so I could park my truck somewhere while she was on the road. Set her off again. Then she started cussing me in French. I guess she thought some dumb country hick like me wouldn't understand her."

"What did you do?" Michelle asked.

He shrugged. "Gave it back to her in fluent and formal French. That made her madder, so she switched to Farsi." He grinned. "I'm also fluent in that, and I know the slang. She called on the sheriff to arrest me for obscenity, but he said he didn't speak whatever language we were using so he couldn't arrest me." He smiled blithely. "I like your husband," he told Minette. "He was nice about it, but he sent her on her way. Her parting shot, also in Farsi, was that no woman in North America would be stupid enough to marry a man like me. She said she'd rather remain single forever than to even consider dating someone like me."

"What did you say to her then?" Michelle wanted to know.

"Oh, I thanked her."

"What?" Minette burst out.

He shrugged. "I said that burly masculine women didn't appeal to me whatsoever, and that I'd like a nice wife who could cook and have babies."

"And?" Minette persisted.

"And she said I wanted a malleable female I could chain to the bed." He shook his head.

"What did you say about that?"

"I said it would be too much trouble to get the stove in there."

Michelle almost doubled up laughing. She could picture Sara trying to tie this man up in knots and failing miserably. She wondered if she dared repeat the conversation when she got home.

Wolf anticipated her. He shook his finger at her. "No carrying tales, either," he instructed. "You don't arm the enemy."

"But she's nice," she protested.

"Nice. Sure she is. Does she keep her pointed hat in the closet or does she wear it around the house?" he asked pleasantly.

"She doesn't own a single one, honest."

"Make her mad," he invited. "Then stand back and watch the broom and the pointy hat suddenly appear."

"You'd like her if you got to know her," Michelle replied.

"No, thank you. No room in my life for a woman who shares her barn with flying monkeys."

Michelle and Minette laughed all the way back to the office.

"Oh, what Sara's missing," Minette said, wiping tears of mirth from her eyes. "He's one of a kind."

"He really is."

"I wish I could tell her what he said. I wouldn't dare. She's already scored a limousine driver. I expect she could strip the skin off Wofford Patterson at ten paces."

"A limousine?"

Michelle nodded. "The driver was texting someone at the wheel and almost wrecked the car. She reported him to the agency that sent him."

"Good for her," Minette said grimly. "There was a wreck a few months ago. A girl was texting a girlfriend and lost control of the car she was driving. She killed a ten-year-old boy and his grandmother who were walking on the side of the road."

"I remember that," Michelle said. "It was so tragic."

"It's still tragic. The girl is in jail, pending trial. It's going to be very hard on her parents, as well as those of the little boy."

"You have sympathy for the girl's parents?" Michelle ventured.

"When you work in this business for a while, you'll learn that there really are two sides to every story. Normal people can do something impulsive and wrong and end up serving a life term. Many people in jail are just like you and me," she continued. "Except they have less control of themselves. One story I covered, a young man had an argument with his friend while he was skinning a deer they'd just killed in the woods. Impulsively, he stabbed his friend with the knife. He cried at his trial. He didn't mean to do it. He had one second of insanity and it destroyed his life. But he was a good boy. Never hurt an animal, never skipped school, never did anything bad in his life. Then he killed his best friend on an impulse that he regretted immediately."

"I never thought of it like that," Michelle said, dazed.

"Convicted felons have families," she pointed out.

"Most of them are as normal as people can be. They go to church, give to charity, help their neighbors, raise good children. They have a child do something stupid and land in jail. They're not monsters. Although I must confess I've seen a few parents who should be sitting in jail." She shook her head. "People are fascinating to me, after all these years." She smiled. "You'll find that's true for you, as well."

Michelle leaned back. "Well, I've learned something. I've always been afraid of people in jail, especially when they work on the roadways picking up trash."

"They're just scared kids, mostly," Minette replied. "There are some bad ones. But you won't see them out on the highways. Only the trusted ones get to do that sort of work."

"The world is a strange place."

"It's stranger than you know." Minette chuckled. She pulled up in front of the newspaper office. "Now, let's get those photos uploaded and cropped and into the galleys."

"You bet, boss," Michelle said with a grin. "Thanks for the ride, too."

"You need to learn to drive," Minette said.

"For that, you need a car."

"Roberta had one. I'll talk to Blake Kemp. He's our district attorney, but he's also a practicing attorney. We'll get him going on probate for you."

"Thanks."

"Meanwhile, ask Gabriel about teaching you. He's very experienced with cars."

"Okay," she replied. "I'll ask him." It didn't occur to her to wonder how Minette knew he was experienced with cars.

Chapter Seven

"No, no, no!" Gabriel said through gritted teeth. "Michelle, if you want to look at the landscape, for God's sake, stop and get out of the car first!"

She bit her lower lip. "Sorry. I wasn't paying attention."

The truck, his truck, was an inch away from going into a deep ditch.

"Put it in Reverse, and back up slowly," he instructed, forcing his voice to seem calm.

"Okay." She did as instructed, then put it in gear, and went forward very slowly. "How's this?"

"Better," he said. He drew in a breath. "I don't understand why your father never taught you."

Mention of her father made her sad. "He was too busy at first and then too sick," she said, her voice strained. "I wanted to learn, but I didn't pester him."

"I'm sorry," he said deeply. "I brought back sad memories for you."

She managed a faint smile. "It's still not that long since he, well, since he was gone," she replied. She couldn't bring herself to say "died." It was too harsh a word. She concentrated on the road. "This is a lot harder than it looks," she said. She glanced up in the rearview mirror. "Oh, darn."

He glanced behind them. A car was speeding toward them, coming up fast. The road was straight and clear, however. "Just drive," he told her. "He's got plenty of room to pass if he wants to."

"Okay."

The driver slowed down suddenly, pulled around them and gave her a sign that made her flush.

"And that was damned well uncalled for," Gabriel said shortly. He pulled out his cell phone, called the state highway police, gave them the license plate number and offered to press charges if they caught the man. "She's barely eighteenand trying to learn to drive," he told the officer he was speaking to. "The road was clear, he had room to pass. He was just being a jerk because she was female."

He listened, then chuckled. "I totally agree. Thanks."

He closed the cell phone. "They're going to look for him."

"I hope they explain manners to him. So many people seem to grow up without any these days," she sighed. She glanced at her companion. It had made him really angry, that other man's rudeness.

He caught her staring. "Watch the road."

"Sorry."

"What's wrong?"

"Nothing. I was just…well, it was nice of you, to care that someone insulted me."

"Nobody's picking on you while I'm around," he said with feeling.

She barely turned her head and met his searching black eyes. Her heart went wild. Her hands felt like ice on the wheel. She could barely get her breath.

"Stop that," he muttered, turning his head away. "You'll kill us both."

She cleared her throat. "Okay."

He drew in a breath. "You may be the death of me, anyway," he mused, giving her a covert glance. She was very pretty, with her blond hair long, around her shoulders, with that creamy complexion and those soft gray eyes. He didn't dare pay too much attention. But when she was fully grown, she was going to break hearts. His jaw tautened. He didn't like to think about that, for some reason.

"Now make a left turn onto the next road. Give the signal," he directed. "That's right. Look both ways. Good. Very good."

She grinned. "This is fun."

"No, fun is when you streak down the interstate at a hundred and twenty and nobody sees you. That's fun."

"You didn't!" she gasped.

He shrugged. "Jags like to run. They purr when you pile on the gas."

"They do not."

"You'll see." He smiled to himself. He already had plans for her graduation day. He and Sara had planned it very well. It was only a couple of months away. He glanced at his companion. She was going to be absolutely stunned when she knew what they had in mind.

*   *   *

The piece on Wofford Patterson ran with Michelle's byline, along with photos of his native grasses, his water conservation project, and his huge bull. People she didn't even know at school stopped her in the hall to talk to her. And not only other students. Teachers paid her more attention, as well. She felt like a minor celebrity.

"I actually had someone to sit with at lunch," she told Sara, all enthusiasm, when she got home from school that day. "Mostly I'm always by myself. But one little article in the paper with my name and just look!"

Sara managed a smile. "It was well written. You did a good job. Considering the material you had to work with," she added with smoldering black eyes

Then Michelle remembered. Wofford Patterson. Mortal enemy. Sara's nemesis.

"Sorry," she said, flushing.

"The man is a total lunatic," Sara muttered, slamming pans around as she looked for something to boil pasta in. Her beautiful complexion was flushed. "He backed into me and tried to blame me for it! Then he said I rode a broom and kept flying monkeys in the barn!"

Michelle almost bit through her lower lip. She couldn't laugh. She couldn't laugh…

Sara glanced at her, rolled her eyes, and dragged out a big pot. "You like him, I gather?"

"Well, he didn't accuse me of keeping flying monkeys," Michelle said reasonably. "He's very handsome, in a rough-cut sort of way, and he loves animals."

"Probably because he is one," Sara said under her breath.

"He has this huge rottweiler. You wouldn't believe what he calls her!"

"Have you seen my hammer?" Gabriel interrupted suddenly.

Both women turned.

"Don't you keep it in the toolbox?" Michelle asked.

"Yes. Where's my toolbox?" he amended.

The two women looked at each other blankly. Then Sara flushed

"I, uh, had to find a pair of pliers to turn the water spigot on outside. Not my fault," she added. "You have big hands and when you turn the water off, I can't turn it back on. I took the whole toolbox with me so I'd have access to whatever I needed."

"No problem. But where is it?" Gabriel added.

"Um," Sara frowned. "I think I remember…just a sec." She headed out the back door.

"Don't, for God's sake, tell her the name of Patterson's dog!" Gabriel said in a rough whisper.

She stared at him. "Why?"

He gave her a speaking look. "Who do you think Patterson's unknown buddy in World of Warcraft is?" he asked patiently.

Her eyes widened with glee. "You mean, they're buddies online and they don't know it?"

"In a nutshell." He grinned. "Two lonely people who can't stand each other in person, and they're soul mates online. Let them keep their illusions, for the time being."

"Of course." She shook her head. "She'd like him if she got to know him."

"I know. But first impressions die hard."

Sara was back, carrying a beat-up brown toolbox. "Here." She set it down on the table. "Sorry," she added sheepishly.

"I don't mind if you borrow stuff. Just put it back, please." He chuckled.

She shrugged. "Sometimes I do. I'm just scatter-brained."

"Listen," he said, kissing the top of her head, "nobody who speaks six languages fluently could even remotely be called scatterbrained. You just have a lot on your mind all the time."

"What a nice way to put it. No wonder you're my favorite brother!"

He gave Michelle a droll look.

"Well, if I had other brothers, you'd still be my favorite," Sara amended.

"Are we going to drive some more today?" Michelle asked him hopefully.

"Maybe tomorrow," he said after a minute. He forced a smile. He left, quickly.

Michelle sighed. "I can't follow orders," she explained while Sara put water on to boil and got out spaghetti.

"He's just impatient," Sara replied. "He always was, even when we were kids." She shook her head. "Some habits you never grow out of."

Michelle knew a lot about Sara, and her childhood. But she was too kindhearted to mention any of what Gabriel had told her. She just smiled and asked what she could do to help.

Graduation was only days away. So much had happened to Michelle that she could hardly believe how quickly the time had gone by. Marist College had accepted her, just as Gabriel had told her. She was scheduled for orientation in August, and she'd already had a conversation online with her faculty advisor.

"I'm so excited," she told Gabriel. They were sitting on the front porch, watching a meteor shower. There were a couple of fireballs, colorful and rare. "I'll be in college. I can't believe it."

He smiled. "You'll grow. College changes people. You see the world in a different way when you've studied courses like Western Civilization and math."

"I'm not looking forward to the math," she sighed. "People say college trig is a nightmare."

"Only if you don't have a tutor."

"But I don't…"

He glanced down at her. "I made straight A's."

"Oh." She grinned. "Okay. Thanks in advance."

He stretched. "No problem. Maybe you'll do better at math than you do at driving."

She thumped his arm. "Stop that. I can drive."

"Sort of."

"It takes practice," she reminded him. "How can I practice if you're always too busy to ride in the truck with me?"

"You could ask Sara," he pointed out.

She glowered at him. "I did."

"And?"

"She's always got something ready to cook." She pursed her lips. "In fact, she has pots and pans lined up, ready, in case I look like I'm even planning to ask her to ride with me." Her eyes narrowed suspiciously. "I have reason to believe you've been filling her head with irrelevant facts about how many times I've run into ditches."

"Lies."

"It was only one ditch," she pointed out.

"That reminds me." He pulled out his cell phone and checked a text message. He nodded. "I have a professional driving instructor coming out to work with you, starting Saturday afternoon."

"Coward," she accused.

He grinned. "I don't teach."

"I thought you were doing very well, except for the nonstop cursing."

"I thought you were doing well, except for the non-stop near accidents."

She threw up her hands and sighed. "Okay. Just push me off onto some total stranger who'll have a heart attack if I miss a turn. His family will sue us and we'll end up walking everywhere…"

He held up a hand. "I won't change my mind. I can't teach you how to drive with any efficiency. These people have been doing it for a long time."

She gave in. "Okay. I'll give it a shot." She looked up at him. "You and Sara are coming to graduation, aren't you?"

He smiled down at her. "I wouldn't miss it for the whole world, *ma belle.*"

Her heart jumped up into her throat. She could walk on air, because Gabriel teased her in that deep, soft tone that he used only with her.

He touched her long hair gently. "You're almost grown. Just a few more years."

"I'm eighteen."

He let go of her hair. "I know." He turned away. She was eighteen years old. Years too young for what he was thinking of. He had to let her go, let her grow, let her mature. He couldn't hold her back out of selfishness. In a few years, when she was through college, when she had a good job, when she could stand alone—then, yes, perhaps. Perhaps.

"You're very introspective tonight," she remarked.

"Am I?" He chuckled. "I was thinking about cows."

"Cows?"

"It's a clear night. If a UFO were to abduct a cow, we would probably see it."

"How exciting! Let's go looking for them. I'll drive!"

"Not on your life, and don't you have homework? Finals are coming up, I believe?"

She made a face. "Yes, they are, and I can't afford to make a bad grade." She glanced at him. "Spoilsport."

He shrugged. "I want you to graduate."

She folded her hands on her jeans-clad thighs. "I've never told you how much I appreciate all you and Sara have done for me," she said quietly. "I owe you so much…"

"Stop that. We were happy to help."

It had just occurred to her that she was going away, very soon, to college. She was going to live in the dormitory there. She wouldn't live with Sara and Gabriel again. Her holidays would be spent with fellow students, if anyone even stayed on campus—didn't the campus close for holidays?

"I can see the wheels turning," he mused, glancing down at her. "You'll come to us for holidays and vacations," he said. "Sara and I will be here. At least until you're through college. Okay?"

"But Sara has a place in Wyoming—" she began.

"We have a place in Wyoming, and we have a competent manager in charge of it," he interrupted. "Besides, she likes it here in Texas."

"I did notice she was up very late last night on the computer," she said under her breath.

"New expansion on her game," he whispered. "She and her unknown pal are running battlegrounds together. She's very excited."

Michelle laughed softly. "We should probably tell her."

"No way. It's the first time I've seen her happy, really

happy, in many years," he said wistfully. "Dreams are precious. Let her keep them."

"I suppose it won't hurt," she replied. "But she's not getting a lot of sleep."

"She hasn't slept well in a long time, despite therapy and prescriptions. This gaming might actually solve a few problems for her."

"You think?"

"We can wait and see, at least." He glanced at his watch, the numbers glowing in the darkness. "I have some paperwork to get through. You coming in?"

"In just a minute. I do love meteor showers."

"So do I. If you like astronomy, we'll have to buy a telescope."

"Could we?" she asked enthusiastically.

"Of course. I'll see about it."

"I would love to look at Mars!"

"So would I."

"I would love to go there," she ventured.

He shrugged. "Not going to happen."

"It was worth a try."

He chuckled, ruffled her hair and went back inside.

Graduation day was going to be long and exciting. Michelle had gone to the rehearsal, which had to be held inside because it was pouring rain that day. She had hoped it wouldn't rain on graduation day.

Her gown and cap fit perfectly. She wasn't going to graduate with honors, but she was at least in the top 10 percent of her class. Her grades had earned her a small scholarship, which would pay for textbooks. She didn't want Gabriel and Sara to be out of pocket on her account, regardless of their financial worth.

Her gown was white. It made her look almost angelic,

with her long blond hair down to her waist, her peaches-and-cream complexion delicately colored, her gray eyes glittering with excitement.

She didn't see Gabriel and Sara in the audience, but that wasn't surprising. There was a huge crowd. They were able to graduate outside because the skies cleared up. They held the graduation ceremonies on the football field, with faculty and students and families gathered for the occasion.

Michelle accepted her diploma from the principal, grinned at some of her fellow students and walked off the platform. On the way down, she remembered what a terrifying future she was stepping into. For twelve years, she'd gone to school every day—well, thirteen years if you counted kindergarten. Now, she was free. But with freedom came responsibility. She had to support herself. She had to manage an apartment. She had to pay bills....

Maybe not the bills part, totally. She would have to force Gabriel and Sara to let her pay rent. That would help her pride. She'd go off to college, to strangers, to a dormitory that might actually be unisex. That was a scary thought.

She ran to Gabriel and Sara, to be hugged and congratulated.

"You are now a free woman." Sara chuckled. "Well, mostly. Except for your job, and college upcoming."

"If it's going to be a unisex dorm," Michelle began worriedly.

"It's not," Gabriel assured her. "Didn't you notice? It's a Protestant college. They even have a chaplain."

"Oh. Oh!" She burst out laughing, and flushed. "No, I didn't really notice, until I thought about having to share my floor with men who are total strangers."

"No way would that happen," Gabriel said solemnly,

and his dark eyes flashed. "I'd have you driven back and forth first."

"So would I," Sara agreed. "Or I'd move up to San Antonio, get an apartment and you could room with me."

Tears stung Michelle's cheeks. She was remembering how proud her father had been of her grades and her ambitions, how he'd looked forward to seeing her graduate. He should have been here.

"Now, now," Gabriel said gently, as if he could see the thoughts in her mind. He brushed the tears away and kissed her eyelids closed. "It's a happy occasion," he whispered.

She was tingling all over from the unexpectedly intimate contact. Her heart went wild. When he drew back, everything she felt and thought was right there, in her eyes. His own narrowed, and his tall, muscular body tensed.

Sara coughed. She coughed again, to make sure they heard her.

"Lunch," Gabriel said at once, snapping out of it. "We have reservations."

"At one of the finest restaurants in the country, and we still have to get to the airport."

"Restaurant? Airport?" Michelle was all at sea.

Gabriel grinned. "It's a surprise. Someone's motioning to you." He indicated a female student who was waving like crazy.

"It's Yvonne," Michelle told them. "I promised to have my picture taken with her and Gerrie. They were in my geography class. Be right back!"

They watched her go, her face alive with pleasure.

"Close call, masked man," Sara said under her breath.

He stuffed his hands into his slacks and his expression hardened.

"You have to be patient," Sara added gently, and touched his chest with a small hand. "Just for a little while."

"Just for years," he said curtly. "While she meets men and falls in love...."

"Fat chance."

He turned and looked down at her, his face guarded but full of hope.

"You know how she feels," Sara said softly. "That isn't going to change. But she has to have time to grow up, to see something of the world. The time will pass."

He grimaced and then drew in a breath. "Yes. I suppose so." He laughed hollowly. "Maybe in the meantime, I can work up to how I'm going to explain my line of work to her. Another hurdle."

"By that time, she'll be more likely to understand."

He nodded. "Yes."

She hugged him impulsively. "You're a great guy. She already knows it."

He hugged her back. "I'll be her best friend."

"You already are." She drew back, smiling. The smile faded and her eyes sparked with temper as she looked past him.

"My, my, did you lose your broom?" came a deep, drawling voice from behind Gabriel.

"The flying monkeys are using it right now," Sara snarled at the tall man. "Are you just graduating from high school, too?" she added. "And I didn't get you a present."

He shrugged. "My foreman's daughter graduated. I'm her godfather."

"So many responses come to mind. But choosing just one," she pondered for a minute. She pursed her full lips.

"Do you employ a full-time hit man, or do you have to manage with pickups?"

He raised his thick eyebrows. "Oh, full-time, definitely," he said easily, hands deep in his jean pockets. He cocked his head. "But he doesn't do women. Pity."

Sara was searching for a comeback when Michelle came running back.

"Oh, hi, Mr. Patterson!" she said with a grin. "How's that bull doing?"

"Eating all he can get and looking better by the day, Miss Godfrey," he replied, smiling. "That was a good piece you wrote on the ranch."

"Thanks. I had good material to work with."

Sara made a sound deep in her throat.

"What was that? Calling the flying monkeys in some strange guttural language?" Wolf asked Sara with wide, innocent eyes.

She burst out in Farsi, things that would have made Michelle blush if she understood them.

"Oh, my, what a thing to say to someone!" Wolf said with mock surprise. He looked around. "Where's a police officer when you need one?"

"By all means, find one who speaks Farsi," Sara said with a sarcastic smile.

"Farsi?" Jacobsville police chief Cash Grier strolled up with his wife, Tippy. "I speak Farsi."

"Great. Arrest her," Wolf said, pointing at Sara. "She just said terrible things about my mother. Not to mention several of my ancestors."

Cash glanced at Sara, who was glowering at Wolf, and totally unrepentant.

"He started it," Sara said angrily. "I do not ride a broom, and I have never seen a flying monkey!"

"I did, once," Cash said, nodding. "Of course, a man threw it at me…"

"Are you going to arrest her?" Wolf interrupted.

"You'd have to prove that she said it," Cash began.

"Gabriel heard her say it," Wolf persisted.

Cash looked at Gabriel. So did Sara and Michelle and Tippy.

"I'll burn the pasta for a week," Sara said under her breath.

Gabriel cleared his throat. "Gosh, I'm sorry," he said. "I wasn't paying attention. Would you like to say it again, and this time I'll listen?" he asked his sister.

"Collusion," Wolf muttered. He glowered at Sara. "I still have my handcuffs from my FBI days…"

"How very kinky," Sara said haughtily.

Cash turned away quickly. His shoulders were shaking.

Tippy hit him.

He composed himself and turned back. "I'm sorry, but I really can't be of any assistance in this particular matter. Congratulations, Michelle," he added.

"Thanks, Chief Grier," she replied.

"Why are you here?" Wolf asked the chief.

"One of my young brother-in-law's older gaming friends is graduating," he replied with a smile. "We came to watch him graduate." He shook his head. "He's awesome at the Halo series on Xbox 360."

"So am I," Wolf said with a grin. He glanced at Gabriel. "Do you play?"

Gabriel shook his head. "I don't really have time."

"It's fun. I like console games. But I also like…" Wolf began.

"The reservations!" Gabriel interrupted, checking his watch. "Sorry, but we've got a flight to catch. Graduation present," he added with a grin and a glance at Michelle. "See you all later."

"Sure," Wolf replied. He glanced at Sara and his eyes twinkled. "An airplane, huh? Having mechanical problems with the broom…?"

"We have to go, right now," Gabriel said, catching Sara before she could move toward Wolf.

He half dragged her away, to the amusement of the others.

"You should have let me hit him," Sara fumed as they sat comfortably in the business-class section of an aircrat bound for New Orleans. "Just one little slap…"

"In front of the police chief, who would have been obliged to arrest you," Gabriel pointed out. "Not a good thing on Michelle's graduation day."

"No." She smiled at Michelle, who looked as amused as Gabriel did. "Sorry. That man just rubs me the wrong way."

"It's okay," Michelle said. "I can't believe we're flying to New Orleans for lunch." She laughed, shaking her head. "I've never been on a plane before in my life. The takeoff was so cool!" she recalled, remembering the burst of speed, the clouds coming closer, the land falling away under the plane as she looked out the window. They'd given her the window seat, so that she had a better view.

"It was fun, seeing it through your eyes," Sara replied, smiling. "I tend to take it for granted. So does he." She indicated Gabriel, who laughed.

"I spend most of my life on airplanes, of one type or another," Gabriel confessed. "I must admit, my flights aren't usually this relaxed."

"You never did tell me what you do," Michelle said.

"I'm sort of a government contractor," he said easily.

"An advisor. I go lots of places in that capacity. I deal with foreign governments." He made it sound conventional. It really wasn't.

"Oh. Like businessmen do."

"Something like that," he lied. He smiled. "You have your first driving lesson tomorrow," he reminded her.

"Sure you wouldn't like to do it instead?" she asked. "I could try really hard to avoid ditches."

He shook his head. "You need somebody better qualified than I am."

"I hope he's got a good heart."

"I'm sure he'll be personable…"

"I hope he's in very good health," she amended.

Gabriel just chuckled.

They ate at a five-star restaurant downtown. The food was the most exquisite Michelle had ever tasted, with a Cajun spiced fare that teased the tongue, and desserts that almost made her cry they were so delicious.

"This is one of the best restaurants I've ever frequented," Gabriel said as they finished second cups of coffee. "I always stop by when I'm in the area." He looked around at the elegant decor. "They had some problems during Hurricane Katrina, but they've remodeled and regrouped. It's better than ever."

"It was delicious," Michelle said, smiling. "You guys are spoiling me rotten."

"We're enjoying it," Sara replied. "And there's an even bigger surprise waiting when we get home," she added.

"Another one? But this was the best present I've ever had! You didn't need to…"

"Oh, but we did," Gabriel replied. He leaned back in his chair, elegant in a navy blue jacket with a black turtleneck and dark slacks. Sara was wearing a simple black dress with pearls that made her look both expensive and beautiful. Michelle, in contrast, was wearing the only good dress she had, a simple sheath of off-white, with her mother's pearls. She felt dowdy compared to her companions, but they didn't even seem to notice that the dress was old. They made her feel beautiful.

"What is it?" Michelle asked suddenly.

She was met with bland smiles.

"Wait and see," Gabriel said with twinkling black eyes.

Chapter Eight

It was very late when they got back to the ranch. There, sitting in the driveway, was a beautiful little white car with a big red ribbon tied around it.

Michelle gaped at it. Her companions urged her closer.

She touched the trunk, where a sleek silver Jaguar emblem sat above the keyhole.

"It's a Jag," she stammered.

"It's not the most expensive one," Sara said quickly when Michelle gave them accusing glances. "In fact, it's a midrange automobile. But it's one of the safest cars on the road. Which is why we got it for you. Happy Graduation!"

She hugged Michelle.

"It's too much," Michelle stammered, touching the body with awe. She fought tears. "I never dreamed... Oh, it's so...beautiful!" She turned and threw herself into Sara's arms, hugging her close. "I'll take such good care of it! I'll polish it by the inch, with my own hands...!"

"Don't I get a hug, too? It was my idea," Gabriel said.

She laughed, turned and hugged him close. "Of course you do. Thank you! Gosh, I never dreamed you'd get me a car as a present!"

"You needed one," Gabriel said at the top of her head. "You have to be able to drive to work for Minette in the summer. And you'll need one to commute from college to home on weekends. If you want to come home that often," he added.

"Why would I want to stay in the city when I can come down here and ride horses?" she asked, smiling up at him. He was such a dish, she thought dreamily.

Gabriel looked back at her with dark, intent eyes. She was beautiful. Men would want her. Other men.

"Well, try it out," Sara said, interrupting tactfully. "I'll help you untie the ribbon."

"I'm never throwing the ribbon away!" Michelle laughed. "Oh. Wait!" She pulled out her cell phone and took a picture of the car in its bow.

"Stand beside it. We'll get one of you, too," Gabriel said, pulling out his own cell phone. He took several shots, smiling all the time. "Okay. Now get inside and try it out."

"Who's riding shotgun?" Michelle asked.

They looked worriedly at each other.

"It's too late to take it out of the driveway," Gabriel said finally. "Just start it up."

Michelle stood at the door. It wouldn't open.

"The key," Sara prompted Gabriel.

"The key. Duh." He chuckled. He dug it out of his pants pocket and handed it to Michelle. It was still warm from his body.

She looked at the fob in the light from the porch. "There's no key."

"You don't need one."

She unlocked the car and got inside. "There's no gear-shift!"

"See the start button?" Gabriel prompted. "Press it."

She did. Nothing happened.

"Hold down the brake with your foot and then press it," he added.

She did. The car roared to life. She caught her breath as the vents opened and the gearshift rose up out of the console. "Oh!" she exclaimed. She looked at the controls, at the instrument panel, at the leather seats. "Oh!" she said again.

Gabriel squatted by the door, on the driveway. "Its creator said something like, 'we will never come closer to building something that is alive.' Each Jaguar is unique. Each has its own little idiosyncrasies. I've been driving them for years, and I still learn new things about them. They purr when they're happy, they growl when they want the open road." He laughed self-consciously. "Well, you'll see."

She leaned over and brushed her soft mouth against his cheek, very shyly. "Thanks."

He chuckled and got to his feet. "You're welcome."

"Thanks, Sara," she called to the other woman.

"It was truly our pleasure." Sara yawned. "And now we really should get to bed, don't you think? Michelle has an early morning, and I'm quite tired." She hesitated. "Perhaps we should check to make sure the flying monkeys are locked up securely...?"

They both laughed.

The driving instructor's name was Mr. Moore. He had a small white round patch of hair at the base of his skull. Michelle wondered if his hair loss was from close calls by students.

He was very patient. She had a couple of near-misses, but was able to correct in time and avoid an accident. He told her that it was something that much practice would fix. She only needed to drive, and remember her lessons.

So she drove. But it was Sara, not Gabriel, who rode with her that summer. Gabriel had packed a bag, told the women goodbye, and rushed out without another word.

"Where is he going?" Michelle had asked Sara.

The other woman smiled gently. "We're not allowed to know. Some of what he does is classified. And you must never mention it to anyone. Okay?"

"Of course not," Michelle replied. She bit her lip. "What he does—it's just office stuff, right? I mean he advises. That's talking to people, instructing, right?"

Sara hesitated only a beat before she replied, "Of course."

Michelle put it out of her mind. Gabriel didn't phone home. He'd been gone several weeks. During that time, Michelle began to perfect her driving skills, with Sara's help. She got her driver's license, passing the test easily, and now she drove alternately to work with Carlie.

"This is just so great," Carlie enthused on the way to work. "They bought you a Jaguar! I can't believe it!" She sighed, smoothing her hand over the soft leather seat. "I wish somebody would buy me a Jaguar."

Michelle chuckled. "It was a shock to me, too, let me tell you. I tried to give it back, but they wouldn't hear of it. They said I needed something safe. Like a big Ford truck wouldn't be safe?" she mused.

"I'd love a big brand-new Ford truck," Carlie sighed. "One of those F-Series ones. Or a Dodge Ram. Or a Chevy Silverado. I've never met a truck I didn't love."

"I like cars better," Michelle said. "Just a personal

preference." She glanced at her friend. "I'm going to miss riding with you when I go to college."

"I'll miss you, too." Carlie glanced out the window. "Just having company keeps me from brooding."

"Carson is still giving you fits, I gather?" Michelle asked gently.

Carlie looked down at her hands. "I don't understand why he hates me so much," she said. "I haven't done anything to him. Well, except make a few sarcastic comments, but he starts it," she added with a scowl.

"Maybe he likes you," Michelle ventured. "And he doesn't want to."

"Oh, sure, that's the reason." She shook her head. "No. That isn't it. He'd throw me to the wolves without a second thought."

"He spends a lot of time in Cash Grier's office."

"They're working on something. I'm not allowed to know what, and the chief makes sure I can't overhear him when he talks on the phone." She frowned. "My father's in there a lot, too. I can't imagine why. Carson isn't the praying sort," she added coldly, alluding to her father's profession. He was, after all, a minister.

"I wouldn't think the chief is the praying sort, either," Michelle replied. "Maybe it's something to do about that man who attacked your father."

"I've wondered about that," her companion replied. "Dad won't tell me anything. He just clams up if I mention it."

"You could ask the chief."

Carlie burst out laughing. "You try it," she replied with a grin. "He changes the subject, picks up the phone, drags someone passing by into the office to chat—he's a master at evasion."

"You might try asking Carson," she added.

The smile faded. "Carson would walk all over me."

"You never know."

"I know, all right." Carlie flushed a little, and stared out the window again.

"Sorry," Michelle said gently. "You don't want to talk about him. I understand."

"It's okay." She turned her head. "Is Gabriel coming back soon?"

"We don't know. We don't even know where he is," Michelle said sadly. "Some foreign country, I gather, but he didn't say." She shook her head. "He's so mysterious."

"Most men are." Carlie laughed.

"At least what he does is just business stuff," came the reply. "So we don't have to worry about him so much."

"A blessing," Carlie agreed.

Michelle did a story about the local fire department and its new fire engine. She learned a lot from the fire chief about how fires were started and how they were fought. She put it all into a nice article, with photos of the firemen. Minette ran it on the front page.

"Favoritism," Cash Grier muttered when she stopped by to get Carlie for the drive home that Friday afternoon.

"Excuse me?" Michelle asked him.

"A story about the fire department, on the front page," he muttered. He glared at her. "You haven't even done one about us, and we just solved a major crime!"

"A major crime." Michelle hadn't heard of it.

"Yes. Someone captured old man Jones's chicken, put it in a doll dress, and tied it to his front porch." He grinned. "We captured the perp."

"And?" Michelle prompted. Carlie was listening, too.

"It was Ben Harris's granddaughter." He chuckled. "Her grandmother punished her for overfilling the bathtub by taking away her favorite dolly. So there was this nice red hen right next door. She took the chicken inside, dressed it up, and had fun playing with it while her grandparents were at the store. Then she realized how much more trouble she was going to be in when they noticed what the chicken did, since it wasn't wearing a diaper."

Both women were laughing.

"So she took the chicken back to Jones' house, but she was afraid it might run off, so she tied it to the porch rail." He shook his head. "The doll's clothes were a dead giveaway. She's just not cut out for a life of crime."

"What did Mr. Jones do?" Michelle asked.

"Oh, he took pictures," he replied. "Want one? They're pretty cool. I'm thinking of having one blown up for my office. To put on my solved-crime wall." He grinned.

They were laughing so hard, tears were rolling down their cheeks.

"And the little girl?" Michelle persisted.

"She's assigned to menial chores for the next few days. At least, until all the chicken poop has been cleaned off the floors and furniture. They did give her back the doll, however," he added, tongue in cheek. "To prevent any future lapses. Sad thing, though."

"What is?"

"The doll is naked. If she brings it out of the house, as much as I hate it, I'll have to cite it for indecent exposure..."

The laughter could be heard outside the door now. The tall man with jet-black hair hanging down to his waist wasn't laughing.

He stopped, staring at the chief and his audience.

"Something?" Cash asked, suddenly all business.

"Something." Carson's black eyes slid to Carlie's face and narrowed coldly. "If you can spare the time."

"Sure. Come on in."

"If you don't need me, I'll go home," Carlie said at once, flushed, as she avoided Carson's gaze.

"I don't need you." Carson said it with pure venom.

She lifted her chin pugnaciously. "Thank God," she said through her teeth.

He opened his mouth, but Cash intervened. "Go on home, Carlie," he said, as he grabbed Carson by the arm and steered him into the office.

"So that's Carson," Michelle said as she drove toward Carlie's house.

"That's Carson."

Michelle drew in a breath. "A thoroughly unpleasant person."

"You don't know the half of it."

"He really has it in for you."

Carlie nodded. "Told you so."

There really didn't seem to be anything else to say. Michelle gave her a sympathetic smile and kept her silence until they pulled up in front of the Victorian house she shared with her father.

"Thanks for the ride," Carlie said. "My turn to drive tomorrow."

"And my turn to buy gas." She chuckled.

"You don't hear me arguing, do you?" Carlie sighed, smiling. "Gas is outrageously high."

"So is most everything else. Have a good night. I'll see you tomorrow."

"Sure. Thanks again."

Michelle parked her car in front of the house, noted that she really needed to take it through the car wash, and started toward the front door. Sara's car was missing. She hadn't mentioned being away. Not a problem, however, since Michelle had a key.

She started to put it into the lock, just as it opened on its own. And there was Gabriel, tanned and handsome and smiling.

"Gabriel!" She threw herself into his arms, to be lifted, and hugged, and swung around once, twice, three times, in an embrace so hungry that she never wanted to be free again.

"When did you get home?" she asked at his ear.

"About ten minutes ago," he murmured into her neck. "You smell of roses."

"New perfume. Sara bought it for me." She drew back just enough to see his face, her arms still around his neck, his arms still holding her close. She searched his eyes at point-blank range and felt her heart go into overdrive. She could barely breathe. He felt like heaven in her arms. She looked at his mouth, chiseled, perfect, and wondered, wondered so hard, how it would feel if she moved just a little, if she touched her lips to it...

His hand caught in her long hair and pulled. "No," he said through his teeth.

She met his eyes. She saw there, or thought she saw, the same burning hunger that was beginning to tauten her young body, to kindle needs she'd never known she had.

Her lips parted on a shaky breath. She stared at him. He stared back. There seemed to be no sound in the world, nothing except the soft rasp of her breathing and the increasing heaviness of his own. Against her flattened breasts, she could feel the warm hardness of his chest, the thunder of his heartbeat.

One of his hands slid up and down her spine. His black eyes dropped to her mouth and lingered there until she almost felt the imprint of them, like a hard, rough kiss. Her nails bit into him where her hands clung.

She wanted him. He could feel it. She wanted his mouth, his hands, his body. Her breath was coming in tiny gasps. He could feel her heartbeat behind the soft, warm little breasts pressed so hard to his chest. Her mouth was parted, moist, inviting. He could grind his own down into it and make her moan, make her want him, make her open her arms to him on the long, soft sofa that was only a few steps away....

She was eighteen. She'd never lived. There hadn't been a serious romance in her young life. He could rob her of her innocence, make her a toy, leave her broken and hurting and old.

"No," he whispered. He forced himself to put her down. He held her arms, tightly, until he could force himself to let go and step back.

She was shaky. She felt his hunger. He wasn't impervious to her. But he was cautious. He didn't want to start anything. He was thinking about her age. She knew it.

"I won't...always be eighteen," she managed.

He nodded, very slowly. "One day," he promised. "Perhaps."

She brightened. It was like the sun coming out. "I'll read lots of books."

His eyebrows arched.

"You know. On how to do...stuff. And I'll buy a hope chest and fill it up with frothy little black things."

The eyebrows arched even more.

"Well, it's a hope chest. As in, I hope I'll need it one day when you think I'm old enough." She pursed her lips and her gray eyes twinkled. "I could fake my ID...."

"Give it up." He chuckled.

She shrugged. "I'll grow up as fast as I can," she promised. She glowered at him. "I won't like it if I hear about you having orgies with strange women."

"Most women are strange," he pointed out.

She hit his chest. "Not nice."

"How's the driving?" he asked, changing the subject.

"I haven't hit a tree, run off the road or approached a ditch since you left," she said smugly. "I haven't even dinged the paint."

"Good girl," he said, chuckling. "I'm proud of you. How's the job coming along?"

"It's great! I'm working on this huge story! It may have international implications!"

Odd, how worried he looked for a few seconds. "What story?"

"It involves a kidnapping," she continued.

He frowned.

"A chicken was involved," she added, and watched his face clear and become amused. "A little girl whose doll was taken away for punishment stole a chicken and dressed it in doll's clothes. I understand she'll be cleaning the house for days to come."

He laughed heartily. "The joys of small-town reporting," he mused.

"They never end. How was your trip?"

"Long," he said. "And I'm starving."

"Sara made a lovely casserole. I'll heat you up some."

He sat down at the kitchen table and watched her work. She made coffee and put a mug of it, black, at his place while she dealt with reheating the chicken casserole.

She warmed up a piece of French bread with butter to go with it. Then she sat down and watched him eat while she sipped her own coffee.

"It sure beats fried snake," he murmured.

She blinked. "What?"

"Well, we eat what we can find. Usually, it's a snake. Sometimes, if we're lucky, a big bird or some fish."

"In an office building?" she exclaimed.

He glanced at her with amusement. "It's not always in an office building. Sometimes we have to go out and look at…projects, wherever they might be. This time, it was in a jungle."

"Wow." She was worried now. "Poisonous snakes?"

"Mostly. It doesn't really affect the taste," he added.

"You could get bitten," she persisted.

"I've been bitten, half a dozen times," he replied easily. "We always carry antivenin with us."

"I thought you were someplace safe."

He studied her worried face and felt a twinge of guilt. "It was just this once," he lied, and he smiled. "What I do is rarely dangerous." Another lie. A bigger one. "Nothing to concern you. Honest."

She propped her face in her hands, her elbows on the table, and watched him finish his meal and his coffee.

"Stop that," he teased. "I can take care of myself. I've been doing it for twenty-odd years."

She grimaced. "Okay. Just checking."

"I promise not to get killed."

"If you do, I'm coming after you. Boy, will you be sorry, too."

He laughed. "I hear you."

"Want dessert? We have a cherry pie."

He shook his head. "Maybe later. Where's Sara?"

"I have no idea. She didn't even leave a note."

He pulled out his cell phone and pressed the speed dial. He got up and poured more coffee into his cup while he waited.

"Where are you?" he asked after a minute.

There was a reply. He glanced at Michelle, his lips pursed, his eyes twinkling. "Yes, she's right here."

Another silence. He sat back down. He was nodding.

"No, I think it's a very good idea. But you might have asked for my input first....No, I agree, you have exquisite taste....Yes, that's true, returns are possible. I won't tell her. How long?...Okay. See you then." He smiled. "Me, too. Thanks."

He hung up.

"Where is she?" she asked.

"On her way home. With a little surprise."

"Something for me?" she asked, and her face brightened.

"I'd say so."

"But you guys have already given me so much," she began, protesting.

"You can take that up with my sister," he pointed out. "Not that it will do you much good. She's very stubborn."

She laughed. "I noticed." She paused. "What is it?"

"You'll have to wait and see."

Sara pulled up into the driveway and got out of her car. She popped the truck and dragged out several big shopping bags. She handed some to Gabriel and one to Michelle. She was grinning from ear to ear.

"What in the world...?" Michelle exclaimed.

"Just a few little odds and ends that you're going to need to start college. Come on inside and I'll show you. Gabriel, get your nose out of that bag, it's private!"

He laughed and led the way into the house.

Michelle was speechless. Sara had exquisite taste in clothing, and it showed in the items she'd purchased for their houseguest. There was everything from jeans and sweats to dresses and handbags and underwear, gossamer gowns and an evening gown that brought tears to Michelle's eyes because it was the loveliest thing she'd ever seen.

"You like them?" Sara asked, a little worried.

"I've never had things like this," she stammered. "Daddy was so sick that he never thought of shopping with me. And when Roberta took me, it was just for bras and panties, never for nice clothes." She hugged Sara impulsively. "Thank you. Thank you so much!"

"You might try on that gown. I wasn't sure about the size, but we can exchange it if it doesn't fit. I'll go have coffee with Gabriel while you check the fit." She smiled, and left Michelle with the bags.

They were sipping coffee in the kitchen when Michelle came nervously to the doorway. She'd fixed her hair, put on shoes and she was wearing the long, creamy evening gown with its tight fit and cap sleeves, revealing soft cleavage. There was faint embroidery on the bodice and around the hem. The off-white brought out the highlights in Michelle's long, pale blond hair, and accentuated her peaches-and-cream complexion. In her softly powdered face, her gray eyes were exquisite.

Gabriel turned his head when he caught movement in his peripheral vision. He sat like a stone statue, just staring. Sara followed his gaze, and her face brightened.

"It's perfect!" she exclaimed, rising. "Michelle, it's absolutely perfect! Now you have something to wear to a really formal occasion."

"Thanks," she replied. "It's the most beautiful thing I've ever owned." She glanced at Gabriel, who hadn't spoken. His coffee cup was suspended in his hand in midair, as if he'd forgotten it. "Does it…look okay?" she asked him, wanting reassurance.

He forced his eyes away. "It looks fine." He put the mug down and got to his feet. "I need to check the livestock." He went out the back door without a glance behind him.

Michelle felt wobbly. She bit her lower lip. "He didn't like it," she said miserably.

Sara touched her cheek gently. "Men are strange. They react in odd ways. I'm sure he liked it, but he's not demonstrative." She smiled. "Okay?"

Michelle relaxed. "Okay."

Out in the barn, Gabriel was struggling to regain his composure. He'd never seen anything in his life more beautiful than Michelle in that dress. He'd had to force himself out the door before he reacted in a totally inappropriate way. He wanted to sweep her up in his arms and kiss her until her mouth went numb. Not a great idea.

He stood beside one of his horses, stroking its muzzle gently, while he came to grips with his hunger. It was years too soon. He would have to manage the long wait. Meanwhile, he worried about the other men, young men, who would see Michelle in that gown and want her, as he wanted her. But they would be her age, young and untried, without his jaded past. They would be like her, full of passion for life.

It wasn't fair of him to try to keep her. He must distance himself from her, give her the chance to grow away from him, to find someone more suitable. It was going to be hard, but he must manage it. She deserved the chance.

* * *

The next morning, he was gone when Michelle went into the kitchen to help Sara fix breakfast.

"His truck's gone," Michelle said, her spirits dropping hard.

"Yes. I spoke to him late last night," Sara replied, not looking at her. "He has a new job. He said he might be away for a few weeks." She glanced at the younger woman and managed a smile. "Don't worry about him. He can take care of himself."

"I'm sure he can. It's just…" She rested her hand on the counter. "I miss him, when he's away."

"I'm sure you do." She hesitated. "Michelle, you haven't started to live yet. There's a whole world out there that you haven't even seen."

Michelle turned, her eyes old and wise. "And you think I'll find some young man who'll sweep me off my feet and carry me off to a castle." She smiled. "There's only one man I'll ever want to do that, you know."

Sara grimaced. "There are so many things you don't know."

"They won't matter," Michelle replied very quietly. She searched Sara's eyes. "None of it will matter."

Sara couldn't think of the right words. So she just hugged Michelle instead.

Chapter Nine

Michelle was very nervous. It was the first day of the semester on campus, and even with a map, it was hard to find all her classes. Orientation had given the freshmen an overview of where everything was off the quad, but it was so confusing.

"Is Western Civilization in Sims Hall or Waverly Hall?" she muttered to herself, peering at the map.

"Waverly," came a pleasant male voice from just behind her. "Come on, I'll walk you over. I'm Randy. Randy Miles."

"Michelle Godfrey," she said, shaking his hand and smiling. "Thanks. Are you in my class?"

He shook his head. "I'm a junior."

"Should you be talking to me?" she teased. "After all, I'm pond scum."

He stopped and smiled. He had dark hair and pale

eyes. He was a little pudgy, but nice. "No. You're not pond scum. Trust me."

"Thanks."

"My pleasure. Are you from San Antonio?"

"My family is from Jacobsville, but I lived here with my parents while they were alive."

"Sorry."

"They were wonderful people. The memories get easier with time." She glanced around. "This is a huge campus."

"They keep adding to it," he said. "Sims Hall is brand-new. Waverly is old. My father had history with old Professor Barlane."

"Really?"

He nodded. "Just a word of warning, never be late for his class. You don't want to know why."

She grinned. "I'll remember."

On the way to Waverly Hall, Randy introduced Michelle to two of his friends, Alan Drew and Marjory Wills. Alan was distantly pleasant. Marjory was much more interested in talking to Randy than being introduced to this new student.

"You're going to be late for class, aren't you?" Alan asked Michelle, checking his watch. "I'll walk you the rest of the way."

"Nice to have met you," Randy said pleasantly. Marjory just nodded.

Michelle smiled and followed Alan to the towering building where her class was located.

"Thanks," she said.

He shrugged and smiled. "Those two." He rolled his eyes. "They're crazy about each other, but neither one will admit it. Don't let them intimidate you, especially Marjory. She has…issues."

"No problem. I guess I'll see you around."

"You will." He leaned forward, grinning. "I'm in the class you're going to right now. And we'd better hurry!"

They barely made it before the bell. The professor, Dr. Barlane, was old and cranky. He gave the class a dismissive look and began to lecture. Michelle was grateful that she'd learned how to take notes, because she had a feeling that this class was going to be one of the more demanding ones.

Beside her, Alan was scribbling on scraps of paper instead of a notebook, like Michelle. He wasn't bad-looking. He had dark hair and eyes and a nice smile, but in her heart, there was only Gabriel. She might like other men as friends, but there was never going to be one to compare with Gabriel.

After class, Alan left her with a smile and whistled as he continued on to his next class. Michelle looked at her schedule, puzzled out the direction to go and went along the walkway to the next building.

"Well, how was it?" Sara asked that night on the phone.

"Very nice," she replied. "I made a couple of friends."

"Male ones?" Sara teased.

"What was that?" Gabriel spoke up in the background.

"She made friends," Sara called to him. "Don't have a cow."

He made a sarcastic sound and was quiet.

"How do you like your roommate?" Sara continued.

Michelle glanced into the next room, where Darla was searching frantically for a blouse she'd unpacked and couldn't find, muttering and ruffling her red hair.

"She's just like me. Disorganized and flighty," Michelle said, a little loudly.

"I heard that!" Darla said over her shoulder.

"I know!" Michelle laughed. Darla shook her head, laughing, too.

"We're going to get along just fine," Michelle told Sara. "Neither of us has half a mind, and we're so disorganized that we're likely to be thrown out for creating a public eyesore."

"Not likely," Sara replied. "Well, I'm glad things are going well. If you need us, you know where we are, sweetie."

"I do. Thanks. Thanks for everything."

"Keep in touch. Good night."

"Good night."

"Your family?" Darla asked, poking her head into the room.

Michelle hesitated, but only for a second. She smiled. "Yes. My family."

Michelle adjusted to college quite easily. She made some friends, mostly distant ones, and one good one—her roommate, Darla. She and Darla were both religious, so they didn't go to boozy parties or date promiscuous boys. That meant they spent a lot of time watching rented movies and eating popcorn in their own dorm room.

One thing Sara had said was absolutely true; college changed her. She learned things that questioned her own view of the world and things about other cultures. She saw the rise and fall of civilizations, the difference in religions, the rise of science, the fascination of history. She continued her study of French—mainly because she wanted to know what Sara and Gabriel spoke about that they didn't want her to hear—and she sweated first-year biology. But by and large, she did well in her classes.

All too soon, final exams arrived. She sat in the library with other students, she and Darla trying to absorb what they needed to know to pass their courses. She'd already lived in the biology lab for several days after school with a study group, going over material that was certainly going to come up when they were tested.

"I'm going to fail," she moaned softly to Darla. "I'll go home in disgrace. I'll have to hide my head in a paper sack...."

"Shut up," Darla muttered. "You're going to pass! So am I. Be quiet and study, girl!"

Michelle sighed. "Thanks. I needed that."

"I'm going to fail," one of the boys nearby moaned to Darla. "I'll go home in disgrace..."

She punched him.

"Thanks." He chuckled, and went back to his books.

Michelle did pass, with flying colors, but she didn't know it when she went back to Comanche Wells for the holidays.

"I'll have to sweat it out until my grades come through," she said to Sara, hugging her warmly. "But I think I did okay." She looked past Sara and then at her, curious.

"He's out of the country," Sara said gently. "He was really sorry, he wanted to be home for the holidays. But it wasn't possible. This was a rush thing."

Michelle's heart fell. "I guess he has to work."

"Yes, he does. But he got your presents, and mine, and wrapped them before he left." Her dark eyes twinkled. "He promised that we'd love the gifts."

"I'd love a rock, if he picked it out for me," Michelle sighed. "Can we go shopping? Minette said I could work for her over the holidays while I'm home, so I'll have a little money of my own."

"Whenever you like, dear," Sara promised.

"Thanks!"

"Now come and have hot chocolate. I want to hear all about college!"

Minette had some interesting assignments for Michelle. One was to interview one of Jacobsville's senior citizens about Christmas celebrations in the mid-twentieth century, before the internet or space travel. It had sounded rather boring, honestly. But when she spoke to Adelaide Duncan, the old woman made the past come alive in her soft, mellow tones.

"We didn't have fancy decorations for the Christmas tree," Mrs. Duncan recalled, her pale blue eyes dancing with delightful memories. "We made them from construction paper. We made garlands of cranberries. We used candles set on the branches to light the tree, and we used soap powder mixed with a little water for snow. Presents were practical things, mostly fruit or nuts or handcrafted garments. One year I got oranges and a knit cap. Another, I got a dress my mother had made me in a beautiful lemon color. My husband kissed me under the mistletoe when we were still in school together, long before we married." Her face was wistful. "He was seventeen and I was fifteen. We danced to music that our parents and relatives made with fiddles and guitars. I wore the lemon-yellow dress, ruffled and laced, and I felt like I had possession of the whole world's treasures." She sighed. "We were married for fifty-five years," she added wistfully. "And one day, not too long away now, I'll see him again. And we'll dance together...."

Michelle had to fight tears. "Fifty-five years," she repeated, and couldn't imagine two people staying together for so long.

"Oh, yes. In my day, people got married and then had children." She shook her head. "The world has changed, my dear. Marriage doesn't seem to mean the same as it used to. History tends to repeat itself, and I fear when the stability of a civilization is lost, society crumbles. You'll study the results in your history classes in college," she added, nodding. "Do you have Dr. Barlane for history by any chance?"

"Yes," Michelle said, stunned.

The old woman laughed. "He and I graduated together from Marist College, both with degrees in history. But he went on to higher education and I got married and had a family. By and large, I think my life was happier than his. He never married."

"Do your children live here?" she asked.

"Oh, no, they're scattered around the world." She laughed. "I visit with them on Skype and we text back and forth every day, though. Modern technology." She shook her head. "It really is a blessing, in this day and time."

Michelle was surprised. "You text?" she asked.

"My dear," the old lady mused, laughing, "I not only text, I tweet and surf, and I am hell on wheels with a two-handed sword in World of Warcraft. I own a guild."

The younger woman's idea of elderly people had gone up in a blaze of disbelief. "You...play video games?"

"I eat them up." She shrugged. "I can't run and jump and play in real life, but I can do it online." She grinned from ear to ear. "Don't you dare tell Wofford Patterson, but I creamed one of his Horde toons last night on a bat-tleground."

Michelle almost fell over laughing.

"And you thought you were going to interview some dried up old hulk who sat in a rocking chair and knitted, I bet," the woman mused with twinkling eyes.

"Yes, I did," Michelle confessed, "and I am most heartily sorry!"

"That's all right, dear," Mrs. Duncan said, patting her hand. "We all have misconceptions about each other."

"Mine were totally wrong."

"How nice of you to say so!"

Michelle changed gears and went back to the interview. But what she learned about elderly people that day colored her view of them forever.

"She plays video games," Michelle enthused to Minette, back at the office. She'd written her story and turned it in, along with her photos, while Minette was out of the office. Now she was elaborating on the story, fascinated with what she'd learned.

"Yes, there have been a lot of changes in the way we perceive the elderly," Minette agreed. "I live with my great-aunt. She doesn't play video games, but I did catch her doing Tai Chi along with an instructor on public television. And she can text, too."

"My grandparents sat and rocked on the porch after supper," Michelle recalled. "He smoked a pipe and she sewed quilt tops and they talked." She shook her head. "It's a different world."

"It is." She hesitated. "Has Gabriel come home?"

Michelle shook her head. "It's almost Christmas, too. We don't know where he is, or what he's doing."

Minette, who did, carefully concealed her knowledge.

"Well, he might surprise you and show up on Christmas day. Who knows?"

Michelle forced a smile. "Yes."

She and Sara decorated the tree. Two of the men who worked for Gabriel part-time, taking care of the horses and the ranch, had come in earlier with a big bucket, holding a tree with the root ball still attached.

"I can't bear to kill a tree," Sara confided as the men struggled to put it in place in the living room. "Sorry, guys," she added.

"Oh, Miss Sara, it's no trouble at all," the taller of the two cowboys said at once, holding his hat to his heart. He grinned. "It was our pleasure."

"Absolutely," the shorter one agreed.

They stood smiling at Sara until one thumped the other and reminded him that they had chores to do. They excused themselves, still smiling.

"You just tie them up in knots." Michelle laughed, when they were out of the room. "You're so pretty."

Sara made a face. "Nonsense."

"Hide your head in the sand, then. What are we going to decorate it with?" she added.

"Come with me."

Sara pulled down the ladder and the two women climbed carefully up into the attic.

Michelle caught her breath when she saw the heart of pine rafters. "My goodness, it's almost a religious experience to just look at them!" she exclaimed. "Those rafters must be a hundred years old!"

Sara glanced at her with amusement. "I believe they are. Imagine you, enthralled by rafters!"

"Heart of pine rafters," she replied. "My grandfather built houses when he was younger. He took me with him a time or two when he had to patch a roof or fix a leak. He was passionate about rafters." She laughed. "And especially those made of heart of pine. They're rare, these days, when people mostly build with green lumber that hasn't been properly seasoned."

"This house has a history," Sara said. "You probably already know it, since your people came from Jacobs County."

Michelle nodded, watching Sara pick up two boxes of ornaments and stack them together. "It belonged to a Texas Ranger."

"Yes. He was killed in a shoot-out in San Antonio. He left behind two sons, a daughter and a wife. There's a plaque in city hall in Jacobsville that tells all about him."

"I'll have to go look," Michelle said. "I haven't done any stories that took me there, yet."

"I'm sure you will. Minette says you're turning into a very good reporter."

"She does?" Michelle was all eyes. "Really?"

Sara looked at her and smiled. "You must have more confidence in yourself," she said gently. "You must believe in your own abilities."

"That's hard."

"It comes with age. You'll get the hang of it." She handed Michelle a box of ornaments. "Be careful going down the steps."

"Okay."

They spent the afternoon decorating the tree. When they finally plugged in the beautiful, colored fairy lights, Michelle caught her breath.

"It's the most breathtaking tree I've ever seen," she enthused.

"It is lovely, isn't it?" Sara asked. She fingered a

branch. "We must keep it watered, so that it doesn't die. When Christmas is over, I'll have the men plant it near the front steps. I do so love white pines!"

"Do you ever miss Wyoming?" Michelle asked, a little worried because she knew Sara was only here so that Michelle could come home, so that she wouldn't be alone with Gabriel.

Sara turned to her. "A little. I lived there because Gabriel bought the ranch and one of us needed to run it. But I had no real friends. I'm happier here." Her dark eyes were soft. She smoothed over an ornament. "This belonged to my grandmother," she said softly. It was a little house, made of logs, hanging from a red silk ribbon. "My grandfather whittled it for her, when they were dating." She laughed. "Wherever I am, it always makes me feel at home when the holidays come."

"Your mother's parents?"

Sara's face went hard. "No. My father's."

"I'm sorry."

Sara turned back to her. In her lovely face, her dark eyes were sad. "I don't speak of my mother, or her people. I'm sorry. It's a sore spot with me."

"I'll remember," Michelle said quietly. "It's like my stepmother."

"Exactly."

Michelle didn't betray her secret knowledge of Sara's early life, of the tragedy she and Gabriel had lived through because of their mother's passion for their stepfather. She changed the subject and asked about the other ornaments that Sara had placed on the tree.

But Sara wasn't fooled. She was very quiet. Later, when they were sipping hot chocolate in the kitchen, her dark eyes pinned Michelle.

"How much did he tell you?" she asked suddenly.

In her hands, the mug jumped, almost enough to spill the hot liquid on her fingers.

"Careful, it's hot," Sara said. "Come on, Michelle. How much did Gabriel tell you?"

Michelle grimaced.

Sara took in a long breath. "I see." She sipped the liquid gingerly. "He never speaks of it at all. Yet he told you." Her soft eyes lifted to Michelle's worried gray ones. "I'm not angry. I'm surprised."

"That he told me?"

"Yes." She smiled sadly. "He doesn't warm to people. In fact, he's cold and withdrawn with almost everyone. You can't imagine how shocked I was when he phoned me and asked me to come down here because of a young girl he was going to get custody of." She laughed, shaking her head. "I thought he was joking."

"But he's not. Cold and withdrawn, I mean." Michelle faltered.

"Not with you." She stared into Michelle's eyes earnestly. "I haven't heard Gabriel laugh in years," she added softly. "But he does it all the time with you. I don't understand it. But you give him peace, Michelle."

"That would be nice, if it were true. I don't know if it is," Michelle replied.

"It's fairly obvious what you feel for him."

She flushed. She couldn't lift her eyes.

"He won't take advantage of it, don't worry," Sara added gently. "That's why I'm here." She laughed. "He's taking no chances."

"He doesn't want to get involved with a child," Michelle said heavily.

"You won't be a child for much longer," the other woman pointed out.

"I'm sure he meets beautiful women all the time," Michelle said.

"I'm sure it doesn't matter what they look like," Sara replied. She smiled. "You'll see."

Michelle didn't reply to that. She just sipped her hot chocolate and felt warm inside.

It was the week before Christmas, a Friday about lunchtime, when the women heard a truck pull up in the driveway.

Michelle, who was petting one of the horses in the corral, saw the truck and gasped and ran as fast as she could to the man getting out of it.

"Gabriel!" she cried.

He turned. His face lit up like floodlights. He held out his arms and waited until she ran into them to pick her up and whirl her around, holding her so close that she felt they were going to be joined together forever.

"Oh, I've missed you," she choked.

"I've missed you." His voice was deep at her ear. He lifted his head and set her on her feet. His black eyes were narrow, intent on her face. He touched her mouth with just the tip of his forefinger, teasing it apart. His eyes fell to it and lingered there while her heart threatened to jump right out of her throat.

"Ma belle," he whispered roughly.

He framed her oval face in his big hands and searched her eyes. *"Ma belle,"* he repeated. His eyes fell to her mouth. "It's like falling into fire…"

As he spoke, his head started to bend. Michelle's heart ran away. She could hear her own breathing, feel his breath going into her mouth, taste the coffee and the faint odor of tobacco that came from him, mingled with some masculine cologne that teased her senses.

"Gabriel," she whispered, hanging at his mouth, aching to feel it come crashing down on her lips, crushing them, devouring him, easing the ache, the hunger that pulsed through her young, untried body...

"Gabriel!"

Sara's joyful cry broke them apart just in the nick of time. Gabriel cleared his throat, turned to his sister and hugged her.

"It's good to have you home," Sara said against his chest.

"It's good to be home." He was struggling to sound normal. His mind was still on Michelle's soft mouth and his hunger to break it open under his lips, back her into a wall and devour her.

"Have you eaten? I just made soup," Sara added.

"No. I'm starved." He made an attempt not to look at Michelle when he said that. He even smiled.

"I could eat, too," Michelle said, trying to break the tension.

"Let's go in." Sara took his arm. "Where did you come from?"

"Dallas, this time," he said. "I've been in the States for a couple of days, but I had business there before I could get home." He hesitated. "I got tickets to the ballet in San Antonio when I came through there this morning." He glanced at Michelle. "Want to go see *The Nutcracker* with me?" he added with a grin.

"Oh, I'd love to," she said fervently. "What do we wear?"

"A very dressy evening outfit," Sara said. "I bought you one once, and you never even wore it."

Michelle grinned. "Well, I haven't been anywhere I'd need to wear it," she replied, not guessing what it told Gabriel, whose eyes twinkled brightly.

Michelle flushed and then grinned at him. "No, I'm not dating anybody at college," she said. She shrugged. "I'm too busy studying."

"Is that so?" Gabriel laughed, and was relieved.

"When are you leaving?" Sara asked.

"At six, and you'd better start dressing as well, because we're all three going," Gabriel added, and he exchanged a speaking look with Sara.

"All of us? Oh. Oh! That's nice!" Michelle worked at sounding enthusiastic.

Sara just winked at her. "I'd better go through my closet."

Gabriel looked down at Michelle with the Christmas tree bright and beautiful behind her. "I wouldn't dare take you out alone, *ma belle,*" he said under his breath. "You know it. And you know why."

Her eyes searched his hungrily. She knew. She'd felt it, when he held her beside the truck. She knew that he wanted her.

She'd had no idea what wanting really was, until Gabriel had come into her life. Now she was aware of a hunger that came around when he was close, that grew and surged in her when he looked at her, when he spoke to her, when he touched her....

"Yes, you know, don't you?" he breathed, standing a little too close. He rubbed his thumb against her lips, hard enough to make her gasp and shiver with delight. His black eyes narrowed. "It's too soon. You know that, too."

She ground her teeth together as she looked at him. He was the most perfect thing in her life. He was preaching caution when all she wanted to do was push him down on the floor and spread her body over him and...

She didn't know what would come next. She'd read books, but they were horribly lacking in preliminaries.

"What are you thinking about so hard?" he asked.

"About pushing you down on the floor," she blurted out, and flushed. "But I don't know what comes next, exactly…"

He burst out laughing.

"You stop that," she muttered. "I'll bet you weren't born knowing what to do, either."

"I wasn't," he confessed. He touched her nose with the tip of his finger. "It's just as well that you don't know. Yet. And we aren't going to be alone. Yet."

She drew in a long sigh and smiled. "Okay."

He chuckled.

"I've never been to the ballet," she confessed.

"High time you went," he replied, and he laughed. "Go on."

Sara had laid out the most beautiful black velvet dress Michelle had ever seen. It had a discreet rounded neckline and long sleeves, and it fell to the ankles, with only a slight tuck where the waistline was.

"It's gorgeous!" Michelle enthused.

"And you'll look gorgeous in it," Sara replied. She hugged Michelle. "It's yours. I have shoes and a purse to match it."

"But, I have a dress," Michelle began.

"A summer dress," Sara said patiently, and smiled. "This one is more suitable for winter. I have one similar to it that I'm wearing. We'll look like twins." She grinned.

"Okay, then. And thank you!" Michelle said heartily.

"You're very welcome."

Chapter Ten

Gabriel wore a dress jacket with dark slacks and a black turtleneck sweater. He looked classy and elegant. Sara wore a simple sheath of navy blue velvet with an expensive gold necklace and earrings and looked exquisite, with her silky black hair loose almost to her waist and her big, dark eyes soft in her beautiful face.

Michelle in her black velvet dress felt like royalty. The trio drew eyes as they filed into the auditorium where the ballet was being performed.

Up front, in the orchestra pit, the musicians were tuning up their instruments. Gabriel found their seats and let the women go in first before he took his place on the aisle.

"There's quite a crowd," Michelle remarked as more people filed in.

"Oh, dear." Sara's voice was full of consternation.

Before Michelle could ask what was wrong, she saw it for herself. Wofford Patterson, in a dinner jacket with a white tie and black slacks was escorting a beautiful blonde, in an elegant green velvet gown, down the aisle—directly to the seats beside Sara.

"Mr. Brandon," Wolf said, nodding. "This is Elise Jorgansen. Elise, Gabriel Brandon. That's his sister, Sara. And that's his ward, Michelle."

"Nice to meet you," Elise said, and smiled at them all with genuine warmth.

"I believe our seats are right there," Wolf told the pretty woman. He escorted her past Gabriel and the women with apologies, because it was a tight squeeze. He sat next to Sara, with Elise on his other side.

Sara tensed and glared straight ahead. Wolf grinned.

"I didn't know that you liked the ballet, Miss Brandon," Wolf said politely.

"I like this one. It's *The Nutcracker*," she added with a venomous look at the man beside her.

He pursed his lips. "Left the flying monkeys at home, did we?"

"I'd love to drop a house on you, dear man," she said under her breath.

"Now, now, it's the ballet," he pointed out. "We must behave like civilized people."

"You'd need so much instruction for that, Mr. Patterson," Sara said, her voice dripping honey.

"Isn't the music lovely?" Michelle broke in.

The music was the instruments being tuned, but it shattered the tension and everyone laughed.

"Behave," Gabriel whispered to his sister.

She gave him an irritated look, but she kept her hands in her lap and sat quietly as the ballerinas came onstage one by one and the performance began, to Michelle's utter fascination and delight. She'd never seen a live performance of the ballet, which was her favorite.

At intermission, Sara excused herself and left the row.

"I'm not getting up," Wolf said. "I'd never get back in here."

"Neither am I," Gabriel mused. "It's quite a crowd."

"You seem to be enjoying the music, Miss Godfrey," Wolf said politely.

"I've never been to a ballet before," she replied, laughing. "It's so beautiful!"

"You should see it in New York City, at the American Ballet Company," Gabriel said gently.

"They do an excellent performance," Wolf agreed. "Have you seen it at the Bolshoi?" he added.

"Yes," Gabriel agreed. "Theirs is unbelievably beautiful."

"That's in Russia, isn't it?" Michelle asked, wide-eyed.

"Yes," Gabriel said. He smiled down at her. "One day, Sara and I will have to take you traveling."

"You should see the world," Elise agreed, from beside Wolf. "Or at least, some of it. Travel broadens your world."

"I can't think of anything I'd love more," Michelle replied, smiling back at the woman.

"Elise studied ballet when she was still in school," Wolf said. "She was in line to be a prima ballerina with the company she played with in New York."

"Don't," Elise said gently.

"Sorry," Wolf said, patting her hand. "Bad memories. I won't mention it again."

"That life is long over," she replied. "But I still love going to see the ballet and the theater and opera. We have such a rich cultural heritage here in San Antonio."

"We do, indeed," Gabriel agreed.

The musicians began tuning their instruments again,

just as Sara came back down the aisle, so graceful and poised that she drew male eyes all the way.

"Your sister has an elegance of carriage that is quite rare," Elise said to Gabriel as she approached.

"She also studied ballet," Gabriel replied quietly. "But the stress of dancing and trying to get through college became too much. She gave up ballet and got her degree in languages." He laughed. "She still dances, though," he added. "She just doesn't put on a tutu first."

"It wouldn't go with the broom," Sara said to Wolf, and smiled coldly as she sat down.

"Broom?" Elise asked, curious.

"Never mind. I'll explain it to you later," Wolf replied.

Sara gave him a look that might have curdled milk and turned her attention to the stage as the curtain began to rise.

"Well, it was a wonderful evening," Michelle said dreamily as she followed them out to the car. "Thank you so much for taking us," she added to Gabriel.

He studied her in the lovely dress, smiling. "It was my pleasure. We'll have to do this more often."

"Expose you to culture, he means," Sara said in a stage whisper. "It's good for you."

"I really had a good time."

"I would have, except for the company," Sara muttered. She flushed. "Not you two," she said hastily when they gaped at her. "That…man! And his date."

"I thought Elise was very nice," Michelle ventured.

Sara clammed up.

Gabriel just chuckled.

Christmas Eve was magical. They sat around the Christmas tree, watching a program of Christmas music on television, sipping hot chocolate and making s'mores in the fireplace, where a sleepy fire flamed every now and then.

In all her life, Michelle couldn't remember being so happy. Her eyes kept darting to Gabriel, when she thought he wasn't looking. Even in jeans and a flannel shirt, he was the stuff of dreams. It was so hard not to appear starstruck.

They opened presents that night instead of the next morning, because Sara announced that she wasn't getting up at dawn to see what Santa had left.

She gave Michelle a beautiful scarf of many colors, a designer one. Michelle draped it around her neck and raved over it. Then she opened Gabriel's gift. It was pearls, a soft off-white set in a red leather box. They were Japanese. He'd brought them home from his last trip and hidden them to give at Christmas. The necklace was accompanied by matching drop earrings.

"I was right," he mused as Michelle tried them on enthusiastically. "They're just the right shade."

"They are, indeed. And thank you for mine, also, my sweet." Sara kissed his tan cheek, holding a strand of white ones in her hand. They suited her delicate coloring just as the off-white ones suited Michelle's.

"I like mine, too." He held up a collection of DVDs of shows he particularly liked from Michelle and a black designer turtleneck from Sara.

Sara loved her handmade scarf from Michelle. It was crocheted and had taken an age to finish. It was the softest white knit, with tassels. "I'll wear it all winter," she promised Michelle, and kissed her, too.

Michelle had hung mistletoe in strategic places, but she hadn't counted on Gabriel's determined reticence. He kissed her on the cheek, smiled and wished her the happiest of Christmases and New Years. She pretended that it didn't matter that he didn't drag her into an empty room and kiss her half to death. He was determined not to treat her as an adult. It was painful. But in some sense, she did understand.

So three years went by, more quickly than Michelle had dreamed they would. She got a job part-time with a daily newspaper in San Antonio and did political pieces for it while she got through her core courses and into serious journalism in college.

She went to class during summer to speed up her degree program, although she came home for the holidays. Gabriel was almost always away now. Sara was there, although she spent most of her time in Wyoming at the ranch she and Gabriel owned. Michelle had gone up there with her one summer for a couple of weeks during her vacation. It was a beautiful place. Sara was different somehow. Something had happened between her and Wofford Patterson. She wouldn't talk about it, but she knew that it had changed Sara. Gabriel had mentioned something about Sara going back into therapy and there had been an argument in French that Michelle couldn't follow.

Wofford Patterson had also moved up to Catelow, Wyoming. He bought a huge ranch there near Sara's. He kept his place in Comanche Wells, but he put in a foreman to manage it for him. He had business interests in Wyoming that took up much of his time, he said, and it was hard to commute. Sara didn't admit that she was glad to have him as a neighbor. But Michelle suspected that she did.

Sara was still playing her online game with her friend, and they fought battles together late into the night. She still didn't know who he really was, either. Gabriel had made sure of it.

"He's such a gentleman," Sara mused over coffee one morning, her face bright with pleasure. "He wants to meet me in person." She hesitated. "I'm not sure about that."

"Why not, if you like him?" Michelle asked innocently, although she didn't dare let on that she knew exactly who Sara's friend was, and she knew that Sara would have a stroke if she saw him in person. It would be the end of a lovely online relationship.

"People aren't what they seem," Sara replied, and pain was in her eyes. "If it seems too good to be true, it usually is."

"He might be a knight in shining armor," Michelle teased. "You should find out."

"He might be an ogre who lives in a cave with bats, too." Sara chuckled. "No. I like things the way they are. I really don't want to try to have a relationship with a man in real life." Her face tensed. "I never wanted to."

Michelle grimaced. "Sara, you're so beautiful…"

"Beautiful!" She laughed coldly. "I wish I'd been born ugly. It would have made my life so much easier. You don't know…" She drew in a harsh breath. "Well, actually, you do know." She managed a soft smile. "We're all prisoners of our childhoods, Michelle. Mine was particularly horrible. It warped me."

"You should have been in therapy," Michelle said gently.

"I tried therapy. It only made things worse. I can't talk to total strangers."

"Maybe you just talked to the wrong person."

Sara's eyes were suddenly soft and dreamy and she flushed. "I think I did. So much has changed," she added softly.

Michelle, who had a good idea what was going on up in Wyoming, just grinned.

Sara's eyes took on an odd, shimmering softness. "Life is so much sweeter than I dreamed it could be." She smiled to herself and looked at her watch. "I have some phone calls to make. I love having you around." She added, "Thanks."

"For what?"

"For caring," Sara said simply.

Michelle was looking forward to her last Christmas in college. She got talked into a blind date with Darla's boyfriend's friend. He turned out to be a slightly haughty man who worked as a stockbroker and never stopped talking on his cell phone for five seconds. He was at it all through dinner. Bob, Darla's boyfriend, looked very uncomfortable and apologetic.

"Bob feels awful," Darla whispered to Michelle in the restroom after they'd finished eating. "Larry seemed to be a normal guy."

"He just lives and breathes his job. Besides," she added, "you know there's only one man who interests me at all. And it's never going to be someone like Larry."

"Having seen your Mr. Brandon, I totally understand." Darla giggled. She shook her head. "He is a dreamboat."

"I think so."

"Well, we'll stop by the bar for a nightcap and go home. Maybe we can pry Larry away from his phone long enough to say good-night."

"I wish I was riding with you and Bob," Michelle sighed. "At least he stops talking while he's driving."

"Curious, that he didn't want to ride with Bob," Darla said. "Well, that's just men, I guess."

But Larry had an agenda that the girls weren't aware of. He knew that Bob and Darla were going dancing and wouldn't be home soon. So when he walked Michelle to the door of the apartment she and Darla shared, he pushed his way in and took off his jacket.

"Finally, alone together," he enthused, and reached for her. "Now, sweetie, let's have a little payback for the meal and the drinks…"

"Are you out of your mind?" she gasped, avoiding his grasping arms.

"I paid for the food," he said, almost snarling. "You owe me!"

"I owe you? Like hell I owe you!" She got to the door and opened it. "I'll send you a check for my part of the meal! Get out!"

"I'm not leaving. You just want to play hard to get." He started to push the door closed. And connected with a steely big hand that caught him by the arm, turned him around and booted him out into the night.

"Gabriel!" Michelle gasped.

"You can't do that to me…!" Larry said angrily, getting to his feet.

Gabriel fell into a fighting stance. "Come on," he said softly. "I could use the exercise."

Larry came to his senses. He glanced at Michelle. She went back inside, got his jacket, and threw it at him.

"Dinner doesn't come with bed," she told him icily.

Larry started to make a reply, but Gabriel's expression was a little too unsettling. He muttered something under his breath, turned, slammed into his car and roared away.

Gabriel went inside with Michelle, who was tearing up now that the drama had played itself out.

"Ah, no, *ma belle,*" he whispered. "There's no need for tears." He pulled her into his arms, bent his head, and kissed her so hungrily that she forgot to breathe.

He lifted his head. His black eyes were smoldering, so

full of desire that they mesmerized Michelle. She tasted him on her mouth, felt the heavy throb of his heart under her hands.

"Finally," he breathed, pulling her close. He brushed his lips over her soft mouth. "Finally!"

She opened her mouth to ask what he meant, and the kiss knocked her so off balance that she couldn't manage a single word in reply. She held on with all her might, clung to him, pushed her body into his so that she could feel every movement of his powerful body against her. He was aroused, very quickly, and even that didn't intimidate her. She moaned. Which only made matters worse.

He picked her up, still kissing her, and laid her out on the couch, easing his body down over hers in a silence that throbbed with frustrated desire.

"Soft," he whispered. "Soft and sweet. All mine."

She would have said something, but he was kissing her again, and she couldn't think at all. She felt his big, rough hands go under her dress, up and up, touching and exploring, testing softness, finding her breasts under the lacy little bra.

"You feel like silk all over," he murmured. He found the zipper and eased her out of the dress and the half slip under it, then out of the bra, so that all she had left on were her briefs. He kissed his way down her body, lingering on her pert breasts with their tight little crowns, savoring her soft, helpless cries of pleasure.

It excited him to know that she'd never done this. He ate her up like candy, tasting her hungrily. He nuzzled her breasts, kissing their soft contours with a practiced touch that made her rise up in an aching arch to his lips.

Somehow, his jacket and shirt ended up on the floor. She felt the rough, curling hair on his chest against her bare breasts as his body covered hers. His powerful legs eased between her own, so that she could feel with him an intimacy she'd never shared with anyone.

She cried out as he moved against her. Sensations were piling on each other, dragging her under, drowning her in pleasure. She clung to him, pleading for more, not even knowing exactly what she wanted, but so drawn with tension that she was dying for it to ease.

She felt hot tears run down her cheeks as his mouth moved back onto hers. He touched her as he never had before. She shivered. The touch came again. She sobbed, and opened her mouth under his. She felt his tongue go into her mouth, as his hands moved on her more intimately.

Suddenly, like a fall of fire, a flash of agonized pleasure convulsed the soft body under his. He groaned and had to fight the instinctive urge to finish what he started, to go right into her, push inside her, take what was his, what had always been his.

But she was a virgin. His exploration had already told him that. He'd known already, by her reactions. She was very much a virgin. He didn't want to do this. Not yet. She was his. It must be done properly, in order, in a way that wouldn't shame her to remember somewhere down the line.

So he forced his shivering body to bear the pain. He held her very close while she recovered from her first ecstasy. He wrapped her up tight, and held her while he endured what he must to spare her innocence.

She wept. He kissed away the tears, so tenderly that they fell even harder, hot and wet on her flushed cheeks.

She was embarrassed and trying not to let him see.

He knew. He smiled and kissed her eyes shut. "It had to be with me," he whispered. "Only with me. I would rather die than know you had such an experience with any other man."

She opened her eyes and looked up into his. "Really?"

"Really." He looked down at her nudity, his eyes hungry again at the sight of her pink-and-peach skin, silky and soft and fragrant. He touched her breasts tenderly. "You are the most beautiful woman I will ever see."

Her lips parted on a shaky breath.

He bent and kissed her breasts. "And now we have to get up."

She stared at him.

"Or not get up," he murmured with a laugh. "Because I can't continue this much longer."

"It would be...all right," she whispered. "If you wanted to," she added.

"I want to," he said huskily. "But you won't be happy afterward. And you know it. Not like this, *ma belle*. Not our first time together. It has to be done properly."

"Properly?"

"You graduate from college, get a job, go to work. I come to see you bringing flowers and chocolates," he mused, tracing her mouth. "And then, eventually, a ring."

"A ring."

He nodded.

"An...engagement...ring?"

He smiled.

"People do it all the time, even before they get engaged," she said.

He got to his feet. "They do. But we won't."

"Oh."

He dressed her, enjoying the act of putting back onto her lovely body the things he'd taken off it. He laughed at her rapt expression. "You have a belief system that isn't going to allow a more modern approach to sex," he said blandly. "So we do it your way."

"I could adjust," she began, still hungry.

"Your happiness means a lot to me," he said simply. "I'm not going to spoil something beautiful with a tarnished memory. Not after I've waited so long."

She stared up into his black eyes. "I've waited for you, too," she whispered.

"I know." He smoothed back her hair just as they heard a car door slam and footsteps approaching.

Michelle looked horrified, thinking what could have happened, what condition they could have been in as Darla put her key into the lock.

Gabriel burst out laughing at her expression. "Now was I right?" he asked.

The door opened. Darla stopped with Bob in tow and just stared at Gabriel. Then she grinned. "Wow," she said. "Look what Larry changed into!"

And they all burst out laughing.

Michelle graduated with honors. Gabriel and Sara were both there for the ceremony, applauding when she walked down the aisle to accept her diploma. They went out to eat afterward, but once they were home, Gabriel couldn't stay. He was preoccupied, and very worried, from the look of things.

"Can you tell me what's wrong?" Michelle asked.

He shook his head. He bent to kiss her, very gently. "I'm going to have to be out of the country for two or three months."

"No!" she exclaimed.

"Only that. Then I have a job waiting, one that won't require so much travel," he promised. "Bear with me. I'm sorry. I have to do this."

She drew in a long breath. "Okay. If you have to go."

"You've got a job waiting in San Antonio, anyway," he reminded her with a smile. "On a daily newspaper. It has a solid reputation for reporting excellence. Make a name for yourself. But don't get too comfortable there," he added enigmatically. "Because when I get back, we need to talk."

"Talk." She smiled.

"And other things."

"Oh, yes, especially, other things," she whispered, dragging his mouth down to hers. She kissed him hungrily. He returned the kiss, but drew back discreetly when Sara came into the room. He hugged her, too.

He paused in the doorway and looked back at them, smiling. "Take care of each other." He grinned at his sister. "Happy?" he asked, referring to the changes in her life.

Sara laughed, tossing her long hair. "I could die of it," she sighed.

"I'll be back before you miss me," he told Michelle, who was looking sad. He wanted to kiss her, right there in front of the world. But it wasn't the time. And he wasn't sure he could stop.

"Impossible," Michelle said softly. "I miss you already."

He winked and closed the door.

Michelle liked the job. She had a desk and three years of solid education behind her to handle the assignments she was given.

A big story broke the second month she'd been with the newspaper. There was a massacre of women and children in a small Middle Eastern nation, perpetrated, it was said, by a group of mercenaries led by a Canadian national named Angel Le Veut. He had ties to an anti-terrorism school run by a man named Eb Scott in, of all places, Jacobsville, Texas.

Michelle went on the offensive at once, digging up everything she could find about the men in the group who had killed the women and children in the small Muslim community that was at odds with a multinational occupation force.

The name of the man accused of leading the assault was ironic. One of the languages she'd studied was French. And if loosely translated, the man's name came out as "Angel wants it." It was an odd play on words that was used most notably in the sixteenth century by authorities when certain cases were tried and a guilty verdict was desired. The phrase *"Le Roi le Veut"* meant that the king wanted the accused found guilty—whether or not he really was, apparently. The mysterious Angel was obviously an educated man with a knowledge of European history. Michelle was puzzled over why such a man would choose a lifestyle that involved violence.

Her first stop was Jacobsville, Texas, where she arranged an interview with Eb Scott, the counterterrorism expert, whose men had been involved in the massacre. Michelle knew him, from a distance.

Her father had gone to school with him and they were acquaintances. Her father had said there wasn't a finer man anywhere, that Eb was notorious for backing lost causes and fighting for the underdog. That didn't sound like a man who would order the murder of helpless women and children.

Eb shook her hand and invited her into his house. His wife and children were gone for the day, shopping in San Antonio for summer clothing. It was late spring already.

"Thank you for seeing me," Michelle said when they were seated. "Especially under the circumstances."

"Hiding from the press is never a good idea, but at times, in matters like this, it's necessary, until the truth can be ferreted out," Eb said solemnly. His green eyes searched hers. "You're Alan Godfrey's daughter."

"Yes," she said, smiling.

"You used to spend summers in Comanche Wells with your grandparents." He smiled back. "Minette Carson speaks well of you. She did an interview with me yesterday. Hopefully, some of the truth will trickle down to the mass news media before they crucify my squad leader."

"Yes. This man, Angel," she began, looking over her notes while Eb Scott grimaced and tried not to reveal what he really knew about the man, "his name is quite odd."

"Le Veut?" He smiled again. "He gets his way. He's something of an authority on sixteenth-century European history. He and Kilraven, one of the feds who's married to a local girl, go toe-to-toe over whether or not Mary Queen of Scots really helped Lord Bothwell murder her husband."

"Has this man worked for you, with you, for a long time?" she asked.

He nodded. "Many years. He's risked his life time and time again to save innocents. I can promise you that when the truth comes out, and it will, he'll be exonerated."

She was typing on her small notebook computer as he spoke. "He's a Canadian national?"

"He has dual citizenship, here and in Canada," he corrected. "But he's lived in the States most of his life."

"Does he live in Jacobsville?"

Eb hesitated.

She lifted her hands from the keyboard. "You wouldn't

want to say, would you?" she asked perceptibly. "If he has family, it could hurt them, as well. There wouldn't be a place they could go where the media wouldn't find them."

"The media can be like a dog after a juicy bone," Eb said with some irritation. "They'll get fed one way or the other, with truth or, if time doesn't permit, with lies. I've seen lives ruined by eager reporters out to make a name for themselves." He paused. "Present company excepted," he added gently. "I know all about you from Minette."

She smiled gently. "Thanks. I always try to be fair and present both sides of the story without editorializing. I don't like a lot of what I see on television, presented as fair coverage. Most of the commentators seem quite biased to me. They convict people and act as judge, jury and executioner." She shook her head. "I like the paper I work for. Our editor, even our publisher, are fanatics for accurate and fair coverage. They fired a reporter last month whose story implicated an innocent man. He swore he had eyewitnesses to back up the facts, and that he could prove them. Later, when the editor sent other reporters out to recheck—after the innocent man's attorneys filed a lawsuit—they found that the reporter had ignored people who could verify the man's whereabouts at the time of the crime. The reporter didn't even question them."

Eb sighed, leaning back in his recliner. "That happens all too often. Even on major newspapers," he added, alluding to a reporter for one of the very large East Coast dailies who'd recently been let go for fabricating stories.

"We try," Michelle said quietly. "We really try. Most reporters only want to help people, to point out problems, to help better the world around us."

"I know that. It's the one bad apple in the barrel that pollutes the others," he said.

"This man, Angel, is there any way I could interview him?"

He almost bit through his lip. He couldn't tell her that. "No," he said finally. "We've hidden him in a luxury hotel in a foreign country. The news media will have a hell of a time trying to ferret him out. We have armed guards in native dress everywhere. Meanwhile, I've hired an investigative firm out of Houston—Dane Lassiter's—to dig out the truth. Believe me, there's no one in the world better at it. He's a former Houston policeman."

"I know of him," she replied. "His son was involved in a turf war between drug lords in the area, wasn't he?"

"Yes, he was. That was a while back."

"Well, tell me what you can," she said. "I'll do my best not to convict the man in print. The mercenaries who were with Angel," she added, "are they back in the States?"

"That's another thing I can't tell you right now," he replied. "I'm not trying to be evasive. I'm protecting my men from trial by media. We have attorneys for all of them, and our investigator hopes to have something concrete for us, and the press, very soon."

"That's fair enough."

"Here's what we know right now," Eb said. "My squad leader was given an assignment by a State Department official to interview a local tribesman in a village in Anasrah. The man had information about a group of terrorists who were hiding in the village—protected by a high-ranking government official, we were told. My squad leader, in disguise, took a small team in to interview him, but when he and his men arrived, the tribesman and his entire family were dead. One of the terrorists pointed the finger at Angel and accused his team of the atrocity. I'm certain the terrorist was paid handsomely to do it."

Michelle frowned. "You believe that?"

Eb stared her down with glittering green eyes. "Miss Godfrey, if you knew Angel, you wouldn't have to ask me that question."

"Sorry," she said. "It's my job, Mr. Scott."

He let out a breath. "You can't imagine how painful this is for me," he said. "Men I trained, men I've worked with, accused of something so inhuman." His face hardened. "Follow the money. It's all about the money, I assure you," he added curtly. "Someone stands to lose a lot of it if the truth comes out."

"I can only imagine how bad it must be," she said, and not without sympathy.

She asked questions, he answered them. She was impressed by him. He wasn't at all the sort of person that she'd pictured when she heard people speak of mercenaries. Even the word meant a soldier for hire, a man who sold his talents to the highest bidder. But Eb Scott's organization trained men in counterterrorism. He had an enormous operation in Jacobsville, and men and women came from around the world to learn from his experts. There were rumors that a few government agents had also availed themselves of his expertise.

The camp was state-of-the-art, with every electronic gadget known to modern science—and a few things that were largely experimental. They taught everything from evasive driving techniques to disarming bombs, improvised weapons, stealth, martial arts, the works. Michelle was allowed to photograph only a small section of the entire operation, and she wasn't allowed to photograph any of his instructors or the students. But even with the reservations on what she was shown, what she learned fascinated her.

"Well, I'll never think of mercenaries the same way

again, Mr. Scott," she said when she was ready to leave. "This operation is very impressive."

"I'm glad you think so."

She paused at the door and turned. "You know, the electronic media have resources that those of us in print journalism don't. I mean, we have a digital version of our paper online, like most everyone does. But the big networks employ dozens of experts who can find out anything. If they want to find your man, they will. And his family."

"Miss Godfrey, for the sake of a lot of innocent people, I hope you're wrong."

The way he said it stayed on her mind for hours after she left.

Chapter Eleven

Michelle wrote the story, and she did try to be fair. But when she saw the photographs of the massacre, the bodies of small children with women and men weeping over them, her heart hardened. If the man was guilty, he should be hanged for this.

She didn't slant the story. She presented the facts from multiple points of view. She interviewed a man in Saudi Arabia who had a friend in Anasrah with whom he'd recently spoken. She interviewed a representative of the State Department, who said that one of their staff had been lead into the village by a minor government official just after the attack and was adamant that the mercenaries had been responsible for the slaughter. She also interviewed an elder in the village, through an interpreter, who said that an American had led the attack.

There was another man, also local, who denied that a foreigner was responsible. He was shouted down by the others, but Michelle managed to get their representative in Saudi Arabia to go to Anasrah, a neighboring country, and interview the man in the village. His story contradicted the others. He said that it was a man well-known in terrorist circles who had come into the village and accused the tribesmen of betraying their own people by working with the government and foreigners. He said that if it continued, an example, a horrible example, would be made, he would see to it personally.

The local man said that he could prove that the terrorists themselves had perpetrated the attack, if he had time.

Michelle made the first big mistake of her career in journalism by discounting the still, small voice in the wilderness. The man's story didn't ring true. She took notes, and filed them on her computer. But when she wrote the story, she left out what sounded like a made-up tale.

The story broke with the force of bombs. All of a sudden, it was all anyone heard on the media. The massacre in Anasrah, the children murdered by foreigners, the mercenaries who had cut them down with automatic weapons while their parents pleaded for mercy. On television, the weeping relatives were interviewed. Their stories brought even hardened commentators to tears on-screen.

Michelle's story, with its unique point of view and Eb Scott's interview—which none of the national media had been able to get, because he refused to talk to them—put her in the limelight for the first time. Her story was reprinted partially in many national papers, and she was interviewed by the major news networks, as well. She respected Eb Scott, she added, and she thought he was sincere, but she wept for the dead children and she thought the mercenary responsible should be tried in the world court and imprisoned for the rest of his life.

Her impulsive comment was broadcast over and over. And just after that came the news that the mercenary had a sister, living in Wyoming. They had her name, as well. Sara.

It could have been a coincidence. Except that suddenly she remembered that the man, Angel, had both American and Canadian citizenship. Now she learned that he had a sister named Sara. Gabriel was gone for long periods of time overseas on jobs. Michelle still tried to persuade herself that it wasn't, couldn't, be Gabriel.

Until Sara called her on the phone.

"I couldn't believe it when they said you broke the story," she said in a cold tone. "How could you do this to us?"

"Sara, it wasn't about anyone you know," she said quickly. "It was about a mercenary who gunned down little children in a Middle Eastern village…!"

"He did nothing of the sort," Sara said, her voice dripping ice. "It was the tribesman's brother-in-law, one of the terrorists, who killed the man and his family and then blamed it on Angel and his men."

"Do you know this man Angel?" Michelle asked, a sick feeling in her stomach because Sara sounded so harsh.

"Know him." Her laugh was as cold as death. "We both know him, Michelle. He uses Angel as an alias when he goes on missions for Eb Scott's clients. But his name is Gabriel."

Michelle felt her blood run cold. Images flashed through her mind. Dead children. The one dissenting voice, insisting that it was the terrorists not the Americans who perpetrated the horror. Her refusal to listen, to print the other side of the story. Gabriel's side. She'd convinced herself that it couldn't be Gabriel. Now she had to face facts.

"I didn't know," she said, her voice breaking. "Sara, believe me, I didn't know!"

"Eb told you it wasn't him," Sara said furiously. "But you wouldn't listen. I had a contact in the State Department send a man to tell your newspaper's agent about the dead man's brother-in-law. And you decided not to print it. Didn't you? God forbid you should run against the voice of the world press and risk your own glowing reputation as a crusader for justice by dissenting!"

"I didn't know," Michelle repeated through tears.

"You didn't know! If Gabriel ends up headfirst in a ditch somewhere, it will be all right, because you didn't know! Would you like to see the road in front of our ranch here in Wyoming, Michelle?" she added. "It looks like a tent city, surrounded by satellite trucks. They're certain they'll wear me down and I'll come out and accuse my brother for them!"

"I'm so sorry." Michelle didn't have to be told that Gabriel was innocent. She knew he was. But she'd helped convict him.

"You're sorry. I'll be certain to tell him when, and if, I see him again." There was a harshly indrawn breath. "He phoned me two days ago," she said in a haunted voice. "They're hunting him like an animal, thanks to you. When I told him who sold him out, he wouldn't believe me. It wasn't until I sent him a link to your story that he saw for himself."

Michelle felt every drop of blood draining out of her face. "What...did he say?"

"He said," Sara replied, enunciating every word, "that he'd never been so wrong about anyone in his life. He thought that you, of all people, would defend him even against the whole world. He said," she added coldly, "that he never wanted to see you or hear from you again as long as he lived."

The words were like bullets. She could actually feel their impact.

"I loved you like my own sister," Sara said, her voice breaking. "And I will never, never forgive you!" She slammed down the phone.

Michelle realized after a minute that she hadn't broken the connection. She hung up her own telephone. She sat down heavily and heard the recriminations break over her head again and again.

She remembered Eb Scott's certainty that his man would never do such a thing. Sara's fierce anger. It had been easy to discount them while Angel was a shadowy figure without substance. But Michelle knew Gabriel. And she was certain, absolutely certain, that the man who'd saved her from suicide would never put another human being in harm's way.

It took two days for the effects of Sara's phone call to wear off enough that she could stop crying and blaming herself. The news media was having a field day with the story, running updates about it all day, every day, either in newscasts or in banners under the anchor people. Michelle finally had to turn off the television to escape it, so that she could get herself back together.

She wanted, so desperately, to make up for what she'd done. But she didn't even know where to start. The story was everywhere. People were condemning the American mercenaries on every news program in the world.

But Gabriel was innocent. Michelle had helped convict him in the press, without knowing who she was writing about. Now it was her turn to do her job properly, and give both sides of the story, however unpopular. She had to save him, if she could, even if he hated her forever for what she'd done.

So she went back to work. Her first act was to contact the newspaper's man in Saudi Arabia and ask him to repeat the story his informant in Anasrah had told him. Then she contacted Eb Scott and gave him the information, so that he could pass it on to his private investigator. Before she did that, she asked him to call her back on a secure line, because she knew how some of the tabloid news bureaus sometimes had less scrupulous agents digging out information.

"You're learning, Miss Godfrey," Eb said solemnly.

"Not soon enough. I know who Angel is now," she added heavily. "His sister hates me. He told her that he never wanted to see or speak to me again, either. And I deserve that. I wasn't objective, and people are paying for my error. But I have to do what I can to undo the mess I helped make. I'm sorry I didn't listen."

"Too little, and almost too late," he said brutally. "Learn from it. Sometimes the single dissenting voice is the right one."

"I won't forget," she said.

He hung up.

She tried to phone Sara back and apologize once again, to tell her she was trying to repair the damage. But Sara wouldn't accept the first phone call and after that, her number was blocked. She was heartsick. The Brandons had been so good to her. They'd made sacrifices to get her through school, through college, always been there when she needed help. And she'd repaid them like this. It wounded her as few things in life ever had.

When she tried to speak to her editor in confidence, to backtrack on the story she'd written, he laughed it off. The man was obviously guilty, he said, why make waves now? She'd made a name for herself in investigative reporting, it was all good.

She told him that Angel wasn't the sort of person to ever harm a child. Then he wanted to know how she knew that. She wouldn't reveal her source, she said, falling back on a tried and true response. But the man was innocent.

Her editor had just laughed. So she thought the guy was innocent, what did it matter? The news was the thing that mattered, scooping all the other media and being first and best at delivering the story. She'd given the facts of the matter, that was the end of it. She should just enjoy her celebrity status while it lasted.

Michelle went back to her apartment that night saddened and weary, with a new sense of disillusionment about life and people.

The next morning, she phoned Minette Carson and asked if she had an opening for a reporter who was certain she wasn't cut out for the big dailies.

Minette was hesitant.

"Look, never mind," Michelle said gently. "I know I've made a lot of enemies in Jacobsville with the way I covered the story. It's okay. I can always teach journalism. I'll be a natural at showing students what not to do."

"We all have to start somewhere when we learn how to do a job," Minette replied. "Usually, it's a painful process. Eb Scott called and asked me, before you did the interview, if you knew who Gabriel really was. I told him no. I knew you'd have said something long before this. I should have told you."

"I should have suspected something," came the sad

reply. "He was away from home for long stretches, he spoke a dozen impossible languages, he was secretive about what sort of work he did—I just wasn't paying attention."

"It amused everyone when he took you in as his ward," Minette said. "He was one of the coldest men Eb Scott ever hired—well, after Carson, who works for Cy Parks, that is." She chuckled. "But once you came along, all of a sudden Gabriel was smiling."

"He won't be anymore," Michelle said, feeling the pain to the soles of her feet.

"Give it time," was the older woman's advice. "First, you have some work to do."

"I know. I'm going to do everything in my power to prove him innocent. Whatever it takes," Michelle added firmly.

"That's more like it. And about the job," she replied. "Once you've proven that you aren't running away from an uncomfortable assignment, we'll have a place for you here. That's a promise."

"Thanks."

"You're welcome."

Michelle convinced Eb Scott to let her talk to his detective. It worked out well, because Dane Lassiter was actually in San Antonio for a seminar that week and he agreed to meet with her in a local restaurant.

He wasn't exactly what she'd expected. He was tall, dark-haired and dark-eyed, with an easygoing manner and a wife who was thirtysomething and very attractive. She, like Michelle, was blonde.

"We always go together when he has to give seminars." Tess laughed. "At least once I've had to chase a pursuing woman out of his room." She shook her head, sighing as she met her husband's amused gaze. "Well, after all, I know he's a dish. Why shouldn't other women notice?"

Michelle laughed with them, but her heart wasn't in it. There had been a snippet of news on television the night before, showing a camp of journalists on the road that led to the Brandons' Wyoming property. They were still trying to get Sara to talk to them. But this time they were met with a steely-eyed man Michelle recognized as Wofford Patterson, who was advising them to decamp before some of Sara's friends loosed a few bears on the property in a conservation project. Patterson had become Sara's personal protector and much more, after many years of antagonism.

"I've been watching the press reports on Brandon," Dane said, having guessed the train of her thoughts. "You watch six different reports and get six different stories."

"Yes," Michelle said sadly. "Not everyone tries for accuracy. And I can include myself in that company, because I should have gone the extra mile and presented the one dissenting opinion. It was easy to capitulate, because I didn't think I had any interest in the outcome," she added miserably.

Tess's pale eyes narrowed. "Mr. Brandon was your guardian."

She nodded. He was more, but she wasn't sharing that news with a virtual stranger. "I sold him out. I didn't mean to. I had no idea Angel was Gabriel. It was hard, going against a majority opinion. Everyone said he was guilty as sin. I saw the photographs of the women and children." Her face hardened. "It was easy to believe it, after that."

"I've seen similar things," Dane said, sipping black

coffee. "But I can tell you that things are rarely what they seem."

She told him about her contacts, and he took notes, getting names and telephone numbers and putting together a list of people to interview.

He put up his pen and notebook. "This is going to be a lot of help to the men who were blamed for the tragedy," he said finally. "There's a violent element in the country in question, dedicated to rooting out any hint of foreign influence, however beneficial. But at the same time, in their ranks are a few who see a way to quick profit, a way to fund their terrorism and inflict even more horror on our overseas personnel. This group that put your friend in the middle of the controversy is made up of a few money-hungry profiteers. Our State Department has worked very hard to try to stifle them. We have several oil corporations with offices there, and a good bit of our foreign oil is shipped from that country. We depend on the goodwill of the locals to keep the oil companies' officials and workers safe. The terrorists know that, and they see a way to make a quick profit through kidnappings and other attacks. Except that instead of holding people for ransom, they threaten violence if their demands aren't met. It's almost like a protection racket..."

"That's what he meant," Michelle said suddenly.

"Excuse me?"

"Eb Scott said, 'follow the money,'" she recalled.

"Eb's sharp. Yes, that's apparently what's behind all this. The terrorist leader wanted millions in bribes to protect oil company executives in his country. The brother-in-law of the leader was selling him out to our State Department. A lot of local men work for the oil companies and don't want any part of the terrorist's plans. It's a poor country, and the oil companies provide a secure living for the village. But nobody makes waves and gets away with it. The terrorist leader retaliated, in the worst possible way, and blamed it on Angel and his men—a way of protecting his own men, whom he ordered to kill his brother-in-law to keep him from talking. It was also a way of notifying foreigners that this is how any future attempts to bypass his authority would be handled."

"I'm not telling you anything you didn't already know," she said suddenly.

"I knew it. I couldn't prove it," he added. "But you've given me contacts who can back up the protester's story. I'll have my investigators check them out and our attorneys will take depositions that will hold up in court. It will give the State Department's representatives the leverage they need to deal with the terrorists. And it will provide our news media with a week of guaranteed stories," he added coldly.

She sighed. "I think I'm in the wrong business."

"Good reporters can do a lot of good in the world," Tess interrupted. "It's just that there's more profit in digging up dirt on people."

"Amen," Dane said.

"Well, if I can help dig Gabriel out of the hole I put him into, I'll be happy," Michelle told him. "It's little enough in the way of apology."

"If you hear anything else, through your sources, you can call me anytime," he told her.

"I'll remember."

Dane went to pay the check, against Michelle's protests.

Tess smiled at her. "You really care about the mercenary, don't you?" she asked.

"More than you know," Michelle replied. "He and his

sister sacrificed a lot for me. I'll never be able to pay them back. And now, this has happened...."

"At least you're trying to make up for it," she replied. "That's worth something."

"I hope it's worth enough. I'm grateful to you and your husband for meeting with me."

"It was a nice interlude between the rehashing of horrible cases." Tess laughed. "I work as a skip tracer, something Dane would never let me do before. My father planned to marry his mother, but they were killed in a wreck, so Dane became sort of responsible for me," she added surprisingly. "He wasn't very happy about it. We had a rocky road to the altar." She smiled. "But a son and a daughter later, we're very content."

"You don't look old enough to have two children." Michelle laughed. "Either of you."

"Thanks. But believe me, we are."

Dane was back, putting away his wallet. He handed Michelle a business card. "My cell's on there, as well as the office number."

"I'll cross my fingers, that our contacts can help you get Gabriel and his men off the hook," Michelle said.

His eyes narrowed. "I'm surprised that the national news media hasn't been camped on your doorstep," he remarked.

"Gabriel didn't advertise his involvement with me," she replied. "And nobody in Jacobsville, Texas, will tell them a thing, believe me."

He smiled. "I noticed the way the locals shut them out when they waltzed into town with their satellite trucks. Amazing, that the restaurants all ran out of food and the motels were all full and nobody had a single room to rent out at any price."

She smiled angelically. "I'm sure that was mostly true."

"They did try Comanche Wells, I hear," Dane added.

"Well, see, Comanche Wells doesn't have a restaurant or a motel at all."

"That explains it."

She went back to work, only to find her desk piled high with notes.

"Hey, Godfrey, can't you get your answering machine to work?" Murphy, one of the older reporters whose desk was beside hers, asked. "My old hands are too gnarled to take notes from all your darned callers."

"Sorry, Murph," she said. She was frowning when she noticed who the notes were from. "They want to send a limo for me and have me stay at the Plaza?" she exclaimed.

"What it is to be a celebrity," Murph shook his head. "Hey, there was this cool video that Brad Paisley did, about being a celebrity…!"

"I saw it. Thanks," she said, waving the notes at him. She picked up her purse and left the building, just avoiding her editor on the way out the door.

Apparently the news media had found somebody in Jacobsville who was willing to talk to them. She wondered with droll cynicism what the informant had been paid.

She discovered that if she agreed to do an exclusive interview with just one station, the others would have to leave her alone. Before she signed any papers, she spoke with an attorney and had him check out the agreement.

"It says that I agree to tell them my story," she said.

"Exactly," he replied.

She pursed her lips. "It doesn't specify which story."

"I think they'll assume it means the story they want to hear," he replied. "Although that's implied rather than stated."

"Ah."

"And I would advise caution when they ask you to name the person overseas whom your newspaper provided as a reference regarding the informer," he added. "That may be a protected source."

"I was hoping you'd notice that. It is a protected source."

He only smiled.

She sat down in front of the television cameras with a well-known, folksy interviewer who was calm, gentle and very intelligent. He didn't press her for details she couldn't give, and he understood that some sources of information that she had access to were protected.

"I understand from what you told our correspondent that you don't believe the men in question actually perpetrated the attack, which resulted in the deaths of several women and small children," he began.

"That's correct."

"Would you tell me why?"

"When I first broke the story, I went on the assumption that because the majority of the interviewees placed the blame on the American mercenaries, they must be guilty. There was, however, one conflicting opinion. A villager, whom I cannot name, said that extortion was involved and that money was demanded for the protection of foreign workers. When a relative of the extortionist threatened to go to the authorities and reveal the financial aspect, he and his family were brutally murdered as a warning. These murders were blamed on the Americans who had, in fact, been working for the government trying to uncover a nest of terrorists threatening American oil company employees there."

The interviewer was frowning. "Then the massacre was, in fact, retaliation for the villager's threat to expose the extortionist."

"That is my information, yes."

He studied a sheet of paper. "I see here that the newspaper which employs you used its own foreign sources to do interviews about this story."

"Those sources are also protected," Michelle replied. "I can't name them."

He pursed his lips and, behind his lenses, his blue eyes twinkled. "I understand. But I believe the same sources have been named, in the press, by attorneys for the men allegedly implicated by the international press for the atrocities."

She smiled. "I believe so."

"In which case," he added, "we have elicited permission to quote one of the sources. He has signed an affidavit, which is in the hands of our State Department. Please welcome Mr. David Arbuckle, who is liaison for the U.S. Department of State in Anasrah, which is at the center of this matter. Mr. Arbuckle, welcome."

"Thank you, Mr. Price," a pleasant-looking, middle-aged man replied. He was in a studio in Washington, D.C., his image provided via satellite.

"Now, from what Ms. Godfrey has told us—and we have validated her story—a terrorist cell had infiltrated the village in question and made threats against foreign nationals including ours. Is this true?"

"It is," Mr. Arbuckle said solemnly. "We're very grateful to Ms. Godfrey for bringing this matter to our attention. We were told that a group of mercenaries muscled their way into the village, demanding tribute and killed people when their demands were not met. This is a very different story than we were able to verify by speaking, under offer of protection, to other men in the same village."

He coughed, then continued, "We were able to ascertain that a terrorist cell with links to another notorious international organization was going to fund itself by extorting money from oil corporations doing business near the village. They were using the village itself for cover, posing as innocent tribesmen."

"Abominable," the host replied.

"Yes, killing innocents to prove a point is a particularly bloodthirsty manner in which to operate. The local people were terrified to say anything, after the massacre, although they felt very sad that innocent men were blamed for it. In fact, the so-called mercenaries had provided medical supplies and treatment for many children and elderly people and even helped buy food for them."

"A laudable outreach effort."

"Indeed," Mr. Arbuckle replied grimly. "Suffice it to say that we have used our influence to make sure that the terrorists no longer have a foothold in the village, and the international community has moved people in to assure the safety of the tribesmen who provided us with this information."

"Then the American mercenaries are being cleared of any involvement with the massacre?"

"I can assure you that they have been," Mr. Arbuckle replied. "We were provided with affidavits and other documents concerning the massacre by an American private detective working in concert with the mercenaries' attorneys. They were allowed to leave the country last night and are en route to a secure location while we deal with the terrorists in question. The terrorists responsible for the massacre will be brought to trial for the murders and held accountable. And the mercenaries will return to testify against them."

"I'm sure our viewers will be happy to hear that."

"We protect our people overseas," Mr. Arbuckle replied. "All of them. And in fact, the mercenaries in question were private contractors working for the United States government, not the sort of soldiers for hire that often involve themselves in foreign conflicts."

"Another surprise," Mr. Price said with a smile.

"In this day and time, we all have to be alert about our surroundings abroad," Mr. Arbuckle said. "We take care of our own," he added with a smile.

"Thank you for your time, Mr. Arbuckle."

"Thank you for yours, Mr. Price."

Mr. Price turned back to Michelle. "It was a very brave thing you did, Ms. Godfrey, going up against the weight of the international press to defend these men. I understand that you know some of them."

"I know Eb Scott, who runs an international school of counterterrorism," Michelle corrected, unwilling to say more. "He has great integrity. I can't imagine that any agents he trained would ever go against basic humanitarianism."

"He has a good advocate here." He chuckled.

"I learned a lesson from this, as well," she replied quietly. "That you don't discount the single small voice in the wilderness when you write a story that can cost lives and reputations. It is one I hope I never have to repeat." She paused. "I'd like to thank my editor for standing by me," she added, lying because he hadn't, "and for teaching me the worth of integrity in reporting."

Mr. Price named the newspaper in San Antonio and thanked her for appearing on his program.

* * *

Back in the office, her editor, Len Worthington, was ecstatic. "That was the nicest plug we ever got from anybody! Thanks, kid!" he told her, shaking her hand.

"You're welcome. Thanks for not firing me for messing up so badly."

"Hey, what are friends for?"

He'd never know, she thought, but she only smiled. She'd seen a side of journalism that left her feeling sick. It wasn't pretty.

She didn't try to call Sara again. The poor woman probably hadn't seen the program Michelle was on. It was likely that she was avoiding any sort of press coverage of what had happened. That wasn't hard anymore, because there was a new scandal topping the news now, and all the satellite trucks had gone in search of other prey. Michelle's phone had stopped ringing. There were no more notes on her desk, no more offers of limos and five-star hotels. She didn't mind at all.

She only hoped that one day Sara and Gabriel would forgive her. She went back to work on other stories, mostly political ones, and hoped that she'd never be in a position again where she'd have to sell out her nearest and dearest for a job. Not that she ever would. Nor would she have done it, if she'd had any idea who Gabriel really was.

Michelle had thought about asking Minette for a job again. She wasn't really happy living in the city and she cringed every time someone mentioned her name in connection with the past big news story.

She still hadn't heard from Gabriel or Sara. She didn't expect to. She'd hoped that they might contact her. But that was wishful thinking.

She now owned the home where her father and, before him, her grandparents had lived in Comanche Wells.
She couldn't bear to drive the Jaguar that Gabriel and
Sara had given her…driving it made her too sad. So
she parked it at Gabriel's house and put the key in the
mail slot. One day, she assumed, he'd return and see it.
She bought a cute little VW bug, with which she could
commute from Jacobsville to work in San Antonio. She
moved back home.

At first, people were understandably a little stand-
offish. She was an outsider, even though she was born
in Jacobs County. Perhaps they thought she was going
to go all big-city on them and start poking her nose into
local politics.

When she didn't do that, the tension began to ease a
little. When she went into Barbara's Café to have lunch
on Saturdays, people began to nod and smile at her. When
she went grocery shopping in the local supermarket, the
cashier actually talked to her. When she got gas at the
local station, the attendant finally stopped asking for
identification when she presented her credit card. Little
by little, she was becoming part of Jacobs County again.

Carlie came to visit occasionally. She was happily
married, and expecting her first child. They weren't as
close as they had been, but it made Michelle feel good to
know that her friend was settled and secure.

She only wished that she could be, settled and secure.
But as months went by with no word of or from the Brandons, she gave up all hope that she might one day be forgiven for the things she'd written.

She knew that Sara had a whole new life in Wyoming
from the cashier at the grocery store who had known
her. Michelle didn't blame her for not wanting to come

back to Texas. After all, she'd only lived in Comanche Wells as a favor to Gabriel, so that he could be Michelle's guardian.

Guardian no more, obviously. He'd given up that before, of course, when she turned twenty-one. But sometimes Michelle wished that she still had at least a relationship with him. She mourned what could have been, before she lost her way. Gabriel had assured her that they had a future. But that was before.

She was hanging out sheets in the yard, fighting the fierce autumn breeze to keep them from blowing away, when she heard a vehicle coming down the long road. It was odd, because nobody lived out this way except Michelle. It was Saturday. The next morning, she'd planned to go to church. She'd missed it for a couple of Sundays while she worked on a hot political story.

These days, not even the Reverend Blair came visiting much. She didn't visit other people, either. Her job occupied much of her time, because a reporter was always on call. But Michelle still attended services most Sundays.

So she stared at the truck as it went past the house. Its windows were tinted, and rolled up. It was a new truck, a very fancy one. Perhaps someone had bought the old Brandon place, she concluded, and went back to hanging up clothes. It made her sad to think that Gabriel would sell the ranch. But, after all, what would he need it for? He only had a manager there to care for it, so it wasn't as if he needed to keep it. He had other things to do.

She'd heard from Minette that Gabriel was part of an international police force now, one that Eb Scott had contracted with to provide security for those Middle Eastern oilmen who had played such a part in Gabriel's close call.

She wondered if he would ever come back to Comanche Wells. But she was fairly certain he wouldn't. Too many bad memories.

Chapter Twelve

Michelle finished hanging up her sheets in the cool breeze and went back into the house to fix herself a sandwich.

There were rumors at work that a big story was about to break involving an oil corporation and a terrorist group in the Middle East, one that might have local ties. Michelle, now her editor's favorite reporter for having mentioned him on TV, was given the assignment. It might, he hinted, involve some overseas travel. Not to worry, the paper would gladly pay her expenses.

She wondered what sort of mess she might get herself into this time, poking her nose into things she didn't understand. Well, it was a job, and she was lucky to even have one in this horrible economy.

She finished her sandwich and drank a cup of black coffee. For some reason she thought of Gabriel, and how much he'd enjoyed her coffee. She had to stop thinking about him. She'd almost cost him his life. She'd destroyed his peace of mind and Sara's, subjected them both to cameras and reporters and harassment. It was not really a surprise that they weren't speaking to her anymore. Even if she'd gone the last mile defending them, trying to make up for her lack of foresight, it didn't erase the damage she'd already done.

She was bored to death. The house was pretty. She'd made improvements—she'd redecorated Roberta's old room and had the whole place repainted. She'd put up new curtains and bought new furniture. But the house was cold and empty.

Back when her father was alive, it still held echoes of his parents, of him. Now, it was a reminder of old tragedies, most especially her father's death and Roberta's.

She carried her coffee into the living room and looked around her. She ought to sell it and move into an apartment in San Antonio. She didn't have a pet, not even a dog or cat, and the livestock her father had owned were long gone. She had nothing to hold her here except a sad attachment to the past, to dead people.

But there was something that kept her from letting go. She knew what it was, although she didn't want to remember. It was Gabriel. He'd eaten here, slept here, comforted her here. It was warm with memories that no other dwelling place would ever hold.

She wondered if she couldn't just photograph the rooms and blow up the photos, make posters of them, and sacrifice the house.

Sure, she thought hollowly. Of course she could.

She finished her coffee and turned on the television. Same old stories. Same programs with five minutes of commercials for every one minute of programming. She switched it off. These days she only watched DVDs or streamed movies from internet websites. She was too antsy to sit through a hundred commercials every half hour.

She wondered why people put up with it. If everyone stopped watching television, wouldn't the advertisers be forced to come up with alternatives that compromised a bit more? Sure. And cows would start flying any day.

That reminded her of the standing joke she'd had with Grier and Gabriel about cows being abducted by aliens, and it made her sad.

Outside, she heard the truck go flying past her house. It didn't even slow down. Must be somebody looking at Gabriel's house. She wondered if he'd put it on the market without bothering to put a for-sale sign out front. Why not? He had no real ties here. He'd probably moved up to Wyoming to live near Sara.

She went into the kitchen, put her coffee cup in the sink, and went back to her washing.

She wore a simple beige skirt and a short-sleeved beige sweater to church with pretty high heels and a purse to match. She left her hair long, down her back, and used only a trace of makeup on her face.

She'd had ample opportunities for romance, but all those years she'd waited for Gabriel, certain that he was going to love her one day, that she had a future with him. Now that future was gone. She knew that one day, she'd have to decide if she really wanted to be nothing more than a career woman with notoriety and money taking the place of a husband and children and a settled life.

There was nothing wrong with ambition. But the few career women she'd known seemed empty somehow, as if they presented a happy face to the world but that it was like a mask, hiding the insecurities and loneliness that accompanied a demanding lifestyle. What would it be like to grow old, with no family around you, with only friends and acquaintances and business associates to mark the holidays? Would it make up for the continuity of the next generation and the generation after that, of seeing your features reproduced down through your children and grandchildren and great-grandchildren? Would it make up for laughing little voices and busy little hands, and soft kisses on your cheek at bedtime?

That thought made her want to cry. She'd never thought too much about kids during her school days, but when Gabriel had kissed her and talked about a future, she'd dreamed of having his children. It had been a hunger unlike anything she'd ever known.

She had to stop tormenting herself. She had to come to grips with the world the way it was, not the way she wanted it to be. She was a grown woman with a promising career. She had to look ahead, not behind her.

She slid into her usual pew, listened to Reverend Blair's sermon and sang along with the choir as they repeated the chorus of a well-loved old hymn. Sometime during the offering, she was aware of a tingling sensation, as if someone were watching her. She laughed silently. Now she was getting paranoid.

As the service ended, and they finished singing the final hymn, as the benediction sounded in Reverend Blair's clear, deep voice, she continued to have the sensation that someone was watching her.

Slowly, as her pew filed out into the aisle, she glanced toward the back of the church. But there was no one there, no one looking at her. What a strange sensation.

* * *

Reverend Blair shook her hand and smiled at her. "It's nice to have you back, Miss Godfrey," he teased.

She smiled back. "Rub it in. I had a nightmare of a political story to follow. I spent so much time on it that I'm thinking I may run for public office myself. By now, I know exactly what not to do to get elected," she confided with a chuckle.

"I know what you mean. It was a good story."

"Thanks."

"See you next week."

"I hope." She crossed her fingers. He just smiled.

She walked to her car and clicked the smart key to unlock it when she felt, rather than saw, someone behind her.

She turned and her heart stopped in her chest. She looked up into liquid black eyes in a tanned, hard face that looked as if it had never known a smile.

She swallowed. She wanted to say so many things. She wanted to apologize. She wanted to cry. She wanted to throw herself into his arms and beg him to hold her, comfort her, forgive her. But she did none of those things. She just looked up at him hopelessly, with dead eyes that looked as if they had never held joy.

His square chin lifted. His eyes narrowed on her face. "You've lost weight."

She shrugged. "One of the better consequences of my profession," she said quietly. "How are you, Gabriel?"

"I've been better."

She searched his eyes. "How's Sara?"

"Getting back to normal."

She nodded. She swallowed again and dropped her eyes to his chest. It was hard to find something to say that didn't involve apologies or explanations or pleas for forgiveness.

The silence went on for so long that she could hear pieces of conversation from other churchgoers. She could hear the traffic on the highway, the sound of children playing in some yard nearby. She could hear the sound of her own heartbeat.

This was destroying her. She clicked the key fob again deliberately. "I have to go," she said softly.

"Sure."

He moved back so that she could open the door and get inside. She glanced at him with sorrow in her face, but she averted her eyes so that it didn't embarrass him. She didn't want him to feel guilty. She was the one who should feel that emotion. In the end she couldn't meet his eyes or even wave. She just started the car and drove away.

Well, at least the first meeting was over with, she told herself later. It hadn't been quite as bad as she'd expected. But it had been rough. She felt like crying, but her eyes were dry. Some pain was too deep to be eased by tears, she thought sadly.

She changed into jeans and a red T-shirt and went out on the front porch to water her flowers while a TV dinner microwaved itself to perfection in the kitchen.

Her flowers were going to be beautiful when they bloomed, she decided, smiling as they poked their little heads up through the dirt in an assortment of ceramic pots all over the wooden floor.

She had three pots of chrysanthemums and one little bonsai tree named Fred. Gabriel had given it to her when she first moved in with them, a sort of welcome present. It was a tiny fir tree with a beautiful curving trunk and feathery limbs. She babied it, bought it expensive fertilizer, read books on how to keep it healthy and worried herself to death that it might accidentally die if she forgot to water it. That hadn't happened, of course, but she loved it dearly. Of all the things Gabriel had given her, and there had been a lot, this was her favorite. She left it outside until the weather grew too cold, then she carried it inside protectively.

The Jaguar had been wonderful. But she'd still been driving it when she did the story that almost destroyed Gabriel's life and after that, she could no longer bear to sit in it. The memories had been killing her.

She missed the Jag. She missed Gabriel more. She wondered why he'd come back. Probably to sell the house, she decided, to cut his last tie with Comanche Wells. If he was working for an international concern, it wasn't likely that he'd plan to come back here. He'd see the Jag in the driveway, she thought, and understand why she'd given it back. At least, she hoped he would.

That thought, that he might leave Comanche Wells forever, was really depressing. She watered Fred, put down the can, and went back into the house. It didn't occur to her to wonder what he'd been doing at her church.

When she went into the kitchen to take her dinner out of the microwave, a dark-haired man was sitting at the table sipping coffee. There were two cups, one for him and one for her. The dinner was sitting on a plate with a napkin and silverware beside it.

He glanced up as she came into the room. "It's getting cold," he said simply.

She stood behind her chair, just staring at him, frowning.

He raised an eyebrow as he studied her shirt. "You

know, most people who wore red shirts on the original *Star Trek* ended up dead."

She cocked her head. "And you came all this way to give me fashion advice?"

He managed a faint smile. "Not really." He sipped coffee. He let out a long breath. "It's been a long time, Michelle."

She nodded. Slowly, she pulled out the chair and sat down. The TV dinner had the appeal of mothballs. She pushed it aside and sipped the black coffee he'd put at her place. He still remembered how she took it, after all this time.

She ran her finger around the rim. "I learned a hard lesson," she said after a minute. "Reporting isn't just about presenting the majority point of view."

He lifted his eyes to hers. "Life teaches very hard lessons."

"Yes, it does." She drew in a breath. "I guess you're selling the house."

His eyebrows lifted. "Excuse me?"

"I saw a truck go out there yesterday. And I read that you're working with some international police force now. So since Sara's living in Wyoming, I assumed you'd probably be moving up there near her. For when you're home in the States, I mean."

"I'd considered it," he said after a minute. He sipped more coffee.

She wondered if her heart could fall any deeper into her chest. She wondered how in the world he'd gotten into the house so silently. She wondered why he was there in the first place. Was he saying goodbye?

"Did you find the keys to the Jag?" she asked.

"Yes. You didn't want to keep it?"

She swallowed hard. "Too many bad memories, of what I did to you and Sara," she confessed heavily.

He shook his head. After a minute, he stared at her bent head. "I don't think you've really looked at me once," he said finally.

She managed a tight smile. "It's very hard to do that, after all the trouble I caused you," she said. "I rehearsed it, you know. Saying I was sorry. Working up all sorts of ways to apologize. But there really isn't a good way to say it."

"People make mistakes."

"The kind I made could have buried you." She said it tautly, fighting tears. It was harder than she'd imagined. She forced down the rest of the coffee. "Look, I've got things to do," she began, standing, averting her face so he couldn't see her eyes.

"Ma belle," he whispered, in a voice so tender that her control broke the instant she heard it. She burst into tears.

He scooped her up in his arms and kissed her so hungrily that she just went limp, arching up to him, so completely his that she wouldn't have protested anything he wanted to do to her.

"So it's like that, is it?" he whispered against her soft, trembling mouth. "Anything I want? Anything at all?"

"Anything," she wept.

"Out of guilt?" he asked, and there was an edge to his tone now.

She opened her wet eyes and looked into his. "Out of...love," she choked.

"Love."

"Go ahead. Laugh..."

He buried his face in her throat. "I thought I'd lost you for good," he breathed huskily. "Standing there at your car, looking so defeated, so depressed that you couldn't even meet my eyes. I thought, I'll have to leave, there's nothing left, nothing there except guilt and sorrow. And then I decided to have one last try, to come here and talk to you. You walked into the room and every single thing you felt was there, right there, in your eyes when you looked at me. And I knew, then, that it wasn't over at all. It was only beginning."

Her arms tightened around his neck. Her eyes were pouring with hot tears. "I loved you...so much," she choked. "Sara said you never wanted to see me again. She hated me. I knew you must hate me, too...!"

He kissed the tears away. He sat down on the sofa with Michelle in his lap and curled her into his chest. "Sara has a quick, hot temper. She loses it, and it's over. She's sorry that she was so brutal with you. She was frightened and upset and the media was hunting her. She's had other problems as well, that you don't know about. But she's ashamed that she took it all out on you, blamed you for something you didn't even do deliberately." He lifted his head and smoothed the long, damp hair away from her cheek. "She wanted to apologize, but she's too ashamed to call you."

"That's why?" she whispered. "I thought I would never see her again. Or you."

"That would never happen," he said gently. "You're part of us."

She bit her lower lip. "I sold you out...!"

"You did not. You sold out a mercenary named Angel, someone you didn't know, someone you thought had perpetrated a terrible crime against innocent women and children," he said simply. He brushed his mouth over her wet eyes. "You would never have sold me out in a million years, even if you had thought I was guilty as sin."

He lifted his head and looked into her eyes. "Because you love me. You love me enough to forgive anything, even murder."

The tears poured out even hotter. She couldn't stop crying.

He wrapped her up close, turned her under him on the sofa, slid between her long legs and began to kiss her with anguished hunger. The kisses grew so long and so hard and so hot that she trembled and curled her legs around the back of his, urging him into greater intimacy, pleading with him to ease the tension that was putting her young body on the rack.

"If you don't stop crying," he threatened huskily, "this is going to end badly."

"No, it isn't. You want to," she whispered, kissing his throat.

"Yes, I do," he replied deeply. "But you're going to need a lot of time that I can't give you when I'm out of control," he murmured darkly. "You won't enjoy it."

"Are you sure?" she whispered.

He lifted his head. His eyes were hot and hungry on her body. His hands had pushed up the red shirt and the bra, and he was staring at her pert, pretty breasts with aching need. "I am absolutely sure," he managed.

"Oh."

The single word and the wide-eyed, hopeless look in her eyes broke the tension and he started laughing. "That's it? 'Oh'?"

She laughed, too. "Well, I read a lot and I watch movies, but it's not quite the same thing…"

"Exactly."

He forced himself to roll off her. "If you don't mind, could you pull all this back down?" he asked, indicating her breasts. He averted his eyes. "And I'll try deep breaths and mental imagery of snow-covered hills."

"Does it work?"

"Not really."

She pulled down her shirt and glanced at him with new knowledge of him and herself, and smiled.

"That's a smug little look," he accused.

"I like knowing I can throw you off balance," she said with a wicked grin.

"I'll enjoy letting you do it, but not until we're used to each other," he replied. He pulled her close. "The first time has to be slow and easy," he whispered, brushing his mouth over hers. "So that it doesn't hurt so much."

"If you can knock me off balance, I won't care if it hurts," she pointed out.

His black eyes twinkled. "I'll remember that."

She lay back on the sofa and looked up at him with wide, wondering eyes. "I thought it was all over," she whispered. "That I had nothing left, nothing to live for..."

"I felt the same way," he returned, solemn and quiet. "Thank God I decided to make one more attempt to get through to you."

She smiled gently. "Fate."

He smiled back. "Yes. Fate."

"Where are you going? Come back here." She pulled him back down.

He pursed his lips. "We need to discuss things vertically, not horizontally."

"I'm not going to seduce you, honest. I have something very serious I need to talk to you about."

"Okay. What?"

She pursed her own lips and her eyes twinkled. "Cow abductions."

He burst out laughing.

* * *

They were married in the Methodist church two weeks later by Reverend Blair. Michelle wore a conventional white gown with lace inserts and a fingertip veil, which Gabriel lifted to kiss her for the first time as his wife. In the audience were more mercenaries and ex-military and feds than anyone locally had seen in many a year.

Eb Scott and his wife, along with Dr. Micah Steele and Callie, and Cy Parks and Lisa, were all in the front row with Minette Carson and her husband Hayes. Carlie and her husband were there, too.

There was a reception in the fellowship hall and Jacobsville police chief Cash Grier kept looking around restlessly.

"Is something going on that we should know about?" Gabriel asked with a grin.

"Just waiting for the riot to break out."

"What riot?" Michelle asked curiously.

"You know, somebody says something, somebody else has too much to drink and takes offense, blows are exchanged, police are called in to break up the altercation…"

"Chief Grier, just how many riots at weddings have you seen?" she wanted to know.

"About half a dozen," he said.

"Well, I can assure you, there won't be any here," Michelle said. "Because there's no booze!"

Cash gaped at her. "No booze?"

"No."

"Well, damn," he said, glowering at her.

"Why do you say that?" she asked.

"How can you have altercations without booze?" He threw up his hands. "And I had so looked forward to a little excitement around here!"

"I could throw a punch at Hayes," Gabriel offered, grinning at the sheriff. "But then he'd have to arrest me, and Michelle would spend our honeymoon looking for bail bondsmen...."

Cash chuckled. "Just kidding. I like the occasional quiet wedding." He leaned forward. "When you're not busy, you might want to ask Blake Kemp about *his* wedding reception, though," he added gleefully. "Jacobsville will never forget that one, I swear!"

Michelle lay trembling in Gabriel's arms, hot and damp in the aftermath of something so turbulent and thrilling that she knew she could live on the memory of it for the rest of her life.

"I believe the chief wanted a little excitement?" She laughed hoarsely. "I don't think anyone could top this. Ever."

He trailed his fingers up her body, lingering tenderly on a distended nipple. He stroked it until she arched and gasped. "I don't think so, either." He bent his head and slipped his lips over the dusky peak, teasing it until it grew even harder and she shivered. He suckled it, delighting in the sounds that came out of her throat.

"You like that, do you?" he whispered. He moved over her. "How about this?"

"Oh...yes," she choked. "Yes!"

He slid a hand under her hips and lifted her into the slow penetration of his body, moving restlessly as she accepted him, arched to greet him, shivered again as she felt the slow, hungry depth of his envelopment.

"It's easier now," he whispered. "Does it hurt?"

"I haven't...noticed yet," she managed, shuddering as he moved on her.

He chuckled.

"I was afraid," she confessed in a rush of breath.

"I know."

She clung to him as the rhythm lifted her, teased her body into contortions of pure, exquisite pleasure. "I can't believe...I was afraid!"

His hips moved from side to side and she made a harsh, odd little cry that was echoed in the convulsion of her hips.

"Yes," he purred. "I can make you so hungry that you'll do anything to get me closer, can't I, *ma belle?*"

"Any...thing," she agreed.

He ground his teeth together. "It works...both ways... too," he bit off. He groaned harshly as the pleasure bit into him, arched him down into her as the rhythm grew hard and hot and deep. He felt his heartbeat in his head, slamming like a hammer as he drove into her welcoming body, faster and harder and closer until suddenly, like a storm breaking, a silver shaft of pleasure went through him like a spear, lifting him above her in an arch so brittle that he thought he might shatter into a thousand pieces.

"Like...dying," he managed as the pleasure took him.

She clung to him, too involved to even manage a reply, lifting and pleading, digging her nails into his hard back as she welcomed the hard, heavy push of his body, welcomed the deep, aching tension that grew and swelled and finally burst like rockets going off inside her.

She cried out helplessly, sobbing, as the ecstasy washed over her like the purest form of pleasure imaginable and then, just as quickly, was gone. Gone. Gone!

They clung together, damp with sweat, sliding against each other in the aftermath, holding on to the echoes of the exquisite satisfaction that they'd shared.

"Remind me to tell you one day how rare it is for two people to find completion at the same time," he whispered, sliding his mouth over her soft, yielding body. "Usually, the woman takes a long time, and the man only finds his satisfaction when hers is over."

She lifted an eyebrow. "And you would know this, how?" she began.

He lifted his head and looked into her eyes with a rakish grin. "Oh, from the videos I watched and the books I read and the other guys I listened to...."

"Is that so?" she mused, with a suspicious look.

He kissed her accusing eyes shut. "It was long before I knew you," he whispered. "And after the first day I saw you, sitting in the road waiting for me to run over you, there was no one. Ever."

Her eyes flew open. "Wh-what?"

He brushed the hair from her cheeks. "I knew then that I would love you one day, forever," he said quietly. "So there were no other women."

Her face flushed. "Gabriel," she whispered, overcome.

He kissed her tenderly. "The waiting was terrible," he groaned. "I thought I might die of it, waiting until you grew up, until you knew something of the world and men so that I didn't rob you of that experience." He lifted his head. "Always, I worried that you might find a younger man and fall in love..."

She put her fingers over his chiseled mouth. "I loved you from the day I met you," she whispered. "When I stared at you, that day in town with my grandfather, before I was even sixteen." She touched his cheek with her fingertips. "I knew, too, that there could never be anyone else."

He nibbled her fingers. "So sweet, the encounter after all the waiting," he whispered.

"Sweeter than honey," she agreed, her eyes warm and soft on his face.

"There's just one thing," he murmured.

She raised her eyebrows.

He opened a drawer and pulled out an item that he'd placed there earlier. An item that they'd forgotten to use.

She just smiled.

After a minute, he smiled back and dropped the item right back into the drawer.

Sara was overjoyed. "I can't wait to come down there and see you both," she exclaimed. "But you've only been married six weeks," she added.

Gabriel was facing the computer with Michelle at his side, holding her around the waist, his big hands resting protectively over her slightly swollen belly as they talked on Skype with Sara in Wyoming. "We were both very sure that it was what we wanted," he said simply.

"Well, I'm delighted," Sara said. She smiled. "The only way I could be more delighted is if it was me who was pregnant. But, that will come with time," she said complacently, and smiled. "I'm only sorry I couldn't be at the wedding," she added quietly. "I was very mean to you, Michelle. I couldn't face you, afterward."

"I understood," Michelle said gently. "You're my sister. Really my sister now," she added with a delighted laugh. "We're going to get a place near yours in Wyoming so that we can be nearby when the baby comes."

"I can't wait!"

"Neither can I," Michelle said. "We'll talk to you soon."

"Very soon." Sara smiled and cut the connection.

"Have you ever told her?" Michelle asked after a minute, curling up in Gabriel's lap.

He kissed her. "We did just tell her, my love..."

"Not about the baby," she protested. "About Wolf. About who he really is."

"You mean, her gaming partner for the past few years?" He grinned. "That's a story for another day."

"If you say so."

He kissed her. "I do say so. And now, how about a nice pickle and some vanilla ice cream?"

Her eyebrows lifted. "You know, that sounds delicious!"

He bent his head and kissed the little bump below her waist. "He's going to be extraordinary," he whispered.

"Yes. Like his dad," she replied with her heart in her eyes.

And they both grinned.

* * * * *

She was paralysed by the heat in his eyes, warming her through from head to toe, settling in the pit of her stomach, awakening a sweet, insistent ache she hadn't felt for so long.

The naked desire in his face provoked pride, need, want.

And she wanted him too.

She'd wanted him since the moment he had sauntered into her office, arrogant and demanding, making her think and making her do and making her feel. Not just because he looked so good, was so tall and so broad and so solid, and not just because he had eyes that caressed and a mouth that made her knees tremble, but because he was a man who cared, hide it as he might.

But he was a man who was leaving. A man with itchy feet, who lived his life on the edge of civilisation, risking his life every day.

Right now it was hard to remember why that was a problem.

HIS RELUCTANT CINDERELLA

BY
JESSICA GILMORE

Published in Great Britain 2014
by Mills & Boon, an imprint of Harlequin (UK) Limited,
Eton House, 18-24 Paradise Road, Richmond, Surrey, TW9 1SR

© 2014 Jessica Gilmore

ISBN: 978-0-263-91322-4

23-1014

After learning to read aged just two, **Jessica Gilmore** spent every childhood party hiding in bedrooms in case the birthday girl had a book or two she hadn't read yet. Discovering a Mills & Boon® novel on a family holiday, Jessica realised that romance-writing was her true vocation and proceeded to spend her maths lessons practising her art, creating *Dynasty*-inspired series starring herself and Morten Harket's cheekbones. Writing for Mills & Boon really is a dream come true!

A former au pair, bookseller, marketing manager and Scarborough seafront trader—selling rock from under a sign that said 'Cheapest on the Front'—Jessica now works as a membership manager for a regional environmental charity. Sadly, she spends most of her time chained to her desk, wrestling with databases, but likes to sneak out to one of their beautiful reserves whenever she gets a chance. Married to an extremely patient man, Jessica lives in the beautiful and historic city of York, with one daughter, one very fluffy dog, two dog-loathing cats and a goldfish named Bob.

On the rare occasions when she is not writing, working, taking her daughter to activities or tweeting, Jessica likes to plan holidays—and uses her favourite locations in her books. She writes deeply emotional romance with a hint of humour, a splash of sunshine and usually a great deal of delicious food—and equally delicious heroes.

For my parents

To Mum, thank you for weekly trips to the library,
for never telling me to "put that book down", for
the gift of words and stories and dreams.

And to Dad for proving that families are more than
genes, that blood isn't thicker than water, that nurture
totally trumps nature—and for being the
best grandpa in the world.

I love you both x

CHAPTER ONE

'IF YOU TELL ME where my sister is, I'll give you ten thousand pounds.'

The down-turned head in front of him lifted slowly and Raff found himself coolly assessed by a pair of the greenest eyes he had ever seen, their slight upward tilt irresistibly feline, the effect heightened by high, slanting cheekbones and a pointed chin.

If this lady had a tail, it would definitely be swishing slowly. A warning sign.

He'd never been that good at heeding warnings. He liked to see them more as a challenge.

'I beg your pardon?' Her voice was as cold as her stare. Maybe he should have tried charm before hard cash, but somehow Raff doubted that even his patented charm would work on this cool cat.

Her dismissal should have annoyed him, he was used to people snapping to attention when he needed them, but he had to admit he was intrigued. He smiled, slow and warm. 'Clara Castleton?'

There was no answering upturn of her full mouth as she nodded at the name tag, displayed neatly on the modern oak desk. 'As you can see. But I don't believe you introduced yourself?'

'I don't believe I did.' Raff hooked the wooden chair

out from opposite her desk and slid into it. He knew his six-foot-two frame could be intimidating, used it to his advantage sometimes, but for some reason, standing before her incredibly neat desk, he was irresistibly reminded of being summoned to the headmaster's office.

Although that was where any resemblance to his long-suffering former headmaster ended despite her severely cut suit—her strawberry-blonde hair might be ruthlessly scraped back but it looked as if it was all there and she lacked the terrifying bushy eyebrows. Hers were rather neat lines, adding a flourish to what really was a remarkably pretty face, although the hair, the discreet make-up and the suit were all designed to hide the fact. Interesting. Raff filed that fact away for future use. He sensed he was going to need all the weapons he could get.

He leant back in his chair, keeping his eyes fixed on her face. 'Castor Rafferty, but you can call me Raff. I believe you know my sister.'

'Oh.' Her eyes flickered away from his searching expression. 'I was expecting you a couple of days ago.'

'I've been busy dropping everything and rushing back to England. So, are you going to tell me where Polly is?'

Clara Castleton shook her head. 'I wouldn't tell you if I knew,' she said. 'But I don't.'

Raff narrowed his eyes. He didn't believe her, didn't want to believe her. Because if she was telling the truth he was at an utter dead end. 'Come now, Clara. I can call you Clara, can't I? This short and simple email…' he held up his phone with the email displayed. Not that he needed to be reminded what it said; he knew it off by heart '…tells me quite clearly that in an emergency my sister can be contacted via Clara of Castleton's Concierge Consultancy. Nice alliteration by the way.'

She took the phone and read the message, those intriguing eyebrows raised in surprise. 'Sorry, I have an email address, nothing more.'

'I've tried emailing a couple of times.' Try ten. Or twenty. 'Maybe she'll read it if it comes from you,' he suggested hopefully. 'My original offer still stands.'

'Keep your money, Mr Rafferty.' Her voice was positively icy now. Raff was already finding the anaemic English spring chilly; her tone brought the temperature down another few degrees. 'Your sister has taken care of my fees. She asked me to help settle you in, to continue to make sure the house is cared for. This I can do, it's *what* I do. But unless there is a real emergency I won't be sending any emails.'

It was a clear dismissal—and it rankled, far more than it should do. Time for a change of tactic; he needed to get this right so Polly would be back where she belonged, managing Rafferty's, the iconic department store founded by their great-grandfather.

And he would be back in the field where *he* belonged. He'd barely had a chance to unpack, to assess what was needed, how to play his own small yet vital part in stopping the humanitarian crisis unfolding before him from becoming a full-blown disaster, when he'd received Polly's email ordering him home.

Typical of his family, to think their petty affairs were worth more than thousands of lives. And yet here he was.

Raff looked around the neat, organised room for inspiration. Such a contrast from his last office: a tent on the outskirts of the camp. Even the office before that, situated in an actual building, had been a small room, almost a cupboard, piled high with crates, paperwork and supplies. He couldn't imagine having all this space to himself.

Occupying the corner at the end of the quaint high

street, Clara's office took up the entire ground floor of a former terraced shop, the original lead-paned bow windows now veiled with blinds, the iron sign holder above the front door empty, replaced by a neat plaque set in the wall.

Outside looked like a still from a film set in Ye Olde England but the inside was a sharp modern contrast. The large room was painted white with only bright-framed photographs to alleviate the starkness, although through the French doors at the back Raff could see a paved courtyard filled with flowering tubs and a small iron table and chairs, a lone hint of homeliness.

Clara's very large and very tidy desk was near the back by the far wall, facing out across the room. Two inviting sofas clustered by the front window surrounding a coffee table heaped with glossy lifestyle magazines. The whole room was discreet, tasteful and gave him no clue whatsoever to its owner's personality.

Maybe it was time to try the charm after all.

Raff leaned forward confidingly. 'I'm worried about Polly,' he said. 'It's so out of character for her to disappear like this. What if she's ill? I just want to know that she's all right.' He allowed a hint of a rueful smile to appear.

The look on Clara's face oozed disapproval. Yep, she was still giving out the whole 'disappointed headmaster' vibe. 'Mr Rafferty, you and I both know that your sister hasn't just disappeared. She's gone on holiday after making sure that both her job and home are taken care of. There really is no mystery.'

'It may be a *little* out of character.' Was that doubt creeping into her voice? 'I haven't known her to take even a long weekend before—but that's probably exactly why she needs this break. Besides, isn't it your company too?'

Unfortunately. 'Just what has my sister said to you?'

A faint flush crept over the high cheekbones. 'I don't understand.'

Oh, she understood all right.

'She didn't use the words irresponsible or lazy?' Polly's email might have been short but it had been to the point. *Her* point of view. As always, they differed on that.

The flush deepened. Not so cool after all. The colour gave her warmth, emphasising the curve of her cheek, the lushly dark lashes veiling those incredible eyes. An unexpected jolt of pure attraction shot through him. Before she had been like a marble statue, nice to look at but offputtingly chilly. This hint of vulnerability gave her dimensions. Unwanted, unneeded dimensions. He wasn't here to flirt. With any luck he'd hardly be here at all.

'Our communication was purely business,' but she couldn't meet his eye. 'Now, I do happen to have a half-hour free right now. Is this a convenient time for me to show you the house?'

No, Raff wanted to snap. No, actually it wasn't convenient. None of this was. Not Polly's most uncharacteristic disappearance, nor her SOS ordering him home right now. She couldn't expect him to drop everything and step in so she could go on some extended holiday.

Even though he hadn't been home in over four years. He pushed the thought away. He wasn't needed here, not as he was out in the field. Besides, his absence had given Polly the opportunity she had wanted; the two circumstances were entirely different.

Which made this whole disappearing act even odder. If he allowed himself to stop feeling irritated he might start getting worried.

'Mr Rafferty?'

'Raff,' he corrected her. 'Mr Rafferty makes me think I'm back at school.'

Or even worse back in the boardroom, sitting round a ridiculously large table listening to never-ending presentations and impenetrable jargon, itching to get up, stop talking and *do*.

'Raff,' she said after a reluctant pause. He liked the sound of his name on her tongue. Crisp and cool like a smooth lager on a hot summer's day. '*Is* now a convenient time?'

Not really but Polly had backed him into a hole and until he had a chance to work out what had happened he didn't have much choice.

He *was* still joint Vice CEO of Rafferty's, after all. Someone had to take over the reins, stop Grandfather working himself into an early grave; in Polly's absence that person had to be him.

She had planned it well. The contrary streak in Raff wanted to ensure she didn't get her way. To walk away from her home, her company. Show her he couldn't be manipulated.

But of course he couldn't. Despite everything Polly was his twin—and pulling a stunt like this was completely out of character. Polly didn't just quit; she was the hardest worker he knew. The sooner he found out what had happened and fixed it, the sooner they could both return to their lives.

And he was sure that the woman in front of him could help him, if he could just find a way to make her crack, like a ripe and rather inviting nut.

'Okay, then, Clara Castleton,' he said. 'Lead the way.'

'Is there something wrong?'

Clara knew she sounded cold. Raff Rafferty might

have turned on the charm but she preferred to keep a professional distance, especially when her new client owned an easy smile and a devilish glint in blue, blue eyes.

And a disconcerting way of looking at her as if he could see straight through her barriers, as if the suit didn't fool him at all. Her skin fizzed with awareness of his intense gaze—or with irritation at his high-handed ways.

Either way he was dangerous. The sooner she settled him in and got out, the better.

The tall blond man wasn't actually her client but his sister had made sure Clara was fully briefed. The Golden Boy, apple of his grandfather's eye. Clara knew men like Raff Rafferty all too well. It wasn't a type she admired at all. Not any more.

Look at him now, leaning against her van, a smirk playing on those finely sculpted lips.

'This yours?'

Clara held up the keys. 'Why?'

His eyes swept assessingly over the large, practical van, her logo and contact details tastefully picked out on the side. 'I imagined you driving something a little more elegant.'

Clara took a breath, an unexpected flutter in her stomach at the idea of something elegant, that she was featuring in his imagination at all. She pushed the thought resolutely away.

'Save your imaginings,' she said. 'The van is practical.'

'It's practical all right.'

His lips were pressed together; Clara had the distinct impression that he was laughing at her. 'I'm sure it's not your usual style,' she said as evenly as she could. 'If you'd rather walk I can meet you there.'

'Don't worry about me. I'm not fussy.'

'Great.' She was sure that her attempted smile looked more like a grimace. She should make him sit in the back amongst the cleaning supplies and tools. See how fussy he was then.

At least, Clara reflected as she pulled the van out into the narrow main road that ran through the town, he hadn't offered to drive. Some men found it hard to be driven by a woman, especially in a large van like this. Raff was the very definition of relaxed, leaning back in his seat, lean jean-clad legs outstretched.

Practical it might be, but the large van always felt out of place on Hopeford's narrow windy streets. It took all Clara's skills and concentration to negotiate the small roads. The overhanging houses and cobbled pavements might be picturesque enough to pull in tourists and Londoners looking for a lengthy if direct commute, but they were completely ill suited for work vans.

And it was easier to concentrate on the driving than it was trying to make conversation with someone who seemed to suck all the air out of the van. It had always felt so spacious before.

Unfortunately Raff didn't seem to feel the same way. 'How long has Polly lived here?'

Clara negotiated a particularly tight turn before answering as briefly as was polite. 'About three years, I believe.'

He looked about him. 'It seems quiet, not her kind of place at all.'

Clara glanced over at him. She knew that he and Polly were twins and the relationship was obvious. They both had straight, dark blond hair, although his was far more dishevelled than his sister's usual sleek chignon, straight, almost Roman noses and well-cut mouths. But the similarity seemed only skin deep. Polly Rafferty was quiet, always working, whether at home or on her long train journey into the capital. She was reserved and polite; Clara was the closest thing she had in Hopeford to a friend.

On balance she much preferred the sister's reservation to the brother's easy charm and devilish grin. They were dangerous attributes, especially if you had once been susceptible to a laid-back rich boy's style.

Clara knew all too well where that led. Nowhere she ever wanted to go again.

'The town is increasingly popular,' she said, carefully keeping her voice neutral. 'It's pretty, we have good schools and we're on a direct train line into London.'

'Ye—es…' He sounded doubtful. 'But Polly doesn't have kids and last I saw she wasn't that bothered about quiet either. If she wanted pretty there are plenty of places in London that fit the bill. It's not like she's short of money.'

His tone was disparaging and the look on his face as he stared out at the picturesque street no better. Clara gripped the steering wheel tightly. She might moan about incomers flooding the place, driving prices up and her friends out, but at least they appreciated the town.

'You don't have to stay here,' she said after a moment. 'There are plenty of hotels in London.'

His lips tightened. 'The key to Polly's whereabouts is here. I can feel it. Until I know where she is—and how I can get her to come home—I'm staying.'

Polly Rafferty's house was just a short drive away from Clara's office, a pretty cottage situated on a meandering lane leading out to the countryside. It was one of Clara's favourite houses; many of her clients had bought the huge new builds that had sprung up on gated estates around the town, large and luxurious certainly but lacking in Hopeford charm.

'Picturesque.' It wasn't a compliment, not with that twist of the mouth.

'Isn't it?' she said, deliberately taking his statement at face value. 'This is the most sought-after area in town, close to the countryside and the train station. There's a good pub within walking distance too.'

'All amenities,' Raff said, looking about him, his expression one step removed from disdainful.

The condescension prickled away at her. It was odd. She had so many clients who talked down to her and her staff and it never got to her; twenty minutes in this man's sardonic company and she was ready to scream.

Ignoring him, Clara unlocked the front door and stood back to let the tall man enter. He stood there for a second, clearly conflicted about preceding her into the house. She waited patiently, a thrill of satisfaction running through her when he finally gave in, ducking to fit his tall frame through the small door.

He was as out of place in the low-ceilinged, beamed cottage as a cat at Crufts. The house was sparingly and tastefully decorated but the designer had worked with the history rather than against it. Rich fabrics, colour and flowers predominated throughout, a sharp contrast with the casually dressed man in jeans and desert boots, an old kitbag hoisted over his shoulder.

He didn't look much like a playboy. He looked like a weary soldier who wanted nothing more than a hot shower and a bed.

'The bedrooms are upstairs,' Clara said, gesturing towards the small creaky staircase that wound up to the next floor. 'I had the main guest room made up for you.

It's the second door on the right. There's an en-suite shower room.'

She should offer to show him up there but every nerve was screeching at her to stay downstairs, to keep her distance. Noticing the weary slant to his shoulders led to seeing the lines around his eyes, the dark hollows under them emphasising the dark navy blue, leading in turn to a disturbing awareness of the lines of his body under the rumpled T-shirt, the way his battered jeans clung to lean, muscled legs.

She squeezed her eyes shut. What was she doing ogling clients? *Pull yourself together.*

Maybe her mother *was* right: it might be time to consider dating again. Her hormones were clearly so tired of being kept under rigid control they were running amok for the most unsuitable of men.

Clara took a deep breath, feeling her nails bite into her palms as she tried to summon her habitual poise. 'The kitchen's through here,' she said, marching back into the hallway and leading the way into the light spacious room that took up the entire back of the cottage. She had always envied Polly this room. It was made for a family, not for one lone workaholic who ate standing up at the counter. She didn't look back as she continued to briskly outline the preparations she had made.

'I stocked up with the usual order but if there is anything else you'd like write it here.' She gestured towards the memo pad on the front of the fridge.

She turned to check if he was following and skidded to a halt, backing up a few steps as she nearly collided with his broad chest. 'Erm, there's a lovely courgette and feta quiche in the freezer, which will make a nice, simple dinner tonight.' Clara could feel the telltale burn spreading across her cheeks and knew she was turning red. She backed away another step, turning her back on him once again, finding safety in the sleek chrome fridge door. 'If you want your dinner provided then Sue, the regular cleaner, will pop a stew or a curry into the slow cooker for you but you must leave a note on the morning you require it or email the office before ten a.m.'

She was babbling. She *never* babbled but everything felt out of kilter. Her whole body was prickled with awareness of his nearness. She turned, smiled brightly. 'Any questions?'

Raff's mouth quirked. 'Is there anything you don't do around here?'

'Your sister employs me to keep the house clean, the cupboards stocked, to take care of any problems. She's a busy woman,' she said, unnaturally defensive as she saw the disbelief in his face. 'I offer a full housekeeping service without the inconvenience of live-in staff.'

'She pays you to stock the fridge with quiche?' But the smirk was playing around his mouth again. Annoyingly.

'My father's quiche,' she corrected him. 'Don't knock it until you've tried it. There's also plenty of salad, fruit and hummus.'

'Beer, crisps, meat?'

'Put it on the list,' she said, wanting to remain professional, aloof, but she could feel her mouth responding to his smile, wanting to bend upwards.

She needed to get out. Get some air and give herself a stern talking-to. 'The pub does food if you want something different,' she said. 'Or there are some takeaway menus on the memo board. You'll be fine.'

'I usually am.'

'Okay, then.' She paused, made awkward by the intensity of his gaze. With an effort Clara pulled on her professional persona like a comfort blanket. 'If you have any problems at all just get in touch.' She held out her card.

He reached out slowly and plucked it out of her hand, his fingers slightly brushing against hers as he did so. She jerked her hand away as if burnt, the heat shocking her. She swallowed back a gasp with an effort, hoping she hadn't given away her discomfort.

'I'll do that.' He was looking right into her eyes as he said it.

'Good.' Damn, she sounded breathless. 'That's everything. Have a nice evening.'

Clara began to back out of the kitchen, not wanting to be the one to break the eye contact. It was as if he had a hypnotic effect on her, breaking through her usual calm, ruffling the feathers she kept so carefully smoothed down.

'Ouch.' Something underfoot tripped her up and she put a hand out to steady herself, her eyes wrenched from his.

'Are you all right?'

'Yes, thanks.' Steadier in more ways than one, relieved to be free of his gaze. She looked down at the trip hazard, confused by the large hessian mouse. 'Oh, how could I forget? Mr Simpkins' usual routine is biscuits first thing in the morning and more biscuits and some fish in the evening. He has his own cupboard under the sink.'

'Mr Simpkins?' He sounded apprehensive.

'The man of the house.' She smiled sweetly. 'I do hope you like cats.'

And surprisingly cheered up by the horrified look on his face, Clara swivelled and walked away.

CHAPTER TWO

CLARA ALWAYS MULTITASKED. She had to—she couldn't manage the homes and lives of the over-privileged if she wasn't capable of sorting out babysitters, dog walkers and hedge trimmers whilst ordering a cordon bleu meal and cleaning a loo. Usually all at the same time. Driving was the perfect opportunity to gather her thoughts and make mental lists.

But not tonight. Her to do lists were slithering out of her mind, replaced by unwanted images of smiling eyes, a mobile mouth and a firmly confident manner.

Her own personal kryptonite.

Luckily this was probably the last she'd see of him. He would be on the early train to London each morning, return to Hopeford long after she had finished for the night and it wasn't as if she personally cleaned the house anyway.

Besides, Polly would be home soon and he would return to whichever beach he had reluctantly pulled himself away from faster than Clara could change the sheets and vacuum the rug. Things would be safe and steady.

So she had felt a little awareness. A tingle. Possibly even a jolt. It was allowed—she was twenty-nine, for goodness' sake, and single, not a nun. It wasn't as if she had taken vows of chastity.

It just felt that way sometimes. Often.

She should enjoy the moment—and make sure it didn't happen again.

Pulling into her parents' driveway, Clara took a moment and sat still in the fading light. This was usually one of her favourite times, the calm after a full and busy day, the moment's peace before other ties, welcome, needed, unbreakable ties, tugged at her, anchoring her firmly.

The house lights were on, casting a welcoming glow, beckoning her in. She knew she would step into warmth, love, gorgeous aromas drifting out of the kitchen, gentle chatter—and yet she sat a minute longer, slewing off the day, the last hour, until she could sit no more and slid down out of the van onto the carefully weeded gravel.

Clara's parents lived in a traditional nineteen-thirties semi-detached house in what used to be the new part of town. Now the trees had matured, the houses weathered and the new town had become almost as desirable as the old with families adding attic conversions, shiny glass extensions and imposing garages. The Castleton house was small by comparison, still with the original leaded bay windows and a wooden oval front door.

It was ten years since Clara had occupied the small bedroom at the back but the house itself was reassuringly gloriously unchanged.

'Evening,' she called out, opening the front door and stepping into the hallway.

'In here,' her father called from the kitchen and, lured by the tantalising smell, she followed his voice—and her nose.

'Something smells good.' Clara dropped a fond kiss on her father's cheek before bending down to sneak a look inside the oven.

'Spiced chickpea and spinach pastries in filo pastry.'

'I'd have thought you'd had enough kneading during the day,' she teased.

'It relaxes me. Have you got the list?'

'Of course.' Clara produced a neatly printed out list from a file in the cavernous bag she rarely ventured anywhere without. She used her father's deli for her customers' food requests whenever possible. He wasn't the cheapest, although, she thought loyally, he was definitely the best, but not one person ever balked at the hefty bill topped up with Clara's own cut. The prestige of knowing it was all locally made and sourced was enough for most people although she knew many of them also shopped at the local discount supermarket whilst making sure her father's distinctive purple labels were at the front of their pantries and fridges.

Clara put the list down onto the one clear part of the counter and mock glared at her father. 'It would save us both a lot of time if you let me email it to you.'

'Email me,' he scoffed as he pulled a selection of dressed salads out of the cavernous fridge. 'I'll be up making bread at six. When do I have time to read emails? Hungry?'

'For your pastry? Always. I'll be back in a moment.' She shook her head at him. Clara was always nagging her father to get more high tech, to get a website, engage on social media. The delicatessen was doing well, more than well, but with just a little marketing spur she didn't see why it couldn't do better, expand into neighbouring towns. The problem was her father liked to do everything himself.

Pot, kettle, she thought with a grin as she tore herself away from the kitchen and walked into the main room of the house where the sitting and dining room had been knocked through to create one big family space.

A large oak table dominated the back and Clara felt the usual lift in her heart when she spotted a small dark head bowed over a half-completed gothic Lego castle. This was what made it all worthwhile: the long hours, the repetitive work, the nights in alone.

'Impressive,' she said. 'Good day, sweetie?'

The head lifted, revealing a large pair of dark brown eyes. 'Mummy! You're late again.'

And just like that the happiness became swirled with guilt even though the comment hadn't been accusatory. The matter-of-factness was worse. Summer didn't expect her to be on time: she hardly ever was.

'Sorry, Sunshine. How was school?'

'Fine.'

Of course it was; everything was fine. Unless it was awesome, the ultimate accolade.

'I'm just going to eat and then we'll head home. Have you finished your homework?'

'Of course,' her daughter replied with quiet dignity before breaking into a most undignified grin as Clara walked around the table and gathered her in close for a long moment. Summer was getting taller, her head close to Clara's shoulders, the baby plumpness replaced by sharp bones and long limbs, but she still gave the most satisfying cuddles. Clara breathed her daughter in, steadying herself with the familiar scent of shampoo, fresh air and sweetness before releasing her reluctantly.

'I'll be no more than ten minutes,' she promised. 'We might have time for a quick half-hour's TV. Your turn to choose. Okay?'

It was like being a child herself, sitting at the kitchen table with a plate full of her father's trial runs whilst he quietly measured, stirred and tasted and her mother bustled from one room to the other whilst relating a long and very involved story about a dimly remembered school friend of Clara's who was, evidently, getting married. According to her mother the entire single population of Hopeford was currently entering wedlock, leaving Clara as the sole spinster of the parish.

Clara knew her mother was proud of her—but she also knew she would give a great deal to see her married. Or dating.

Heck, her mother would probably be more relieved than shocked if she spent every Saturday night cruising the local nightspots for casual sex.

Not that there were any real local nightspots other than a couple of pubs and even if she wanted to indulge the pickings were slim. A grin curved her lips at the thought of strutting into her local and coming onto any of the regulars. They'd probably call her parents in concern that she'd been taken ill!

'Clara.' The insistence in her mother's voice was a definite sign that she had moved on from a discussion of Lucy Taylor's appalling taste in bridesmaids' dresses and wanted her attention.

'Sorry, Mum. Miles away.'

'I was just thinking, why not leave Summer here with us tonight so you can go out?' Clara repressed a sigh. It was as she had feared. All this talk of weddings had addled her mother's brain.

'Go out?'

'Your cousin is back home for a couple of weeks. I know she's planning to go to The Swan tonight. It would be lovely if you joined her.'

For just one moment Clara experienced a rare shock of envy. That had once been her plan, a job and a life away from the well-meaning but prying eyes of her hometown.

'I've got a lot of work to do—I've promised Summer

some time before bed but then I must spend a fun couple of hours with the timetables.' She attempted a smile. It wasn't that she minded working all hours but it didn't sound very glamorous.

'Come on, love,' her mother urged. 'You never get to go out. Just one drink.'

It would be so easy to give in. Put the computer away for the evening, go out and get all the gossip about her cousin Maddie's impossibly exciting life as a stylist on a popular reality show. But duty called. She had to remain firm.

She couldn't just drop everything for an unscheduled night out. No, it was absolutely impossible.

'I've been thinking.' Clara wound her hand around the half-pint glass, pointedly avoiding her cousin's eyes. 'Maybe it's time I should consider internet dating.'

Clara knew she was fairly stubborn. Unfortunately it was a trait she had inherited from her mother and passed down to her daughter. United they were a formidable team and when her dad had added his gentle voice to theirs she had been quite outgunned.

Clara had been sent out for fun whether she liked it or not.

And now she was out, she was beginning to wonder again whether her mother might be right about more than Clara's need for a night off.

'Internet dating?' Maddie squealed at a pitch that could cause serious discomfort to dogs. 'Any dating would be a good start. Isn't there anyone closer to home though? I have stories about internet disasters that would make your hair curl. I know you, one disaster and you'll give the whole thing up. And there will be a disaster.' She nodded sagely. 'There always is.'

'Nope. I went to school with, babysat for, employed or have been employed by every single man I know in a ten-mile radius without a single spark. And this way I can profile them first, make sure they're suitable.'

'*If* they tell you the truth,' Maddie said darkly. 'Don't contact anyone without clearing them with me first. I know the language they use.'

Clara laughed, trying to quell the unease Maddie's words conjured up. How would she know who to trust? It had been such a long time ago—and she'd got it horribly wrong then. It wasn't just her pride at stake now; there was Summer too. She'd messed up so badly with Summer's own father, any new man in their lives had to be perfect. Her daughter deserved the best. 'I promise, you get first approval.'

'Ooh, we could have a look now.' Maddie had pulled out her phone and was jabbing away at the screen. 'What are you looking for?'

'Sensible, hardworking with good values.' It didn't take Clara long to think. These things counted for far more than the tilt of a mouth or a warm glint in a pair of navy-blue eyes.

'Very exciting. Any speciality? I have accounts with Uniformly Single, Farmers for You, Country Ladies and Gents and Parents Need Love Too. We could see who is available locally! So, hot fireman, beefy farmer or a fabulous father?'

'They are not all real accounts.' Clara stared at Maddie's phone in disbelief. 'I thought you were happy with Olly.'

'I *am*, but he's an actor. First whiff of success and he'll be off. There's no harm in keeping my accounts open and having the occasional peep.'

'Isn't there anyone, you know, normal?' This was a

bad idea. What had she been thinking, mentioning it to Maddie? She'd meant to do some research first. Approach the whole thing in a sensible businesslike way.

'I still think you're better off warming up on someone you know.' Maddie was scanning around the pub hopefully like a hound on the scent. 'Get back in the saddle before you start galloping. There must be *someone* in here you can practise on.'

It was only Tuesday but that hadn't stopped a constant stream of people popping in for a quick drink or settling in for a longer session. The cousins had bagged a prime position at the corner of the L-shaped room and from her comfortable armchair Clara could see all the comings and goings in the friendly local.

She was out so rarely she felt vaguely guilty, as if she were seventeen again, illicitly consuming half a lager shandy and hoping that the barman didn't ask for ID, jumping every time the door opened in case her parents came in to march her home.

Although these days they would buy her another and beg her to stay.

'Hang on.' Maddie froze as she zoomed in on some unsuspecting prey like the expert hunter she was. 'He looks promising. How about him?'

Clara's chest tightened, an unsettling feeling quivering in her stomach as she saw just who Maddie was staring at. This wasn't who she had been looking for all evening, was it? Wasn't the reason her heart had jumped in painful anticipation each time the door opened?

Stop it, she told herself fiercely.

Raff Rafferty was standing at the entrance looking around the pub. As his eyes swept over Clara they stopped and he smiled slightly, raising one tanned hand in greeting. How embarrassing; he'd seen her staring.

Hoping she wasn't blushing too much, Clara snapped her eyes away, regarding her empty glass with every appearance of absorbed interest.

'You *know* him?' Maddie was still staring in undisguised admiration at Raff. 'Things *have* changed around here, and for the better. You've kept him quiet.'

'I don't actually know him.' Clara was aware how unnaturally defensive she sounded and tried to rein it back in. 'He's new—to town, I mean, but he's not staying for long. He's completely unsuitable.'

'Hot and temporary, sounds perfect for a trial run to me. Sure you're not tempted?'

Clara couldn't quite meet Maddie's enquiring gaze. 'Quite sure. His sister is a client of mine.'

'Oh,' Maddie sighed. 'What a shame he's not a new permanent resident. We could do with some eye candy in this town. Hang on.' Maddie perked up. 'He's coming this way!'

Clara's stomach gave that peculiar twist again. It was a shame that stomachs couldn't qualify for the Olympics because by the feel of the double somersault hers was doing right now she was pretty sure she would score highly on rhythmic gymnastics.

'Clara Castleton.' It was said politely but there was a gleam in Raff Rafferty's eye that unnerved her. As if he was laughing at her.

She looked up as coolly as she could. 'The quiche didn't suit after all?'

'It was delicious,' he assured her. 'But I fancied a drink. Can I get you two ladies a top up?'

Raff turned the full beam of his blue eyes onto Maddie and Clara felt her jaw clench as her cousin beamed back. 'That would be lovely,' Maddie said as Clara blurted out, 'Thank you but we are fine.'

'Come and join us,' Maddie invited, shooting a con-spiratorial look at Clara.

'I'm sure Mr Rafferty has somewhere he would rather be.' It was Clara's turn to be signalling her cousin with a meaningful look but Maddie wasn't being very receptive.

'That's a shame.' Maddie smiled up at Raff. 'Do you?'

'I don't think so.' Raff was looking amused. 'I don't have any friends here so I'd love to join you, thanks. I'm Raff.'

'Maddie.' She was positively purring. 'Raff Rafferty, that's an unusual combination. Your parents liked it so much they used it twice?'

He grinned, annoyingly at his ease. 'I wish. No, my mother was into Greek mythology so when she knew she was having twins she decided to name us after the heavenly twins, Castor and Pollux. My sister escaped with Polly. I wasn't so lucky.'

'I like it,' Maddie said. 'It's unusual.'

Clara caught Raff's eye in a moment of shared amuse-ment, an intoxicating warmth spreading through her at the laughter in his eyes.

'You wouldn't like being called Sugar all the time,' Raff assured her cousin. 'After one week at prep school and five fights I changed it to Raff. Now only my grand-parents use my real name.'

'It could have been worse.' Clara had been thinking. 'If she'd known you were a boy and a girl you might have been Apollo and Artemis.'

'Good God, literally!' Raff looked horrified. 'I will never despise my name again. What a lucky escape I had. For that I absolutely must get you a drink. What are you drinking?'

Clara opened her mouth fully intending to say no again and more firmly this time, but something extraordinary happened and the words in her head changed as soon as they left her mouth. 'Thank you,' she said. 'I'm drinking the local pale ale.'

Raff hadn't intended to leave the house tonight. It had taken him over two days to get back to England and once the plane had touched down at Gatwick he had headed straight to Hopeford like a homing pigeon aiming for a new world record.

He'd hoped that the key to finding Polly would be right here in the surprisingly shapely form of Clara Castleton or hidden somewhere in Polly's house—and he was going to find it whatever it took.

Only it turned out that being mad with his twin wasn't enough; he simply couldn't invade her privacy. One step into her study and he had frozen. He might not like it but Polly was entitled to her secrets.

For a long time they had only really had each other. Now they didn't even have that. The moment she'd started blaming Raff for their grandfather's blatant favouritism it had all fallen apart and everything Raff did made it worse. Even when he'd finally left, finally had the courage to follow his own path, he couldn't make it right.

He didn't know *how* to repair the damage—if it was even repairable. But whatever she thought, she could rely on him. He'd find out where she was, what was wrong and he'd fix it. Fix them.

So here he was. She'd asked him—told him—to come home and he had. But now what?

His mood had turned dark, exhaustion and frustration making rest impossible, introspection unbearable. Five minutes of television channel hopping later and Raff had had enough. It was time to go and check out the ridiculously quaint town his sister had bequeathed him.

Otherwise he was going to end up having a conversation with the cat. Mr Simpkins knew more than he was letting on; he was sure of it.

It didn't take Raff long to explore. Hopeford defined sleepy small town, was the epitome of privileged. The narrow streets closed in around him, making it hard to breathe. This rarefied atmosphere was exactly what he had been running from the last four years.

He'd breathed a sigh of relief at the familiar sign hanging outside a half-timbered building. A pub, a chance to get his head together, regroup. Four years of changing places, of new jobs, new challenges all had one thing in common. A local watering hole. A place to find out the lie of the land, find some compatible companionship and quench his thirst. The Swan was a little older, a lot cleaner and a great deal safer than his last local but he didn't hold that against the place.

Especially when he walked in and clapped eyes on Clara Castleton.

It had taken a moment or two to recognise her. Sure there was the same feline tilt to her long-lashed eyes, the same high cheekbones but that was where the similarity ended. This version had let her hair down, metaphorically as well as physically, the strawberry-blonde length allowed to fall in a soft half-ponytail rather than ruthlessly pulled back.

Even more disturbingly the lush full mouth was curved in a generous smile.

But none of that mattered. Clara was a means to an end, that was all. Mr Simpkins might not be ready to talk but a friendly night in the pub and he might have Clara telling him anything he needed to know. She must know more than she was letting on—she ran every aspect of Polly's life.

'Thank you for the drink…' oh, no, prim was back '…but I really need to be going.'

Raff glanced at his battered old watch. His grandfather had given him a Breitling for his twenty-first but he preferred the cheap leather-strapped watch he had bought first trip out. Bought with money earned by his own sweat, not by family connections.

'It's still early. Are you sure you don't want to stay a bit longer?'

'It's a work night,' she reminded him. Raff had been doing his best to forget. Tomorrow he was going to have to try and dig up something smart, get up ridiculously early and join all the other pack rats on an overpriced, overcrowded train. No matter he hadn't made this exact journey before. He knew the drill.

The only surprise was whether his particular carriage would be overheated or freezing cold. Unlike Goldilocks, Raff was under no illusions that it would be just right.

'Yes, it is,' he agreed. 'Unless you tell me where Polly is and save me from a day in the office tomorrow?'

She sighed as she got to her feet, gathering her bag and coat in her arms. 'I already told you…'

He'd blown it. He was too tired to play the game properly. He made one last-ditch attempt. 'I'm sorry. Let me walk you home.'

'Why? So you can interrogate me some more?' She shook her head, the red-gold tendrils trembling against her neck.

'No.' Well, only partly. 'It's good manners.' In some of the places Raff had lived you always saw the girl home. Even if it was the tent next to yours.

She shot him an amused glance. 'I think I'll be okay.'

'I won't,' he assured her. 'I'll lie awake all night worrying I failed in my chivalric duty. And I'll have to go to work tomorrow all red-eyed and pale from worry and they will all think I've been out carousing all night. Which will be most unfair as it's barely nine p.m.'

'I don't live far.' But it wasn't a no and she didn't complain as he drained his drink and followed her out, noting the blush that crept over her cheeks as she said goodbye to her cousin, who pulled her close for a hug and to whisper something in her ear.

'Where to?' he asked as he fell into step beside her. She walked just as he'd thought she would, purposeful, long strides in her sensible low-heeled boots.

'I live above the office.'

That wasn't a surprise. 'All work and no play…' he teased. It wasn't meant with any malice but to his surprise she stopped and turned, the light from the lamp post highlighting the colour in her cheeks.

'Why do people think it's a bad thing to concentrate on work?' she asked. Raff didn't reply; he could tell the question wasn't really aimed at him. 'So I work hard. I want to provide stability for my daughter. Is that such a bad thing?'

Daughter?

'I didn't know you were married,' he said and wanted to recall the words as soon as he said them. This wasn't the nineteen fifties and she wasn't wearing a ring.

'I'm not,' she said coldly and resumed walking even faster than before.

Way to go, Raff, nice building of rapport, he thought wryly. *You'll get Polly's address out of her in no time.*

He cast about for a safer topic. 'How old is she? Your daughter?'

'Ten,' she said shortly but he could feel her soften, see her shoulders relax slightly. 'Her name's Summer.'

'Pretty.'

'I was in a bit of a hippy stage at the time,' she confessed. 'Summer says she's glad she was born then because I'd probably call her something sensible and boring now. But it suits her.'

'Does she live with you?'

'I know the flat's not ideal for a child,' she said. Why did she assume every question was a criticism? 'But there's a garden at my parents' and she spends a lot of time there.'

'I spent a lot of time with my grandparents too.' During the school holidays it had been the only home he'd known.

'Polly said they brought you up.' It was a simple statement; there was no curiosity or prying behind it but it shocked him all the same. Polly was confiding in Clara, then. No wonder she hadn't put the welcome mat out for him.

What else had his twin said?

'Do you see a lot of Polly?' The question was abrupt and he tried to soften it. 'We're not really in touch any more. I'm glad she has a friend here.'

'We're both busy but we catch up when we can.' It wasn't enough but he didn't know how to push the issue without frightening her off.

And at least Polly had someone looking out for her. He tried again. 'If you care for all your clients the way you look after Polly, no wonder you're so busy.'

'Not all of them. Some just want cleaners and gardeners, others like to outsource all their home maintenance. Or I can provide babysitters, a shopping service, interior designers. Often it's just putting people in touch with the right services.'

'And taking a cut?'

Clara smiled. 'Of course. But some people need me

on call twenty-four seven, to pick up dry-cleaning, pick the kids up from school, buy last-minute gifts. Whatever they need I supply.'

She sounded so calm, so utterly in control and yet she was what? Late-twenties? A couple of years younger than Raff.

'Impressive.' He meant it.

'Not really.' She sounded a little less sure. 'None of it was really planned.' She had slowed down, her step less decisive, nervously twisting the delicate silver bangle on her wrist round and round. 'I had Summer and I needed to work. Oh, I know my parents would have let us live there. They wanted me to go to university but I couldn't just offload my responsibilities onto them. There's a lot of incomers in Hopeford, busy commuters with no time and a lot of money. I started cleaning for them and things kind of snowballed.'

She made it sound so easy but Raff was in no doubt that building her business up from cleaning services to the slick operation she ran today had taken a lot of grit and determination.

'I'd love Summer to have a proper home.' She sounded a little wistful. 'A kitchen like Polly's and a huge garden. But living above the office is practical—and it's ours. It was a better investment than a house at this stage in our lives.'

Investment, plans. It was like an alternative universe to a man who lived out of a kitbag and changed countries more frequently than he had his hair cut.

'This is me.' Clara had come to a stop outside the leaded bow window. She stood at the door calm, composed. 'Do you think you can find your way back or do I need to walk *you* home now?'

Her face was unreadable and there was no hint of flirtatiousness in her manner. Was she trying to be funny or was she completely serious? Raff couldn't figure her out at all. 'I have an excellent sense of direction,' he assured her. 'So…'

'Goodnight, then.' She offered him her hand, a quaintly old-fashioned gesture. Their eyes met, held; Raff could see uncertainty in her gaze as she stood there for one long second before she abruptly stepped back and turned, hands fumbling with her keys.

And she was gone without even one last backward glance.

Raff let out a long breath, an unexpected stab of disappointment shocking him. *Fool,* he told himself. *You're not here to flirt and, even if you had the time or inclination, since when were ice maidens your style?* He was tired, that was all, the jet lag clouding his judgement.

He had a job to do: find Polly, get her home, return to his real life. Nothing and no one, especially not the possessor of a pair of upwardly tilted green eyes, was going to get in his way.

CHAPTER THREE

WHAT WAS THAT?

Clara looked up as the front door creaked, but it was only someone walking by. Old buildings and narrow pavements equalled many creaks and bangs. It was a good thing she wasn't a nervous type.

Nor was she usually the door-watching type.

But it was getting to be a habit.

First at the pub, now today. And yesterday.

She was pathetic.

Especially as she knew only too well that Raff Rafferty hadn't even set foot in Hopeford in the last three days. He had, she guessed, boarded the train to London on Wednesday morning along with all the rest of the commuters but, according to Sue, the woman who usually cleaned the Rafferty house, he hadn't been back since. His bed was unrumpled, no dishes had been used, no laundry left. Either he was extraordinarily tidy, so tidy even Sue's legendary forensic skills couldn't find any trace of him, or he was staying in London.

This was all Maddie's fault. If she hadn't pulled her aside, told her to invite him in for coffee. 'It's not always a euphemism,' she'd said, mischief glinting in those green eyes so like Clara's own. Only brighter, livelier, flirtier. 'Not unless you want it to…'

Of course she didn't. And coffee at that time of night was irresponsible anyway—inviting someone in for a cup of peppermint tea was probably never misconstrued. She could have done that. But did she want to? Want that tall, confident man in her flat? Even for one innocent cup of hot herbal beverage?

Because there was one moment when he had looked down at her and her breath had caught in her throat, every nerve end pulsing with an anticipation she hadn't felt in years. If she had stepped forward rather than back-wards, if he had put his hands on her shoulders, angled his mouth down to hers, what would she have done?

Clara slumped forward. This all proved that she had taken the whole not-dating, stability-for-Summer thing just a tiny bit too far. If she had allowed her mother to set her up, just occasionally, for dinner and drinks with one of the many eligible men she had suggested over the years, then one measly hour in the pub, one small drink, wouldn't have thrown her so decidedly off kilter.

Raff Rafferty had been a tiny drop of water after a long drought. It didn't mean he was the *right* kind of water but just one taste had reminded her of what she was missing. What it felt like to have an attractive man's attention focused solely on her.

Even if he did have an ulterior motive that had noth-ing to do with Clara herself.

'That's a fearsome frown. Planning to murder some-one?'

After all that waiting she hadn't even heard the door open.

She hoped he hadn't seen her jump, that the heat in her cheeks wasn't visible. 'I exact a high penalty for un-paid bills.'

Clara had been hoping that three days' absence had

exaggerated Raff's attractiveness. They hadn't. He was just as tall, as broad as she remembered but the weary air she had glimpsed last time was unequivocal. He looked as if he hadn't slept for a week.

Dark circles shadowed his eyes, unfairly emphasising the navy blue, his face was pale under the deep tan, the well-cut shirt was wrinkled.

'I need a favour.' He didn't even crack a smile. 'Just how full a service do you offer?'

Clara gaped at him. 'I beg your pardon?'

'I asked...' he spoke slowly, clearly, enunciating every word '...how full a service you offer. I need a girlfriend and I need one now. Can you supply me with one, or not?'

If he hadn't been so tired... If he hadn't been quite so desperate, then Raff might have phrased his request slightly differently. As it was it took a while for the outrage on Clara's face to penetrate the dense fog suffocating what was left of his brain.

'You're not the first person to ask me for extra services,' she said finally, contempt dripping through her words. 'I admit, though, you have surprised me. I would have thought you were quite capable of hiring your own special help.'

Something was wrong, Raff could dimly tell, but he fixed on the positive.

'So you can help me?'

'Normally it's the bored wives that ask for something extra. Someone to help *clean out the guttering, trim the borders.*' She put a peculiar emphasis on the last few words. 'I do like to help them when I can. I usually send Dave round. He might be seventy-three but he's steady up a ladder. They don't ask again.'

Raff tried to sort out her meaning from her words. He was quite clearly missing something. 'Do the gutters need doing?' he asked. 'Surely that's your preserve, not mine. Do what you think best. Look, it's been a long day, a long week. Can you help me or not?'

She looked at him levelly but to his astonishment there was a cold anger in her eyes. 'Not. This is a concierge service not an escort service. Now please leave. Now.'

'What?' Raff shook his head in disbelief as her words sank in. 'I don't want... I didn't mean. For crying out loud, Clara, what kind of man do you think I am?'

'I don't know,' she retorted, eyes hot with fury now. 'The kind of man who walks away from his family, the kind of man who doesn't have to work for anything worth having! The kind of man who wants to rent a girlfriend—'

'Yes! A girlfriend. Not an escort or a call girl or whatever your dirty little brain has conjured up.' Now his anger was matching hers, the righteous fury waking him up. 'If I was looking for someone to sleep with I could find them, don't worry your pretty little head about that, but that's not what I'm looking for. I need someone to come to a few functions with me, to gaze lovingly into my eyes and to convince an autocratic old man that I might just settle down with her. Now, is that something you can help me with?'

If he thought his words might make her feel guilty, get her to back down, then he rapidly realised he was wrong. She uncoiled herself from her seat, rising to her feet to look up into his face, her eyes fixed on his, full of righteous anger.

'This is about fooling your grandfather? Why? So he doesn't cut you off? I have had it up to here with poor little rich boys who live their lives according to who holds the purse strings. I wouldn't help you if I had a hundred suitable girls working for me. Now please leave.'

Raff choked back a bitter laugh. 'I don't have to justify myself to you, Miss Castleton, but for your information my grandfather is ill. He's in the hospital and I am under strict orders not to upset him. So I either start dating one of the unfortunate women on the shortlist he drew up for me, fake a relationship or be responsible for yet another dangerous rise in blood pressure.'

He smiled over at her, sweet and dangerous. 'Tell me, Miss Know-it-all, which do you recommend?'

'A shortlist?'

That had stopped Miss Judgemental in her tracks.

Raff didn't want to let go of the anger and frustration, didn't want to try and tease a responsive grin from that pursed-up mouth, coax a glint out of those hard emerald eyes.

Especially as her words had cut a little deeper than they should. No virtual stranger should have the power to penetrate beneath the shield he so carefully erected yet her words had been like well-aimed arrows piercing straight into his Achilles heel.

Whether it was the lack of sleep, the taut tension in the room or the craziness of the situation, he didn't know but, despite his best intentions, a slow smile crept over his face.

'Do you want to see it?'

Clara's eyes widened. 'You have it with you?'

'I needed something to read on the train. Here.' He pulled the sheaf of papers out of his coat pocket and held them out. 'Names, pedigrees, biographies and photographs.'

She made no attempt to take them. 'Thorough.'

'He means business,' Raff agreed, letting the papers fall down onto the desk with an audible thump. It felt as if he had put down a heavy burden. 'Now do you understand?'

She still wasn't giving an inch. 'Couldn't you just talk to him?'

Raff laughed. 'No one *just talks* to Charles Rafferty. We all tug our forelock and scuttle away to do his bidding. Or run away. Both Polly and I took that route.'

He sighed and picked the papers up again, shuffling them. 'I owe you an apology. It doesn't matter even if you do know where Polly is...' she opened her mouth to interject and he held up his hand '...but I'm sure you don't. She's covered her traces well and I don't blame her.'

The only person he could blame right now was himself. They were so estranged she couldn't, wouldn't confide in him.

Concern was etched onto Clara's face. 'Is she okay?'

Raff shook his head. 'I doubt it. It turns out that great profits and great PR aren't enough. My grandfather showed his gratitude for an another excellent year's trading by telling Polly he was never going to make her CEO, and he is going to sign the company over to me.'

'Ouch.'

Clara sank back into her seat, a sign the battle was over. Thank goodness. Raff had been through enough emotional wars in the last few days. He leant against her desk, grateful for the support. 'That was just the start of it.' Raff ran a hand through his hair. Damn, he was tired. What a ridiculous mess. 'We owe him a lot, Polly and me. It's hard to stand up to him. But this was so wrong I had to say something.' His mouth twisted as he pictured the scene. 'I managed to stay calm but he got completely worked up and ended up collapsing in the most dramatic fashion.'

Raff was aware that he was making light of the situation, but the moment his grandfather had clutched his chest and collapsed was branded in his mind. 'I thought we'd lost him.'

Clara reached a tentative hand across the desk, then pulled it back, seemingly unsure how to react. 'Is he okay?'

'Angina. Apparently he's kept that a secret along with his plans. He's to be kept quiet and not allowed to get worked up, which is a little like telling a baby not to cry. And he is taking full advantage of the situation.' Despite himself Raff grinned. He had to admire his grandfather's sheer bloody-mindedness.

'As soon as I walked through the hospital-room door today he handed me this list.' He held up his hands. 'I know I should have told him the truth right then but seeing as the last time I upset him he collapsed, I didn't. I admit I panicked—next thing I knew I was telling him I had a girlfriend already, it was pretty serious and I was agreeing to bring her along to meet him on Sunday. Two days isn't a long time to find a convincing fake girlfriend, you know.'

Clara leant back in her chair and regarded him solemnly but Raff could swear those cat's eyes of hers were sparkling. 'You seem to be in somewhat of a predicament.'

'I am.' He nodded, trying his best to look downcast as hope shot through him. He needed someone cool, someone professional, someone who understood the rules. She would be perfect, if he could just make her see it.

'I don't understand why you lied in the first place. A

few dates isn't going to kill you, is it?' She was looking stern again.

Raff sighed. It was so hard to explain without sounding like an arrogant idiot. 'I have no intention of sticking around and raising expectations would be unfair.'

'Presumptuous.'

'Hardly.' He laughed but there was little humour in it. 'These women aren't the sort to get carried away, at least not where their futures are concerned. The Rafferty name and fortune is old enough and big enough to put me on several "most eligible bachelor" lists. Why do you think I stay out of the country?'

'Is marriage and a family really so terrible?' For a moment Raff thought he saw sadness shimmering in her face but one blink and it was gone, replaced by her usual cool professionalism.

'No,' he admitted. 'But not for me, not yet. There's a lot I need to do before I'm ready for that kind of commitment.'

If he ever was. He'd seen firsthand just what marriage could do. He still didn't know what was worse: his grandmother staying put out of martyred duty or his mother fleeing as soon as things got tough. Either way it had been hard for Polly and him.

Not that any of his school friends had fared much better. Outside gravy adverts, he still wasn't entirely sure that happy families existed.

'Look, I appreciate that I approached this all wrong but I could really use your help.'

She shook her head. 'It doesn't feel right.'

'Clara, please.' He wasn't too proud to beg. 'You would be perfect: you own your own business, know Polly. My grandfather will adore you.'

'Me!' Was that panic on her face? But there was something else too. She was trying to hide it but she was intrigued.

Raff pressed the point home. 'Look, I'll pay you by the day, even if I only need you for a couple of hours, and I'll owe you. There must be something I can do for you. Don't you need an eligible date at all? Wedding, christening, bar mitzvah?'

'My diary's empty.' But her lush mouth was tilted up into a smile. 'Socially at least.'

'Even better,' he said promptly. 'I'm promising you fine dining, glamorous parties and a clothes allowance. Think of me as a particularly masculine fairy godfather whisking you away to the ball.'

'I can't just drop everything.' But, oh, she looked tempted. 'I have a business, a daughter. What's she supposed to do whilst I'm out gallivanting with you?'

'Gallivanting and drumming up business,' Raff said slyly. Bullseye. Temptation was giving way to interest. 'Think of the contacts you'll make.'

'Contacts in London,' she demurred.

'With your talents it wouldn't matter if they lived in Antarctica,' he assured her. 'You'll be soothing out the wrinkles in half of London's lives in no time. And it won't be for long. I'm hoping to get everything sorted out within a month, six weeks tops. I'm sure your parents won't mind babysitting.'

'No.' She looked down at her computer screen, shielding her expression from him. 'I don't know, Raff. I'd have to call in a lot of favours, for work and Summer. I need to think about it.'

'I'll pay you double your daily rate and cover all costs. And if we're successful a bonus. Ten thousand pounds.'

'That's the second time this week you've offered

me ten thousand pounds.' Clara smiled sweetly at him. 'Burning a hole in your pocket?'

Ten thousand pounds. Small change to someone like Raff Rafferty but not to her. Add the daily double rate and this job looked as if it could be pretty lucrative.

A much-needed cash injection. Sure, things were ticking along nicely, turnover was healthy. But so were her outgoings. She chose her staff carefully and paid them well, used the best products, made sure she had people on call at all hours. She had a brilliant reputation but maintaining it cost money. It made it hard to save enough to expand and she was wary of borrowing.

If this extra job lasted six weeks she could make fifteen thousand pounds more than she had budgeted for. Enough for recruitment and advertising in a wider area, another small van. Maybe she could even engage a part-time PA for the office? She handled so many of the emails and calls whilst she was out and about. Keeping the office open and staffed in business hours would be fantastic.

It would be added security. For her and for her daughter.

But it would mean spending those next six weeks with Raff Rafferty. A man who unnerved her, flustered her. Could she handle it?

He was still perched on her desk, affecting nonchalance, but the tense set of his shoulders was a giveaway. He wasn't as relaxed as he liked to make out. He needed her.

Automatically she tapped at her keyboard, lighting up the dormant screen and clicking onto her emails, the very act beginning to calm her taut nerves. The long list of unread emails in bold might daunt some people but she found them soothing, purposeful and she scanned through the subject lines looking for an answer, a reason to turn him down.

Or an excuse to say yes.

Her inbox was the usual mixture of confirmations, enquiries, queries, staff correspondence and sales, nothing meaty, nothing distracting at all. She was about to close it down when a name caught her eye. Pressure filled her chest, making it hard to breathe, and for one long moment everything, the room, Raff Rafferty, her work disappeared.

An email from Byron.

Clara blinked, unsure whether she was seeing things or if the email was actually there. Her hand hovered over her mouse, unable to click as dizzying possibilities filled her mind. *He was coming over, he wanted to see Summer, to be involved.*

Her daughter wanted for nothing, except for an interested, loving father. Could that be about to change? This was the first time he had contacted her in ten years—that had to be a good sign, right?

'Clara, are you okay? If you don't want to do it that's fine. I'll call in a favour or two. I'd have preferred to keep things professional, that's all.'

'What?' With difficulty Clara fought her way past all the possibilities and emotions swirling dizzily around her brain. 'Sorry, I just need to read this. I'll be with you in a second.'

She noticed detachedly that her hand was shaking as she clicked on the email, the words were dancing in front of her eyes, making no sense at all. She blinked again, forcing herself to concentrate.

Dear Miss Castleton…

The opening line made her reel back, shocked by its formality, but, grimly determined, she read on.

Both Mr Byron Drewe and Mr Archibald Drewe will be visiting London the first week in May and would like to know if it is convenient for you to meet with them to discuss your daughter's future. Her presence is not required at the meeting.

Please send me any dates and times that week that would be convenient for you to meet and I will let you know the final arrangements and venue nearer the time. Any expenses you incur will of course be covered. Please provide the relevant receipts.

On behalf Mr Drewe Jr

Her first communication in years—and it was from Byron's secretary.

Her head was suddenly clear, the dizziness and anticipation replaced with hotly righteous anger. How dared they? How dared they dismiss Summer, summon Clara as if she were a servant? How dared they offer to pay her expenses—as long as she provided receipts like an untrustworthy employee?

Although Byron's father had always thought she was a gold-digging good-time girl, she had just naively hoped Byron believed in her, believed in their daughter. Despite everything.

Byron had spent so much time stringing her along, promising her they would be a family, but he hadn't even had the guts to tell his father about the baby. And once his father found out that was the end.

It was a straight choice: Clara and Summer or his family fortune. Turned out it was no choice at all.

Even then he had lied, promised he'd find a way, that

he loved her, loved Summer. Her heart twisted painfully. He had just wanted her to leave quietly, to not make a scene.

Clara's eyes locked onto the photo that sat on her otherwise clutter-free desk and the anger left just as suddenly as it had arrived. Dark hair, dark eyes, just like her father. Clara's feelings didn't matter here; Byron's behaviour didn't either. Summer was the one who counted and this was the first communication she had had from her daughter's father in years. He wanted to meet. Maybe he wanted to be involved.

Or maybe not. But she had to try. If only she didn't have to do it all alone. Of course her parents would come with her if she asked, but she didn't trust them not to threaten to castrate Byron with the butter knife—or actually do it. Not that he didn't deserve it but it wasn't quite the reconciliation she was hoping for.

Her parents were amazing. Supportive and loving and endlessly giving with their time. Clara couldn't have managed without them. But every now and then she couldn't help but wonder what it would be like to be part of a couple, to have a co-parent. Someone who was there all the time to laugh with at the funny bits, to burst with pride at all the amazing things only a parent could truly understand. To help when things got a little bumpy.

It wasn't that she minded being both mother and father to her daughter, she just wished for Summer's sake that she didn't have to be.

Clara scrolled back to the top of the email and reread it intently. If it were just going to be Byron, then meeting him alone would have been difficult, probably emotional, but eminently doable. His father's presence changed everything. He was a hard, harsh man. Clara sagged. She tried so hard to be strong but she really didn't want to do this alone.

'Here, drink this.' A coffee slid across the desk, rich and dark. 'You look like you've had a shock.'

Clara reached out for the white mug, absurdly touched by the gesture. 'Thanks,' she said, blinking rapidly. *No, don't you dare cry,* she told herself fiercely.

'I make a good listener, you know.' He was back leaning against her desk, cradling a mug of his own, concern in his eyes. 'Besides, you know a lot of my family secrets.'

Clara opened her mouth, a polite rebuff on the tip of her tongue, but closed it as a thought hit her.

Maybe she didn't have to be alone after all?

The memory of his earlier offer hung there tempting, intoxicating. He owed her a favour. Anything she wanted. What if she didn't have to face Byron and his father alone?

'I'll do it.' The words were sudden, abrupt, loud in the quiet office. 'If you guarantee me double time in office hours, treble at evenings and weekends, the bonus at the end of the six weeks and...' she swallowed but forced herself to look up, to meet his eyes '...and you will accompany me to one meeting. Agreed?'

It was Raff's turn to pause, the blue eyes regarding her quizzically, probing beneath her armour. 'Agreed,' he said finally.

Clara exhaled the breath she didn't even know she was holding. 'It's a deal.' She held out her hand. 'I'll see you on Sunday.'

His hand reached out to take hers, folding over it in a gesture that was far more like a caress than a handshake. 'Tomorrow. I'll pick you up at noon.'

'But...' Clara tried to withdraw her hand but it was

held fast in his cool grip '…I thought you needed a date to meet your grandfather on Sunday.'

He smiled, the devilry back in his eyes. 'I do, but we need to get to know each other first. You and I are going on a date.'

CHAPTER FOUR

IT WAS BECOMING an annoying habit, somehow agreeing to the outrageous when she meant to refuse.

She'd felt sorry for him, fool that she was. She'd been lured in by a weary expression, candour and charm. A moment of personal weakness.

And yet there was a certain excitement about getting dressed up, about going somewhere other than The Swan. About going out with an undeniably attractive man.

Even if it wasn't a real date.

It was probably a good thing she had said yes. It was so long since she had been on any kind of date she was bound to be a little rusty, a little awkward. This was an opportunity to practise without any pesky expectations hanging over her.

And that was all this fizz in her veins was. It certainly had nothing to do with Raff Rafferty. It was about a pretty dress, a chance to wear her hair down, to put on a lipstick a little darker, a little redder than she wore for work. A chance for heels.

No, Clara decided, eying herself critically in the mirror, she didn't look too shabby. The vintage-style green tea dress was flattering and demure teamed with black patent Mary Janes and her hair was behaving for once, falling in a soft wave onto her shoulders.

She glanced at her watch. Five minutes. She wanted to be downstairs, sitting at her desk, working when he arrived. She might be all dressed up but this was work. Letting him upstairs, into her private space, was a step far too far.

And there could be no blurred lines.

She took a long look around the small, cosy sitting room. It wasn't the grandest of homes, the fanciest. But it was hers, hers and Summer's. Her sanctuary.

She'd bought it, paid for it, chosen the wallpaper, decorated it. Okay, there was a patch where it wasn't perfectly lined up but it was hers.

Raff would dominate the room, suck all the air out of the space.

Make it unsafe.

The urge to sink onto the overstuffed velvet sofa was almost overwhelming. To play hooky from work, from responsibilities, from this devil's pact. She could curl up with a large bar of chocolate and a Cary Grant film, block out the world for a few blissful hours. She pulled her phone out of her bag—one call and this whole crazy arrangement would be over before it had even begun.

Just one click. So easy.

Her finger moved to the contact list icon and hovered there.

Brrriiiing! The doorbell's loud chime echoed through the room, making her jump.

Panic caught in her throat, making breathing difficult for one long second. Clara put her hand to her stomach and took a deep breath, purposefully clearing her mind, filling her lungs, allowing herself a moment to calm.

This isn't real, she told herself. *This is work. This is my business. I'm happy to clean loos, I'll stock shelves, I even pick up dog dirt. I should be looking forward to a few weeks of socialising instead. Any of my staff would kill to swap with me.*

She could do this.

But a part of her would much rather be scrubbing a room out from top to bottom, picture rail to skirting boards, than spend any more time alone with Raff Rafferty.

And the other part of her was looking forward to it just a little bit too much.

'Relax, this is supposed to be fun.' Raff threw an amused look over at his passenger. Clara sat up ramrod straight, clutching the seat as if it were her last hope. 'I'm a safe driver.'

'In a very old car.'

'She's not old, she's vintage.' He patted the steering wheel appreciatively. 'These Porsche 911s were *the* It Car in their day.'

'In the middle of the last century.'

'She's not quite that old. This is a seventies' design classic.' It was the only car Raff had ever owned. She might be red, convertible and need a lot of loving maintenance but she was a link to his father, the only link he had.

'The seventies,' Clara scoffed. 'The decade that taste forgot.'

Raff grinned. 'Sit back, Clara. Enjoy it—the wind in your hair—if you'd let me put the top down that is, the green of the countryside flashing by. What's not to love?'

Clara was twisting the silver bangle she was wearing round and round. 'A date, you said. I thought you meant a drink in The Swan or, if you wanted to go crazy, a meal at Le Maison Bleu. This isn't a date. This is kidnap.'

'We are supposed to have been together for a few

months. Mad about each other.' Her body got even more rigid if that was at all possible. Raff suppressed a smile. 'So, we need to create a relationship full of memories in just one day. Now we can do this the easy way and actually enjoy ourselves or we can endure a torturous afternoon full of monosyllables and long silences.' His mouth quirked. 'Now, if we were faking a marriage then the latter would be fine.'

Was that a smile? An infinitesimal relaxation of all those rigid muscles?

'What's your favourite colour?'

'My what?' That made her move. Her head swung round so fast he thought she might get whiplash.

'Your favourite colour?'

She shook her head. 'I don't even…why on earth do you want to know that?'

'I'll go first.' He leant back into the leather seat, enjoying the cold of the steering wheel under his hands, the purr of the engine. 'Okay, my favourite colour is sea blue, the sea on a perfect sunny day. Favourite food is a good old-fashioned roast dinner, which is the boarding school boy in me, I know, but there are times when just the thought of Yorkshire puddings keeps me going. I didn't think I was a cat or a dog person but after three days of Mr Simpkins I am definitely veering towards the canine. You?'

He sneaked a look over at his passenger. She was still gripping onto the seat but her knuckles were no longer white. 'If I'd known there was going to be a quiz I'd have prepared,' she said, but her voice was less frosty.

It took a few long moments before she spoke again. 'Okay, green, I think. Spring is my favourite season. I hate it when the trees are bare. I grew up with cats so I'll stick up for Mr Simpkins. What was the other one?

Food? It's not sophisticated but when I was travelling and eating all this amazing street food I craved cheese sandwiches. My dad's cheese sandwiches. Home-made bread, cheddar so mature it can't remember being young and his patented plum chutney.'

'Just a simple sandwich?'

'As simple as it gets in my house. Dad's a foodie.'

'You went travelling?' That was unexpected. Maybe they had something in common after all. 'I can't exactly visualise you with a backpack! How old were you?'

There was a long pause. 'Eighteen,' she said finally.

'Where did you go?' As Raff knew all too well, most people jumped at the opportunity to recount every second of their travels. It could be worse than listening to other people's dreams. Clara Castleton was obviously the exception; her silence was so chilly it was as if he'd asked her to recite *The Rime of the Ancient Mariner*. Backwards.

'Thailand to start with,' she said reluctantly after the pause got too long. 'Cambodia, Vietnam and then Bali and on to Australia.' She paused again. 'I was there for two years.'

Raff shook his head. 'When I was eighteen I could barely find my own way to university, let alone travel halfway across the world. Your parents must have been worried sick.'

She laughed, a dry hard laugh with no humour in it. 'I was so sure I was invincible I think I had them fooled too.'

Fooled? Interesting word.

'I planned for so long I don't think there was room to worry, really.' She wasn't really talking to him, he realised, more lost in the past. 'My grandfather was in the merchant navy and he had always told me all these stories of places he had been to. I wanted to see it all. Other kids have posters of pop stars on their wall, I had maps and routes and pictures of magical places I wanted to go to. I was babysitting at thirteen, running errands for neighbours and every penny went into my travel fund. I was going to start out in Asia then Australia, New Zealand, on to Japan then South America, finishing off with a Greyhound trip round the States.'

He could picture her. Intent, focused, planning on conquering the world. 'Did you get to go? Did you see all of those places?'

'No.' Her voice was colourless. 'I had Summer instead.'

'Hang on.' He turned and looked at her rigid profile. 'Did you have your daughter while you were away?'

'She was born in Australia.'

He whistled softly. 'That must have been tough. So you cut your adventures short, flew home and became the responsible, capable woman you are today.' He shook his head. 'Quite some achievement.'

He thought he was such a tough guy but his adventures were orderly by comparison. He always knew where he was going to sleep that evening even if it was in a sleeping bag in a shared tent; he had a ticket back arranged, plans for a month of surfing and partying organised. He even got a wage, for goodness' sake. Clara had taken off at an age most people were still figuring out the Tube and had spent three years travelling. Even a pregnancy and a baby hadn't slowed her down.

When she didn't answer he turned to look at her; she was looking out of the window but her body was slumped. It wasn't the posture of someone who had achieved something remarkable. It was more like despair.

'Are you going to tell me where we are going?' she

asked, straightening and turning to him with a polite smile.

The confidences were obviously at an end.

'I don't need to tell you,' he said as he smoothly turned the car through a pair of metal gates, the only break in a sea of barbed-wire fencing that ran along one side of the road screening off the fields beyond. 'We're here.'

'We're what?' Clara twisted in her seat and looked around her, horror on her face as she took in the barbed wire. 'You *are* kidnapping me. Where are we? What is this?'

'*This* is one of the premier activity sites in the country.' Raff flashed her a smile. 'I hope you like mud.'

'You want me to do what?'

Clara wasn't sure what was worse. She ticked the offending items off on a mental list. Lists usually were soothing, bringing order and meaning.

She wasn't sure anything could bring meaning to her current situation.

First, the mud. There was certainly a lot of it, all greeny-brown, glutinous and deep. Second, the outfit. All that time spent wondering what to wear, turned out she needed baggy camouflage trousers, desert boots that had been worn by who knew how many other smelly, sweaty, muddy feet and a shapeless T-shirt that was the exact colour of the mud. Yep, it all came back to mud.

Mud that she, Clara Castleton, was supposed to be trampling, running, heck, apparently she was supposed to be crawling in it. On her belly.

Which brought her to number three. Men. Smirking men. Okay, toned, built men, the kind that actually stretched out their T-shirts in all kinds of good ways, who filled out the baggy trousers with bulging thighs, who wore the mud on their faces with aplomb. Men who belonged here as she most definitely did not.

The most annoying of the men, 'Call me Spiral', as *if* that were really his name, began to repeat the instructions in the same loud bark. 'Run through that trough, climb that rope, go over that bridge, swing across the ravine, crawl under the net, slide…'

'I heard all of that the first two times.' Clara folded her arms and glared up at him, deliberately ignoring the fourth and most annoying thing of all: a palpably amused Raff Rafferty. 'I'm still not clear why.'

'Because I told you to,' Spiral said with no hint of irony. 'Now get your butt over to the starting line.'

'Come on, Clara.' Raff was openly grinning. 'This is supposed to be fun. Where's your sense of adventure?'

Back in Australia. Left behind with her backpack, her travel journals and her well-thumbed traveller's guide.

'*This* is your idea of a date?' She rounded on him. 'What's wrong with a walk, a picnic, doves and flowers?'

'Too obvious. Besides, I had the chance to try this place out and see if I want to hire it for a staff conference. I'm multitasking. I thought you'd approve,' he said with a self-righteous air that made Clara want to smack him—or tip him into the mud that suddenly looked a lot more tempting.

'This isn't just a lousy date, it's a cheap date?'

Raff leant in close, his breath sweet on her cheek. 'It's a fake date and you are on triple time. Enjoy it. Think about what a lovely story it makes.'

Clara gritted her teeth. 'One for the grandkids?'

'In our case one for my grandfather. Do you want to go first or shall I show you how it's done?'

Eying the long trail of ropes, platforms, nets and pits, Clara felt her stomach drop. This was going to be incredibly undignified. But there was no way she was going to look weak in front of him. 'I'll go.'

She refused to look back as she walked to the start line, painfully aware that all the conversation had stopped and every khaki-clad man was staring at her, lips curled with amusement. They were waiting for her to fail. To give up.

They were in for a surprise. She hoped.

'Come on,' Clara told herself fiercely as she stood at the rope marking the beginning and stared out at what looked like miles of hell. The trail started with a long, shallow trough that Clara was supposed to run through. Correction, wade through. The trough was filled with the ubiquitous mud and led to a cargo net that she was sure was higher than her house.

That was just the start.

Weekly Pilates might be good for her stress levels but it hadn't prepared her for this.

'On the count of three,' Spiral roared. 'One, two, three!'

Clara hesitated for less than a second and then, with a muttered curse, pushed herself forward, managing not to yell as she sank calf deep into the cold, gloopy mud.

'Faster,' Spiral yelled. 'Are you a man or a mouse?'

Answering him would have used up more oxygen than he was worth. Clara set her mouth mutinously and forged on. Too slow and she would prove the smirking men right, too fast and she knew she'd pitch face first into the mud. She set herself a steady trot, trying to ignore the cold, clamminess on her lower legs and the sucking noise as she pulled her leg out of the mud and put one hand onto the rope net, ready to pull herself up the impossible height.

Her eyes were focused on each obstacle; there was

no room in her mind for anything but the task. Spiral's encouraging shouts, the cheers of the other staff were just background noise. Clara was aware of nothing but the hammering of her heart, the pounding of the blood in her ears, the burn in her thighs and her arms as she pulled, swung, jumped, waded and crawled. She had no idea how long she had been there. Minutes? Hours?

Heck, it could have been days.

'Come on, Clara.' How on earth had Raff caught up with her? He was breathing hard, his hair damp with exertion, the dark blue eyes alight with life. She should be mad with him; she was absolutely filthy, totally exhausted, every muscle hurt and people kept yelling at her. And yet…

Adrenaline was pumping through her so fast she was almost weightless; the whole world had contracted to this place, this task. She was alive. Really, truly alive.

She reached out for the rope swing, and missed. Immediately Raff was there, one arm steadying her as she leant further forward off the narrow wooden platform, reaching out into thin air.

'Got it!' Giddy with triumph, she grabbed the rope and pulled it towards her. Putting both hands firmly on it, she wrapped one leg around it and tried to jump on it, slithering back down to the platform as she missed. 'Darn it!'

'Here, let me.'

Clara wanted to tell him no, that she had this, but he was too quick, steadying the rope and, as she jumped again, giving her a quick push up. A jolt of electricity ran through her as his hand pressed against her back but before she could react he had pushed and she was off, swinging through the air.

Her limbs were trembling with the exertion as she

reached the last obstacle, the crawl net. To conquer it successfully she had to lie down, fully face down, in the mud and wiggle her way under ten metres of tight net.

She took a deep breath, the oxygen a welcome tonic to her tired, gasping lungs, and flung herself down into the oozing depths, pushing herself under the net and wiggling through the endless claustrophobic dark, wet mud until she reached the final rope. Once her head was through she gulped in welcome, blessed, clean air before painfully pulling the rest of her out. She lay there collapsed in the mud for five seconds, too exhausted to try and get to her feet.

The mud didn't seem so bad any more. She couldn't tell where it ended and she began. She had turned into some kind of swamp monster.

'That was a very good try.' Spiral's loud tones intruded on the muddy peace and Clara forced herself to pull onto her knees. 'Well done, Clara.'

A glow of pride warmed her. 'Thanks,' she said, drawing her hand across her face, realising too late that rather than wipe the mud off she was adding to it. Spiral held out one meaty hand and effortlessly pulled her to her feet, wrapping a blanket—khaki, of course, she noted—around her shoulders and, grabbing a mug from a plastic picnic table, pressed it into her hands.

Tea. Milky, sugary, the opposite of how she usually liked it. It was utterly delicious.

'You survived.' Raff had eschewed his blanket but was cradling his tea just as eagerly as she was. 'What did you think?'

'That was...' filthy, hard, undignified, unexpected '...exhilarating.'

He broke into an open grin. 'Wasn't it? Do you think

my staff will enjoy it? I thought that it could be the performance award this year. Followed by dinner, of course!'

'That sounds good.' As the adrenaline wore off Clara was increasingly aware of how cold she was; she suppressed a shiver. 'I hope you're going to let them get changed before dinner.'

'I'm kind like that.' He eyed her critically. 'Talking of which, you look freezing. The showers are back in the changing room. Go, warm up, get changed and then I owe you lunch, anything you want.'

Hot water, clean clothes, food. They all sounded impossibly, improbably good. 'You do owe me,' she agreed, putting the mug back onto the table before taking a few steps towards the low stone building where nirvana waited. She paused, impelled by a sudden need to say something, something unexpected.

'Raff,' she said. 'I had fun. Thank you.'

It was the last thing he had expected her to say. Standing there completely covered in mud, the baggy trousers plastered to her legs, the filthy T-shirt clinging to every curve. Raff had expected sulking or yelling, even downright refusal. He didn't expect her to thank him.

He'd known the challenge would shake her up, had secretly enjoyed the thought of seeing prim and judgemental Clara Castleton pushed so far out of her comfort zone—turned out the joke was on him.

'I'm glad,' he said, aware of how inadequate his response was. 'I thought you'd enjoy it.'

Clara smiled. A proper, full-on beam that lightened her eyes to a perfect sea green, emphasised the curve of her cheeks, the fullness of her mouth. She was dirty, bedraggled and utterly mesmerising. The breath left his body with an audible whoosh.

'Liar,' she said. 'You thought I'd hate it. And you were this close…' she held up her hand, her forefinger and thumb just a centimetre apart '…this close to being right.'

'Yes.' The blood was hammering through his veins, loud, insistent. All he could focus on was her wide mouth, the lines of her body revealed so unexpectedly by her wet clothes. What would it be like to take that step forward? To pull her close? To taste her?

Dangerous.

The word flashed through his mind. It would be dangerous; she would be dangerous. Workaholic single mothers were not his style no matter how enticing their smile. Women like Clara wanted commitment, even if they didn't admit it.

They played by different rules and he needed to remember it—no matter how tempted he was to forget.

CHAPTER FIVE

'THAT WASN'T TOO BAD.' Clara's smile and tone were more than a little forced. At least she was trying.

Which was more than his grandfather had.

'It was terrible.' Raff shook his head, unsure who he was more cross with: his grandfather for being so very rude, or himself for expecting anything different.

He *had* expected his grandfather to be terse and angry with him; it would take more than a suspected heart attack and a week in hospital for Charles Rafferty to get over any kind of insubordination even from his favourite grandson. It was the way he had spoken to Clara that rankled most.

'He's not feeling well and it can't be easy being cooped up in bed.'

Raff appreciated what Clara was trying to do but it was no good; her determined 'little miss sunshine' routine wasn't going to fix this.

'He practically accused you of being a gold-digger,' he pointed out. 'I shouldn't have let him speak to you like that.' He had been poised to walk out, stopped only by her calming hand on his arm, holding him in place, the pressure of her fingers warning him to keep still, keep quiet.

'I wasn't going anywhere.' Clara stopped as they reached the hospital foyer; the marbled floor, discreet wooden reception desk and comfortable seating areas gave it the air of an exclusive hotel—if you ignored the giveaway scent of disinfectant and steamed vegetables. 'I've been called worse.' A wounded expression flashed across her face, so fleeting Raff wasn't sure if he had imagined it.

'Thank you.' The words seemed inadequate. Despite his grandfather's antipathy she had been a dignified presence by his side, not too close, not clingy but affectionate and believable. He was torn between embarrassment that she had witnessed his grandfather's most petulant behaviour and an uncharacteristic gratitude for her silent support.

'No problem.' She was saying all the right things but her tone lacked conviction. 'It's my job after all.'

'Come on.' He needed to get out of here, away from the hospital, away from the toxic mixture of guilt and anger, to push it all firmly away. This was why he preferred to be abroad. He could be his own man out in the field. 'Let's go.'

Clara opened her mouth, about to ask where they were going, and then she slowly shut it again. At least they were in the centre of London—it might be a little damp but whatever Raff had in mind it was unlikely to involve mud.

And Raff obviously needed to blow off steam. He was keeping himself together but his jaw was clenched tight and a muscle was working in his cheek. Clara had been treated like dirt before, dismissed out of hand— but her own family had always been there to support her. She couldn't imagine her own grandfather looking at her with such cold, disappointed eyes. Even a teen pregnancy hadn't shaken his love and belief in her.

Polly had called Raff 'The Golden Boy' but it seemed

to her that his exalted position came with a heavy price. No wonder he had needed to employ Clara, to take some of the pressure his demanding grandfather was heaping on as he took advantage of his illness and frailty. An unexpected sympathy reverberated through her—Raff's need to be as far away from his family as possible was a little more understandable.

She kept pace with a silent, brooding Raff as he walked briskly through the busy streets expertly avoiding the crowds of tourists, the busy commuters and the loitering onlookers. Clara rarely visited London despite the direct rail link; if you asked her she would say she was too busy but the truth was it scared her. So noisy, so crowded, so unpredictable. The girl who once planned to travel the world was cowed by her own capital city.

But here, today, it felt different. Friendlier, more vibrant, the way it had felt when she was a teenager, down for the day to shop for clothes in Camden and hang out in Covent Garden where Maddie hoped to be talent-spotted by a model agency whilst Clara spent hours browsing in the specialist travel bookshop. Was it even still there? All her books and maps were boxed away at her parents' house. Maybe she should retrieve some of them, show them to Summer.

'I need to organise a nurse to look after him,' he said, breaking the lengthy silence. 'The hospital won't allow him home without one. He needs to have a specialist diet too, and he is going to hate that.' His mouth twisted. 'At this rate it's going to be weeks before I can talk about the company with him again.'

'Isn't there anyone else who can intercede? Your grandmother?'

Raff shook his head. 'They're separated. She'll have

a go, if I ask her to, but he's never quite forgiven her for leaving.'

Clara knew that Polly and Raff had been raised by their grandparents but not that they had split up. She swallowed, her throat tight; it was becoming painfully apparent how little she knew of Polly's life. They were supposed to be friends and yet she had no idea where she was or why she'd gone.

But was Clara any better? She didn't confide either, happy to keep the conversation light, to discuss work and plans but never feelings, never anything deep. Maybe that was why they were friends, both content with the superficial intimacy, their real fears locked safely away.

'Have they been split up long?'

'Nearly twelve years.' He gave her a wry smile. 'She waited until after Christmas our first year at university. Didn't want to spoil the holidays, she said. We were just amazed she made it that long. She'd wanted out for a long time.'

'I can't imagine your grandfather is easy to live with.' That was an understatement.

He huffed out a dry laugh. 'He's not. Poor Grandmother, from things she let slip I think she was on the verge of leaving when we came to live with them. She only stayed for Polly and me. Now she lives in central London and takes organised trips, volunteers at several museums and spends the rest of her time at the theatre or playing bridge. She's very happy.'

'What about your parents?' She flushed; curiosity had got the better of her. 'I'm sorry, I don't mean to pry.'

'That's okay. We are meant to be dating, after all, and none of this is exactly state secrets.' He didn't look okay though, his eyes shadowed, his mouth drawn into a straight line. 'My father had a stroke when we were eight.'

'I am so sorry.' Tentatively she reached out and touched his arm, awkward comfort. 'That must have been awful.'

'We thought he was sleeping. The ambulance man said if we had called 999 earlier...' His voice trailed off.

Cold chilled her, goosebumping her arms, her spine as his words hit her—they'd found their father collapsed? Her heart ached for the two small children who had to suddenly grow up in such a terrible way.

'The stroke was devastating.' There was a darkness in his voice, the sense of years of regret, of guilt. 'He had to go into a home—oh, the very best home, you know? All luxury carpets and plush chairs but we still knew, even at that age, that it was a place where people went to die.'

Clara felt for the familiar cold curve of her bangle and began to twist it automatically; she wanted to reach out and hold him, hold the small boy who had to watch his father disintegrate before his eyes.

'Our mother couldn't handle it,' Raff continued, still in that same bleak tone. 'She went away for a rest and just stayed away. So my grandparents stepped in, sent us to boarding school and gave us a home in the holidays—and my poor grandmother had to wait ten years for her escape.'

'Her choice.' Clara knew she sounded brisk, the way she sounded when encouraging Summer to sleep without a nightlight, to go on a school trip, to walk to the corner shop on her own. 'It was the right thing for her at the time. There's no point dwelling on what-might-have-beens. You go mad that way.'

She knew all about that. If she hadn't stayed in that particular hostel, hadn't met Byron. If she'd tried harder with his father, if she'd stayed in Australia. 'Our lives are littered with the paths not taken,' she said. 'But if we spend all our time staring wistfully at them we'll never see what's right in front of us.'

'A sick, unreasonable grandfather, a missing twin and an unwanted job?' But the dark note had gone from his voice and Clara was relieved to see a small smile playing around the firm mouth. He stopped in front of her and turned to look at the golden building in front of them. 'We're here. Welcome to the millstone round my neck.'

It had been a long time since Clara had set foot in Rafferty's. The flagship department store occupied a grand art deco building just off Bond Street and, although it was a little out of the way of the tourists pounding bustling Oxford Street and Regent Street, it was a destination in its own right. Discreet, classy and luxurious; just the name Rafferty's conjured up another era, an era of afternoon tea, cocktails and red, red lipstick.

Tourists flocked here, desperate to buy something, anything, so they could walk away with one of the distinctive turquoise and gold bags; socialites, It Girls and celebrities prowled the halls filled with designer items. Anyone who was anybody—and those who aspired to be—drank cocktails at the bar. Rafferty's was a well-loved institution, accessible glamour for anybody with money to spend.

As a child Clara had visited the store every Christmas to see the spectacular window displays, admire the lights, to confide her wish-list to Father Christmas. It had been one of the highlights of her year—and yet she had never brought Summer. She had never even made the seventy-five-minute-long journey into London with her daughter. London was too big, too noisy, too unpredictable.

But as she stood on the edge of the marble steps, remembering the breathless excitement of those perfect days out, Clara's throat tightened. Choosing the perfect gift, admiring the other shoppers, having afternoon tea in the elegant restaurant, those memories meant Christmas to her. How could she not have passed those memories on to her daughter?

To keep Summer safe? Or to keep Clara herself safe?

Maybe, just maybe, she was a little overprotective.

'Are you going to stand there all day or are you actually coming in?'

Clara swallowed. It must be nice to be Raff Rafferty. Adored heir to all this. So sure of yourself, so confident that you could treat life as one big joke.

And yet there were contradictions there. She might disapprove of the lies he was feeding his grandfather—although after the cold, hostile meeting this morning she understood them. But what was he fighting for? The right to live on his trust fund? The right not to do a day's work?

Clara tried to remember what exactly Polly had told her about him. Not much, which was odd in itself; they were twins after all. She said he was spoilt, that she had to work three times as hard and still didn't receive equal recognition. That he was 'messing around abroad somewhere'. Clara had assumed that he was travelling, partying, having fun. After twenty-four hours in his company she wasn't so sure.

He was arrogant and annoying and treated life as one big joke but he didn't *seem* lazy, didn't seem careless of his family's ties and expectations. He had come running the second he'd thought Polly was in trouble and according to the nurse had spent three days and nights at his grandfather's bedside.

Yep, he was definitely a puzzle but, she reminded herself, he was none of her business. And none of this was real, no matter how surprisingly easy it was to forget that.

'I thought you went away to escape Rafferty's,' she said, walking up the famous curved steps to meet him.

'To escape *running* Rafferty's,' he corrected her, escorting her through the famous gilt and glass revolving doors with a light touch on her elbow.

As soon as he took his hand away the spot he had touched felt cold. Clara had to resist the temptation to rub it, to try and get the heat back.

They had entered a massive circular room topped with an ornate glass dome. It was the heart of Rafferty's, an iconic image, immortalised in film, photos and books. Looking up, Clara saw the famous galleries ringing the dome, three storeys of them. Each storey took up the entire block and was filled with a myriad of desirable items: food, clothes, jewellery, books, accessories, pictures, lamps, rugs.

Down here on the beautifully tiled ground floor the world's leading make-up and perfume brands plied their wares, stalls set out in a semi-circle around the foot of the dome. The middle was always reserved for themed displays and, at Christmas, the giant tree that dominated the room.

It was a wonderland. And the man standing next to her wanted to throw it all away.

'It's not that I'm not proud of Rafferty's,' he said, as if he could read her thoughts. 'It was like having our very own giant playground. We could go anywhere, do anything. Polly would walk around talking to all the staff, finding out what they did and how everything worked. I'd usually be hidden away with a stash of sugary contraband in a stock cupboard somewhere.'

'Sounds idyllic.' She could see it too, a cheeky-faced blond urchin charming his way through the store.

'It was,' he sighed, a faraway look in his eye. 'This was our real home. We held every birthday party here. I had my first kiss in this very room with Victoria Embleton-Jones. She was taller than me and a lot more sure of herself. I was in love for a whole week and then she dumped me for an older man with less sweaty hands and a car. I was devastated.'

'My heart's breaking. How old were you?'

'Fourteen. It took me a whole month to get over her. I still get nervous shakes when I meet anyone called Victoria.' His face was solemn but he couldn't hide the gleam dancing in his eyes.

Clara resisted the urge to snort. 'No wonder this place is so special to you, filled with such poignant memories.' She looked around at the bustling, chattering, spending throngs. 'I used to come here when I was a child.' It felt oddly like a confession. 'Afternoon tea was always a highlight of the holidays. I felt so sophisticated.' She sighed at the memory of delicate porcelain teapots and plates filled with cakes. Clara put a hand to her suddenly hollow stomach; it had been a long morning. 'Is that why we're here?' She tried not to sound too hopeful.

'It's not time for a tea break yet, Miss Castleton.' He shook his head. 'I don't know, can't get the staff these days. First we work and then we reward ourselves with as much cake as you can manage.'

'Work?' Heat washed over her; how had she misread the situation so badly? 'If you need a PA I can certainly supply one.'

'I have a perfectly good if rather terrifying PA. She disapproves of me almost as much as you do.' Raff grinned at her flushed and confused denial. 'No, it's time we went shopping.'

'Shopping? I do grocery shopping, as you know, presents as well, but I contract out personal shopping and interior designing…' She was babbling again but couldn't seem to stop.

'Look around, Clara. You're in the world's most famous department store. I could click my fingers and summon a personal shopper for almost anything you could imagine. No, we are going to get you some clothes.'

She gaped at him. 'I have clothes!'

Raff looked her over, sweeping her up and down assessingly. Clara had to fight every individual muscle to make it stay still; the urge to cover herself protectively, shield herself from those keen eyes, was almost overwhelming.

'You have suits,' he said finally. 'Sharp, businesslike suits. Which is great for the office but no use when you're with me. You have jeans and T-shirts and you have a few pretty dresses like the one you are wearing. That's all fine but none of that will do for black-tie dos, for cocktail parties or any of the other dull but apparently necessary events Polly wastes her free time at.'

'Cocktail parties?' The nearest Clara got to a cocktail party was trying to decide between red or white wine at Sunday lunch. 'I didn't expect…'

'I told you it would be time consuming.' His gaze was steely now. 'I also said I would pay you handsomely and make it worth your while in any way necessary. Unfortunately Rafferty's needs to be present at these events. Grandfather can't and Polly won't, until I track her down and beg her to come home. So it's down to me.'

He looked as if he would rather be sitting alone with Mr Simpkins.

'But you, Clara Castleton, are both my secret weapon and my shield. Your very presence will hopefully steer conversation away from dull topics like where I have been and what my plans are whilst simultaneously saving me from match-making mothers and their eager daughters. For that you need clothes. And luckily for you I am temporarily running an establishment that supplies pretty much any outfit you desire.'

'Wait a minute.' She eyed him suspiciously. 'Have you been sneaking through my things?' Raff's assessment of her wardrobe had been depressingly close to the mark.

Raff took another step closer and took her arm, the touch sending a jolt of electricity shooting up, settling at the base of her stomach, his proximity making every nerve buzz. 'I don't need to. I started working here when I was fourteen and spent at least six months in every department.' He shot her an amused grin. 'I was very successful in ladies' wear.'

'That doesn't surprise me,' she muttered.

'So if you're ready…' he ignored the interruption '…let's shop.'

'You will make someone a very good husband one day.' Clara eyed the rail of clothes that Raff and Susannah, the personal shopper he had co-opted to help them, had picked out. 'Forget the name and fortune, any man who can shop like you will be snapped up.'

Raff leant back against the wall. In a stark contrast to the opulence of the outer store the private changing rooms, exclusively for the use of those rich or lucky enough to secure the services of a personal shopper, were a study in sleek minimalism. The walls were a steely grey, the sofas chic, uncomfortable-looking studies in white and black; in this environment the clothes were the stars.

'It's a good thing one of us showed some interest,' he said. 'Poor Susannah certainly earned her commission today. I don't think she's ever met anyone who dislikes clothes as much as you do.'

Clara bit just as he knew she would. 'I like clothes well enough,' she said indignantly. 'I'm just not into fancy clothes or fancy designers or fancy prices.'

Raff suppressed a smile. He might be playing fairy godfather but this Cinderella wasn't at all interested. She'd probably be far more comfortable cleaning the hearth and making the pumpkin into pies than going to the ball.

'Or fancy shoes...' he said provocatively.

'If feet were supposed to be that elevated...' Clara began.

'Then our bone structure would be quite different,' he finished. 'I know, you told me at least three times and poor Susannah twenty. Normally women weep with gratitude after she supplies them with shoes, not lecture her about osteology. Come on, Cinders, enjoy the glass slippers.'

'Cinderella probably almost broke her neck rushing down those stairs in just one shoe.'

She wasn't giving an inch. He shook his head, his grin wide. 'Fairy tales must be a barrel of laughs at your house. It's important that you play the part well and that means dressing the part too. You don't have to keep any of it after we're finished: sell them and give the proceeds to charity, turn them into bunting. They're yours. Personally I'd say enjoy them. There must be a huge demand for sequinned shifts in Hopeford.'

Her mouth tilted upwards. Her smile was irresistible;

maybe it was a good thing she didn't unleash it often. 'Oh, there is. Perfect for a quiet drink at The Swan.'

'We don't have to take them all,' he pointed out. 'I think you need about six cocktail dresses, the same amount in day dresses and shoes and bags as well. Come on, Cinders, the sooner you try them on and make some decisions, the sooner you can have that cake.'

'I think I preferred the mud,' Clara said, but she unhooked the silver sequinned shift and began to carry it to the curtained-off area at the back. She paused at the curtain and turned back, her eyes lowered, cheeks flushed. 'I feel really uncomfortable about this, Raff, you buying me these clothes. It's one thing paying me for my time but this feels a step too far.' She raised her eyes, meeting his with obvious difficulty. 'I can't begin to offer to pay you for them. I'm sure that I can manage with what I have.'

Raff found himself short of breath, unable to formulate any kind of reply. He had been out with enough women to consider that he had a pretty good grip on the feminine mind even if he had been thrust into a single-sex school long before puberty, but he hadn't seen this coming.

Not one ex, from the trust fund socialite to the vegan gardener, had ever turned down a free outfit from Rafferty's.

He wasn't sure whether he admired her pride—or found her stubbornness frustrating. 'Well technically I won't be buying you anything, they're a gift from Rafferty's, but remember I'm not playing Professor Higgins,' he said as offhandedly as he could. 'I'm just ensuring you have the right outfits for the job I have hired you to do. I supply the, what did you call them? Instruments of torture? You wear them.'

She looked at him searchingly for a long moment before nodding, a short reluctant agreement. 'Of course,' she grumbled, 'these clothes aren't designed for real women. If I was a size-zero giraffe I might find this easier.'

Raff ran his eyes over her approvingly. Clara wasn't built like a model, it was true, nor did she eat like one, thank goodness. The year after university, full of pent-up energy he couldn't expel at work, he had partied hard and dated several models and socialites. He had soon got bored with the shallow crowd he was running with.

And women who thought a piece of lettuce meant a full dinner.

No, give him someone like Clara, not too tall, not too small, curves in all the right places. That shift she was holding, for instance, it would fall to mid-thigh, showcase those fantastic legs, cling to the curve of her bosom.

The room felt very small, just a curtain separating him from the area where Clara would be unbuttoning all those tiny buttons, slipping her dress off, replacing it with the short shift.

He took in a deep breath. It was warm in here, roasting in fact. He should talk to someone about the temperature.

'I think you'll look perfect,' he said hoarsely. 'Why don't you get started? I'll just be…' He waved at the entrance. 'I need to get something.' A brandy, a cold shower, some air.

Left alone, Clara felt curiously deflated. There had been something in Raff's eyes. Something hot, something terrifyingly honest. Something that had awakened feelings she had spent so long hiding from: what it was like to be wanted, what it was like to want.

Clara sank down into the hard-backed chair, the sole

piece of furniture in the spacious curtained-off area. For the first time in a really long time she wished she had someone to lean on, to confide in.

Raff, Byron's impending visit, deciding how to best use the money Raff was paying her. There was so much going on she didn't know where to turn.

But there was no one. She didn't want to worry her mother, Summer was too young, Maddie so busy. She had nobody. It hit her like a blow to the stomach as hot, unwanted tears pricked at the backs of her eyes; she blinked them away, wrapping her arms around herself as if she could ward off the unwanted knowledge. She would be so ashamed if her mother or cousin or the handful of friends she kept in contact with guessed just how she felt.

Lonely.

'Come on, Clara, where will self-pity get you?' She hadn't succumbed when she found out she was pregnant, only eighteen, thousands of miles away from home. She had stayed strong when Byron walked out of her life a month before their baby was born.

She wouldn't, *couldn't* give in now. She had a wonderful, healthy daughter, a thriving business. She was lucky, even if it was hard to remember that sometimes.

Slowly, feeling a little punch drunk, Clara rose to her feet and began to unbutton her dress. She was here to do a job. Feelings had nothing to do with it.

The shift was heavy and yet it felt wonderfully cool and soft against her skin, the sequins sparkling as the spotlights hit it. Reflected in the many mirrors that lined the room, Clara gave in to the temptation to pirouette, loving the way the fabric flattered her. Raff was right: annoyingly, she did feel more confident, more sociable in this fabulous, exorbitantly expensive dress.

Muttering, she forced her feet into a pair of strappy

heels. She had thought that pairing silver shoes with a silver dress would be too much, that she would end up resembling a giant glitterball, but she had been wrong. The outfit looked amazing even with bare, pale legs, minimal make-up and a ponytail. Her stomach fluttered at the thought of really going out dressed like this; hair, make-up, accessories. Raff on her arm.

If she could just walk in the shoes that would be a considerable bonus.

A rustle from the other side of the curtain alerted her to another person's presence. Raff must have returned.

Clara took another look in the mirror. Was that really her? So elegant? The shoes added another four inches to her height, giving her legs the illusion of endless length. The urge to hide, tear off this costume and become her own safe self again was almost overwhelming but Clara sucked in a deep breath. She *would* walk through the curtain; she *would* show Raff.

She would hopefully see that heat in his eyes again.

Heart hammering, the wobble in her step not solely caused by the unfamiliar heels, Clara pulled the curtain open, a self-deprecating remark on her lips. But there was no need to utter it.

The room was empty. Another rail of clothes and matching accessories had joined the first one.

Her stomach plummeted as the adrenaline disappeared. It must have been Susannah she had heard. 'Fool,' she muttered. Clara chewed her cheek, indecisive. Should she wait, try on something else, look for him? Unsure, she walked to the door and peeked out, worry turning to irritation as she saw him, right in front of the door, deep in conversation with a small brunette who was smiling up at him.

'Clara?' Darn it, he had spotted her. 'Sorry, I bumped

into an old colleague.' Was it her imagination or did he hesitate over the word 'colleague'?

'Hi, I'm Lisa.' The brunette smiled over at Clara. 'It's so great to see Raff. I thought he was in Afghanistan.'

She thought what? Beach bum or adrenaline junkie, either way Afghanistan was the last place Clara imagined Raff Rafferty.

Or was it? A picture flashed into her mind. That first afternoon, his face grey with weariness, the kind of weariness from hours and hours of travel, sitting in trucks and small airport waiting rooms not from the pampered world of First Class. The battered jeans, the old kitbag.

None of it had added up at the time but she'd been so convinced that she knew the man she was dealing with she hadn't even stopped to consider that her preconceptions might be skewed.

'No, not this time,' he said with a quick glance over at Clara. Was that embarrassment in his eyes? 'I was in Jordan. We're trying to make sure there are some medical facilities in the camps there but I was needed at home so had to take some leave. How about you?'

Lisa blushed. 'I'm based back in the UK at the moment. Did you know I married Mike, Dr Hardy?'

'I had heard. Congratulations. I did a brief stint with him out in Somalia. He's a great bloke.' Again a swift, almost pleading glance at Clara.

Somalia, Afghanistan, Jordan? Polly had said that Raff was abroad, she had been dismissive, giving Clara the impression that he was partying on a beach somewhere, not working in some of the most dangerous places in the world. Wasn't she worried about him?

'Mike is setting up a paediatric programme here in London for kids that just can't be treated in the field so I'm based here too now. It's not the same but there's a lot to do. Actually…' Lisa eyed him speculatively '…this could be a massive piece of luck running into you like this. What are you doing in five weeks' time? Will you still be here?'

'I think so. Why?'

Lisa clasped her hands together and looked up at Raff hopefully. 'We're holding a fundraising ball, all the great and the good digging deep, you know the kind of thing! We had Phil lined up to speak but he had to pull out. Could you speak in his place?'

Raff shifted from foot to foot, his expression one of deep discomfort. Clara watched him with some amusement.

Good, she thought, *let him get out of this.*

'People don't want to hear from me,' he said eventually. 'They want to hear from the medical teams. They're the ones with the real stories.'

'We have doctors and nurses and helicopter pilots and patients,' Lisa assured him. 'But no one understands that without you guys there wouldn't be a hospital— or water or electricity or a single bed. Turning a dusty piece of desert into a hospital? That's the real heroism. We just turn up when it's ready for us. Don't you agree?' she asked Clara.

Clara looked at Raff with her most innocent expression. 'I really do,' she said. 'He'll be there, don't worry. I guarantee it.'

'Really? That's brilliant. Raff, come along to the office this week and we'll sort out slides and I'll let you know how long you have to speak for. Make it funny but real as well, try and make them cry. That's always worth a few more noughts on the cheque!'

'I'll see what I can do.' He slid his gaze over to Clara. 'I'm sure Clara will be happy to help me. You'll have a bit longer to wait for that cake though, Clara. You need a dress fit for a ball, and a pair of glass slippers too.' His eyes dropped to her feet, wobbling in the thin-heeled sandals. 'I'll tell Susannah to bring the highest she can find.'

CHAPTER SIX

CLARA UNZIPPED THE silver shift and let it spill to the floor. She knew Raff was on the other side of the curtain but his silence was absolute.

Fine, if that was the way he wanted to play it, there was no way she was going to be the one to crack.

She bent down and picked up the dress, carefully putting it on the hanger. Still no sound, not even a sigh. Anticipation clenched at her stomach as she slipped the next outfit, a wide-skirted silk affair in a vivid green, off the rail and put it on, barely bothering to check the mirror before wrenching the curtain aside.

'And?'

He was sitting on the sofa, lounging back seemingly without a care in the world. 'The shoes don't go.'

'They go with the other dress. I didn't change them.' Seriously? Shoes? That was what he was thinking? She wouldn't ask, she wouldn't, she wouldn't... 'Okay. Spill.' For goodness' sake, her self-control was legendary. She prided herself on it! But the need to know was burning her and she didn't want to examine why. 'Who was that?'

Raff got to his feet with leonine grace and sauntered over to the rail. 'I think we agreed on the red shoes for that outfit, didn't we? It'll work very well for lunches.

What?' He was regarding her with faint surprise. No wonder. Clara was aware she resembled a fishwife more than a lady-who-lunches, hands on hips and head back. 'I did introduce you. That was Lisa. We worked together.'

'Yes, in Somalia,' Clara said as patiently as she could manage. 'Why were you in Somalia?'

'I worked with her husband in Somalia,' Raff corrected her. 'I knew Lisa in Sri Lanka. I think…' he finished doubtfully. 'It might have been Bangladesh.'

'Mercenary or spy?' The words burst out before she could stop them.

'What?' The look of utter shock on his face was almost comical.

'You keep quiet about what you do, you work in some of the most dangerous places on earth, it has to be one or the other.' It was the only thing that made sense.

'Because spies and mercenaries love to throw fundraising balls?' How she hated that amused smile. He had of course honed in on the only flaw in her thinking.

'Part of your cover.' Okay, not the best idea she'd ever had.

'Interesting theory. I like it. I always fancied myself as a suave, martini-drinking type. Sorry to burst your little fantasy but nothing so exciting.' He paused and handed her another dress, a fifties-style halterneck that Clara secretly rather liked. 'Here, try this on. I'm a project manager for Doctors Everywhere.'

Oh.

Kitbags, dangerous places, fundraising balls, hospitals. That made sense. Reluctantly Clara let go of her visions of chase scenes, fancy cars, an evil mastermind bent on world domination.

'Doctors Everywhere?' she echoed as she obediently accepted the outfit and tottered her way back to the curtain.

Of course she had heard of them; they provided healthcare in the Third World, in refugee camps, in war spots.

They were incredibly well respected. Not the natural playground of playboys. Which meant that every little preconception she had was wrong.

Clara changed on autopilot, so many thoughts tumbling around her brain it was as if her head had joined the circus.

Somehow the emotion she could most easily identify was anger. She pushed away the thought that this might be a little unreasonable. After all, what Raff Rafferty did with his time was really none of her business.

He had made it her business, she argued back as she fumbled with the buttons at the back and cautiously zipped up the tight bodice. Employing her, introducing her to his grandfather, buying her these exquisite, over-priced, really very flattering clothes.

He had made her complicit.

The curtain made a most satisfying swoosh as she pulled it open, and she stomped forward only wobbling twice. Damn, she was still wearing the stupid sliver shoes. No wonder Cinderella had discarded her glass slippers; she was probably in agony by midnight.

'Doctors Everywhere?'

'Yep.' He was still standing up, leaning against the back wall. The plain colour of the backdrop suited him, made the hair a little blonder, the eyes even bluer. Not that she was noticing. Not at all.

Oh, no, she was putting her hands on her hips again. Ten years of careful, calm control and yet one day with this man and she was unleashing her inner harpy. 'Which is obviously such a terrible thing for you to do you had no choice but to lie to your sister and grandfather?' Clara could hear the sarcasm dripping from her voice and tried to calm down.

This wasn't her family. Why did she care so much?

He looked at her for one long moment and Clara thought he wasn't going to answer. After all, the annoying voice of reason whispered, he didn't have to explain himself to her, but after a moment he sighed. 'I didn't lie. They know what I do.'

'They *know*? Then why does your grandfather want you to take over Rafferty's? And why has Polly never mentioned it?' Clara twisted the heavy curtain fabric around her hand and studied him curiously.

'According to Grandfather it's just a phase I'll grow out of. As for Polly…' He glanced away, staring at the stark walls as if the answer would be found there. 'I don't know what she hates more—that Grandfather always wanted me to have this place or that I *don't* want it. I hoped that if I went away she would be able to convince him that she was the better candidate but she accused me of running away. Maybe she was right.'

'Why?' So she was curious; it wasn't a crime.

He pushed himself off the wall and walked over to the small table, which held a jug of iced water and a bunch of grapes, nothing that could mark the valuable clothes. 'Want one?' he offered and she shook her head.

He poured himself a glass. Clara watched as he took a long, deep drink, her eyes drawn to the way his tanned throat worked as he swallowed. He set the glass down and, with a purposeful manner, as if he had come to some kind of internal decision, he turned and faced her squarely, eyes holding hers.

'Because I *was* running away,' he said. 'Away from expectations and responsibility and guilt and family. I was at a really low point, Polly and I were fighting,

Grandfather kept promoting me higher and higher whilst passing her over—and believe me it wasn't on merit—and then I met up with a friend who was volunteering with Doctors Everywhere. He mentioned that they always needed people with good project-management skills and a second language—to be honest I didn't think I had a chance. A pampered boy like me who thought travelling second class was slumming it?

'Nobody was as surprised as me when they took me. But I didn't ever consider not going.' He grimaced. 'I genuinely thought it was a one-off. That I'd be back in three months relieved to be back behind my desk.' His mouth twisted with a wry humour as he remembered. 'I nearly was. That first three months was the most difficult, stressful three months of my life. It made prep school seem like a holiday camp. I couldn't wait for it to be over.

'But I signed up for my next assignment the day after I was released.' He shrugged. 'I didn't know then that I had been broken in easy—an existing brick-built hospital, my own bedroom, not a war zone. Somalia was a horrid shock. But I signed up again as soon as I returned from there, for six months that time. It's like a drug. I think I can walk away any time but I always go back for more.

'Because…it makes a real difference, Clara. Everything I did changed somebody's world. I might not be the person performing the operations—but I was the person making sure that the operations could take place. That we had beds and kits and food and water. It mattered.'

'And Rafferty's doesn't?'

'Not to me.'

Raff heard his words echo around the room. He'd thought them many times but had never said them aloud.

But the sky didn't fall in, the world didn't end, his

grandfather didn't appear in a puff of smoke to blast him away like a vengeful god. He was still the same man, still standing there.

Only everything had changed. He couldn't fool himself or his family any longer. He wasn't working away for a sabbatical or a career break or for an adventure. It was what he *did*, what he needed to do, what he was. And it didn't matter whether his grandfather left him Rafferty's or not, he would just sign it over to Polly. It was hers; she deserved it.

There was no point waiting and hoping that things would work out his way; he had to make them happen.

Clara was still looking at him, that green gaze of hers intent. He didn't know what he had expected. Shock? Disapproval? Horror? It was hard to remember sometimes that to other people Rafferty's was no more than a place to buy beautifully gift-wrapped socks or get an expensive but perfect afternoon tea. It wasn't the centre of everyone's world.

What was it about this woman that made him want to confess, to spill all the secrets that he preferred to keep locked away so tightly? Was it her directness, her transparency? The unexpected way she lit up when she smiled?

Their eyes were locked, the colour rising faint on her cheeks, her breath coming a little quicker. The full mouth parted slightly. Heat rose through him, sudden and shocking. The walls of the room seemed to contract; all he could see was her. The red-gold hair tumbling around her creamy shoulders, delicate tempting shoulders exposed by the deceptively demure halterneck dress, shoulders that were begging for a man to touch them, to kiss the triangle of freckles delicately placed like an old-fashioned patch.

Raff swallowed, blood thrumming round his body, his heartbeat accelerating. She was so very close, green eyes darkening until they resembled the storm-tossed sea. Just a few short steps…

'That suits you.' Raff jumped as Susannah heeled in a third rail. 'Although I don't think those are the right shoes.'

Clara pulled her eyes from his, pulling at the hem of the dress. The room felt a good ten degrees colder and suddenly a lot bigger. 'No,' she agreed, throwing Raff a faint, complicit smile that warmed him through. 'After ten minutes in these shoes I am completely convinced that they are absolutely not the right shoes.'

'Have you made any decisions yet? I've brought a few formal evening gowns as Mr Raff instructed.' Susannah gestured towards the rail. 'He didn't specify but with your colouring I thought greens, blacks and golds might be most suitable. Do you want me to stay and help you try them on?' She picked up a long, dark dress and carried it into the curtained area, hanging it onto one of the silver rails that hung between the floor-length mirrors.

'That's very kind but I think I'll manage, thanks. They all look lovely.' Clara threw the rail a helpless look. 'I'm only on my third dress. I'd better hurry up or I'll never get my reward.'

Cake, she meant cake, Raff reminded himself, fingers curling into a fist as other, equally sweet ways of rewarding her flashed through his head.

Clara took a step back, retreating behind the curtain as Susannah left. Raff paced around the room trying not to interpret every sound he heard. The rustle of a button, the slow, steady zip as the dress was undone, the faint slither of material falling to the floor.

Maybe he should have some more water.

'Have you ever tried to tell them how you feel?' Her voice floated through the curtain.

It took a few seconds for the words to penetrate through his brain, for him to remember the conversation they had been halfway through before time slowed, before his brain had gone into lockdown and his body into overdrive.

'No,' he admitted, running one hand through his hair. It was a relief in some ways to spill the feelings he had carried around for so long, locked inside so tight he barely recognised them himself. Clara was unconnected; she was safe.

In this context at least.

And she was invisible, hidden away behind the curtain; it felt as if he had the seal of the confessional. That he could say anything and be absolved.

'Rafferty's means everything to Grandfather, to Polly too. But it bores me. Merchandise and pricing and advertising and thinking about Christmas in June,' he said slowly, trying to pick his words carefully as he articulated the feelings he barely admitted to himself. 'Polly and I owe my grandfather everything and all he wanted, all he wants, is for me to take this place over. To take my father's place by continuing his work, accepting my great-grandfather's legacy. I didn't know how to tell him I didn't want it. Not ever. What kind of spoiled brat breaks his grandfather's heart?'

She didn't reply. How could she? But her silence didn't feel hostile or loaded.

'I tried.' He leant back against the wall and gazed unseeingly at the ceiling, the long years of thwarted hopes and unwanted expectations heavy on his conscience. 'I really, really tried, worked here after school and every holiday, gave up my dreams of studying medicine and struggled through three years of business management instead. I even did an MBA and I took up the role awaiting me here—and every day, for six years, I hated coming to work.'

He sighed. 'But ironically Polly loved it. I hoped that if Grandfather saw how well she did then he would switch his attention to her. But he's old-fashioned. He doesn't even realise how much he's hurt her by leaving the company to me.'

'You have to tell him.' She sounded so matter of fact. As if it were that easy.

'I know. Unfortunately last time I tried he ended up in hospital.' Raff tried to make his voice sound light but he knew he was failing.

'What's your plan? To spend another six years here hating every moment, you miserable, Polly miserable?'

'No!' he protested. Her words cut a little deeper than he liked. After all, he *had* taken the path of least resistance, hoping it would all work out somehow. He had only postponed the inevitable.

He had run through every possible conversation in his head. None of them ever ended well. If he had to he would just walk away, refuse to be involved, but the old man had lost one son already. If only there was a way to keep the family together and live his own life.

If only he could make his grandfather see…

Unless…

'I could invite him to the ball,' he said, his brain beginning to tick over with ideas. 'Let him see for himself what I've been up to.'

'Will he be fit?' She didn't sound convinced.

There was the flaw. 'It's five weeks away. He'll be back home this week and resting. If I make sure he's escorted at all times, order a special low-fat dinner and keep him away from the wine he should be okay. He never was the sort to dance the night away. I could take a table, fill it with business cronies. He'd enjoy that.'

'And then what?' She still sounded doubtful.

He was over thirty. It was time to be a man, banish the guilt-ridden small boy, eager to please whatever the cost. 'Then, after the ball, when he's seen the difference we make, the difference I make, I'll talk to him again. Honestly and firmly.'

It wasn't a foolproof plan by any means. Nor was it an instant answer. Raff would have to stick around for nearly two months—but he'd planned for that after all, booked Clara for up to six weeks.

It felt like the best shot he had. And regardless of whatever his grandfather decided his own decision was made.

It was only now that he realised just how heavy his burden had been: guilt, expectations, responsibility weighing him down. He wasn't free of it, not yet, but freedom was in sight. It was strange how talking it through with someone, sharing his burden, had helped.

Would anyone have done or was it Clara herself? Raff wasn't sure he wanted to explore that thought any further.

'It could work.' She sounded a little more enthusiastic. 'You better make sure your presentation is spectacular.'

'Our presentation,' he said silkily. 'You're the one who promised we'd be there, agreed to all this. I want your help with every aspect. You don't just get to turn up late and leave early, Cinders. You have to work for your dress and glass slippers.'

Talking of which, she had been a long time getting changed. 'Are you okay in there?'

'Ah…' she sounded embarrassed '…is Susannah there?'

'No, why?'

'Can you find her?' Embarrassment was replaced with curt impatience.

Raff's mouth quirked. 'Are you in need of help? Maybe I can assist? I am fully trained, remember?'

'Raff Rafferty, please find Susannah right now.'

Grinning, Raff sauntered to the door and looked around. No sign. 'I can't see her,' he called. 'I can page her but she might be at the other end of the building, or I can help. Your choice.'

He could almost hear the wheels turning as Clara deliberated her choices.

'Okay. But not one quip, and no looking.'

Interesting.

'I'm a professional,' he assured her. But he didn't feel professional as he walked over; he felt more like an overeager schoolboy who'd been promised an over-the-bra fumble. Inappropriate, he scolded himself.

And yet he couldn't stop thinking about creamy, bare shoulders and those three little freckles.

Deep breath. Focus on the job at hand. Raff pulled the curtain a little to one side and stepped into the changing room.

Where he stopped still. He didn't want to stare, he knew it was wrong and yet, and yet…

'Well, don't just stand there.' Clara gestured to her side. 'Help me. It's stuck and have you seen the price tag? I can't exactly yank it.'

She was wearing a floor-length strapless dress in a shade of blue so dark it almost looked black.

Revealing both her shoulders and a generous amount of cleavage, the dress clung as tightly as a second skin, emphasising the dip at her waist, the curve of her bottom, the length of her legs. Raff swallowed.

'The zip,' she said with killing emphasis as he remained static. 'It's stuck.'

Trying, with little success, to get some air into his suddenly oxygen-deprived lungs, Raff walked over. It seemed to take an eternity. He was a fool, to think he could walk in here, to the intimacy of a room where clothes were discarded, a room of lingerie and limbs and clinging silks. A fool to think he could step so close to naked arms, inhale the light floral scent she wore, watch one curl tumble down onto a bare shoulder. To touch her.

'Just here.' Hadn't she noticed the effect she was having on him? 'Can you see?'

Raff put one hand onto her ribs, holding her still as with utter concentration his other hand worked at the tiny zip, trying to free it from the thread that held it prisoner. Her skin was hot, burning him through the silk; he wasn't sure whether he could really hear her heart hammering or whether it was his imagination.

Or if it was his heart he heard, deafening him with its beat.

'I think I've got it.' His voice was gruff. 'There!'

As he freed the thread the zip shot down with alarming ease, his hand skimming her waist, her hip, and as it did so the top of the dress collapsed into graceful folds.

It all happened so fast, Clara didn't manage to grab at the dress or shield herself, and he, God help him, he didn't look away.

I'm sorry, he wanted to say, wanting to turn, to walk away, allow her a chance to get herself together but he was glued to the spot, desire hot, sweet and dark burning through him. She was perfect, the swell of her breasts, the dip of her waist, the faint silvery marks on her lower belly a badge of motherhood.

She should pull the dress up, turn away, slap his face,

scream, at least, at the very least she should cover herself up. She didn't even sunbathe topless and here she was, standing like a glamour model, exposed.

Only she was paralysed by the heat in his eyes, warming her through from head to toe, settling in the pit of her stomach, awakening a sweet, insistent ache she hadn't felt for so long. The naked desire in his face provoking pride, need, want.

And she wanted him too. She'd wanted him since the moment he had sauntered into her office, arrogant and demanding, making her think and making her do and making her feel. Not just because he looked so good, was so tall and so broad and so solid, not just because he had eyes that caressed and a mouth that made her knees tremble, but because he was a man who cared, hide it as he might.

But he was a man who was leaving. A man with itchy feet, who lived his life on the edge of civilisation, risking his life every day.

Right now it was hard to remember why that was a problem.

For all the strength apparent in him, held tightly coiled in that strong, muscled body, Clara knew she had all the control here. One look, one word and he would walk away with a sincere apology.

But one move forward and… Anticipation shivered through her.

She had spent the last ten years playing it safe, hiding from any experience that might test her, pouring all her emotions into motherhood. But the moment she had swung off that platform yesterday, the moment she had agreed to Raff Rafferty's offer, a new world had opened up. Not safe, not cosy, unplanned, a world that made her pulse beat and her blood hum and desire swirl sweetly inside her like honey.

And, oh, how she wanted.

Without thinking, without planning, she took another step forward, allowing the dress to fall to the ground as she did so. A wanton part of Clara, long locked away, smiled; the rest of her shivered in anticipation as she took in the expression on his face as Raff drank every inch of her in: fierce, hot need.

She felt utterly desirable.

Another step and she was close, so close. Millimetres separated them. Clara was trembling, tiny, anticipatory shivers running through her every nerve and sinew, her veins humming with excitement. She looked up at him boldly, allowing her want to shine out, and with a muffled growl Raff moved forward, closing the infinitesimal gap, pulling her hard against him. Clara found herself on her tiptoes, straining towards him.

It could only have been a second, two at the most before his lips touched hers but it felt like an eternity and Clara was sure she would explode if he didn't kiss her right there and then. And then his mouth was on hers sure and sweet, his hands were holding her close, one on the small of her back, holding her tight, the other in the nape of her neck and Clara wanted to climb onto him, into him and never let go. The lazy circles his fingers were making on her back, each one teasing hot, sensitised skin to the point of insanity, the way his hand cupped her tender neck, fingers buried in her hair, the way his mouth claimed her, demanding, expecting, giving.

Nothing had ever felt so right.

And when he let her go, staggered back with a look of total disbelief on his face, she was utterly bereft. 'The door's unlocked.' He was breathing hard, his voice ragged.

It took a moment for his words to penetrate her overheated brain. 'Oh.' Anyone could have come in, seen her practically naked, draped all over him. She should feel shamed. But she wasn't; she just wanted to be back in his arms, fused into him.

'I could lock it…'

Her eyes fastened on him, on the question implicit in eyes darkened by desire.

'You could, you probably should.' It wasn't the most eloquent response but it was all he needed. Powerful long strides across the room and the key was turned firmly, the outside world shut away.

Raff turned, eyes glittering dangerously. 'Clara?'

This was it, this was her chance to turn back, to get this relationship back on a professional footing. There was nothing she wanted less. 'I'm standing here in my underwear,' she said as calmly as she could, allowing a purr to enter her voice, tossing her hair back over her shoulder. 'And you're all the way over there and fully dressed…'

'That,' he said grimly, advancing on her with meaningful intent, 'can soon be remedied.'

Clara found herself being walked backwards until her back hit the wall. Panting, she looked up at him, a teasing smile on her lips, a smile he claimed as he swung Clara up in strong arms and she gave in to the sensation of his mouth, his hands, all thoughts drifting away and instinct taking over until she was no longer sure who she was or where she was. All she knew was that right now, in this moment, she was his.

CHAPTER SEVEN

'ARE YOU ENJOYING YOURSELF?'

'Yes, thank you.' Polite, cool, collected. Of course she was, just as she always was.

Clara was playing her part to perfection. His house, his life were seamlessly run by her employees while she stepped into her role as his girlfriend with grace. His employees liked her, she had charmed every business associate he had introduced her to and even his grandfather was showing signs of thawing.

But as soon as they were alone she retreated behind a shield of courtesy and efficiency. A shield he made no attempt to push aside.

It was better that way even if he did keep getting flashbacks of hot kisses, silky skin and fevered moans. After all, he usually kept his relationships short and sweet, superficial. Just not usually this short.

Or this sweet.

'I think we've shown our faces long enough if you want to leave.' Raff liked music as much as the next man but the benefit for ill and destitute musicians was a little out of his comfort zone. 'Unless, of course, you're enjoying it.'

The corners of her mouth tilted up, as close as she had got to a genuine smile in weeks. 'The violinist sounds just like Summer when she's practising,' she whispered, her breath sweet on his cheek. 'I had no idea I was raising a musical genius.'

'He sounds like Mr Simpkins when I've forgotten his evening fish,' Raff retorted. 'I think they're trying to extort money from us with menaces. Pay up or the music continues.'

'The percussionists were good and the harpist wasn't too bad…' She broke off, biting her lip, laughter lurking in her eyes.

'Until she started singing.' Raff glared over at the harp. 'If she isn't some sort of banshee then that voice was genetically engineered for warfare. There's no way those howls could be natural.'

'Come on.' Clara placed her hand upon his arm, just as she had done at every party, every dinner, every benefit over the last few weeks. His blood began to heat up until he was surprised his sleeve didn't burst into flames, but he didn't betray his discomfort by a single twinge.

'Only if you want,' he demurred. 'There's still the Cymbal Concerto to go. I'd hate for you to miss out.'

'So considerate.' She might look as if she were wafting along on his arm but her hand was inexorably steering him towards the open doors. 'Successful night?'

'When it was quiet enough to hear myself speak. Polly must be exhausted, spending her free time at these things.' Raff routinely worked twelve-, fourteen-hour days out in the field but give him those any day over his sister's routine of office by day, business socialising by night. 'I would give anything for a quiet night in The Swan.'

'Me too. You know, I thought my life was in danger of getting into a rut.' Clara breathed in a deep sigh as they left through the double doors that led from the ornate banqueting hall into the equally ornate but much quieter and cooler vestibule. 'But after several weeks of social events I am yearning for my sofa, a film and something really plain to eat. A jacket potato, salad, a piece of grilled chicken.'

'That sounds amazing.' It really did. Canapés and fancy dinners had lost any novelty after just a few days. 'Can I join you?'

It was supposed to be a joke but he made the mistake of looking directly at her; their gazes snagged, held and colour rose over the high cheekbones. 'It would be a rom-com,' she warned him, looking away, her voice light.

'My favourite.' Right then he almost meant it; a night lazing on a sofa, something undemanding on the TV, sounded like paradise. But he could feel the phone in his pocket almost physically weighting him down stuffed as it was with commitments and appointments and functions, all as serious and important and necessary as tonight's. 'I might have a spare evening in, oh, about three weeks.'

Rafferty's had to be represented, had to be seen to be there. This was where business was discussed, decided, where deals were struck. Under the sparkling lights, a glass of something expensive in one hand, a canapé in the other.

'Actually…' Clara sounded almost shy, tentative, completely unlike her usual assertive self '…I wondered if you were free tomorrow morning?'

'On a Sunday?' Raff didn't even try to hide his shock. Apart from that very first week, Clara had kept Sundays sacrosanct. They were her family day, a day she was very firmly off duty.

Did that mean her daughter would be there? Raff rubbed the back of his neck, suddenly a little warm. Just because he and Clara had shared a moment didn't mean he was ready to play at happy families. Especially as that particular moment had been well and truly brushed under the carpet.

And although there were times when he wished it hadn't been quite so rigorously filed under 'let's never mention this again', this was a stark reminder why it had to be.

Families, children, commitment. All very nice in principle, but tying. Even more weighty than the phone.

'I know we don't usually work on a Sunday.' She made the statement sound like a question and Raff shrugged non-committally.

It was chilly outside, cold enough for Clara to pull her wrap around her shoulders as they exited the building and began to make their way down the wide stone steps into the brightness of a London night. If the stars were out Raff couldn't see them, the streetlamps and neon signs colluding to hide the night sky from the city dwellers.

He had arranged to meet their driver on the corner of the street and steered Clara along the cobbled pavement, waiting for the inevitable comment about how much her feet hurt.

It didn't come. 'I have an appointment,' she said instead, looking down at the uneven cobbles. 'I wondered if you would come with me. You said, a few weeks ago…' Her voice trailed off.

'Yes.' He frowned as he remembered. 'Of course.' He *had* said he would attend a meeting with her. Only, that was before.

People *must* be talking about them, about the amount of time they were spending together, about the way he picked her up almost nightly in a chauffeur-driven car— maybe it was his turn to act the graceful escort. Only, it seemed worse somehow. Her family were so close, it felt deceitful.

The thought of getting to know her family, of possibly being accepted by them, twisted his stomach. What if he liked them? Or God forbid felt at home?

'It was the only day they offered me.' She finally looked up, her face pale, her features standing out starkly from the almost unnatural pallor of her skin.

'They?'

She took a deep breath, her body almost shaking. 'Summer's father isn't involved. It's his choice. I really tried.' Raff had to take a deep breath of his own to dampen down a sudden, shocking anger. How could anyone have left her to raise a child on her own?

'I send him photos, videos, school reports, tried to get him to Skype with her. He's never been that interested. But a few weeks ago, the day you asked me to help you out, he emailed.'

'He wants to see you tomorrow.' It wasn't a question.

'He's here with his father. They have money—' She came to an abrupt stop, her throat working.

'So do I.'

She gave him a tiny smile but he wasn't joking. They wanted to play powerful and well connected? He was brought up to play that game.

'Byron's father thought that I, well, it doesn't matter now, but we don't have the best relationship.' She twisted her bangle round. 'I wanted to be strong enough to do it alone.'

Raff's heart squeezed, painfully. It couldn't be easy for her to ask for help. 'Is Summer going?'

She shook her head. 'They don't want her there.'

'Of course I'll be there.' It was just returning a favour, right? The cold, still anger that consumed him when he saw the stricken look in her eyes, heard her voice shake, watched her search for words no mother should have to say had nothing to do with his decision. It was just a favour. No big deal.

'I've been dreading this,' she confessed, the shadows under her eyes making them look even bigger than usual. 'All I've ever wanted is for Byron to be part of Summer's life. And now he's finally here, in London, just an hour away from her, I'm terrified.' She shook her head helplessly. 'I don't know why. I should be stronger than this.'

Raff stopped and turned her around to face him, tilting her chin up, making her look at him, see the truth of his words. 'Clara, you are incredible. You raise Summer alone, you run a business, half of Hopeford relies on you one way or another. You are the strongest woman I know.'

She stared up at him, doubt in her eyes. 'Really?'

'Really.' He squeezed her shoulders, ignoring the urge to pull her in a little closer.

She exhaled. 'Thank you, I appreciate it. I really do.'

Raff knew instinctively that it wasn't easy for her to lean on him; he was honoured, of course, that she had asked him, had confessed her fears to him. It must have hurt her to show him the vulnerable side she kept so locked away. But it was terrifying as well. Physical intimacy was one thing, emotional intimacy, honesty, secrets? Another ballgame altogether.

But she'd been let down enough already. One morning, that was all she was asking. He was capable of that at least.

As they approached the hotel Clara's demeanour subtly changed, as if she were going into battle. There was little outward sign of her stress although her grip tightened on his arm. Her face was utterly calm as if she were going to any business meeting, her hair had been ruthlessly tamed and coiled back in a neat bun, not one curly tendril allowed to fall about her face. It made her eyes look even bigger, emphasised the catlike curve of her cheek; Raff thought she looked vulnerable, a child playing dress up.

She had dressed for battle too, sleek and purposeful in a grey suit.

But Raff could feel the faint tremors running through her body. Her lips were colourless under her lip gloss.

The Drewes were staying at one of the most exclusive hotels in London, an old Georgian town house discreetly tucked away in a square in Marylebone. It was an interesting choice. Not overtly glitzy but it suggested old money, power and taste.

Raff was looking forward to this. He knew all about old money, power and taste. Bring it on.

Clara was all purpose now, marching up the stone steps and through the double doors, turning with no hesitation towards the hotel's sunny dining room.

'Clara.' Both men rose to their feet; although they both wore smiles the brown eyes were alike—cold and assessing.

'Byron, Mr Drewe.' She shook hands in turn, strangely formal considering one of these men was the father of her child. 'This is Raff.' She didn't qualify their relationship. *Good girl,* Raff thought, *keep them guessing.* 'Raff, this is Byron and his father, Archibald Drewe.'

Raff reached over to shake hands in his turn, unable to resist making his own handshake as strong and powerful as he could. So this was Summer's father, this tall, handsome man, whose smile didn't reach his eyes and who wore his privilege with ease.

'Please, sit down.' The elder Drewe looked very similar to his son, the dark hair almost fully grey and the tanned face more wrinkled but with a steely determination behind the affable façade.

Raff pulled out Clara's chair for her, a statement of intent.

'It's been a while,' she said to Byron. 'You've cut your hair.'

'You look great.' The other man was looking at her with open admiration. 'Haven't changed a bit even if you have changed the sarong for a suit.'

He had seen Clara in a sarong. The hot jealousy that burned through Raff at Byron Drewe's words shocked him. Of course he had seen Clara in a sarong—and a lot less too. He was her ex-lover, the father of her child. At some point Clara had been enamoured enough with this guy to have a baby with him.

And at some point he had allowed her to come home, alone. To raise their child alone.

The jealousy ebbed away, replaced with cold dislike and even colder contempt. 'I am trying to persuade her to link her business with mine. But you know Clara.' He smiled at her. 'She has to be in control. Even a name like Rafferty's doesn't reassure her!'

'Rafferty's?' The older man's eyes were now assessing Raff. 'Impressive.'

The contempt deepened. Now they knew who he was his stock had gone up. Raff hated that.

'What do you do now, Clara?' Should Byron Drewe be smiling at her in that intimate way? Raff allowed himself a brief, self-indulgent fantasy of leaning across the table and planting one perfect punch on that perfect nose.

'I run a concierge service.'

'Half of Hopeford couldn't manage without her, including me,' Raff said.

'How interesting.' The older Mr Drewe couldn't sound less interested. Maybe it was his nose that Raff should fantasise about punching.

'It keeps me busy.' If Clara had heard the snub she wasn't reacting. 'And it's thriving. Between work and Summer I don't have much free time.'

Raff bit back a smile as he mentally applauded. *Nicely done, Clara. Remind them why we're here, ignore their put-downs and make sure they realise you're doing them a favour.*

She didn't need him to step in at all. He might as well help himself to the coffee and sit back and enjoy the show.

'And how is Summer?'

Surely Summer's own grandfather shouldn't pronounce her name in that slightly doubtful way, as if he wasn't quite sure it was right.

Or maybe he just didn't like the name. Clara could scrape her hair back and put on a suit but she knew full well that Archibald Drewe still thought of her a teenage hippy with long hair, tie-dye dresses and a happy-go-lucky attitude who had named her daughter accordingly.

She had been that girl once, but it was a long time ago.

'She's good.' Clara pulled out her tablet. 'I have pictures.'

'That won't be necessary, thank you.'

Time stopped for a long moment, the blood freezing in her veins. How could he dismiss her daughter, his own flesh and blood, in that cold, cavalier way?

'She has your hair, your eyes.' She looked directly at Byron, willing him to stand up for her, for his daughter, for once in his pampered life. 'If you ever look at the pictures I send you you'll know that.'

'I look.' He had the grace to sound ashamed. 'She's beautiful.'

'She is, but she is also smart and kind and very funny. You'd like her.'

He shifted in his seat, evidently uncomfortable. Beside her Raff was leaning back, ostensibly totally at his ease, sipping a cup of coffee. But the set of his shoulders, the line of his jaw told her that he was utterly alert, following every word, every intonation.

Every put-down.

Her hands tightened on her cup; it had been like a game of chicken, leaving asking him along to the last possible moment, kidding herself that she might be able to do this alone. Afraid that his presence might make the whole, nasty situation even more humiliating. She'd thought she'd be ashamed, for him to see this side of her. The dismissed, 'unwanted single mother' side. But having him next to her filled her with the strength she needed to battle on. After all, he had his demons too.

She reached over and laid her hand on his forearm, squeezing very slightly, letting his warmth fill her as she lifted her head and stared evenly at her daughter's father.

'I haven't told her you're here but I hope you have got time to meet her.' She wanted to keep it businesslike but she couldn't help babbling a little, trying to sell her daughter to the one person who shouldn't need the pitch, the one person who should be in regardless.

'She has a picture of you in her room and I tell her lots of stories about you and about Sydney. She helps me put the photos together every Christmas, chooses the pictures she wants to send you. She would love to meet you.'

'Clara, I…' Was that pity in his eyes or shame? Either way it wasn't what she wanted to see.

'It's just, while you're here…'

'I'm getting married.'

Clara stared at Byron blankly. This was why they wanted to see her? Did they think she'd be upset after ten years of silence and neglect, that she was so pathetic she still harboured hopes that they would be a family?

The ego of him.

Raff moved his arm so that his hand lay over hers, lacing his fingers through her fingers, a tacit show of support. She should be annoyed at this overt display of ownership but relief tingled through her instead. 'That's great,' she said, injecting as much sincerity into her voice as she could. 'Congratulations, I hope you'll be very happy.'

'He's marrying Julia Greenwood.'

Archibald Drewe obviously expected this to mean something.

'Great!'

'She's heiress to a media empire,' he told her, his voice oozing contempt for her obvious ignorance. 'This is a brilliant match for Byron, and for our business.'

Much better than a penniless English teenager. She'd known she was never good enough for Byron's family. Once it would have hurt that he had allowed them to influence their future. Now she simply didn't care.

As long as it didn't affect her daughter.

'We want you to sign this.' Archibald Drewe slid a sheaf of papers over the table. Aha, this was the real reason for the meeting. Business, the family way.

'What is it?' Clara made no move to take it.

'Byron is about to join together two great businesses, and any children he and Julia will have…' the emphasis here was intentional '…will inherit a very influential business indeed. We don't want anything from Byron's past to jeopardise his future.'

Anything? They meant anyone.

Beside her Raff was rigid, his hand heavy on hers, fingers digging in, almost painfully.

'And what does this have to do with me?'

'I want to make it quite clear…' Archibald Drewe leant forward; obviously the kid gloves were off '…that your daughter has no claim on me, my son or our business. No claim at all. However…' his smile was as insincere as his eyes were hard '…we are not unfeeling. It's not the girl's fault her beginnings were so unorthodox.'

Raff's arm twitched under hers, the only sign he was alive. Otherwise he was completely still. She couldn't look at him, afraid of what might be in his face. She didn't need his anger and she really couldn't handle pity right now.

The room seemed to have got very cold. She knew how Archibald Drewe felt about her; he had made it completely clear ten years ago. She hadn't expected time to soften him; only money and influence could do that.

But, fool that she was, she hadn't expected him to try and wipe his granddaughter out of the family history books.

'We will send no more annual cheques and you will stop with the photos and emails. Julia does not know of your daughter's existence and neither Byron or I wish her to know. If you sign this contract, however, I will give you a one-off payment of one million pounds sterling in complete settlement of your daughter's claim.'

Raff had met people like the Drewes far too many times; with them it always came down to money. What a cold existence they must lead.

'What does the contract say?' Clara's voice was completely still but she was gripping his hand as if he were the only thing anchoring her.

'It says your daughter has no claim now or in the future on our money or any of our business interests. It also states clearly that she may make no attempts to contact Byron or any member of his family.'

'I see.'

'It's a good offer, Clara.' At least Byron didn't try to meet her eye. Coward.

He had promised himself that he wouldn't intercede but it was no good. How dared they treat Clara like this? 'I'll get my lawyer to have a look at it. Clara isn't signing anything today.' Raff made no attempt to keep the contempt out of his voice.

'That won't be necessary.' Clara pushed the contract away and rose to her feet. 'I won't sign away my daughter's right to contact her father or siblings although don't worry, Byron, I'll do my best to talk her out of it. I would hate for her to be humiliated the way I have been today.'

She was amazing. Calm, clear, holding her anger at bay. But it was costing her; he could hear the strain in her voice, see it in the tense way she stood. What if she hadn't asked him to be there, had had to face these two men alone? It wasn't that she couldn't defend herself. She obviously could. No damsel in distress, this lady. But she shouldn't have to.

She should never have been put into this position. They thought their money and influence gave them the right to treat people like dirt. They were everything he despised.

Raff stood up, taking Clara's hand in his as she continued, her eyes as cold as her voice, but he could feel her hand shaking slightly as she held herself together. 'I won't promise not to send you yearly updates—you don't have to open them but she is your daughter and the least you can do is acknowledge that she exists. As for the money, keep it. I work hard and I provide for her. I always have. I've put every cheque you sent away for her future and that's where it stays. I don't need anything from you, Byron, not any more, and I certainly don't need anything from you, Mr Drewe.'

The older man's face was choleric. 'Now don't be so hasty…'

'If you change your mind, if you want to meet her, then you know where I am. Ready, Raff?'

'Ready.' He got to his feet and nodded at the two men. 'I wish I could say it's been a pleasure but I was brought up to be honest.'

It wasn't until they got outside that Clara realised that she was shaking, every nerve jangling, every muscle trembling.

'Come on.' Raff's eyes were still blazing. 'You've had a shock and you need something to eat. And if I stay anywhere near here I will march back in there and tell them exactly what I think of them.'

'They wouldn't care.' She wasn't just shaking, she was cold to the bone. Clara wrapped her arms around herself trying to get some heat into her frozen limbs.

'I'd feel better though.' He shot her a concerned glance. 'Come here.' He pulled Clara into his embrace, wrapping his arms around her, pressing her close. 'You're like ice.'

She had tried so hard to avoid his touch since that afternoon, since she had let down her guard, but the memory of his touch was seared onto her nerve endings and her treacherous body sank thankfully against him.

'Let's get a taxi. We can go to Rafferty's, get you fed.'

'No, honestly.' Clara wasn't ready to face the world yet. 'Let's just walk. I need some air.'

'Whatever you want.' But he didn't let go of her, not fully, capturing her hands in his, keeping her close as they walked. 'I am going to insist on tea full of sugar though. I work in a medical capacity, remember? I am fully qualified to prescribe hot, sweet drinks.'

Clara knew that if she spoke, just one word, she'd start to cry. And she didn't know if she would ever be able to stop. So she simply nodded and allowed him to continue to hold her hands as they ambled slowly through the grey streets.

'You must think I'm a fool,' she said finally. They had continued to wander aimlessly until they had reached Regent's Park. Raff had bought them both hot drinks from a kiosk and they walked along the tree-lined paths in silence.

Raff looked at her in surprise. 'I don't think anything of the sort. Why?'

'Byron.'

He huffed out a laugh. 'If you judged me on my taste in women when I was eighteen your opinion of me would be very low indeed.'

But Clara didn't want absolution. The humiliation cut so deep. 'I thought I was so worldly. I had travelled thousands of miles alone, with a ticket I had saved up for. I had amazing A-level results. I had it all. I was an idiot. An immature idiot.'

She risked looking into his face, poised to see contempt or, worse, pity, but all she saw was warm understanding. 'I didn't really date at school. I was so focused on my future, on leaving Hopeford. So when I met Byron…' She shook her head. 'We were in Bali, staying in the same hostel. He was two years older and seemed so mature. I had no idea he was from a wealthy family. He didn't act like it. It was his suggestion we share a house in Sydney and save to go travelling together. It was his own little rebellion against his father's plans.'

'We all have those.' His mouth twisted.

'At least yours involves saving people's lives.' She wasn't ready for absolution. 'Byron was just playing. But

I didn't see it. I fell for him completely. When I found out I was pregnant I was really happy. I thought we really had a future, travelling the world with a baby. God, I was so naïve.' She stopped and scuffed her foot along the floor, as unsettled as a teenager on her very first date. 'Thank you.'

Raff raised his eyebrows in surprise. 'What for?'

'For standing by me, for allowing me to handle it.'

'Well,' he confessed, 'that wasn't easy. I don't usually resort to violence but I had to sit on my hands to keep from throttling Byron's father when he offered you the money.'

'Why do men keep offering me money? First you and now him. Why do some people think that throwing money at things—at *me*—solves their problems?'

To her horror Clara could hear that her voice was shaking and feel the lump in her throat was growing. *Keep it together, Clara,* she told herself, but there were times when will power wasn't enough.

Clara blinked, hard, but it was too late as the threatened tears spilled out in an undignified cascade. She knuckled her eyes furiously, as if she could force them back.

'Because we're fools?' Raff took her hand in his, his fingers drawing caressing circles on her palm. It wasn't the first time he had touched her today but this wasn't comforting; the slow, lazy touch sent shivers shooting up her arm.

'No, don't.' She pulled her treacherous hand away. 'You don't have to be nice to me. This is all a pretence, isn't it?' The only person she could ask to stand by her wasn't really in her life at all. How pathetic was that?

Her throat ached with the effort of keeping back the sobs threatening to erupt in a noisy, undignified mess, the tears continuing to escape as Raff took hold of her, tilting her chin up so she had no choice but to look him in the eyes.

'Not all of it,' he said, his voice hoarse. 'It's not all pretence, Clara. Is it? I know we haven't talked about it, try and pretend it didn't happen, but it felt pretty real to me.'

'That was just sex.' Easy to say but she knew her tone lacked conviction. There was no such thing as just sex for Clara; she hadn't trusted anyone enough to get close enough for 'just sex' since Byron. Just this man, standing right here, looking down at her with the kind of mixture of concern and heat that could take a girl's breath away.

'I'm on your side, Clara. I'm here for you, whatever you need, whatever you want.'

Hope sprang up, unwanted, pathetic, needy; she pushed it ruthlessly away. 'For as long as we have a deal, right?' Was that sarcastic voice really hers?

'For as long as it takes, as long as you need me.' His hands tightened on her shoulders, his eyes dark, intense as if he could bore the truth of his words into her.

And, oh, how she wanted to believe him. She didn't mean to move but somehow she was moving forward, allowing herself to lean in, rest her head against the broad shoulders, allowing those strong arms to encircle her, pull her close as the desperate sobs finally overwhelmed her, muffled against his jacket. And he didn't move, just held her tight, let her cry it all out. For as long as she needed to.

CHAPTER EIGHT

'You look…' Raff came to a nonplussed stop, trying to find a word, any word, that did Clara justice. It didn't exist.

'Beautiful?' Clara supplied for him. That wasn't the word; it wasn't enough by any measure. 'I hope so. I've spent all day being prodded, plucked and anointed. If I don't look halfway decent at this exact moment in time then there is no hope.'

'Don't worry,' he assured her. 'You're somewhere past halfway.'

The truth was that at the sight of her all the breath whooshed out of his body; in a room full of glitter she shone the brightest. In the end she had eschewed all the designer dresses Rafferty's had to offer and had opted for a vintage dress that had belonged to her great-grand-mother, a ballerina-length full-skirted black silk with a deceptively demure neckline, although it plunged more daringly at the back, exposing a deep vee of creamy skin.

Raff immediately vowed that nobody else would dance with Clara that evening, no other man would be able to put his hand on that bare back, feel the silk of her skin.

'You scrub up nicely as well,' she assured him.

Raff pulled at his bow tie. He'd owned a tux since

his teens but he still felt as if he were dressing up as James Bond.

Or a waiter.

'Nervous?'

'A little,' he admitted. 'Not about the presentation, more how Grandfather will take it. How is he?'

'He's here.' She pulled an expressive face. Her relationship with Raff's grandfather had thawed a little; he was at least polite. But although she told Raff—and herself—that his initial rebuff didn't worry her, she wasn't being entirely honest. It was all too reminiscent of Archibald Drewe's treatment of her, an uneasy and constant reminder of her mistakes.

'Grumpy that he has a special diet and can only drink water but happy he's away from that damned TV and fool nurse. His words not mine.'

'I bet he's glad to be talking work as well.' Raff had mingled business with business and invited some of Rafferty's key suppliers and associates to fill the table he had paid for. It was odd seeing his two very different worlds colliding in this rarefied atmosphere of luxury and wealth.

Opting for something a little unusual, Doctors Everywhere were holding the event in a private garden belonging to the privileged residents of a west London square.

'It's amazing, like a fairy tale.' Clara was looking out at the candlelit gardens, her green eyes shining. Watching the lights play on her hair and face, Raff could only agree.

'We have some very generous—and very rich—patrons,' he said, trying to drag his thoughts back to the business at hand. 'I hadn't even thought about this side of our work. I spend the money, not raise it. I need to talk to Grandfather about allowing them to use Rafferty's for something in the future. We could certainly donate food and staff or raffle prizes.'

And the people he knew could give even more. Helping with the last stages of the fundraiser had been an eye-opener, just not a particularly welcome one.

Raff knew he did a good job out in the field, but anyone with a good grasp of electrics, mechanics and project management could do that. He had other uses that were far more unique: entrée into some of England's richest and most influential echelons and, although he himself didn't value those connections, he knew that no charity could run on good intentions alone. Ensuring the donations came in was a vital role.

But would it be as satisfying? Or would it be a gilded cage just like the one he was working so hard to escape from?

'Is everything set up?' Clara was as cool and collected as ever, on the surface at least, but when he took her arm he felt the telltale tremble.

'Ready to go,' he promised her. 'My mission tonight is to get all these people to remember why they're here and part with as much money as possible.'

And throw the gauntlet down. Show his grandfather that this was where he belonged—and this was where he was staying, no matter what. Only he didn't feel the same burning need to get back out into the field. It helped, of course, that he had been helping to set up the fundraiser, interacting with colleagues, seeing a new side of the charity's work. But it was more than that.

Clara. Everything he didn't want or need in his life. She needed stability and commitment and a father for her daughter, not a travelling jack of all trades whose idea of a perfect day with family meant a day by himself. And yet, and yet...

Somehow she had got under his skin. More than attraction, more than lust. He respected her, admired her strength—but it was those glimpses of carefully hidden vulnerability that really hooked him in. He knew how much she hid it, despised any display of weakness. But she had trusted him enough to lean on him, cry on him, allow him to shoulder her burdens for a short time.

From Clara that was a rare and precious gift. But was he worthy? And was he capable of accepting all that she had to offer?

'They certainly do a lot of good.' Raff's grandfather had been slowly softening throughout the evening, his initial scepticism disappearing when he saw his table companions and the carefully prepared meal that had been specially provided for him. If he still cast a longing look or two at the bottles of very expensive wine that littered the table, he had at least stopped complaining and was sipping the despised mineral water with martyred compliance.

'I had no idea about the sheer scale of their work,' Clara agreed. 'Nor just how desperate things can be. I'll never complain about waiting for a doctor's appointment again.'

Raff and his colleagues spent their lives making sure that people all over the globe, people who lived in poverty, who had fled their homes, who had seen their world turned into warzones still had access to medicine, to doctors. To hope.

He could have taken the easy option, the job provided for him, the family money, enjoyed all that London had to offer the young and the rich. In a way she wished he had; it would be so easy to keep her distance from that man. Much harder to stay away from the man sitting next to her, even though there was no way there could ever be any kind of happy ever after between them.

But in the few days since the meeting with Byron something had changed. They were easier with each other, more intimate. Hands brushed, lingered, eyes met, held. Nothing had happened, not again, but the promise of it hung seductively over them.

Butterflies tumbled around her stomach, a warm tingle spreading through her at the thought.

'I'm sorry.' Raff finally managed to gracefully extricate himself from the conversation he was embroiled in. 'I've been neglecting you all evening.'

'That's okay.' After all, she was being paid for her time.

Not that Clara felt she could charge a penny for tonight; she would ask Raff to donate her fee back to the charity.

Raff pulled a face. 'I'd much rather be talking to you, but I have been promising myself that as soon as the dancing starts I am all yours.' His eyes were full of promise and a shiver ran through her despite the heat in the overcrowded room.

'You didn't say anything about dancing,' Clara protested. 'I can barely walk in these heels, let alone dance.'

'Don't worry.' His expression was pure wicked intent. 'I won't let you fall.'

'You better not. When are you on?'

'In a few minutes. Wish me luck?'

Clara put one hand on his cheek, allowing herself the luxury of touch, rubbing her palm along the rough stubble. 'Good luck,' but she knew he didn't need it. If he managed to get one hundredth of his charm across then he would have the guests clamouring to outbid each other.

The presentations had been spread out throughout the evening. A welcome speech before canapés, then, after the starters, two of the nurses gave an evocative talk that brought their exciting, dangerous and very necessary work alive. A surgeon's visceral yet compelling description of the challenges she faced was an uneasy filler between the main course and pudding.

No one else seemed to notice the incongruity between their surroundings, with the conspicuous display of wealth and luxury, and the poverty and need so eloquently conveyed. Clara saw women wiping tears, the diamonds on their hands and wrists worth more than the total the charity was trying to raise.

'We need to make sure everyone is suitably worked up before the auction,' Raff whispered. 'They'll all be well fed and watered. We want them to go home with their consciences as sated as their stomachs!'

Just the nearness of him, though he was barely touching her, that lightest of contact, sent tremors rippling up and down her body. For so long she had been shut away in a box of her own design, not allowing herself to do or to feel. Constraining herself to the narrowest of lives. And it had worked. She hadn't been hurt, hadn't messed up.

But she hadn't felt either. Hadn't felt this bitter-sweetness ache. That awareness that overtook everything so that all she could see was him; she could feel nothing but his breath on her cheek, sending waves of need shuddering through her.

Clara took a deep breath, trying to regulate her hammering pulse, remember where they were, what he was about to do. 'So it's up to you to seal the deal?'

He grimaced. 'I wish they'd put me on first. Logistics isn't exactly the sexiest subject. They'll be eying up the petits fours and coffee and be in a post-dinner slump by the time the auction comes around.'

'Don't be ridiculous.' Clara reached for his hand and squeezed it, trying to quell the absurd jump every nerve gave as her fingers tangled with his. 'If anybody can make logistics fascinating, you can. Go get them.'

Raff turned and looked at her and for one long moment the tent fell away, the people fading away to nothing but a murmuring backdrop to the scorching intensity of his gaze. 'You think?'

'I do.' And she did. This was a new side to the confident, nonchalant playboy—but then wasn't that playboy just a façade? A mask he wore well but a mask nonetheless. And the more Clara saw the passionate, principled man behind it, the more she wanted to retreat, to run away.

She'd thought playboys were her downfall. She'd been wrong. She had survived Byron, left him with her head held high and her heart only slightly cracked. But a man who cared, a man who carried the weight of the world on his broad shoulders? That was a far scarier prospect.

'I think you can do anything,' she said. 'Including make every person here spend three times more than they budgeted for.'

'That's my aim.' The words were jokey but his face was deadly serious. 'Ready to clap nice and loudly?'

'That's my job.'

'I'll make sure I give you a good reference.'

Was it her imagination or did disappointment pass fleetingly over his face at her words? That would be ridiculous, Clara told herself sternly. They both knew what this was. This was a business arrangement. A glitzy, intimate contract maybe but a contract nonetheless. Money was changing hands, favours were being done. That was all.

'Okay, then.' And he was gone, the eyes of half the women in the room following the tall figure as he strode across the marquee.

Clara sank back in her chair, an unaccountable feeling of melancholy passing over her. What had he wanted her to say? She didn't know; she was no good at this. Had swapped flirting for nappies and never quite got her groove back.

'This means a lot to him.'

She jumped. For a moment she'd forgotten where she was, that she was surrounded by people. 'I'm sorry?'

Charles Rafferty was looking up at the stage where his grandson stood, talking to the computer technician. Raff was relaxed, laughing, totally at home.

'I knew he had this ridiculous hankering to be a doctor—it was because of his father's illness, of course, that's why I persuaded him to switch to business; besides, I needed him. But his heart was never in it. When he said he was off to work for these people I thought that a bit of time and freedom would sort him out. That he'd come back to me.'

She had no idea what to say.

Raff was responsible for people's lives every day. He didn't cut them open, administer the medicine, nurse them, but he made that possible. He worked in impossible conditions in impossible countries for an impossibly tiny wage.

And he loved it. It was good that his grandfather was seeing that, acknowledging it.

'He doesn't want to let you down,' she said, aware what a lame response it was.

'No.' The older man looked at her, really looked at her

for the first time in the weeks since they had met. And for once there was no trace of a sneer on his face. Just hollow loss. 'He's aware of his family responsibilities. I made sure of that. He was only eight when his father had the stroke, when it was obvious his father would never recover. Only eight when I anointed him as my heir.'

'And Polly?' Okay, she was going beyond anywhere she had any right to go. But Polly was her friend. And Raff? He meant something to her, something a little like friendship.

'Polly?' He shook his head. 'I made a mess of it, didn't I? I inherited the company from my father and groomed my son to take my place with Castor waiting in the wings. It didn't even occur to me that he might not want it—or that Polly did.'

'Look, he's ready.' Raff had stepped up onto the temporary stage and was gesturing for quiet. He dominated the marquee, tall, imposing, his sheer force of will stopping the chatter as people turned to listen. 'I'm sure you'll work it out,' she said quietly as the main light dimmed, leaving just one spotlight trained directly onto Raff.

The silence was expectant. Clara was aware of nothing but the ache of anticipation twisting her stomach. *Do well,* she urged him silently. *Make them see.* Looking at her hands, she was surprised to see her nails digging into her palms. She didn't feel any pain but when she unfurled her hands there were crescent marks embedded in the soft skin. When had he started to matter so much? When had she begun to care?

It wasn't just because she had helped him, gone over the presentation over and over until it made no sense to either of them.

'I know you are all ready for your coffees.' Raff hadn't raised his voice at all yet every syllable carried to every corner. 'And listening to me talk about project management isn't going to raise your heart rate the way my very talented colleagues did. I have watched them perform surgeries, vaccinate children and deliver babies in every kind of condition you can think of—and I was still blown away by their talks earlier. So no, I can't compete with them. My job now, as in the field, is to enable their work. And this, ladies and gentleman, is how I do it.'

He raised a hand and pressed a button and immediately the room was filled with the sound of drums building up into a crescendo as the screen behind him burst into life.

Raff had elected not to go for a talk and slides, knowing that the previous presentations would be using photos to great effect. Instead he had put together a video, a montage of photos and film showing a 'typical' day in his life, backdropped by fast, evocative music. The film started by panning around a small dorm room, ending in a different if similar room, and took in five different clinics and hospitals, two camps and four temporary clinics during the ten-minute show.

Raff was shown sitting in an office with paperwork piled on top of a crowded desk, spanner in hand, eying up a battered old truck, in a helicopter, setting up a tent, fixing a tap, spade in hand digging a pit, playing volleyball outside a tent, watching a spectacular desert sunset.

But the main focus of the film was the patients and people using the facilities he built, repaired and managed.

As the camera lingered on a queue of women waiting patiently to vaccinate their children, he spoke. 'We need running water, toilets, moving vehicles, electricity, satellite connections, working kitchens, working sterilisers for the most basic of our clinics. The hospitals are a whole other level. It all needs to be brought in on budget and just to add to my woes our staff and volunteers quite like to be fed, have somewhere to sleep and the chance to get to the nearest city to enjoy their time off. It's exhausting, often sweaty and dirty, and involves spreadsheets, but on the rare occasion when everything is working I can stand back and I see this.'

Another image flashed up and stayed there. A small boy beaming at the camera, one leg wrapped in bandages, his arm encased in plaster. 'I see children with a future, families kept together, mothers who will live to watch their children grow up. I see hope.

'Thanks to you we will be able to keep vaccinating, operating, delivering and curing. Your generous donations mean that children, just like Matthew here, have a future. Thank you. I'm now going to give you the opportunity to show just how generous you can be. There are some fabulous prizes in our auction. Dig deep, dig hard and bid as high as you can.'

The spotlight dimmed and the house lights were switched back on as the room erupted into applause. People were on their feet congratulating Raff as he walked around the room.

'That was different,' Charles Rafferty said drily. But, Clara noted, his eyes were moist.

'It was good, wasn't it?' she agreed. 'Luckily Raff blogs a lot when he's out in the field and often embeds video or pictures so he had a lot of footage he could use.'

'If he goes back,' Raff's grandfather said, his eyes fixed on Clara, the intent gaze eerily similar to that of his grandson, 'what about you?'

Clara's mouth dried. She had kind of got used to having him around, sitting on her desk disrupting her, whispering highly libellous biographies of the people they met, raising an approving eyebrow as she made small talk.

She had got used to those moments when their hands brushed, the sensation that time was slowing and that all she could see or hear was him. The swell that seemed to roar upwards, filling her full of awareness of his every movement, his every gesture.

'We've managed so far,' she said as lightly as she could. 'Skype, letters, it works really well. We're both so busy that time apart gives us a chance to breathe. Excuse me for a moment.'

The tent seemed so bright, so loud. The chatter and the music competing with each other, driving up the noise level to a deafening shriek. Each of the myriad lights seemed to shine directly into her eyes, the heat making her stomach roll. She needed air and quiet and dark. She needed some space.

Clara moved quickly across the tent, swerving to avoid the clustered groups, making sure she didn't catch anyone's eye as the announcer returned to the stage to announce the start of the auction. Thankfully, she reached the marquee entrance and slipped out into the grounds.

What was wrong with her? It had been a highly successful night. Raff's presentation had been sensational, the guests all looked ready to start spending and donating lavishly and if Clara had read him correctly then Raff's grandfather looked ready to do the right thing and give the company to Polly.

Even better, she had made some great contacts and, if she dared, was in a great position to expand out of Hopeford.

If she dared. Was that it? Was that the reason for this melancholy that had fallen on her like a damp dusk? Because starting the business had been absurdly simple; it had all fallen into place with surprising ease. But taking it into the big city meant taking risks and that was something Clara just didn't do any more.

Or was it because this adventure was nearly over? She'd thought that she was finished with adventures but maybe that part of her wasn't as dead and buried as she liked to think. As she had hoped. Compared to backpacking around the world it was a tame adventure, true, but a part of her was thrilling to the unpredictability.

And Raff. Clara sighed, feeling the truth exhale out of her with her heavy breath. There it was. Like a fool she was allowing the pretence to take over. Just because they pretended it was a relationship, acted as if it were a relationship, did not make it one. He didn't want or need ties here; he was doing his best to sever the ones he already had.

There was nothing long term for her. She should be sensible. Just as she always was.

'Here you are.' Clara's heart gave an absurd skip at the low voice; clearly the sensible memo hadn't reached it yet. 'Are you okay?'

'A little hot.' That wasn't a lie. 'Shouldn't you be inside for the auction?'

'There's not much call for exotic villas or cases of fine wine out in the field,' he said, walking up behind her and wrapping his arms around her. All thoughts of caution, of taking a step back, fled at his touch. 'I did purchase an obscene amount of raffle tickets, though. You?'

'I don't think there's any point in me competing against any of those platinum cards.' There had been some amazing items on the auction list but the guide prices alone had made Clara take a hasty gulp of her wine. 'I think your grandfather was planning to bid. Maybe we should go back in.'

'He's quite capable of spending a lot of money without

my help.' Raff's arms tightened a little, his breath hot on her neck, burning her, branding her, sending heat flaming through her veins. 'I'm looking forward to spending some time off duty.' He turned her unresisting body round, cupping her face with his hand. 'I just want a night with no more work talk, a beautiful woman on my arm, in my arms. Music, wine, fun. Are you in? Because…' his voice was low, intimate '…there's no one else I want to be with.'

She had spent the last ten years building up a reputation, one she was proud of. She was often called driven, reliable, honest—and she was proud of those attributes. But beautiful? Fun?

Raff thought she was both of them. And tonight, just tonight, Clara thought she might think so too.

'Just one night?' That was what he had said, right? Was it enough? It had to be.

'Is that all you want?'

'Yes.' That was the right answer, wasn't it? She searched his face for answers but he was giving nothing away. Only his eyes showed any expression: heat, want, need. What was she waiting for? 'No. I don't know. You're going away.'

'I work away,' he corrected her.

She stared at him, confused. 'What are you saying?'

He smiled at her, dangerous and sweet. 'I'm saying there's no need to plan ahead.' His hand slid down her shoulder, moved to caress the exposed skin on her back.

Clara felt her stomach drop, her knees literally weaken; she had never realised that could actually happen in real life. Any second now she was going to have to grab hold of him just to keep herself upright.

'Chemistry like this doesn't come along often…' his hand was drifting up and down, scorching a blazing trail along her spine '…but it's more than chemistry. I like you, Clara. A lot. I like how we are together. I like who I am when I'm with you. I think we should stop fighting it and go with it.' He paused, his gaze moving down to linger on her mouth. 'See where it takes us.'

See where it takes us. Somewhere new, somewhere dangerous. But there had been a flash of something in his eyes when he said he liked her. Something heartfelt.

And she liked him too. More than she wanted to admit to herself. He didn't fit any of the criteria she had pains-takingly typed into the internet dating sites. He wasn't local, didn't have a steady job, wasn't family orientated. But he made her laugh, made her feel safe—and he made her tremble with need.

Was that enough?

She was over-thinking it. She had said she wanted to try dating again and here was this gorgeous man ready and waiting.

Waiting for her to say yes.

She had to say yes. Raff had never before put himself on the line like that, not for anybody. He didn't know what would happen when he was back out in the field, where they would be this time next year, but he didn't care. Even the thought that they might *be* somewhere next year didn't trigger his usual flight reflexes.

Slowly, his eyes on hers, searching for consent, he reached out and trailed a finger along the feline curve of her cheek, down to her full bottom lip. She stared up at him, eyes wide, endlessly green, questioning.

Whatever she was asking he obviously supplied the right answer because she moved. One small step closer, bringing her full body into contact with his. Raff moved his finger, reluctantly, off the smooth, full lip and fol-lowed the curve of her jaw, her skin silky under his touch.

He reached the tip of that pointed little chin and slid his finger under, tilting her face up towards him.

He waited for one torturous second, giving her plenty of time to change her mind before allowing himself to dip his head towards hers for a soft, barely there, sweet leisurely kiss, her mouth opened under his, soft, yielding.

'What do you say, Clara?' he whispered against her mouth. 'Will you come back with me tonight? Come back with me now?'

She leant in and claimed his mouth with hers. 'Yes,' she whispered back. 'I say yes.'

CHAPTER NINE

'I SHOULD HAVE KNOWN I'd find you here. Afraid you'd turn into a pumpkin if you didn't get home before sunrise?' Was that anger in his voice? Clara swallowed, reaching for the hole punch on her desk, settling it back into a perfect line.

'I didn't want anyone to see me leaving.' She couldn't meet his eyes as she answered him. It was the truth, but only half the truth.

She had woken up in the early hours, nestled in his arms, and for one blissful moment had felt happy, sated. Safe. Tempted to wake him up to see if it could be as magical a third or fourth time.

And then reality intruded. How could she face the next morning? The intimacy of early morning conversation, coffee, breakfast—followed by the walk of shame in strappy heels and yesterday's dress. She wasn't sure which scared her more.

She didn't want to be that woman, sneaking out of a bedroom in the dark, shoes in one hand, balled up tights in the other, and yet somehow there she was, tiptoeing through the dark streets until she reached the sanctuary of home and a sleepless night alone in her own cold and empty bed.

'I didn't think you'd mind,' she said in the end. 'I

mean, it's midday and you've only just turned up.' She wanted to recall the words as soon as she'd said them. She didn't want him to know that she'd been watching the door, her phone, her email, half desperately hoping that he would be doing his utmost to track her down.

Half hoping he'd stay well away.

His eyes narrowed. 'I didn't think you were the kind of woman to play games, Clara.'

Ouch. 'I'm not.' Not usually anyway. 'But last night was…' amazing, magical, the best night of her life '…like a fairy tale. I wasn't sure either of us knew what we were doing. Not really.'

They'd spent so much time together, shared so many secrets, danced around the attraction they felt for so long, it was easy to be swept up in the romance. The thought of waking up to regret and apology on his face—or conversely to expectation and hope—was more than she could bear. Far better to run.

She'd never thought of herself as a coward before.

'I knew exactly what I was doing,' he said silkily and she flushed at the sarcastic tone. 'I thought I made it very clear to you that I was in this. With you. But if you can't trust me then there's not really any point, is there?'

'I do trust you.' It was herself she didn't trust; she had got it so very wrong before.

He laughed, a short, hard sound, running his hand through his hair as he shook his head. 'You won't let me in, Clara. You don't want people around here to see us together, to know you stayed over. I haven't met your parents or your daughter. Seriously, when I said I was in, it wasn't as your bit on the side.'

'That isn't fair.' Clara jumped up, sending her chair skittering backwards. 'You told me you liked me yesterday. Yesterday! What does that mean, anyway? We're not in school any more.'

'No, that's why I thought we could try and have an adult relationship.' He sighed. 'Come on, Clara, what do you want? I'm not the kind of guy to offer you hearts and flowers and big romantic gestures. This is new to me too. I thought we could take it one day at a time, find our way into this thing. But if you won't let me in then there's no way it's ever going to work.'

Feel our way in? One day at a time? It was hardly a grand declaration but it was the best he had. Raff wanted this thing, whatever it was, to be honest from the start. His father had treated his mother like a princess, splurged expensive gifts and holidays on her, never allowed her to shoulder a single responsibility. And then the second she had needed to step up she had disintegrated. If Raff was going to try something more serious than a simple fling then it had to be equal.

And that meant honesty.

Damn, he knew relationships were hard but he hadn't expected to feel as bereft as he had this morning. Waking up to find her side of the bed empty, her clothes gone. If it weren't for the faint scent of her perfume in the air he would have thought he had imagined the whole thing.

'I do want to let you in.' She was still standing behind her desk, a physical as well as an emotional barrier between them. 'I'm just not sure how. My parents, Summer, I don't want to let them down again.'

'You think I'll let them down?' Was that really her opinion of him?

'You said yourself one day at a time. How can I risk my daughter's happiness on that?'

Raff huffed out an exasperated laugh. 'All relationships are one day at a time, Clara. Anyone who says otherwise is a liar and a fool.'

He took a deep breath, trying to steady his pulse. 'You want to know why I didn't come rushing round here this morning?' Apart from needing time to calm down before facing her. 'I went to visit my grandfather. To tell him that as much as I love him and appreciate him I can't be who he wants me to be, do what he wants me to do.'

'So you are going back?' She wasn't looking at him, straightening the few items on her desk over and over. He wanted to walk over, remove the stapler and ruler and make her listen. Instead he hung back by the door.

'I was always going back.' He had made that clear right from the start, from the first moment of attraction. 'But it's not full time. We are only ever allowed to do short-term contracts. I could be back in the UK for four months of the year. I've offered to stay on the board at Rafferty's but that's it.'

It hadn't been easy; his grandfather had known all too well what Raff was going to say and had put up some resistance—he wouldn't be Charles Rafferty if he didn't—but in the end he had gracefully bowed down to the inevitable.

It had been a massive relief. Raff didn't want to cut all his ties with his family; imperfect and demanding as they were, they were all he had.

But it didn't have to be that way—if Clara would just allow him in, let them try. Four months a year wasn't a huge amount, he knew that. But it was all he had right now. It was a start.

'And Polly?'

'The company's hers, so all we need is the lady herself. I guess this is when we find out if you've been holding out on me after all.' He meant the words to sound light but they came out dark. Bitter.

Her head shot up. 'Is that what you think?'

'Clara, I don't know what to think.'

She looked stricken, her eyes full of hurt. 'I haven't lied, Raff. All I have is an email address. But she did say to use it if I needed to get in touch so I can send a message letting her know what's happened. If you want me to.'

This could be the moment when he turned around and walked away. He could head back to Jordan completely free. No Rafferty's, no family expectations, no Clara.

Freedom wasn't all it was cracked up to be.

Slowly he moved across the room, his eyes fixed on hers. 'We can do better than this.' His voice was low. 'I wish I could promise you it will all work out but I can't.'

He had reached the side of her desk and held out his hand to her. After a long moment's deliberation she took it, allowing him to draw her out. 'I won't lie to you, Clara. I don't know what's going to happen. And I know four months a year isn't very much. But I think we could be good, if we just tried. If you wanted to.'

'I do want to,' she whispered.

He didn't want to fight with her, didn't want to argue about the future. He just wanted the here and now, to enjoy the present.

He stepped closer, one hand slipping around her waist, the other slipping through the silky tendrils of hair as he finally kissed her good morning. It wasn't the lazy waking-up kiss he had hoped for but right now all he wanted was to taste her, reassure her.

Her mouth was warm and honey sweet; her hands fastened around the nape of his neck, light and cool yet capable of igniting with just one touch. Raff buried one hand in the smooth strands of her hair, anchoring himself to her.

He kept the kiss light, using every ounce of his control to tantalisingly nibble along her bottom lip, resisting her attempts to deepen it, to push it further, harder. Hotter.

His hand splayed out along her waist, tracing the faint outline of her ribs, enjoying knowing that just a couple of inches higher and he would brush against the fullness of her breast, a couple of inches further down and he would brush over the curve of her hips round to her pert bottom. The urge to rush nearly overwhelmed him but he held back with superhuman restraint.

It would be easy, so easy and, oh, so tempting to pick her up, allow those shapely legs to wrap around him, to carry her across the room, lock the door and drop her on one of those plump, inviting sofas.

So tempting. But there was no need to rush. Because part of being an adult meant learning that anticipation was part of the game—and it made the end result all the sweeter.

Slowly, reluctantly, he pulled back. Clara's eyes were glazed, heavy-lidded, her mouth swollen. 'Good morning,' he whispered and was rewarded by a slow, sweet smile.

'Good morning.'

'Shall we start again?'

Her eyes clouded over. It wasn't an encouraging sign. 'Raff...'

Whatever she was going to say was cut short as the front door was flung open, banging against the wall.

Clara jumped back and resumed her official face in less time than it took Raff to register the sound.

'Summer.' She sounded shocked and the look she threw Raff was a mixture of apology and warning. 'What are you doing home?'

Raff turned round and saw a slim girl aged about ten, the pointed chin and high cheekbones clearly marking her kinship to Clara although the dark eyes and hair were her only legacy from her absent father. A stab of anger hit him that Byron had chosen money over fatherhood. The merry-faced girl deserved more.

Every child deserved more.

'Half day.' Summer dropped her satchel onto the sofa. 'Don't you remember?'

'Wasn't Grandma picking you up?' Clara wasn't even looking at him.

'Yes, she dropped me back here though, as I didn't see you yesterday. Who's this?'

Raff watched with interest as the colour rose on Clara's cheeks. 'This is a client of mine…'

'Not any more,' Raff interjected. He smiled at the girl. 'Hi, I'm Raff.'

'Oh.' Summer looked at him with interest. 'The VIC?'

'The what?' Raff didn't spend much time with children. He feared it showed.

'Very Important Client. The reason Mummy has been so busy.'

'That's finished now.' Clara had regained her usual colour. 'Obviously we'll still look after the house but the, er, the project has come to an end. Mr Rafferty has come in to collect his invoice.' She glared meaningfully at Raff.

'And to celebrate.' This was it, the chance to prove to Clara that he was a fit person to be in Summer's life. 'How do you two ladies fancy an afternoon out at Howland Hall?'

'The theme park? Yes, please!'

'I don't think so.'

The two voices spoke at once.

'Mummy, please, I've never been on a roller coaster.' The big eyes turned appealingly to Clara.

'Mr Rafferty, can I just have a quick word?' Clara took Raff's arm and led him to the back of the office, through the French doors and into the courtyard beyond.

'What are you doing?' she snapped. 'This is not okay.'

Unease slithered over him. 'What?'

Clara glared at him. 'Offering to take Summer out.'

He looked at her bemusedly. 'I won a family pass in the raffle last night. I thought it would be nice.'

'You know I don't let Summer meet men I'm dating.' Clara put her hand on her forehead, rubbing distractedly. She looked tired. 'It's not fair on her. What if she gets attached? You're going away.'

'It's an afternoon at a theme park, not an invitation to move in.' What was she getting so worried about? Hang on. 'How many men?'

'What?'

'How many men have you not allowed Summer to meet?' The thought of her out with other men made him lose all focus.

'None yet but there may be. In the future. After all, you said one day at a time…' She didn't finish the sentence; she didn't need to. 'But that's not the point. I don't want Summer going to theme parks and I don't want her going on roller coasters and I don't want her getting attached to you.'

He put his hands on her shoulders. 'Relax, Clara. Every child needs to go on a roller coaster and I promise to be as dull as I can. She'll be so unattached she'll be like a broken jigsaw.'

She chewed her lip. 'I don't know.'

'One afternoon.'

'Roller coasters are dangerous.'

'Not at Howland Hall. They're known for their safety measures. You can't let her grow up without having ever been on a roller coaster. She'll rebel, become a stunt-woman or join the circus. Buy a motorbike for sure.'

'She has promised me she'll never get on a bike!' Clara bit her lip. 'I don't know, Raff.'

'I do,' he said promptly. 'Afternoon of adrenaline-fuelled, gravity-defying fun and then I'll take you both out for dinner somewhere where jeans and trainers are welcomed. If our stomachs can handle it, that is. As a thank-you, to Summer as well. She must have missed you the last few weeks.'

Clara had mentioned that her daughter had found her continued absence difficult; Raff *did* owe her a treat. At least that was what he told himself, pushing away the sudden and unwanted feeling of protectiveness that slammed into him when he thought of her absent father.

Clara twisted the bangle on her wrist round and round, a sure sign she was unsure. 'As long as she knows that's what this is,' she said after a long moment. 'A thank-you. I don't want her getting the wrong idea. And we'll take the van. I'm not letting her into that tiny back seat of yours. I bet it doesn't even have a seat belt.'

'I'll call you Miss Castleton and keep ten metres between us at all times,' Raff promised. 'Now, do you like to be at the front or the back of the roller coaster? The middle is strictly for wimps.'

'This,' Summer said rapturously as she bounced along between Clara and Raff, 'is the best day ever. I only want to do things with VIP tickets, Mummy. It's cool not having to queue.'

'There's nothing wrong with taking your turn,' Clara said, but she didn't even convince herself. Unfair it might be, but there was something to be said for waltzing up to the front of every queue, even though Clara found she couldn't meet the accusing eyes of the people who had been waiting patiently for up to an hour to board one of the world-famous roller coasters.

They had been on the Scorpion twice, Runaway Train three times and the Dragonslayer five times. She'd lost count of how many times they had been on the Rapids. They were all soaked through but luckily as spring slid into summer the weather was complying, and even though she kept checking Summer anxiously her daughter was showing no sign of being chilled.

'I want to go on that one,' Summer said for what must be the twentieth time, pointing over at the Typhoon. Clara shuddered. 'You're too short,' she said firmly.

'I'm not. I'm tall for my age,' Summer insisted.

'Let's go and have a look,' Raff interjected easily. 'There's a height chart just outside and you can have a proper look at it, Summer. You might change your mind when you see how green the people getting off it look.'

It wasn't his place to intercede and part of Clara resented it, but another part of her liked the sharing of the load, the way he interacted with her daughter. The two of them were slightly ahead, strolling along the concrete path. Summer was explaining something involved to Raff, something about roller coasters judging by her expansive hand gestures. It was strange seeing her with a man who wasn't her grandfather, seeing the way she responded to his gentle teasing and laid-back questions.

The old familiar ache twisted around her stomach. She had let Summer down; her daughter needed a father, someone to urge her forward when Clara's instinct was to hold her back, hold her tight.

Raff would be perfect. But would it be fair on Summer when he would be gone so frequently?

Would it be fair to Clara, herself? On the one hand she would keep her independence, wouldn't have to compromise anything in her life. But surely if she was going to take such a big step then there should be some changes.

The theme park was set in the grounds of an old, now abandoned stately home and the owners played up to its heritage. Although there was a vast amount of plastic signage they tried to keep everything vintage-looking; even the food carts and toilets had an Edwardian country-garden look, the staff smart in striped blazers and straw hats,

'It's so cool.' Summer was gazing up at the park's newest ride, her eyes huge. 'Look, Mummy.'

Clara shuddered. 'I feel sick just looking, Sum. How can you want to go on that?' She had never allowed her onto anything faster than a carousel before but there was an adrenaline junkie hidden in her demure daughter. She wanted to try everything.

She reminded Clara of herself when she was young.

'They look like they're flying.'

'If humans were meant to fly, we'd have wings. Honestly, I can cope with any normal roller coaster but this?' The riders were strapped in but their legs were left free, to dangle helplessly as the roller coaster snaked at incredible speed around the twists, turns and loops. That was bad enough but after the first loop the carriages went horizontal, leaving the hapless passengers facing down as the train swooped along the thin rails.

'There's the height sign.' Summer went racing over to it. 'I'm big enough, Mummy, look. Can I go on it, please, please?'

'I don't know.' Her instinct was to say no, just as she

had instinctively wanted to refuse Clara's pleas to go on anything apart from the caterpillar train aimed at the under threes. But she had swallowed down her fears and let her daughter go. And look how happy she was, eyes shining, her face lit up with enthusiasm.

Over the last few weeks it had become painfully apparent just how much she sheltered Summer—and herself—from any kind of physical or mental stress. And that was good, right? Only, maybe, she had crossed the line, just a little, into overprotectiveness.

Better to be overprotective than neglectful. But Summer was growing up, and if she pulled too tightly now she knew it could cause problems later; it was just so hard to let go, even a little.

'I really hate the idea of it, sweetie. I don't think I can.' She'd conquered her own reluctance and gone on every single ride so far, as if sitting by Summer's side would keep her safe, She'd been not so secretly relieved when Summer's age had put a couple of the most terrifying beyond their reach. 'I need to feel something under my feet if I'm travelling at that speed.'

Summer's face fell but she didn't ask again, just nodded in agreement. Despite her good behaviour she couldn't hide her disappointment; her whole body projected it from her drooping shoulders to the tip of her toe scuffing the pavement.

Raff took Clara's arm, pulling her a short distance away, out of Summer's earshot. 'I'll take her on.'

Panic immediately clawed at Clara's chest. 'No, you don't have to.'

He grinned. 'I want to try it. It's meant to be great.'

'You're hanging from a bar looking down at the ground hundreds of feet below and travelling at G-force speeds. How can that be great?'

'Come on, Clara, I know the adrenaline gets you. You're buzzing every time we get off a ride.'

Adrenaline or raw fear? Clara wasn't even sure there was a difference. 'It's not...' She paused. She didn't want to say safe. Not again. Even if every fibre was screaming at her that it wasn't. 'It's not your responsibility.'

'No, but I'm offering. Look, we passed a café just a couple of minutes back up that path. Why don't you go and have a horribly overpriced coffee so you don't even have to watch and we'll find you when we're done?'

'Please, Mummy.' Summer had come dancing over; her eyes pleaded with Clara.

What harm could it do? They had VIP passes so they wouldn't have to join the lengthy queue. In just twenty minutes' time, Summer would be telling her about every twist, turn and scream.

And she would never know that allowing her to go on the ride took far more out of Clara than any roller coaster in the world.

'Okay, then.' She staggered backwards as Summer flung herself onto her with a high-pitched squeal. 'You do everything Raff tells you and remember, if you change your mind just say. No one will be cross or think you're a coward.'

'I won't change my mind. Thank you, Mummy, thank you, Raff. This is totally epic.'

'Totally,' he agreed. 'See you soon, Clara. Enjoy the calm. I think a return to the Rapids after this, don't you? After all, my socks are almost dry now!'

Surely they must be finished now? Clara checked her watch for what felt like the hundredth time. Wanting to block out even the mental image of her daughter queuing and boarding such an unnatural ride, she had opted for a seat at the other side of the café by a large window over-looking a shady pond. Once seated with a latte she had immersed herself in work emails on her mobile. After all, technically it was a work day.

But Sue was proving as ferociously efficient at running the office as she was at running a house and it had only taken Clara twenty minutes to clear the backlog. Without work the old, all-too familiar panic reasserted itself. She swallowed, trying to dislodge the lump in her throat, the clutching sensation at her chest. Summer was fine, she was with Raff, she was on a ride designed to be completely safe despite all outward appearances.

But, oh, if only Summer didn't have to grow up. Maybe the witch in Rapunzel had a point. She was very misunderstood if you ignored the eye-gouging part. In fact, Clara could look up any convenient towers in forests for sale right now and deposit Summer at the top of one.

She sighed. Maybe that was just a little over the top.

Drinking the last bitter, lukewarm dregs, Clara tapped her fingers on the wooden table top. Maybe she should go out there and wait, be at the exit, beaming, ready to welcome her daughter back to solid ground. She needed to hide her fears better, show support for all Summer's whims, schemes and plans just as her parents had for her. Just as they still did.

Mind made up, Clara pushed her chair out and gathered up her bag and jacket and the coats Raff and Summer had left with her. Arms full, she walked towards the exit, deliberately keeping her steps unhurried, hoping if she projected an aura of calm she might even come to believe it herself.

It was only an hour until closing time and the café had been quiet, almost eerily so compared with the hustle and bustle outside. The screams of the riders mingled with the cries of the hot and overtired toddlers and babies punctuated by screeches and laughter from the school groups and gangs of older teenagers. The day was still unseasonably warm and the coats were stuffy in her arms as she walked towards the ride.

It was odd how the noise seemed to dim as she approached the area dedicated to Typhoon. No rattle of wheels, no Tannoy, no adrenaline-fuelled screams, no noisy chatter from the queue. It was almost preternaturally quiet, as if she were in some alternate dimension; in the theme park and yet not of it.

It was as if the ride wasn't running at all...

The blood rushed to her head, pounding loudly in her ears as she looked up at the twisting circular rails, so very thin, so very high. But with hideous clarity Clara already knew what she would see. A train lying like a broken toy along the curve of a loop, completely still, the passengers suspended high above the ground below, immobile.

It doesn't mean she's up there.

But there was no queue; the waiting people were being cleared away from the area by efficient staff members. No jaunty blazers and hats here; they were all purpose with fluorescent jackets and walkie-talkies and grim, unsmiling faces.

Clara turned and walked back to the café. They were meeting her there; she should have waited. Summer would be disappointed at having missed her turn and Raff would just be relieved that they hadn't been on that particular carriage and she would admit that for one terrified moment she had thought they were up there and Summer would roll her eyes and tell her to stop worrying about everything and they would agree to call it a day and walk back to the van...

Clara caught her breath. It was all going to be fine.

She walked back into the café, ready to catch her daughter up in her arms and never let her go.

They weren't there. She looked around, her head buzzing with disbelief. They had to be here.

'Are you all right?' The young man behind the counter was looking at her oddly as if he had never seen a woman utterly paralysed by fear, burdened by coats and indecision and terror before.

'Yes,' she said automatically, barely recognising the high, strained voice coming out of her mouth. 'At least, I don't know what to do. I think my daughter is on that train but I don't know who to ask.'

The room was spinning recklessly round, a rushing sound in her ears, and she swayed as if she were on a roller coaster herself, the coats spilling from her arms. Strong arms caught her, sat her down; voices were jabbering at her, asking questions she had no idea how to answer.

She had taken her eye well and truly off the ball and now her daughter was trapped alone except for a man she didn't know at all. And it was all Clara's fault.

CHAPTER TEN

'What's happening?'

That was a very good question. Unfortunately Raff wasn't sure he knew the answer. Carefully, making sure he didn't rock the carriage in any way, he turned his head to the side so that he could see Summer. She was holding herself still, her body was unnaturally rigid and the pointed little face was pale but she didn't seem to be on the verge of tears, thank goodness, Raff had never had to deal with weeping children before; doing so trapped two hundred metres in the air would definitely be beyond him.

'I think there's been a problem with the power,' he said as calmly as he could, trying not to dwell on just how uncomfortable it was to be suspended on his back strapped into a leather harness.

Although he believed there were clubs that catered for such desires.

At least the carriage hadn't stopped when they were facing down; there might have been mass hysteria. Instead he could look up at the late afternoon sky and pretend the ground was just a few comfortable feet below.

'Will they rescue us?' Her voice sounded small and scared.

'Of course!' Although goodness knew when. It was

hard to see exactly where they were and what was nearby but the ride extended out well over a kilometre and the entrance platform was a long way back. 'They won't want us cluttering up the park much longer.'

'How?'

'I think they'll use a crane,' he said after some thought. 'Although a helicopter would be fun. Have you ever been in one?'

'No.' Summer sounded wistful. 'Nor an aeroplane. Not even the Eurotunnel. We usually go away with Granny and Grandpa and stay in a cottage and walk.' She sounded less than thrilled.

'That sounds fun,' he said gravely.

'I want to stay in a villa with a pool like Natasha. Mummy says one day when our ship comes in. Although I'd rather fly there.'

Raff wanted to promise her that he'd take her away immediately, anywhere she wanted to go, but he managed to stop the words slipping out. He had no right to promise this child anything.

'Where would you want to go? If you could go anywhere?'

'Well,' she said thoughtfully. 'Natasha always goes to Majorca and that does look epic but I really want to go to Florida and go on all the roller coasters.'

She wanted to what? Raff didn't think he was ever going to set foot on a roller coaster again. 'They have alligators in Florida,' he said.

'Awesome! Have you seen one?'

'Yep, and crocodiles too. Big nasty ones in Africa.'

'You've been to Africa?' Her eyes were big with excitement. 'Did you see elephants and lions and zebras?'

'All of them. There's nothing like lying in a tent and listening to a lion roar somewhere in the distance.' He lowered his voice. 'It makes the hairs on the back of your neck stand up.'

'Ooh.' She sounded envious. 'Have you been to Australia?'

'Actually, no.'

'I was born there,' she said proudly.

'So you've been somewhere I haven't been.'

There was another long pause. 'Raff?'

'Mmm?'

'I'm scared.'

'Look at me.' Raff wiped all tension off his face and smiled reassuringly at her. 'Give me your hand.' Her hand was so small it looked lost in his; he clasped it tightly, giving her a reassuring squeeze. 'I promise you, Summer, we'll be absolutely fine. I am going to be with you the whole time, okay?'

'Okay.'

'Now, where else do you want to go? I've never seen the Northern Lights so that's on my list.' He felt the small hand relax and saw a little colour come back into her cheeks. She was going to be fine; he just hoped that rescue wasn't too far away.

If this was just a tiny proportion of the weight of responsibility Clara carried then no wonder she didn't want her daughter to go anywhere or do anything. If he ever became a parent then he would build a house lined with cotton wool and keep his children confined within. How did anybody do it? Carry that burden? No wonder his mother had run the second she had been left solely responsible for Polly and him.

For the first time Raff felt a glimmering of empathy for his sweet, childlike but ultimately weak mother. Pampered, cosseted her whole life, she had been utterly unprepared for life as a single mother. So she had run away; as he had, as Polly had. It must be in the genes.

But they had been so young, even younger than Summer here, and they had put all their faith and trust in her. She had let them down, badly. He couldn't imagine anything that would induce Clara to abandon Summer—or anything that would induce him to abandon his children if he was ever lucky enough to have any.

Children had never been in his life plan. But lying here, looking up at the stars, cradling a small trusting hand and listening to Summer describe her perfect holiday villa, they suddenly didn't seem like such a terrible idea after all.

'Miss.' One voice seemed more insistent than the rest and Clara forced herself to look up, to try and focus. 'Drink this.'

Tea. Hot, milky and full of sugar, utterly disgusting, but she managed a few sips and the room came back into focus. Clara pushed the still-full mug away but the man pushed it back. 'Drink it up, all of it,' he said and, like a child, she obeyed.

He didn't say another word, not until the mug was half empty. 'Your daughter is on Typhoon?'

'I think so.' She sounded more like herself. 'But I wasn't there. I don't know if she got on that train but she was supposed to meet me here.' Clara looked around. There were a few people staring at her curiously, some more openly than others; she focused on a couple of white-faced groups, possibly also worrying about trapped friends and relatives. 'She's only ten.'

'My name is Steve and I'm a customer service manager here. If you feel up to walking then you could accompany me to the site. The camera automatically photos them as the carriage goes horizontal, for souvenir photos, you know? If your daughter is on there then you'll be able to identify her.'

'Where else could she be?'

'We evacuated the area so she may just be waiting for you at the other side,' Steve said calmly. 'Is she on her own?'

Clara shook her head. 'No, she's with my friend, but his phone is here. I was watching their stuff…' Her voice faltered. Watching their coats, phones, but not them.

She should have been there.

'Okay, then, if you're able to walk, let's go.' Clara nodded numbly. But she didn't need to identify any photos. She knew that Summer was stuck on top of the narrow metal loop in the sky.

The next half-hour was the longest of Clara's life. She managed to phone her parents, relieved when they promised to be there as soon as possible. At least Summer wasn't on her own. Raff would be great in a crisis like this; calm, probably finding ways to make the whole thing a big adventure.

He'd keep her daughter safe.

The waiting friends and families had all been asked to wait in the café where tea, coffee and biscuits were on constant supply.

'They have come to a stop in the worst possible place,' Steve explained to the assembled group as they settled in. A few were in tears, a couple more red-faced and angry, demanding they be listened to and threatening lawsuits, but most, like Clara, seemed dazed. 'It's one of the highest points of the ride and there's no infrastructure nearby we can reach them from. Nor can we safely restart the ride. But we do plan for these worst-case scenarios and help is on the way. We've ascertained that no one is injured…' a relieved murmur broke out at his words '…and although they're not comfortable they're steady and despite appearances they are safe. Specialist rescue workers are bringing in cranes and ropes and we hope to begin freeing them within the hour.'

Clara sank into a chair, her hands cradling one in an endless loop of hot teas people kept putting in front of her. She didn't drink any of them, just held them, letting the warmth travel through her numbness, keeping her anchored in the present, keeping away her fears until she finally heard the news the group had been praying for: the first passenger had been safely brought back down to the ground. The rescue mission was working.

'Mummy!'

At last, at last. Clara was on her feet, pulling Summer close as if she could absorb her daughter back into her, inhaling her in. 'Hi, Sunshine.' Her voice was shaky and she tried to control it. 'I don't think I've ever been happier to see you.'

She stood back a little, anxiously checking her daughter over. There were no signs of strain or tears on Summer's face. In fact, she looked as if she had just strolled over from the carousel next ride over.

'Did you know Raff has been in a helicopter and one of those tiny planes?' Summer tucked herself back under Clara's arm, encircling her waist with her arms and squeezing in tight. 'He's heard lions at night and hyenas. Isn't that the coolest?'

'Totally. Are you okay, Sum? Was it scary?'

'A little,' her daughter confessed. 'But Raff made it all okay. He promised we'd be all right and we were. Wait till they hear about this at school. Natasha is going to be epically jealous.'

'Is she all right?'

Clara's heart missed a beat at the low, concerned voice.

'They took her off first. I just wanted to make sure she was okay.'

'Raff!' Summer left her mother's side and threw herself at the tall, broad man. He stood, awkward for a moment, before wrapping his arms around her and cuddling her back.

A lump formed in Clara's throat, making it hard to speak. This was what Summer should have had, had never had.

'If I ever get stuck on a roller coaster again I want to be stuck with you,' Raff told her daughter seriously. 'You were by far the best-behaved person up there.'

'Some of them were making the most awful racket,' Summer said, hanging onto Raff's arm. 'As if crying was going to make it better.'

'That's why I'm so glad you were there to cheer me up.'

Summer turned to Clara, her face lit up with excitement. 'Can we still go to dinner, Mummy, please? I'm totally okay.'

Clara swallowed. 'Sorry, honey.' There, that was normal, wasn't it? Not a quiver in her voice. 'Granny and Grandpa are just through there waiting to take you home. But I think they mentioned something about fish and chips…'

'I wanted to stay with you and Raff.'

'I'm just going to drive Raff home and then I'll be straight there. Come on, sweetie.'

She hadn't looked at him. Not properly. Raff just stood there as Summer was peeled off him and delivered to her grandparents, still protesting that she was okay and wanted to go out for dinner.

He wanted to placate her, promise her that it would happen some other time. But he wasn't sure about that at all.

'I'm sorry about that.' Clara still wasn't looking at him directly. 'I thought she'd be better off going straight back.'

'I could have driven the van back, if you wanted to go with Summer.'

She paused. 'I wasn't sure if you'd be okay to drive. Besides, I thought we should talk.'

Here it came. Raff was suddenly very tired. There had been a few moments up there when he had been concerned, worried that they'd be trapped for several hours, that the actual rescue process would be dangerous. The responsibility had been heavy.

It was funny; he bore a huge amount of responsibility nearly every day of his life. He had to keep all kinds of facilities going; literally hundreds of lives depended on him. He took that responsibility very seriously, lived for it. But it was nothing compared to the fear he had felt when Clara's daughter was in such terrible danger and there was nothing he could do but sit there, talk to her and hold her hand.

He ran a hand through his hair, aware just how much the accident had taken out of him. All he wanted to do at this point was have a beer, a shower and collapse into his bed, but there was no point putting this off.

Clara would say what she had to say; she had every right to. He had messed up.

They walked away from the building, their steps in harmony but several inches apart, not one centimetre of them touching.

'I'm sorry,' he said after a while, not able to bear the silence any longer. 'You must have been terrified.'

Clara stopped and stood stock still for a long, long moment. Raff could see how unnaturally rigid her shoulders were, the lack of colour in her lips. The defeated look in her eyes.

'You had no right.' Her voice was trembling; he didn't know if she was holding back tears or filled with anger. He feared it was both.

Her throat was burning with the effort of keeping the tears held back. Again. For goodness' sake, she had barely cried in years and now she was giving Niobe a run for her watery money.

'You had no right,' she tried again. 'Inviting us here in front of Summer so I had no choice but to agree, offering to accompany her on the ride. I know I could have said no.' She could hear the volume of her voice rising and took a deep breath. 'I could have but you put me in a really difficult position. I've hardly been around lately, thanks to you. The last thing I wanted to be was a killjoy mother as well as an absent one!'

She expected him to defend himself, to get angry back. Instead he stood, facing her, palms outstretched. 'You're right. I was completely out of line.'

If he thought being calm and reasonable was going to calm her down he was in for a big shock. 'She could have been killed up there!' The words were torn out of her, raw and heartfelt. 'Do you know how it feels to see the one person, the one person you would gladly die for, stuck miles up in the sky and know you are utterly, utterly helpless? Of course you don't!' Was that her? So cold and bitter. 'The only person you care for is yourself.'

Raff's face whitened. 'I care about you.'

She didn't want to hear it. 'Yes, one day at a time.' Was that why she was so angry? They hadn't finished the conversation in her office; Summer had interrupted them before it had been resolved. No, she pushed the uncomfortable thought far out of her mind. It had nothing to do with Raff and his piecemeal approach to relationships; this was all about her daughter.

'She could have died,' she repeated and this time the words really hit home. 'She could have fallen and I wasn't there, Raff. I wasn't there.'

'No, you weren't, but I was.' He ran a hand down her arm, looking intently into her eyes and just like that the anger dissipated. Oh, how she wanted to step forward, lean into him and let him hold her. But she stood firm. 'She wasn't alone. And, Clara? Your daughter was amazing. She's brave and interesting and that is down to you. You are a wonderful mother.'

He was saying all the right things and it would be so, so easy to put this behind her, behind them, and let him into her life properly, into Summer's life. Because this was what Summer wanted, what she deserved. Someone who appreciated just how special she was, someone who made her feel safe.

This was what Clara needed.

But Raff wasn't that man as much as she desperately wanted him to be. He was leaving, soon. And both she and Summer deserved better than a part-time Prince Charming.

'Come on.' She resumed walking, relieved to see the van close by. 'I'll drive you home.'

Raff didn't even try and argue, just slid across to the passenger seat as Clara opened the door and settled herself at the wheel. Neither of them spoke during the short drive back to Hopeford. It was no time at all until Clara drew up in front of the pretty cottage and killed the engine—and Raff still had no idea what to say, how to break the deathly silence.

He had always been able to rely on his charm in the past. Now it wasn't enough, not by miles.

'I know people think I keep her too close.' The words made him jump, unexpected in the long silence. 'But they have no idea what she and I have been through. When I first came back I was so young, other mothers used to think I was her au pair or big sister. I always had to do everything better to prove I was as good as they were.'

'Of course you were.' He could see her. Young, independent, tilting her head coolly as she walked past the whispers, the sneers, the judgement. 'Better.'

'I have to put her first,' she said. 'Always.'

'Clara.' He reached over and took her cold hand. 'I know today was horrible. I can't imagine what you went through. But it doesn't have to change anything.'

She was immobile under his touch, the green cat's eyes remote, shuttered. 'You're leaving,' she said. 'There isn't a future for us, so what's the point?'

Fun? Living for today? Attraction? Raff searched through his usual stock of reasons and arguments and found them wanting.

'I think we could be good together.'

'When you're in town, when you can fit us in? I know how amazing your job is, Raff. I think it's great, that you are a very giving person. I really do. But I can't be second best. And nor can Summer. And I don't think you can give us what we need.'

Ouch. Words like arrows, well aimed and sharp. Raff looked at her and could see no indecision; her eyes were steady, the colour of a stormy sea. 'She deserves better than that, Raff. *I* deserve better. She needs a father figure, someone she can rely on. I know you were great with her up there and I am so grateful but I can't have you in her life. I can't have you in my life.'

Raff wanted to reassure her but what could he say? He couldn't offer her more, couldn't *be* more. His life was elsewhere; his calling was elsewhere. She was right. She deserved so much more than an emotionally stilted runaway could offer her.

'You do,' he said, aware how harsh his voice sounded. He swallowed, shocked at the size of the lump in his throat. 'You both do. I hope you find someone who appreciates just how amazing you are.'

'You didn't promise me anything,' she said, looking down at her hands, twisting the bangle round and round her slender wrist. 'You were always very clear what this was and I thought I knew what I was doing. I guess somewhere along the way the lines blurred for me. That was stupid of me.' She looked up at him, held his gaze. 'But things are clear now. You're a good man, Raff Rafferty. I hope you find whatever it is you're looking for.'

She reached across and opened his door. Her intention was clear. Raff searched for something to say but came up with nothing. All he could do was press a kiss to her soft cheek and climb out of the van and watch as she drove away into the deepening twilight, leaving Raff alone with only the birds' evensong for company.

He was free just the way he liked it. Free of family obligations, free of Rafferty's, free of all ties. It was what he had always wanted.

It should feel so good. So why did he feel as if he had suddenly lost everything?

CHAPTER ELEVEN

'WHAT YOU NEED to do,' Maddie said, 'is get back on the horse.'

'I need to *what*?' Clara stared at her cousin suspiciously.

'Get back on the horse. So you fell. Who can blame you? That man was sex on a stick. I would have quite liked to have fallen myself, if I wasn't with Ollie,' Maddie finished, a little unconvincingly, Clara thought. 'And as a starter to get you back into the swing of things he was perfect. But he was never the main course and you know it, so don't let him make you lose your appetite.' She sat back on the sofa, took a sip of her wine and beamed at Clara.

Clara tried to disentangle Maddie's mix of metaphors and gave up. 'I still don't know what to do about this.' She held up the cheque that had arrived with that morning's post. 'It's twice the amount I was expecting.'

'Which is terrible because?'

Clara gave her a level look. 'Because I was sleeping with him.'

'It's guilt money. He knows he should have stayed and fought for you. He hasn't and he's throwing money at his guilty conscience.'

'I didn't want him to stay and fight for me. I'm not Guinevere.' But Clara could feel her cheeks heating up;

even she didn't believe a single word she was saying. She knew with utter certainty that they would echo through her head tonight as she fought off thoughts of him. It was worse at night, what-ifs and might-have-beens spiralling dizzily through her mind until she finally fell into a fitful, dream-filled sleep. 'I don't know if I can accept this. Should I return it, ask for the right amount?'

'Don't you dare.' Maddie sat bolt upright in horror. 'You deserve that money. And as you are giving away that whole gorgeous wardrobe he bought you...'

'*Gave* me and I'm not giving it away, I'm selling it. All proceeds to Doctors Everywhere.' She was never going to wear most of them again; this seemed like the right solution.

'Every item?' Maddie peeped over from under long eyelashes but Clara had seen her cousin perform that trick far too many times before to fall for her beseeching glance.

'Every one.'

'Even the sequinned shift?'

'Even the sequinned shift, well, probably.' She hated to admit it but she did have a secret fondness for the frivolous, shiny, ridiculously short piece of clothing. Nothing to do with the look in Raff's eyes when she had first tried it on.

'Bags me it next time we go out!' Maddie was all smiles again. 'Seriously, Clara, that's one hell of a bonus for a job well done. Whatever his motivation you put in a lot of hours—legitimate hours—and he got the results he wanted. Take the cheque and get yourself signed up to one of these websites before you retreat back into that shell of yours.' She patted the open laptop perched between them. 'Right, what are your interests? Fine dining and culture?'

'No!' Clara shook her head, uneasily aware that she was being a little over-emphatic. 'I did far too much of that with Raff.'

'And you didn't enjoy it?'

An image came into Clara's head. Mud. Mud everywhere, Raff hoisting her up onto the rope. The feeling of freedom, of being able to let go. 'I want someone I can do ordinary things with,' she said slowly. 'Walk, talk, read. But when we do them together they become extraordinary.'

There was a long moment's silence. 'Don't we all?' said Maddie softly.

Clara picked up the cheque again, aware she had said too much, revealed too much even to herself. 'I'm not going to sign up yet, no…' as her cousin tried to interrupt '…I don't mean I won't, just not tonight. Not right now. I think I might take Summer away for a few weeks and I'll do it when we get back.'

'But it's term time. You never let her miss school.'

'I think this is a sign.' Clara looked at the cheque. She had already been considering the trip before the cheque arrived. It just made the logistics easier. 'I'll put the amount I was expecting into the business, just as I always planned to. But the extra I'm going to spend doing something I should have done a long time ago. I'm going to take Summer to Australia.'

Australia. Once it had been the promised land—a land of freedom, of exotic, alien landscapes, of opportunity. And then it had all turned to gritty dust. For the longest time she couldn't even hear an Australian accent without a sense of foreboding, of panic. Had put her wanderlust behind her, packed her need for adventure away along with her backpack and guidebooks and dreams.

But in doing so she had denied Summer her heritage. Her daughter deserved to know who she was. And Clara? Clara needed to find herself again. 'I think I was attracted to Raff because he reminded me of how I used to be.'

Maddie snorted. 'You were attracted to him because he was hot.'

Clara smiled. But the painful thump her heart gave whenever she thought of him, the tightness in her chest, had nothing to do with the way he looked, nice as that was. It was the way he made her feel—as if she could do anything. Once she had had that belief in herself.

'That too,' she agreed. 'But if this whole mess has taught me anything it's that I need to figure some things out about me before I can commit to anyone properly. It's a good thing Raff was always going away.' See, that was convincing. She was totally believable. 'I'm not ready for a relationship. Not yet. But I hope to be.' She smiled brightly. An easy, simple relationship. They existed, right?

'And Byron?'

'I hope he'll meet up with us but if he doesn't?' She shrugged. 'I can't force him, Maddie. I used to think if he just met Summer he'd fall for her but now I just don't know. But she should see where she was born, where she spent her first year.'

It was time to lay some ghosts to rest. And when she came back she'd be ready to move on, Raff Rafferty nothing but a pleasant memory. See, she had a plan. Everything was better with a plan. Even a bruised heart.

And that was all this was. She'd allowed herself to believe their own story, that was all. Hearts didn't get broken, not in real life, not after just a few weeks, not when you were the one to walk away, the one with responsibilities.

No, it was just a little bruised. She just needed time,.

Time, distance and a little bit of hope that it was all going to be all right, somehow.

But later, when Maddie had gone and Clara was sitting alone on her sofa, as she always was, that tiny bit of hope evaporated.

She was a strong woman, she owned her own business, her own home, raised her daughter alone. Was it wrong for her to have wanted him to ride into battle for her? Wanted him to try?

She was no fairy-tale princess but right now she would give anything to see Raff on a charger fighting his way through a forest of thorns, scaling a tower, searching the town for the owner of one small slipper. Instead he had turned and walked away without a word.

As Byron had.

Was she that unlovable? Wasn't she worth fighting for? He hadn't said one word to try and convince her to change her mind.

Clara looked around the small room. At the large framed prints and photos she had carefully chosen and hung, the wallpaper she had spent days cutting, pasting and hanging and smoothing out most of the air bubbles.

The sofa she and Summer hung out on, chatted, watched films, read books, cuddled on. The plants she tried not to kill with alternate bouts of love and neglect. The stuffed bookshelves, an eclectic mix of Summer's old picture books, the ones that were too babyish to stay in her room but that Clara couldn't bear to part with, crime novels and business guides. No travel guides though. Maybe it was time to get them out again.

This was her life, the life she chose and worked every minute to maintain. A safe, ordered life. And now it wasn't enough.

She missed him, a huge aching chasm inside her that

hurt more with every day, every non phone call, every non email. She didn't want any of the perfect matches on the dating sites; she wanted Raff.

But he didn't want her.

It was as if the sun had gone out and she didn't know if she was ever going to get used to living in the dull grey gloom. She had to get away. She would take Summer to Australia and while she was there she would forget all about Raff Rafferty.

It was the only way.

'Castor.' His grandfather stood to meet him, every inch the proprietor. He might have been forced into retirement but here, in the world-famous Rafferty tea rooms, he was still king. 'Good to see you.'

'And you, sir.' Raff took the proffered hand and shook it. 'Good to see you out and about.'

'Got no time to play the damned invalid,' his grandfather grunted as he slowly sat down. Raff watched him anxiously but it didn't seem more than the usual twinges of arthritis that had plagued Charles Rafferty for the last few years. He turned to the discreetly hovering waitress. 'We'll have the usual, Birgitte.'

'Should you be eating afternoon tea? Wouldn't the soup be a better option?'

Charles Rafferty scowled. 'I've been eating pap for the last few weeks. A man can't live on soup alone.'

'Nor can he live long on huge amounts of cream and butter, especially after suffering problems with his heart,' Raff reminded him. He turned to the waitress and smiled. 'Can you make sure there is no cream or butter and just a small selection of cakes? Thank you so much.'

'You always did think you knew best.' But to Raff's relief his grandfather made no attempt to countermand his order. Instead he sat back in his chair and turned his trademark sharp look on Raff. The one that had him confessing all his sins instantly. 'Polly returns soon and all this…' he waved one hand at the tearooms '…all this will be hers. Any regrets?'

'Only that it took this long,' he assured him.

'And you? Where next?'

Now *that* was the million-dollar question. Raff's morning meeting at Doctors Everywhere had changed everything and Raff had no idea how he felt about any of it. He waited until the waitress had unloaded the heavy tray, positioning the silver teapot in the middle of the table, accompanied by a silver jug of hot water, a jug of milk, a small bowl of lemon slices and the silver sugar bowl. It was the same design and arrangement as the very first afternoon tea served in this very room nearly one hundred years ago. Rafferty's were big on tradition.

'Jordan,' he said, pouring out his grandfather's tea, knowing he liked it weak, black and with lemon. He wasn't so fussy; in the camps he took his hot drinks as they were served, grateful for the comfort and the caffeine. 'Just for a few weeks.' He stirred his own tea, finding it hard to look him in the eye, not wanting his response to influence him in any way.

'But they want me to consider basing myself back here. Their Director of Philanthropy is moving on and they've asked me to replace him.'

He continued to stir his tea, the morning's conversation still whirling around his brain.

He had gone to the London office to report for duty and organise his next posting, a normal procedure that had quickly proven to be far from standard when he had been ushered, not to the assignments department but into the CEO's office for a long and frank conversation.

'You're one of our best guys out in the field,' the CEO had said. 'But you're replaceable out there. I'd like you to consider working here instead. We completely beat our targets at that ball, and signed up some committed new sponsors; much of that was through your contacts. With you heading up our philanthropy section, combining your business experience with the work you did with us, I reckon we could bring in some serious money—and that means funding some serious work.'

'Obviously you would be good in that role. I trained you myself.' His grandfather was being as modest as usual. 'But you always hated being deskbound. I thought it was the field work you wanted?'

Raff had to fight the urge to squirm. With his grandfather's keen gaze focused on him like this there was no way he could lie to him—or to himself.

'Honestly? I'd been thinking something along similar lines myself,' he admitted. 'It makes a lot of sense, I know. But it will be hard. I love the unpredictability of what I do now. They've promised it won't all be desk work and meetings and events. I'll need to have a good understanding of our needs so I'll still get to spend some time in the field, but it will be site visits from the HQ, not getting my hands dirty and being part of a team, at least not in the same way. But everyone at HQ needs to do at least one field rotation every two years so I wouldn't have to walk away entirely.'

'Is this about the girl? Your grandmother thinks she's the one.'

'When did you see Grandmother?' Raff didn't want to talk about Clara, not to someone who could read him as well as his grandfather did.

'We *are* still married,' his grandfather pointed out as if separate lives and separate houses for the last ten years were a mere technicality. 'But we're not discussing my love life.' Raff choked on his tea. Thank goodness, now *that* would be an awkward conversation in every way. Grandparents weren't supposed to have love lives, especially not ones who were estranged. Bridge partners? Absolutely. Love lives? Absolutely not. 'Wouldn't this new job work much better if you are considering getting engaged?'

'We're not.' With relief Raff turned to the waitress bearing the heavy stand heaped with dainty finger sandwiches, scones and an array of tiny cakes and pastries. 'Thanks so much, Birgitte. Grandfather, don't get up. I'll serve you.'

'Only to make sure I eat brown bread and no cake,' his grandfather grumbled. He looked keenly at Raff. 'I thought things were serious? You've been inseparable for weeks. I admit I wasn't sure at first but actually I quite like her. She's feisty, good thing for a spoilt chap like you.'

Raff took longer selecting each sandwich than was strictly necessary, placing them carefully on the plate. 'It hasn't worked out,' he said, handing him the plate with the elegant flourish a summer working in this very tea room had instilled in him.

'Why ever not? You were smitten.' Charles Rafferty pointed his fork at Raff in a way that would have got either he or Polly sent from the table when they were children.

Smitten. Clara had obviously fooled everyone even better than he had hoped. It helped that he liked her, that he desired her, that he enjoyed getting behind the barriers she put up, making her laugh. He valued her opinion, enjoyed her company—and sometimes the sight of her almost brought him to his knees.

But *smitten*?

'Clara deserves more than I can give her. She needs someone reliable, someone who won't run away the moment things get difficult.' He had told himself this so many times in the last week it sounded as if he were reciting something he had learned off by heart.

'And why is that someone not you?'

Raff opened his mouth to reply and then shut it again, more than a little nonplussed. His grandfather was sitting bolt upright looking expectantly at him, wanting some sort of answer. How could he not know? He was separated from his own wife after all! The Raffertys were all the same: good workers, terrible husbands. Or wives—Polly was no nearer to being settled than he was. They'd probably end up living together in their nineties in a crumbling mansion somewhere and people would call them 'those peculiar Rafferty twins'.

They were impetuous—he had signed up to a crisis organisation on a whim, for goodness' sake—the absolute opposite of the calm, ordered, organised Clara. Raff curled his fingers into his palm. He had to stop thinking about her. She needed a future with someone stable. Someone unlike him.

The honourable, the only thing to do was to respect her wishes, to walk away.

'You did spend six years working in a business you dislike for my sake.'

'I wouldn't say dislike...'

'Four years working for little money in difficult conditions helping others?'

'Well, I...'

'You came home the second your sister needed you?'

'Of course, but...'

His keen blue eyes softened. 'You wrote to your

mother every week even though she never wrote back. Visited your father every weekend even though he had no idea who you were. Rejected invitations to parties, the chance to be in the school team because they clashed with visiting hours.'

How did his grandfather know all this? Know *him* this well? Raff thought he'd done such a good job of keeping it all hidden well away. 'They were my parents.' He coughed slightly to clear his throat, dislodge the unwanted lump that was suddenly lodged there. He hadn't wanted to turn down those invitations, to lose his coveted spot in the team, but what if that had been the week? What if his father had died and he hadn't visited, hadn't told him once again how sorry he was for not saving him?

His mother seldom replied to the letters he dutifully sent. Occasionally parcels would turn up, books or T-shirts or toys. After a couple of years they had become even less frequent—and the toys were too young, the books too easy, the clothes a size or so too small.

'Of course she wants you,' his grandfather said, taking advantage of Raff's introspection to help himself to several of the cakes. 'You're a good man, Castor, loyal to a fault, hardworking, handsome. Well…' his eyes twinkled '…people do say you take after me. The only person who doesn't believe in you, Castor, is you.'

He put his knife down and looked seriously over the table at Raff. 'Don't make the same mistakes I did. Don't walk away because you're too stubborn or too proud or too afraid. You don't want to be my age and full of regrets. They make lonely bedfellows, you know. If I'd tried harder with your grandmother, then maybe…' He sighed. 'I have hope it's not too late for us. You at your age? You should be beating her door down, begging her to take you back.'

Raff saw his grandfather out to his car, his mind whirling. The job, Clara, his grandfather. Clara again. What if he let her down? Couldn't be the man she needed him to be?

There was more than his pride at stake here. More than his heart. He was willing to risk all he was, all he wanted, all his dreams, gamble them on a chance of happiness. But could he risk Clara's, Summer's stability? Their future?

It was so much responsibility. The stakes were far, far too high. Better to fold now than let them lose everything. That was the right thing to do no matter how very wrong it felt.

But try as he might to convince himself a small beacon of hope refused to flicker and die away. What if it wasn't too late? What if he could somehow make things right?

What if this was the chance he'd been waiting for his whole life? Was he just going to sit back and let the opportunity to be part of a family pass him by? He had salvaged his relationship with his grandfather despite all the odds. Maybe, just maybe there was hope for him after all.

CHAPTER TWELVE

IT SHOULD HAVE BEEN utter bliss, lying on a comfortable chaise, the sun blissfully melting into every one of her weary bones and muscles. She didn't even have Summer to worry about; she was currently enjoying a playdate with an old friend of Clara's, an afternoon of beaches, barbecues and rollerblades. She wouldn't be missing Clara at all.

But no matter how comfortable the chaise, how delicious the sun, how novel the lack of responsibility, Clara just couldn't relax. With an exasperated groan she sat up and checked her phone again, hoping someone, somewhere needed her. No, there were no texts, voicemails, emails or any other type of message.

She was utterly alone.

Looking around the lavish poolside area, Clara tried to shake off the gloom. After all, look where she was! Sitting in a comfortable chair, an iced juice on the table beside her, views to die for spread out all around her; blue, blue water overshadowed by the wings of the famous opera house.

She was living the dream, for a few days at least. She had decided to finish their holiday in luxurious style and you really didn't get much more luxurious than her present location.

If she didn't want her admittedly extortionately expensive drink, then she could go for a swim in the rooftop pool just a few feet in front of her, or work out in the lavishly appointed gym, have a nap in the massive hotel room that Summer swore was bigger than their entire apartment or go for a walk. She was just steps from the Rocks Markets and she still had some gifts to buy. If nothing in the touristy stalls tempted her then there were plenty of shops in Sydney's historic heart.

Or she could go to the Botanic Gardens; after all, she told herself, she'd just be taking a walk. She wouldn't be stressing about tomorrow. About the near miracle that was going to occur.

No. Clara slumped back in her chair with a sigh, her eyes unfocused, barely noticing the spectacular scenery. All she could see was the exotic lush greenery of the gardens and the two people who would be strolling there tomorrow. Would they have anything to say to each other? What would be worse: awkward silences or an instant connection?

This was what you wanted, she told herself, as if repeating the words over and over again would somehow make them true. Summer was finally going to meet her father. Clara just hadn't expected to feel so terrified about it.

If she was honest with herself then she might have to admit it wasn't just today, this loneliness. It had been chilling her for weeks even as she had busied herself with preparations for this trip. They had spent the first ten days here in Sydney staying with old friends before heading out to the Blue Mountains, taking in the vineyard where they had lived when Summer was just a baby.

After that they had undertaken the long, exhausting

journey to the farm where one of Clara's friends had moved to, completely in the middle of nowhere. Her daughter had immediately taken to the outdoor life; loving every minute of her first riding lessons, hanging onto a strap as she was bounced around in the back of the truck, swimming in the local watering hole. *Don't,* Clara had wanted to cry out a hundred times. *Look out for crocodiles, for snakes, for spiders, what if the horse bolts or the truck overturns?*

What if?

But she had held her tongue even though it had physically hurt, even though she had been almost doubled up in fear and dread, and she had watched her daughter blossom.

Meanwhile Clara herself found it harder and harder to work out just who she was any more.

The trip had definitely healed some old wounds, but had also brought up new, troubling ones. Even after all the years away she had friends here, people who she could connect with straight away. There was no one outside her family who she had that connection with back in England. No one but Raff.

Damn, she had said his name. If it weren't bad enough torturing herself with images of Summer and Byron getting on so well she became totally redundant, she had to think of Raff. Again.

Truth be told he was often on her mind. The more she tried to forget about him, the larger he loomed.

Because as good a time as she was having, as much fun as it was showing Australia to her daughter, there was a little part of her that knew that having Raff with them would have made everything perfect. He'd have charmed her friends and adored the outback. And if he were here she would feel so much better about tomorrow, if he were distracting her, reassuring her that she was doing the right thing.

She was, wasn't she? Mechanically Clara reached for the bangle at her wrist, turning it round and round, the familiar feel of the silver slipping through her fingertips a reassurance, a grounding.

Typical Byron to leave his change of heart to the last minute, for the grand reconciliation to eat into their last days. But how could she deny him? Well, she would happily deny him anything and everything but this wasn't about him.

Unfortunately though it was about her, because, sitting here alone, she had to admit that once you took away her work and her daughter there was very little left.

She had allowed her worry for Summer, her drive to provide for her daughter, to consume her. Which was laudable. But, there that word was again, it was a little lonely.

Well, things would change. She would date and she would not compare every man to Raff, no matter how tempting. She would have hobbies and friends and relax and soon she wouldn't even remember Raff's name.

Or think about him whenever she looked at the night sky and saw the Heavenly Twins. Thank goodness they had different stars here in the Southern Hemisphere.

Clara eyed her phone again, her pulse speeding up. What harm would one little peek do? He hadn't blogged for a couple of weeks now; she just wanted to know he was all right. It wasn't stalking or being obsessive. It was caring about a friend.

It was almost embarrassing how quickly her browser picked up the Doctors Everywhere website, how it immediately assumed she wanted to go to the section dedicated to field staff blogs. It was almost as if she had been reading it every day. Every evening. When she couldn't sleep…

Not just Raff's blog, all of them. Trying to get an idea of the world he occupied, the people he worked with, his friends, the way he spent his days. The job that was so all consuming he walked away from his family, his heritage, to be part of it.

That he walked away from her without a backwards look.

Her breath caught as she saw the all-too-familiar photo. It was a couple of years old, she reckoned, the hair shorter, more preppy, his gaze wary. Her finger hovered and for one moment she fooled herself that she had a choice before she touched the screen and watched the blog load.

Nothing new. It was the same short entry she had read far too many times detailing his impressions on arriving at the refugee camp. The same matter-of-fact tone as he described families crammed into tents, all their worldly goods reduced to what they could carry, how they were treating pregnant women who had walked for hundreds of miles, malnourished children, broken men.

It was so vivid she could see it; every time the shock hit her anew. His work was so important, how could she compete? What if she asked him to come back and he regretted it, that regret poisoning whatever it was they had?

Or maybe they had nothing and he wouldn't come back at all.

Or what if she risked it? Let him go and welcomed him home in between postings. Shared him with the job he loved so much. Could she do that? Could she be so selfless, live with the uncertainty and the danger and the long months when he was away?

She turned the bangle round and round. That question had become more and more pressing as the weeks went by. She wanted to answer yes...

'Excuse me, miss?' The polite young waiter had returned, a tall glass on his tray.

'I haven't finished this one yet,' she apologised with a guilty look at the still-full drink. It was her third. She dreaded seeing how much money she had wasted on the freshly squeezed juices. But ordering them, sitting here with a drink and watching the world go by was better than sitting in her room and brooding. Just.

'No, miss, this is a new drink. It's a mudslide.'

'A what?' Clara stared at the drink. It looked like a coffee to her.

'A mudslide,' he repeated. 'Vodka, coffee liqueur and Irish cream, mixed with crushed ice.'

A latte with a kick. 'But I didn't order a drink. There must be some mistake.'

'No, miss, the gentleman over there ordered it. He said you were a big fan of mud.'

Clara stared at him. 'He said I...' Was this some strange Australian chat-up ritual? She had worked in a bar not that far from here throughout her pregnancy and for the first months of Summer's life but that was nearly a decade ago. Maybe this was a cultural reference that was totally lost on her.

The only mud she had been near in years was with Raff. Oh!

Don't be ridiculous, Clara told herself. Raff was in Jordan, but her heart was hammering so loud she was surprised the whole pool area wasn't throbbing with the beat. She swallowed, her mouth dry.

'The gentleman?' She could barely get the words out, torn between embarrassment and a longing so deep, so intense it nearly floored her.

'Over at the bar.' The young man nodded over towards the long pool bar the other side of the terrace.

It wasn't him; it couldn't be him. She was setting herself up for a massive disappointment but all the admonishing thoughts in the world couldn't quell the hope rising helium light inside her.

Clara tugged at her skirt as she rose out of the chair, looking over in the direction the waiter had indicated. *Be cool and say no, thank you,* the sensible side of her was whispering. *It'll be some bored businessman seeing you sitting alone. He thinks he'll liven his business trip up with a flirt. That's all it is.*

And just because he has broad shoulders and a shock of dishevelled dirty blond hair and navy blue eyes, even darker with exhaustion, doesn't mean it's him. It can't be him sauntering slowly towards you.

'I thought it was apt.' He nodded at the drink still sitting on the waiter's tray. Raff lifted it off, discreetly passing the young man a folded note as he slunk gratefully back to the bar. 'In lieu of the real thing.'

Clara stood and stared, drinking him in. It was like the first time she had seen him: an old crumpled shirt, battered jeans, skin almost grey with weariness. Totally irresistible.

'I thought you were in Jordan.' Of all the things to say. But conversation had deserted her; she was stuck to the spot like an incredulous statue, unable to move or feel.

'I was two days ago, or was it three? It may have been a week. It feels like I've been travelling for ever.'

'But what are you doing here?' It was a mirage, surely. She was like a traveller in a desert, Raff the welcome oasis. Which made her a truly pathetic human being but all she wanted to do was look at him, relearn every feature for posterity. Instead she stood, a foot between them, too scared to touch him in case he disappeared.

'I wanted to see you.' Clara gaped at him, a mute question in her eyes. 'Maddie told me where you were. Nice surroundings, by the way. Is this how you backpacked as a teenager?'

'Just like this, five star all the way.' She fastened on his words. 'You came to see me?'

'I'm hoping to see a baby koala as well, it seems a shame to come all this way and not see one, but mainly I've come to see you.'

Heat filled her, whooshing up from her toes and filling every atom, every nerve burning. 'Me?'

'And the baby koala…' Raff gestured to the drink. 'Are you going to drink that?'

'Sorry.' It was such a lovely gesture and she was spoiling it. 'I'm not a huge fan of vodka. Or Irish cream.'

He regarded the brown mixture with distaste. 'It sounded better than it looks. Do you want to take a walk?'

'A walk?' For goodness' sake, it was as if she were under a spell. Raff was here. In the swanky terrace bar. Half the way across the world from where she had seen him last, from where he was supposed to be. She should have squealed, thrown herself at him, made some indication that she was pleased to see him instead of standing here gaping.

'I've not been to Sydney before. So far I have seen the airport, the inside of the taxi and this rather nice swimming pool. I have been reliably informed there is a rather impressive bridge and opera house I should take a look at. Where's Summer?'

'With a friend. Tomorrow she's seeing Byron.' It was

such a relief to tell him, the burden instantly slipping off her shoulders.

Raff raised his eyebrows in shock, letting out a low whistle of surprise.

'I know, I told him we were coming and made sure he knew when we would be in Sydney and heard nothing, which wasn't a surprise at all. Then he called last night. Which was a surprise but what could I say?' It was nice to see him, to hear him, to be able to speak to someone who absolutely, intuitively understood.

More than nice.

He grimaced. 'Anything you wanted but, knowing you, I guess you said that of course you could accommodate him at such short notice.'

Clara shrugged, the warmth in his eyes almost too much for comfort. 'For her sake.'

He nodded. 'I know. What time are you taking her?'

She bit her lip. 'He's going to text.'

'Do you want me to come with you?'

Just eight words. Eight simple words. Words that made all the fear and the loneliness and the worry evaporate in the hot Sydney sun.

'Yes, please.' She glanced at him, almost shyly. 'She'll be so happy to see you. She talks about you all the time.'

'I can't wait to see her either. I'm counting on her to teach me all the Aussie slang. And I bet she knows all the best baby koalas.'

'She knows it all.' Clara rolled her eyes.

The lift down was spacious and cool but to Clara it felt tiny, almost claustrophobic. She was sharing it with Raff. Every nerve tingled with the need, the want to touch him but she couldn't, frightened he'd disappear like a genie back into the bottle of her imagination. The lift opened straight into the impressive marble foyer and she mutely led the way to the exit. As they reached the steps the sun hit them bright and hot, as different from an English sun as a daisy from an orchid. Clara automatically began to walk on the harbourside path, the sea sparkling beneath them.

Raff took her hand, an easy, natural gesture. It felt like coming home. Clara allowed her fingers to curl up, to meet his, a lifeline she had thought she could manage without. 'So Cinderella is all alone in the big city? It's a good thing I've come to cheer you up.'

'You're the fairy godmother?'

He squeezed her fingers. 'Or Buttons, but I did have another role in mind.'

The teasing voice had turned serious as he stopped and turned to face her, still holding her hand in his. 'I walked away because it felt like the right thing to do. But it wasn't. It was the cowardly thing to do.' His fingers tightened, almost painfully but she didn't resist, his firm grip anchoring her down. 'I don't really know how families work, how loving someone works. It seems so easy to get it wrong, to let people down so badly it's worse than trying at all.'

Clara clung onto him, her fingers laced tightly through his, her heart hammering. 'I was afraid too,' she said honestly. 'I was losing my way. I spent so many years trying to keep things secure and safe and then you came along.' She shook her head, trying to blink away the tears threatening to fall. 'You made my life look so small. You made me feel small.'

'I didn't mean to.' He stepped forward in alarm, one hand brushing her cheek, collecting her tears as they overspilt. 'I just wanted to see you smile. God, it was presumptuous, I know, but I admit I liked the idea of shaking you up a little. You were so sorted, it made me feel inadequate.' He grimaced. 'That was wrong, sorry.'

'No, it was good,' she protested, holding his hand to her cheek. 'I needed it. If it wasn't for you I wouldn't be here, moving on. I'd just work and look after Summer and kid myself that I was happy with such a narrow life. But I'm not. And if loving you means long absences and worry and sharing you with your work then I can manage. Because that's a lot better than not having you in my life at all. And I do want you, I do love you.'

She'd said it. She'd said it all. The four-letter word she hadn't even admitted to herself on long, lonely, sleepless nights. The world might still be going on around them but here and now it had stopped as the word reverberated around her head.

Love.

She peeked up to see his reaction but Raff's face was unreadable.

'Would it ruin your plans too much if I was around a bit more than that?' he asked. 'If I was around pretty much full time? Thing is…' he grinned ruefully '…and I am being presumptuous again so please bear with me, the thing is I don't know much about being a good husband and father.' Clara's heart twisted at the words. 'But I am pretty sure being away over half the year is not a good start.'

'But you love your job.' It was a half-hearted statement, as her mind raced at his words. Had he really said husband and father?

'I love you more.' Raff trailed his hand along her cheek; every nerve fired up at the light caress. 'They offered me a job in London a few weeks ago and I said I needed time to think about it, but I was just scared. I defined myself through my job. I wasn't sure who I would be without it. But if I'm honest, I'd been thinking about offering my services full time in London anyway. The ball made me realise just how much I can achieve with my friends and connections—it would be pretty selfish of me not to use them. It's a very different kind of challenge but a good one, I think.

'Then when I was away all I could think about was you. Being out in the field wasn't enough any more. In fact...' his finger brushed her lip '...it was pretty lonely.'

'I've been lonely too.' It didn't feel like an admission of failure, not now.

'Suddenly, it didn't feel like such a big decision at all. I was going to take the job and woo you. Only when I hotfooted it to Hopeford you were gone.'

'So you came all the way to Sydney.' Clara smiled at him, a wide, uninhibited grin of joy. 'We leave in two days. You didn't have that long to wait.'

'What's another twenty-four hours of travel?' he said. 'Besides, waiting was making me anxious. I didn't want to lose my nerve. You can be pretty intimidating, you know, Clara Castleton?'

'Me?' She'd worked hard at it but that wasn't who she wanted to be any more. She was sick of keeping the world at arm's length.'

'You can also be funny and warm and sharp and there is no one I'd rather wade through mud with. I told you once I'm not a hearts and flowers kind of guy. I'm the idiot who takes a beautiful woman on an assault course or gets a kid stuck on top of a roller coaster but I promise, if you take a chance on me, I'll always put you first. I'll always try.'

Clara took a step closer to him, finally allowing herself to lean in against that tall, broad body, to lace her fingers around his neck, to reach up and press a kiss on that firm mouth. 'I know you will,' she whispered. 'You always put everyone else first. And I don't need hearts or flowers or clean and tidy adventure-free dates. I just need you, Raff Rafferty.'

* * * * *